P9-BZC-697

"Cook brings a dose of gritty realism to fantasy."
—*Library Journal*

"Eminently satisfying."
—*Booklist*

## BUGGED OUT

One of John Stretch's pals headed our way. Lugging a beetle as big as a lamb. He didn't editorialize; he just dropped the monster when I didn't offer to take it. He headed back to the wars.

Playmate said, "Hey, Garrett, whack that thing with something. It ain't dead."

It lay on its back. Its legs were twitching. Its wings, ditto. Then it stopped struggling. It seemed to be assessing its situation.

"Garrett!"

It flipped. It faced me. Big brown jaws clacked.

It charged. . . .

The Garrett, P.I., Series by Glen Cook

# CRUEL ZINC
# MELODIES

A GARRETT, P.I., NOVEL

# GLEN COOK

A ROC BOOK

ROC
Published by New American Library, a division of
Penguin Group (USA) Inc., 375 Hudson Street,
New York, New York 10014, USA
Penguin Group (Canada), 90 Eglinton Avenue East, Suite 700, Toronto,
Ontario M4P 2Y3, Canada (a division of Pearson Penguin Canada Inc.)
Penguin Books Ltd., 80 Strand, London WC2R 0RL, England
Penguin Ireland, 25 St. Stephen's Green, Dublin 2,
Ireland (a division of Penguin Books Ltd.)
Penguin Group (Australia), 250 Camberwell Road, Camberwell, Victoria 3124,
Australia (a division of Pearson Australia Group Pty. Ltd.)
Penguin Books India Pvt. Ltd., 11 Community Centre, Panchsheel Park,
New Delhi - 110 017, India
Penguin Group (NZ), 67 Apollo Drive, Rosedale, North Shore 0632,
New Zealand (a division of Pearson New Zealand Ltd.)
Penguin Books (South Africa) (Pty.) Ltd., 24 Sturdee Avenue,
Rosebank, Johannesburg 2196, South Africa

Penguin Books Ltd., Registered Offices:
80 Strand, London WC2R 0RL, England

First published by Roc, an imprint of New American Library,
a division of Penguin Group (USA) Inc.

First Printing, May 2008
10  9  8  7  6  5  4  3  2  1

# 1

It was a marvelous winter. My personal favorite kind of winter. An ever-lovin' blue-eyed kind of winter that slunk in early and got bitter frigid before anybody remembered where they stashed their winter coats. Snow came down more often and heavier than even the old folks could remember, and you know how their recollections work. Everything was bigger, better, sharper, steeper, rougher, and tougher in the good old days.

When it didn't snow there was freezing rain.

The world slowed down.

I favor slow. I like loafing around the house, hard at it doing a whole raft load of nothing. Nothing being what I do best when there are no ladies present.

Dean would maintain that they couldn't be ladies if they were hanging around with me.

The downside of the weather was, what with snow and ice, it was hard to get a replacement keg in. It was almost as hard to get out to those temples of dissolution where the golden elixir was dispensed.

All good things must end. No good deed goes unpunished. Sooner rather than later. These natural laws underpin my life.

Same as it ever was, the idyll killer was a knock on my front door.

Dean shouted, "I can't leave this omelet."

Always an excuse.

I climbed out of my chair, snaked out from behind my cluttered desk, crabbed sideways to the hallway door. Whoever built the house probably intended my office to be a walk-in closet. I glanced at Eleanor, central figure in the grim painting hanging behind my desk. She's running away from a brooding mansion. One weak light burns in a high window. She's beautiful and frightened. The light is in a different window each time I look.

There used to be the hint of a horrible, menacing presence in the dark background. I can't find it anymore. But Eleanor keeps running.

I told her, "You seem gloomy today."

True. I couldn't recall the last time I saw her looking so pessimistic.

Pular Singe popped out of the Dead Man's room. The ratgirl has converted a quarter of that into her own little office. She manages the business side of our racket. Much better than I ever did.

I asked, "You expecting somebody?" She has a half brother who won't stay away. Which can be hard on the nerves. He's a local crime lord. In a time when TunFaire has been suffering from a severe outbreak of law and order.

"No."

"Maybe it's Jerry the beer guy with the new keg." I was whistling past the graveyard. Unexpected visitors never augur well.

I took a peek through the peephole. "Zippity-do!"

"What?" Singe asked. Instantly suspicious.

"Proof that the gods love men."

"It is the beer man, then?"

"No. Even better." I popped the door open. Revealing a stoop chock-full of male fantasies. The closest was Alyx Weider, naughty blond temptress and daughter of Max Weider, dark overlord of the Weider brewing empire. Max has me on retainer.

"Out of the road, Garrett," Alyx ordered. "It's freaking cold out here." She didn't wait for me to move.

I looked past the flock. They had arrived in a coach. Smoke curled from a slim sheet-metal chimney. The coachman had fled into the cabin already. The vehicle was so big it should have had oars and sails. Six matched chestnuts dragged it around. They looked like they wanted to join the coachman.

Three more honeys shoved past. I wished the weather was a little fairer. They wouldn't be so thoroughly bundled. There was one each of the primary colors: blonde, brunette, and redhead, plus a moon-faced, raven-haired exotic with skin the hue and smoothness of honey. They put off so much heat that they should've been immune to the weather. Grizzled old glaciers would melt when they passed.

*Whack!* A hand got me across the back of the head.

Singe snickered.

Uh-oh. Tactical error. Drooling over Alyx and the honey girl with the challenging brown eyes left my back exposed to the redhead.

Singe snickered some more. Ominous, that, coming from the unique sound box of a ratperson throat.

"Tinnie. Sweetheart. What are you doing with this crowd?"

Tinnie Tate, devoutly committed redhead, is my off-and-on main woman. Very main, of late. And possessed of not even the remotest intellectual understanding of my broad appreciation of female folk who are easy on the eyes.

"Making sure your fantasies don't get past the hallucination stage."

Alyx Weider being one of her best friends would factor in. Alyx has been chasing me since she was old enough to get up on her own hind legs.

I asked, "Singe, is Old Bones snoozing?"

"Probably. But he does pretend quite well."

That he does. If he can't sleep for a year at a time, he'd just as soon pretend. Some people are just so lazy.

We were talking about my partner. A unique sort of beast, even in TunFaire, where it's a rare and remarkable day when we don't see the rare and remarkable.

"Let's go in there. My office is too intimate." And there wasn't enough furniture in the small front room. Which we don't use much. It still smells like the Goddamn Parrot.

Singe headed for the kitchen.

The two unfamiliar women made frightened squeaks when they saw my sidekick.

The Dead Man is a near quarter ton of defunct Loghyr, a species now little known and almost extinct. This one looks like a dwarf mammoth minus the hair and tusks. He went around on his hind legs when he was alive. His trunk-like snoot makes his yellowish gray, wrinkled face uglier than you can imagine. There is no twinkle in his eyes.

Loghyr don't die like the rest of us. We croak; the part

that isn't meat and bone hustles off to whatever reward is on the schedule. Or sticks around to make life miserable for the living. Usually the same living we made miserable before we assumed room temperature. But Loghyr stick around and haunt their own corpses. For centuries, sometimes.

It's been four and a half of those since somebody stuck a knife between my partner's ribs.

I'm double haunted. Eleanor was a ghost when I met her, too.

I told the ladies, "He's harmless." Though a huge misogynist. I used to be able to wake him up just by bringing in a female of this caliber.

He's getting used to me having an occasional companion of the obstinate sex. He gets along with Singe and Tinnie. Most of the time. The redhead remains strictly "Miss Tate," however.

Though startled and intimidated, the new girls didn't recognize a Loghyr when they saw one. So they weren't scared.

"Tinnie, my sweetest sweet, who might your friends be? And why do you turn up now, after weeks and weeks of sticking your tongue out and staying away?"

Tinnie said, "Bobbi Wilt and Lindy Zhang." Without indicating which was which. Because I didn't need to know. "Guys, this here is six feet three inches of the prettiest ex-Marine you're ever likely to find underfoot. Look at those big baby blues. Never mind the bad hair, the pockmarks, the scars, and all that stuff. That's just normal wear and tear."

I'd enumerate her physical shortcomings but I haven't found any yet. Everything is there, in all the right places, with a shine on it. Personality-wise, though, one or two sharp corners could be polished off.

"Definitely a problem," Alyx said. Showing me her tongue between sharp little teeth, a come-hither challenge in her eye. "You find one still in good shape, he's too immature to waste time on. You find one like this, that's all broken in, he's like this. All broken down."

"You aren't so old I can't turn you over my knee, Miss Alyx."

"Promises, promises."

"Alyx!" Tinnie was not amused.

I asked, "So, how come I find myself inundated by beautiful women?" Coats were coming off. Being an observer by trade, I was observing. And I was impressed.

I was looking at Tinnie but Alyx answered. "Because I had to see you. And I thought you might not let me in if it was just me."

The honey-tone honey drawled, "Her father wouldn't let her come alone. And Tinnie was there when he decided that you're the answer to our problems." There was a twinkle in her eye. She'd be another one who enjoyed getting a dig in at the expense of her friends.

Alyx said, "Tinnie's got you so whipped. She didn't need to come keep an eye on me."

Who knows? I don't have much backbone around temptations packaged like these. I'd still be telling me what a dumb thing it was to do but be grinning from ear to ear as I went down for the third time.

Tinnie looked grim. Probably because she didn't like that "whipped" pig wriggling out of its poke. Like it was some kind of secret.

Singe returned. Lugging a tea service. She made three of my four visitors uncomfortable. Well-schooled young ladies, they owned manners potent enough to not be rude in someone else's house.

"So," I said. Standing. The available chairs being filled. I didn't go for more. Despite visions of harem girls dancing in my head.

This much glamour doesn't descend on me without bringing bad, bad news. The kind of news that ends up with me having to go to work.

"Alyx?"

Now that she was here she didn't want to talk about her problem.

It happens. People hire me. Then they don't want to tell me why. Usually because they have to admit having done something incredibly stupid.

Tinnie grinned. That lit up the room. "What my friend the blond beer bimbo wants to tell you is, her daddy needs to see you. He sent her because he didn't think you'd open the door to anybody who looked like a wannabe client."

Too true. I wasn't looking for work. I have a regular

income from several sources. And work is so much like . . . well, so much like work.

But prospective clients are always bimbos. Er, make that, there's always a woman involved. As Singe might say, because half of us are female and females are more likely to find themselves in straits nature didn't equip them to handle.

Singe sucks all the fun out sometimes, being boneheaded, literal, and logical.

# 2

"Here's the story," Alyx said. Never an auspicious beginning. People who start that way usually plan on retailing a fictionalized account.

"I'm all ears."

"Not quite, but they are a little ridiculous."

Two paragons snickered. The redheaded fourth seized the named appendages from behind. "But they're so cute!"

"Spin me your tall tale, baby Weider girl."

"Daddy wants to build his own theater."

"Good on Max. Theater is hot right now. He'll milk it for a ton."

"We're gonna be the stars. Us and Cassie Doap. And Heather Soames, maybe."

I gave Alyx the maximum-power raised right eyebrow. The one that makes the nuns renounce their vows. "No. Not Cassie."

Then my mouth got ahead of my brain. "Girls don't go onstage." Not good girls. Only girls who have something to market.

"We can if we want!" Petulant.

Alyx Weider is as spoiled a kid as ever came up in Tun-Faire. And that's all her father's fault.

Max indulged her not only because she was the baby of the family but because of his failures with her older siblings. Like he thought if he invested enough he could buy one perfect kid.

Why not? He'd been able to buy everything else he'd ever wanted since he'd gotten rich.

Alyx wasn't half as rotten as she ought to be, the way she'd been raised.

"You're not being nice!"

"Alyx, what I am is shutting up and listening." Which I proceeded to do with grand determination and limited success.

"Daddy is building a theater. A big one. He already told us we could be stars. Tinnie knows somebody who can write us a play."

I leaned back and turned. My eyebrow query failed to knock Miss Tate down. She must be developing an immunity. "Jon Salvation," she said.

"The Remora? You're kidding."

"He's good. He wrote a comedy about the fairy queen Eastern Star."

"I was talking!" Alyx snapped. "You told me you'd be quiet and listen."

"Being quiet, Alyx. Listening raptly."

Miss Weider offered a halfhearted, grotesquely inappropriate head butt that would've taken out the lynchpin of my fantasy life if I hadn't been a trained martial artist–type. Tinnie growled. She cuts Alyx a lot of slack because they're ancient friends and their families are in business together, but she has her limits.

She snarled, "Goddamnit, Alyx! Cut the shit! Talk!"

Bobbi and Lindy were amused—the way bettors around a dogfight pit might be amused by the antics of future combatants.

"Daddy wants to get into the theater business. He has a theater under construction. The World. It'll put three or four different shows on at the same time."

Max the innovator. How would he do that?

Tinnie interjected, "They'll have staggered starting times. Each play will show three times a day."

"Tinnie, please!" Alyx whined.

So Max had found a way to move a lot more Weider beer. I gave Alyx a nudge. "The problem you need solved is?"

"Sabotage."

Tinnie explained, "It's actually kind of petty but somebody keeps getting in and breaking things."

"Criminals? Trying to shake him down?" That's how the protection racket starts.

Most crooks are smart enough to steer clear. Max Weider

is rich. And doesn't scruple in a fight. He'll play fair, businesswise, but try strong-arming him and there's an excellent chance somebody less personable than me will help you get started on an attempt to swim across the river. With granite in your undies.

Not even the Contagues, the emperors of TunFaire crime, would risk making a run at Max Weider. Unless the payoff prospects were beyond my ability to imagine.

Near as I can tell, all hands are happy with the status quo. Possibly excepting the law-and-order extremists at Watch and Guard headquarters in the Al-Khar.

Alyx chewed her lower lip fetchingly. Reluctantly, she said, "Maybe. But there's, like, ghosts, too. And bugs."

"Ghosts?" Just thinking out loud. Ghosts happen, but I hadn't run into any recently. The residual personality haunting the Eleanor painting being the last. "It's the wrong time of year for bugs." Unless you kept your house too warm. Which nobody can afford to do. Other than on the Hill.

Around here we can see our breath in the winter. Except in the kitchen. And in the Dead Man's room when we have company.

"Tell that to the bugs, big boy."

"Tinnie?"

"It's all hearsay to me. I haven't been to the site."

"Ladies?" Bobbi and Lindy were content to sit quietly and elevate the temperature of the room. The Dead Man offered no remarks. Singe sat in the corner with her dim candle, working her books.

Her rat eyes do let us save on lighting costs.

Tinnie took the opportunity to apply a pinch meant to keep me focused.

Alyx admitted, "What I'm telling you is hearsay to me, too. Daddy won't let me go to the construction site."

Tinnie observed, "He doesn't want her associating with the kind of guys who work construction."

I snickered. "That's because he started out as that kind of guy himself. So. Alyx. What do you want? Other than to indulge in one of your special efforts to get Tinnie mad at me?"

"Daddy wants to talk to you about what's going on."

Max has been good to me. His retainer, meant to inhibit

floor loss and general misconduct at the brewery, has kept me solvent through numerous dry spells.

"Can I catch a ride?"

"We're not headed home. We're going to Tinnie's. To rehearse."

They had a play already?

Tinnie said, "No, we're going to the manufactory. There's more room. And more privacy. The walk will do you good."

"I'm so pleased you're always looking out for me."

"You're very special to me."

"What if I slip on a patch of ice?" She was right. It had been a long winter and I'd spent most of it avoiding going outside.

"I'll bring fresh flowers, lover."

Dean finally wandered in, armed with refreshments. Two steps into the room he froze. His jaw dropped.

He's old. Around seventy, I'd guess. He's skinny, shows a lot of bushy white hair this year, and has dark eyes that can twinkle with mischief. On rare occasions. More often they're alive with disapproval.

"Damn!" I murmured. "The old goat is human."

Tinnie wasn't his problem. He sees her all the time. And he knows Alyx. He's never anything but polite when she's around. But the other two . . .

He pulled it together before he turned into a creepy old man. "Good afternoon, Miss Tate. Miss Weider. Ladies. Would you care for something sweet?"

They all said no, they were watching their figures. And doing a fine job, I have to report. I stayed busy helping them do that. As did Dean. His eyes all but bugged out when the ladies started getting back into their cold-weather duds.

# 3

Back from the front door, I asked, "What happened to you, Dean? You looked like you got a sudden case of young man's fancy."

"The one with the marvelous chestnut hair."

"Bobbi."

"What?"

"Her name is Bobbi. Bobbi Wilt. Tasty, huh?"

He showed me a scowl but it wasn't his best. "It's remarkable how much she resembles someone I used to know."

Someone who'd had a huge impact. Dean was so distracted he was ready to walk into walls.

He has worked for me since I bought the house. In the beginning he lived with one of his brigade of homely nieces. Then it just made sense for him to move into one of the extra rooms upstairs. That kept him from bringing the nieces round, trying to fix them up. He never said much about his olden days. He was in the Cantard the same time as my grandfather. They never met. He knew folks on my mother's side.

None of which matters now. Dean cooks for me and keeps house. And works hard at filling in for my judgmental mom.

Dean shook like a big old dog that just ambled in out of the rain. "I guess when you're my age, everybody looks like somebody you've already met."

"Who does she remind you of?"

"A girl I knew. My own Tinnie Tate. An old regret. It doesn't matter anymore. It was a long time ago."

Clever. He got in a dig even there.

"Must have been something special."

"She was. She was indeed." He drifted toward the kitchen. "We're out of apples again."

Pular Singe is addicted to stewed apples. Dean indulges her shamelessly. Despite ingrained prejudice.

Ninety-eight of a hundred TunFairens loathe ratpeople just for existing. They can't help it.

"I'm not inclined to pay a premium because we're way off season."

"Noted. You aren't inclined to pay more than the minimum for anything in any season."

Sharper than a serpent's tooth, the ingratitude of a servant confident in the security of his position.

"I hope you have something ready for lunch. I have to go out, soon as I fill up."

He paused long enough to benefit me with his full frontal scowl.

# 4

In some parts of town they'd given up trying to keep the streets clear. In others they kept after the snow with a dogged fervor. The city fathers had invoked emergency regulations to keep the more critical thoroughfares passable.

Lucky me, it wasn't my day to help clear my block. Unlucky me, it hadn't snowed. Today's crew wouldn't have much to do.

The sky was a cloudless blue. There was no wind. Light melting had begun in direct sunlight. So ice could form in all the low places once the sun went down.

It's a couple miles to the Weider brewing complex. Not a tough walk. No hills of consequence. A few historical landmarks I never notice because they're always there. Furniture of the world.

There were a lot of people out, enjoying.

I was in a good mood myself by the time I got where I was going. Nobody stalked me. Nobody bopped me on the noggin. Nobody even gave me a second glance.

Some days it's the other way around. Too many days.

The big brewery stinks even in cold weather, because of the fermentation. The employees and neighbors no longer notice.

This was the mother brewery, the heart of the Weider empire. There are several dozen lesser operations around TunFaire, onetime competitors who surrendered their independence to the Dark Lord of the Hops. The lesser breweries concentrate on local and specialty products.

The queen brewery is a Gothic redbrick behemoth. It

looks like a folklore hangout for vampires and werewolves. It is festooned with towers and turrets and odd little gables and dormers and lofts that have no connection with producing nature's holy elixir.

The towers house swarms of bats. Max thinks bats are cool. He enjoys seeing them swarm out on a summer's evening.

The whole strange place is Max's imagination given form, weird because Max wanted it weird. And he could afford to build it that way.

A smaller version faces it from across Delor Street. The Weider family shanty.

Max originally meant that to be his brewery. When it went up it was the biggest beer-making operation in all TunFaire. Two years later it was too small to handle demand. And Max's wife, Hannah, was pregnant for the third time. So he tossed up the monster across the way.

Max and Hannah produced five children: Tad, Tom, Ty, Kittyjo, and Alyx. Alyx was the baby by half a decade. Tragedy stalked the family, maybe punishing Max for his worldly success. Tad died fighting in the Cantard. Tom and Ty survived—with Tom gone mad and Ty condemned to a wheelchair. Kittyjo and I were an item once upon a time but she was too loony for me.

My pal Morley Dotes says the absolute first rule of life is, don't get involved with a woman crazier than you are. A rule I haven't always pursued with due diligence. Because of more immediate distractions.

But like I said, tragedy hounds Max Weider. Tom and Kittyjo were murdered. Hannah died that same night, destroyed by the shock.

I climbed the steps to the main brewery entrance. An old, old man sat behind a small table in a cubby just inside. He was a retiree putting in a few hours of part-time. He was almost blind. But he was aware of me because I came in with a creak of hinges and a blast of cold air.

"Can I help you?"

"It's Garrett, Gerry. Looking for the boss. He here today?"

"Garrett? You ain't been around in a while."

"Cold and snow, Gerry. And nothing happening to worry the boss." My function is to stimulate the consciences of the brew crew. So they don't surrender to temptation. Not too often, in too big a way. "What about the boss?"

"If he's here, he came over underneath. And he don't do that much no more. Less'en it's really foul out. So, chances are, he ain't here. Yet."

Max is a hands-on owner who visits the floor every day.

By "underneath" Gerry meant through the caverns below the brewery. Those were the reason Weider chose to build where he did. The beer is stored there till it's shipped.

"How's business? Any cutbacks because of the weather?"

"I hear tell a ten percent drop-off on account of it's hard to make deliveries. The local brew houses picked up most of the slack. The boss didn't lay nobody off. He's got the extra guys harvesting ice. It's a good year for that."

"So I hear." They would be cutting the ice from the river. "Thanks, Gerry. I'll head on across."

Would he believe I was just looking for the boss? The whole brewery would know I was on the prowl before I found Max. Any villainy would scurry into the shadows to wait the danger out.

Privilege, private law, is vibrantly alive. Max Weider is a comfortable practitioner. He cares for his troops. Most return the favor by limiting their pilferage.

It seemed colder outside. Because it's always hot inside the brewery. From the fires used to boil water and warm the fermenting vats.

The steps up to the Weider mansion door had received only a half-hearted cleaning since the last snow. I understood. We'd all had enough of that.

I knocked.

The man who answered was new. And a disaster on the hoof. If there was a race that could mix with the human, his ancestors had mixed it up. There had to be a half dozen kinds of human in the blend, too.

He would be five feet tall on his tippy-toes on his best day. His head was huge for his height and almost perfectly round. With a couple saucers smashed onto the sides where his ears belonged. The only hair on him was a huge, drooping black mustache. Its twisted ends hung four inches below his nonexistent chin. His eyes were slits stuffed with chips of coal. His mouth was a lipless gash under a nose fit for an elfin princess. He didn't look worried about her showing up to claim it.

His body was another globe. His stubby arms sort of stuck out at his sides. How the hell did he dress himself?

He didn't speak, just stared at me. Filling the doorway. Immovably.

"Name's Garrett. The boss wants to see me."

One bald eyebrow twitched.

"Alyx came by my place. Said the Old Man wanted me to come by."

The other naked eyebrow shivered.

"Be that way. I didn't feel like working today, anyhow."

I could go down to the river, see what it looked like frozen over. It wasn't far past the brewery. I could watch the ice sledges bring the harvest home.

The living art form of ugly did nothing to help me out. He just stood there.

I turned away.

"Hang on, Garrett." Manvil Gilbey, Max's sidekick, materialized behind the short and wide. "Come on in. Don't mind Hector. It's his job to keep the riffraff out."

"Then I'd better start hiking. I'm about as riffy a rack of raff as you're likely to step in."

"Always the charmer."

"One hundred and ten proof."

"We didn't expect you this soon. I would've told Hector to bring you straight to Max."

Gilbey belongs to Dean's generation. Old as original sin. He and Max have been best friends since their Army days, in a war that began before they were born and continued till their grown children were dead. Until a year ago. Devouring Karentine youth all the while.

Hector stepped aside. I followed Gilbey through the foyer, down into the vast ballroom that takes up half the ground floor. *Click-clack* across the bare serpentine floor. Then up to the mezzanine on thick, custom carpeting.

I murmured, "What was that?"

"Hector?"

"Yeah."

"Son of a man Max and I soldiered with. A hero himself, Hector was, but he was having a hard time making it. Life is tough if you don't have pure blood."

"Crap," I said. "We're not getting into all that human rights bullshit again, are we?"

In Karenta, in TunFaire especially, "human rights" means the rights of humans to preferential status. The Other Races and artifact peoples get whatever is left.

"No. Our problems are in a new arena now."

"Alyx said something about building a theater. That seems out of character."

"I'll let Max explain."

I glanced back. Hector was standing by, ready to answer the door. Beside a rack of lethal tools, there in case his immovable object had a showdown with an irresistible force.

"A true exotic. Maybe even a unique." Slang terms for mixed breeds of extreme aspect.

"Would you believe Hector has a wife and five kids?"

"If you say so. But I don't want to meet the kind of woman who finds him attractive."

"He may have hidden assets and unexpected talents."

"He'd have to have, wouldn't he?"

"You've got a bad attitude, Garrett. People could tag you for some kind of racialist."

"I am. The kind that don't give a shit what you are so long as you leave me alone."

It had been a while since I'd seen Max. But when I stepped into his den it seemed I'd been away only minutes.

It was a room twenty people could fill and all be comfortable. A fleet of overstuffed chairs jockeyed for position in front of a big fireplace. A major accessory to that was a lackey whose calling was to feed the flames. The room was sweltering hot. The fireplace end was almost intolerable. But Max was in a chair up close, roasting himself. I guess so he'd make a good-looking corpse when he was done.

Max is not a big man. He stands maybe five feet six when he stands. Which he doesn't do much, anymore. Since Hannah's death he spends most of his time by the fire, waiting. Once a day he ambles over to the brewery, mainly to be seen taking an interest.

# 5

Max rose as I approached.

Max Weider is a round-faced man with rosy cheeks and a twinkle in his eye even when he's down so deep he can't figure out which way is up. He still has hair but his barber isn't getting rich charging by the hour. The part down the middle is six inches wide.

Max's mustache was bushier, maybe to balance the weak crop up top. Though it would never threaten the beast lurking under Hector's nose.

I was startled. There was a definite twinkle in Max's eye this morning. I asked, "Manvil, what's happened?"

Gilbey understood. This was the surprise he'd promised. "He's found a reason to live."

Max shoved a beefy hand at me. "Damned straight. How you doing, Garrett? Enough friggin' snow for you?"

Sounded like he had been taste-testing the product. "I'm filled up on it, yeah. Alyx came by the house. With a covey of—"

"Felt like a rooster in a henhouse, didn't you? That Bobbi makes me wish I was forty years younger, I'll tell you."

I glanced at Gilbey. Manvil had a twinkle in his eye, too. "Have you guys suddenly turned into dirty old men? Suddenly?"

"No," Max said. "We're too far past it even to pretend."

"Speak for yourself, Weider," Gilbey snapped. "This soldier ain't ready to lie down."

"It ain't the lyin' down, Bubba. It's the gettin' up." Old Man Weider made a wave-off gesture, then indicated a chair close by. "Park it. Let's talk."

"I can't take the heat."

"I should remember. I'm the lizard. The rest of you are warm-blooded." He compromised. He moved far enough from the fire that I would just sweat, not drip drops of grease.

"So, what's the story? Alyx was vague."

"That girl's always vague. She ain't right. I need to find her a husband."

"Don't look at me."

"I didn't think you'd volunteer. One of the reasons I like you. Though never too close to my baby girl."

Gilbey asked, "Want a beer while we talk?"

"Sure. And you bringing that up makes me wonder if I shouldn't change my mind."

"About?"

"About marrying. Alyx. I'd have free beer for life."

Max chuckled. "It wouldn't be a long one, Garrett. That girl has notions about how things oughta be, even if she ain't figured out where she fits. Still, you talkin' about marryin' for the beer instead of the money . . . I like that."

Gilbey lugged over three big tankards. He settled. We three made up points of a lopsided triangle.

The professional fire tender left without being invited. Probably part of his job to know when.

I said, "There was talk about ghosts. And bugs."

"At the World, you mean." Gilbey. With foam on his upper lip.

"That's why I'm here, isn't it?"

"Partly," Max admitted.

"Mostly," Gilbey said.

"Mainly." Old Man Weider drained off half a pint. "There's something going on over there that ain't right. I don't believe it's ghosts. I think it's somebody working stunts. With extortion in mind."

"There are bugs, though," Gilbey said.

"In the winter?"

"In the winter. And the World won't work if the customers have to deal with bugs."

I didn't say so but bugs are a fact of life. In my world, anyway. You have to come to a natural understanding with them, so to speak.

"You'll see," Gilbey promised.

My skepticism was too obvious.

Gilbey clambered to his feet. I thought he was going for refills. I was wrong. He collected a drawing board, two feet by three. A sheet of fine handmade paper was affixed. Someone had used writing sticks to create excellent drawings of a building.

I have a small financial interest in the manufactory that produces the writing sticks and a dozen other miraculous gimmicks.

Max has a bigger chunk of the same operation. As does Tinnie's family. They provided the capital. I delivered the inventor.

Max said, "They call those 'elevations,' Garrett. That's what the World will look like when it's done."

"All right. I'll take your word. But these two here look more like maps than pictures."

Gilbey said, "They are maps. This is the ground-level layout. The band pits. The stages. The passageways to the center. We thought we could do the vendor work out of there. A carpenter who knows theater told us that was dumb. So that's where the actors will wait and change and where the ready props will be stored. The vendors will operate from under the second- and first-class seating."

"All right." I followed his finger but didn't really picture it. "It looks like a pie."

"Our clever innovation," Max said. "There are a lot of theaters these days. Not many get a full house after the first week of a play's run. So we'll run three at once. With limited audiences. That will make it harder to get into one of our shows. So, if you do, you've got something to brag about. People want to be part of the elite. We manage it right, we'll have them trying to outdo each other in how many times they've been to one of our plays. We'll use special paper tickets that they can keep and show off."

Max has a knack for creating artificial shortages that spark snob appeal.

Gilbey added, "We're still a ways from a final plan. We'd like to come up with movable walls so we can change the size of the pie slices."

"All right," I said. "I see the layout. What's this?"

"That's the cellar. Under the floor and stage. So people and stuff can come up from there. And for storage. Prop storage is a big problem for theaters."

Max chimed in. "This will be only the second theater in TunFaire built to be a theater."

"And all this is going up now? In the weather we're having?"

"Yep. But it isn't going as fast as it should."

I was amazed. TunFaire's construction people don't like to work in bad weather. On the other hand, they're not fond of not eating.

Gilbey said, "We want to open in time for the spring season."

That *was* ambitious. But Max Weider generally accomplishes what Max Weider sets out to do.

"All right. I know the general plan. What do you want from me?"

Gilbey told me, "What you do across the street. Show up unexpectedly. See what's going on."

"Find out who's sabotaging things," Max said. "It's trivial stuff now. Pranks. Petty theft. Vandalism. Nobody's asked for protection money yet, but it feels like it could turn serious."

"Ghosts and bugs aren't serious?"

"Nuisances add up."

"Finances? In case I need to bring in other people? Assuming you want quick results."

"I haven't caught you robbing me yet. Manvil, give him what he needs. Keep records, Garrett." Not one of my strengths, he knew. "I'm interested in results."

Max is a bottom-line guy. And proof that good things happen when you keep an eye on that end of life's math.

Gilbey prepared papers. I asked, "The Old Man really has a new reason to live?"

"When he forgets Hannah and the kids. The theater excites him."

"And you?"

He lied, "I'm pretty much past the worst."

"And Alyx?"

"Alyx worries us. Alyx hasn't faced it yet."

"All you can do is watch her and be ready when she needs you."

"How are you going to start?"

"Go look around the construction site."

"Use the papers. I'll have your advance against expenses messengered to your place."

"Good. It won't be my fault if the money evaporates somewhere out there."

"No. But Max would take a long, hard look if anything did happen."

People don't have much faith in other people's honesty anymore.

# 6

I didn't recognize the World first time past. I thought they'd just be getting started, not almost finished.

I expected lots of guards, too. Thieves inevitably appear wherever there's something burnable. Even in this brave new postwar world, where law and order threatens to become a universal disease.

I was a hundred yards into the Tenderloin before I realized I'd missed. I turned. There it was. Looking just like one of the elevations Gilbey had shown me, not quite complete. How do you walk right on by a round building without noticing?

Max had used the sheer weight of his own fortune, supported by selective gratuities, to gain possession of a grand tract on the edge of the anything-goes part of town. He'd cleared the tenements and whorehouses, the taverns and feeble storefront-branch churches.

I headed back, wondering if there was something about Max that I'd been missing. The World looked like a monument to an aging man's ego. Gilbey's elevations had done little to betray the scale of the project. Maybe that's how you miss a round building. It's too big to see.

"Where you goin' there, slick?" a bony old man with a peg leg, a ragged white beard, a truncheon, and a wild walleye wanted to know. His other eye was glass and brown instead of a washed-out blue.

"Do you read?"

"Some."

"Here's word from the owner." I produced the paperwork Gilbey had given me. "I'm a security specialist. The Old Man isn't happy with the way things are going."

"Who?"

"Max Weider. Of the brewery Weiders. The man who pays your salary."

"Lego Bunk pays my salary, ace. And he's one cheap-ass mortar forker."

Watching a semiliterate, one-eyed, walleyed man try to read Gilbey's fancy hand was an adventure. My patience got strained before the old boy nodded. "All right, chief. Guess you're real. Mind me asking what you're supposed to do?"

"You have a name?"

"They call me Handsome. I don't know why."

Made no sense to me, either. "Handsome, the boss is worried about delays. Says people are blaming ghosts and bugs. Says he don't believe it. He wants some heads busted. In order to encourage the others."

Handsome understood. I'd referenced a bad habit of Venageta's rulers during the recent conflict. If they thought their troops weren't trying hard enough, they executed a few. In order to encourage the others.

Handsome was a veteran.

The peg leg was a clue.

The war for control of the Cantard and its mines had gone on forever. It defined generations. It bound men together where they had nothing else in common.

"You Corps?" I asked.

Handsome grunted an affirmative.

"Me too." He was way older so we had little else in common. But that was enough.

Two minutes after you start boot training they convince you that Marines are a separate and dramatically superior species. And once a Marine, always a Marine. Rah!

Marines are more family than most brothers and sisters.

And so forth.

You never get over it, either.

We didn't swap stories. You don't do that, except maybe with the guys who were there with you.

Me bringing it up was as good as a secret handshake, though. Handsome became confidential. "I don't believe they's really no ghosts. That's crap. I never heard no music, neither. An' I been here since the start. Somebody's pulling some shit, maybe, trying to fuck up the program. Maybe kids. They's kids around all the time. One day gang-type kids, the next day kids that look like they run away from the Hill. But they's plenty a' fucking bugs, I guaroontee you that. Bugs you ain't gonna believe till they climb your fucking leg."

"Tell me about the bugs."

"They're big. And bold as cats. You go on in there, cap. Prowl around. Won't be that long afore you see." He stepped aside.

No one else challenged my right to visit the site.

Actually, no one seemed to give a rat's whisker, one way or another. Everybody but Handsome was trying to get some construction done.

I went inside. It was warm in there. I saw no obvious reason why.

My familiarity with the theater phenomena was limited. I went to a passion play once with a lost girlfriend, way back. Twice recently I'd gone with Tinnie, to a comedy and a tragedy, both historicals based on rulers from Imperial times. Neither play impressed me.

Interior work on the World was just getting started. Most of the planking meant to become ground-level flooring remained to be pegged into place. No seating or stages or walls had gone up yet. A couple of carpenters pegged away. I strolled over. One worked an augur. The other sanded the head of a peg just driven into place. I peered into the lower-level gloom. "What's the plan for ventilation down there?"

The carpenters looked like brothers separated by five years. The elder said, "I'm a carpenter, chief. You want to know something like that, ask the friggin' architect."

The other said, "Don't mind this asshole. He married my sister. She sucked the nice out of him years ago."

Not brothers, then. The sister must be a walking disaster zone, she had a brother who talked like that.

The younger continued. "They'll be louvered iron windows that can be adjusted from inside. And a stack in the center that's supposed to draw hot, stale air."

"Thank you."

Something brown scooted through the lower murk.

Carpenter the Elder failed to object to his companion's remarks. I assumed the crab-and-grin was a regular act.

Another something moved downstairs. Followed by a bunch of somethings. Rats? "You guys seen any ghosts?"

"Say what?"

"Ghosts. Old Man Weider said you construction guys can't stay on schedule on account of ghosts and bugs."

The crabby carpenter whacked a peg into place with a wooden mallet. "I heard the same shit, slick. But *I* ain't never seen no spooks. Bugs, though? Shit. Yeah. We got them fuckers out the wazoo. Some a' them big enough to rape a dog."

"Not mosquitoes, I hope." In the islands we'd joked about the skeeters being so big they'd hang you in the trees so they could snack on you later.

"Nah. They's cock-a-roaches, mainly. I seen some ugly beetles, too. Shit! Lookit! There's one right over there." He threw his mallet. He missed. The mallet bounced all the way to the wall. Which I noted only in passing. Because I was looking at the biggest goddamned roach that ever lived. And the fastest thing on six feet that I ever saw.

It wasn't big enough to rape a dog. Not even one of those little yappy fur balls favored by old women on the Hill. "Holy shit!" That son of a bitching bug had to be eight inches long. There wasn't anything like that native to TunFaire.

I begged, "Tell me that wasn't a baby."

"Nope." That was the carpenter who wasn't busy retrieving his mallet. "That was the biggest one I ever seen. But they keep getting bigger. We kill as many as we can. Old Man Weider needs to get somebody in here that knows what they're doing."

"He got me instead."

"Kind of takes the optimism out, don't it?"

What the hell? This guy didn't even know me and he was piling on. "I'll be back."

"That a threat or a promise, chief?"

"Pick your poison."

# 7

I took a meandering route home. A little south of the direct route. I stopped by Playmate's smithy and stable. Before he could start carping I told him, "I need to rent a coach. Tomorrow. Big enough for four people and fifty rats. I'll need a driver, too."

"Rent?" He sounded skeptical.

"You always get paid."

"Thanks to Pular Singe."

Playmate skeptical is a vision. Because he's a big black human house. Three hundred pounds, every ounce muscle. A slow-talking, fierce-looking sweetheart of a guy. So soft he's squishy on the inside. A religious sort fully stuffed up with homilies about turning cheeks. He oozes unwarranted faith in the innate goodness of mankind.

My experience suggests the opposite. The species is naturally wicked. People just fake it till opportunity crosses their bows. Only rare, twisted souls and random mutations, like Playmate, rise above the muck.

And Playmate is no fanatic. He'll turn the other one only once. Then he'll bring the hammer down. If you're obviously a bad guy, you won't get the once.

He stared and went right on not understanding. "You're volunteering to pay for use of a coach? Up front?"

"This is unbecoming. How long have we been friends?"

"I don't remember. Five minutes, back when we were kids?"

"Wiseass. That's the attitude that . . . Like I said, when did I ever not pay you?"

"Not once," he admitted. "Since you've had Dean Creech and the Dead Man to keep you honest. And Singe to keep your books."

"And before that, one time, you had to wait a couple days till I tracked down a client who tried to stiff me."

"Let's forget it. We're all even now."

One thing about Play, lately. His sense of humor is severely diminished. And he isn't very patient.

I worry that he may be suffering chronic pain, or something.

"I've just gotten a major commission from Max Weider. He gave me a free hand. The job should be calm, cool, peaceful, and profitable. I almost feel guilty about getting paid for doing it."

Playmate slapped both hands onto his butt. "Where did I leave my chain-mail underwear?"

"Come on, man! It's a walk. There aren't even any damsels in distress. Just Tinnie Tate, Alyx Weider, and a couple of their friends who're scared their theater won't open on time."

"That actually makes sense," Play said when I told him what I meant to do. "It's not the usual Garrett leap into the middle of things, flailing around till you're the last one standing."

My methods are more sophisticated than that. Sometimes.

"You going over to The Palms now?"

"Say what?"

"Your standard routine would be, go sucker Morley next."

He was speaking of my good friend, the half dark elf vegetarian restaurateur Morley Dotes. The semiretired bad guy. "Not this time. John Stretch, Singe, Melondie Kadare, maybe, and a lot of rats. Plus a coach to haul them in. I won't even bother the Dead Man. It'll be heroics on a budget."

"I don't believe you for a second. Even if you believe you."

"You need to root around in your junk room. See if you can't find where you left your positive attitude."

"You could be right, old buddy. The trouble is, you really are my old buddy. I've known you way too long."

My friends. My pals. They never let up.

# 8

I had planned to visit The Palms. I hadn't seen Morley in weeks. But Playmate's attitude made me think it might be more useful to let Dotes lie fallow. I shouldn't need any high-skill bonebreakers this time.

Whatever else he pretends, running his upscale club, Morley is a serious thug.

I gave The Palms a wide berth. Morley could find some excuse to come see me.

It was a nice day. I was humming as I turned into Macunado Street, betraying the fact that I have less musical talent than a wounded water buffalo.

I headed up the slight slope toward home. I wasn't alone in suffering the happy. My neighbors were out, enjoying air that lacked the usual heavy flavor.

The long, cold winter had frozen the ugly out.

People who normally ignore me, or watch me like they expect me to turn berserk, nodded, smiled, lifted a hand in feeble greeting. I do provide local entertainment. And safety. And stability.

Some minion of the law is always hanging around, keeping an eye on me.

I spied a Relway Runner. Not bothering to be discreet. I should be grateful, or flattered, that they watch me when all I'm doing is swilling beer and feuding with Tinnie.

Deal Relway, secret police honcho, is determined to catch me doing something. Anything. Now or a hundred years from now.

Singe opened the front door. "What's gotten into you?"

"You just did a contraction, sweetheart. You know that?" Ratpeople voice boxes aren't built for human speech. They have trouble speaking Karentine at all. The man on the street won't understand one word in ten from your average ratperson. Singe, though, has mastered the vulgate. Almost. Now including contractions.

When first I met Pular Singe she pretended to be deaf. That let her hide her brilliance from Reliance, the then master of the ratpeople underworld. Her half brother eventually replaced Reliance.

"Son of a bitch," she said. "Next thing you know, it'll be standing up on its own hind legs."

Another contraction. And this the first I'd heard that didn't involve a sibilant.

"Are you in a bad mood today?"

"I am in a very good mood, Garrett. While you were away there were deliveries that included two hundredweight of apples, two kegs of beer, and forty-three angels in gold."

"Huh? Angels?"

"A trade coin from the Tamedrow League. A mercantile consortium way up the north coast. These were minted in PeDiart-meng Arl. We do not see their sort often."

"Huh?" More piercing wit.

I'd started to slide off my afternoon high.

Singe can't help it. She has to go all out when she knows something I don't. "Angels are the standard monetary unit for coastal trade as far north as anybody from Karenta ever goes. Somebody must have regular connections up that way."

"Pull the other one now. See if it's got bells on."

*She is one hundred percent correct.*

"You! You're awake?"

*I am. Today was a tutoring day.*

My sidekick and junior partner is mentoring a fifteen-year-old high priestess from a rustic cult. She's almost a pet. Or intern.

There went a scary notion. Him crafting a small, mobile version of himself. A wicked deed I had no trouble seeing him doing.

"I don't get it. She used to be scared to death of you."

*Without cause. While those who should be wary consider themselves immune to enjoying their just deserts.*

I told Singe, "The money is from Max. An advance against expenses."

"We have a commission?"

"Yeah. It looks pretty simple." I explained. And told her what I planned.

The Dead Man tickled the inside of my head. *I suggest that you do not discount the matter of the ghosts.*

"You see something in my head that I don't?"

He has developed a bad habit of assuming my permission to rummage or eavesdrop inside my skull.

*No. Yet ghosts figure prominently in several reports. Though everyone seems inclined to discount their reality. And their music.*

"Where are you going?" I asked Singe. She had finished the bookwork resulting from our receipt of a pot of gold. She's much too efficient.

"To see John Stretch. You'll need his help to make your plan work."

"I wasn't feeling fanatical about getting started right this minute."

Singe said, "The pixies are still hibernating. You will not get help from them."

A pixie colony lives in the void between the inner and outer brickwork in my front wall. They're boisterous, obstreperous, obnoxious, unpredictable, and exasperating. And extremely useful. When they're not doing their damnedest to drive me nuts. Melondie Kadare is queen of the nest. And a dedicated drunk.

"Wave a beer around. They'll fly in their sleep."

Singe made a brief, weird snorting noise. Her excuse for a laugh.

"Go," I told her. "Once your brother gets here we'll adapt the plan."

"You think he will just drop everything and run to help you?"

"I have a bottomless war chest. And it's honest work."

Besides being a crime lord, John Stretch is a ratpeople community leader. Successful crooks are the only real leaders the ratpeople ever produce. The broader society won't tolerate anything more.

Most people, if they think about ratpeople at all, would rather they just went away. Unless they can trick up a way to exploit them.

I throw what work I can to John Stretch. Not that I'm any reformer.

Poor humans have it better. Men can sell their strength and violence. Women can sell their flesh. Not many folks want to boff a ratgirl. And ratmen aren't long on strength, only on sneak.

Pular Singe is mistress of the one special skill a handful of ratfolk can market. She's a tracker. The best there is. She can follow a fish underwater. That and her knack for bookkeeping are what she brings to the team.

She went out.

Dean came in. "Suppertime."

"What are we having?"

"Chicken stew."

I gave him the look.

He ignored it. He's immune.

"Yesterday: fish stew. The day before: rabbit stew. Before that: beef stew. I'm sensing a pattern. What next?"

"Pigeon? Snake? I'll come up with something."

"How about a new job? Could you come up with that?"

"Not working the slave's hours I put in here. I don't have time to look."

*Children. Stop squabbling. Pick up your toys and do your chores.*

# 9

Singe likes having her brother visit. She enjoys socializing but doesn't have the nerve to meet people on her own.

She came back with John Stretch before I could finish supper, have a cup of tea, and get my ego mildly bruised by my partner, who would not tell me what he had discussed with his student.

John Stretch stands four and a half feet tall. Five when he forces himself as upright as he can get. His real name is Pound Humility. To my human eye, he has only his ratness in common with Singe.

They have the same mother but different fathers. Which means nothing in their matrilineal society. The females have little control once they come into season. John Stretch was born in the litter before Singe's. Unusually for their folk, they get along like brother and sister.

John Stretch was dressed flamboyantly, in bright colors and high sea boots. His shirt was a rusty orange. It had fat, loose sleeves. The laces in front were loose. His trousers were baggy, too. They were black. And patched.

He was trying to keep a low profile, though. The shirt had arrived hidden inside a ragged brown coat so long its hem was wet.

When he's in public John Stretch swaggers and is loud. At my house, with nobody to impress, he'll turn mildly intellectual. He's marginally less smart than Singe. And less driven to learn and excel. Even so, he has a knack for insights into motivation, human and rat.

And he has one incredibly useful extra talent.

He can reach inside the heads of ordinary rats. The way the Dead Man taps into mine. He can read them and, I think, can control them. Thus, he can know what they know, see what they see, and smell what they smell.

I extended a hand. John Stretch shook. He still had trouble with the mechanics. I said, "Let me guess. Singe went straight to the kitchen."

"Yes." His sibilants were harsher than Singe's. But he was polishing them. He worked on his Karentine almost as fiercely as she did. He'd leave a mark. If he survived. "She said there is something I can help with."

"On a strictly cash for labor basis." I explained what I wanted to do.

"The bugs are how big?"

"The one I saw up close was about this long." I resisted the temptation to exaggerate.

"Sounds like some good eating. For regular rats," he hastened to add. "They like roaches."

"Then they're living large in this town. TunFaire has the finest herd of roaches anywhere."

I caught a mental sneer from my deceased sidekick. He disagreed. He wasted no time telling me where they were bigger and better, more numerous and tasty, though.

John Stretch disagreed, too, offering as proof testimony from rats off foreign ships. Then Singe arrived with mugs and a pitcher. The mugs came fully charged with proof that mortal men are beloved by the gods. At least, by those gods who favor fermented barley.

Singe and John Stretch are bottomless sumps when it comes to beer.

I asked, "How much organizing time would you need?"

"A few minutes," John Stretch said. "Getting a pack of rats together does not take long if you know where to look."

It wouldn't in this berg. If you had a magic whistle.

"Then I'll just holler whenever Playmate comes up with a coach."

"Sounds good to me."

We got serious about the beer. Singe asked me questions about my childhood. "What're you, writing a book?"

"I have one written already. Now I need some stories to put in it."

"Huh?" Maybe that made sense to her.

"You know that Jon Salvation who follows Winger around?"

"The Remora? The playwright? What about him?"

"He just finished his second story about her adventures. They are making the first one into a play."

"I don't believe it. Stuff like that doesn't happen in the real world. Damn! Who'd come knocking at this time of night?" I looked at my sidekick.

He didn't help out.

Singe was wobbly already. She mumbled something about it not really being all that late.

Dean was preoccupied in the kitchen.

I pried myself out of my chair.

# 10

I opened up after a look through the peephole, mainly out of habit. "What the hell are you doing here?"

Colonel Westman Block stepped forward. I let him come. Because the Dead Man sent, *Let him enter if he wishes. He has no ulterior motive.*

That I did not buy. Block is head of the City Watch and Civil Guard. Lurking behind him, like shadowy, avenging devils, is the Unpublished Committee for Royal Security. Whatever their handle may be this week.

They change names but never stop being the secret police. And they're having a huge impact on TunFaire's darker side.

Block said, "I've been to the Hill. Enjoying a first-class ass-reaming. A certain sorcerer's overly indulged second son is locked up in the Al-Khar. All he did was rape some foreigner's four-year-old daughter. Prince Rupert showed up during the chat. I don't know how he knew what was going on. Maybe Deal. But he told the Windsinger to be grateful that we didn't cut the little asshole's pecker and balls off."

Prince Rupert had a set of his own.

"So you thought you'd drop by, mooch a beer, and fill me in?"

"I did want to ask why a known criminal was seen entering your house an hour ago."

"So now I'm a known criminal?" I failed to steer him away from the Dead Man's room. Once he invited himself in he had no trouble seeing John Stretch.

"I'm not convinced. Deal has fewer doubts."

"Deal thinks everybody but Deal Relway is a crook. And he's keeping an eye on himself."

Block chuckled. "Letting you run free is more profitable than pulling you in. We're like gulls behind a ship. We follow you and pick off the fish you turn up in your wake."

Took me a second to get it. I had to go back to the islands, us moving from one hellhole to the next aboard troop transports.

Singe left the room as we entered. She returned with a new mug and the pitcher refilled. Block accepted the mug. He didn't mind it having been touched by a ratperson.

He took a long drink. "That's good." He eyed the Dead Man.

"He's asleep," I lied. That being Old Bones's preferred state.

"I don't believe you. But it doesn't matter. The world is at peace. I hope winter never ends. So, what do you have going?" He looked at John Stretch.

I saw no reason not to tell him. He wouldn't believe me, anyway.

I didn't betray John Stretch's secret power. The Crown doesn't need to know everything. Especially if that might cause feelings of vulnerability.

"Giant bugs? You're shitting me."

"I might be. By accident. I only saw one. But it was huge. I'm more worried about the ghosts."

"Why would there be ghosts around there?"

"I don't know. An old burial ground?"

"With the tenants just now getting disgruntled? Be rational. The usual reasons ghosts jump up would've brought them out a long time ago."

I'd spotted that flaw on my own. "Weider thinks it might be somebody angling for a payoff."

"Villains. Breathing villains. Stupid, breathing villains."

We were getting sloppy already.

Possibly with a little subtle assistance.

I closed the door behind the colonel. "What was that all about, Chuckles?"

*He was passing by. Feeling lonely. Colonel Block will not admit it, especially to himself, but he is a lonely man. He may have created an adversarial relationship here but it is a relationship.*

*None of which was alive in his surface mind.*

# 11

Another day, half of it wasted on morning. I wakened early, feeling good, and couldn't go back to sleep. I ambled down to the kitchen, where I surprised Dean, though he wouldn't admit it. He just poured tea and started the eggs and sausage. "This could turn into a habit."

"A good one, I'm sure you'll argue."

He wasted no breath responding. "There was a message from Miss Weider."

"Um? What does she want?"

"To know why you haven't cleaned up the world." He seemed both amused and puzzled.

"It's a big place. And I don't run so fast anymore."

"I'm sure that isn't what she meant."

"That kid Penny still running messages?"

"I wouldn't be surprised. But I don't know how to get hold of her."

"Figures."

"You need a message carried?"

"I do. To Playmate."

"There's a new family moved in down by the corner. They have a boy who could do it. Joe Kerr. He seems like a good kid."

I gave him the look. "You're kidding."

"What? How?"

"Joe Kerr?"

"Yes? So? There's a problem with that?"

"Maybe not. Maybe it's just me. Is he trustworthy?"

He shrugged. "I trust people till they give me reason not to."

"I've noticed. But see if you can recruit him."

"Me?"

"They very one. He knows you. He'd think I'm some pervert trying to pull him in."

"I can see how he'd think that. You have that look."

I speared a sausage and ignored him, except to say, "Round him up. As soon as you can."

I met the kid on the stoop. He was nine or ten. There was nothing remarkable about him. Wild red hair. Freckles. Big ears and fat front teeth. Gray-green eyes. Ragged clothes. Nervous smile. I gave him two coppers, the message, and instructions on how to get to Playmate's stable. "Three more coppers when you bring back an answer."

"Yes, sir." Off he went. He acquired an escort of three younger siblings before he got to the intersection with Wizard's Reach.

# 12

Singe wandered into my office. "Playmate is here."

"His own self? Already?"

"Yes. And yes. I'm off to get John Stretch. Close the door behind me."

Instead, I closed the door behind me. Playmate couldn't leave his coach unattended. A coach that wasn't his to lose. He has a mildly disreputable penchant for borrowing vehicles left in his care. Sometimes to help me. We've been fortunate enough not to destroy one yet. But one time we did forget to take a body out.

Play brought the children back. The message kid met me with both hands out. I paid even though he hadn't brought a message.

"What's this?" I asked Playmate. Indicating the huge, burr-headed man leaning on the mahogany coachwork. Play hadn't left the driver's seat. "How you doing, Saucerhead? What're you doing here?"

"I was over to Play's when your message come. I didn't have nothing to do. Any shit involving you usually gets entertaining. So I decided to tag along."

Probably hoping to pick up a few loose coins himself.

Saucerhead Tharpe isn't quite as big as Playmate. And not much smarter than the horses pulling that coach. But he is more social. Than both. And he's handy to have around.

People don't argue with Saucerhead. Not for long.

"I'm not hiring," I said. "Not right now."

Tharpe shrugged. His shoulders were mountain ranges heaving. He needed new clothes to cover them. A bath would contribute something positive, too. And a date with a razor would help. "Don't matter, Garrett. I'm not working. Not right now."

"You'll be the first to hear when I do need help."

"Yeah." He scowled. He knew where I'd turn first. "Thanks."

I throw work his way when I can. He's a good friend, long on loyalty but short on critical life skills. He never learned how to think about tomorrow.

"Tag along if you want. I'm just gonna shake some bugs out of a place Old Man Weider is building."

"You in the extermination racket now?"

"Not quite. These are special bugs. Here they come." Meaning Singe, John Stretch, and several of Stretch's associates. Each lugging a clever wicker cage filled with quarrelsome critters. Up close, those were the nastiest rats I ever saw. Pit bull rats. Champion fighting cock rats. I grumbled, "Did you need to bring the ones that are foaming at the mouth?"

Singe countered, "There you go, exaggerating again. Hello, Mr. Tharpe. How is Grosziella?"

Grosziella? Who would that be?

"We broke up. I . . ." Saucerhead launched a tale told many times. The names change but he keeps connecting, and disconnecting, with the same woman. They could wear the same underwear.

John Stretch told me, "I thought you would want enthusiasm." The last word arrived in a flurry of lisps.

"As long as they save it for the bugs. Everybody set? You bringing all these handlers?"

"Have to. Too many rats for me to manage alone."

Singe said, "I need to run inside for a minute."

I told John Stretch, "I don't see how we can get them and the cages all inside the coach." I watched Singe climb the steps. She's worse than Tinnie, sometimes. And Tinnie must have a bladder the size of a grape.

# 13

John Stretch and his crew began unloading cages.

I frowned at the World. Construction had stopped. "Am I missing a holiday? Did the weekend sneak up on me?"

I went looking for Handsome. I found a pair of Civil Guards instead. They were all shiny and self-important in the new, pale blue uniforms. They wore red flop hats and brandished tin whistles.

They ambled over. One eyed the rat cages, horrified. The other looked away. "Who're you, ace?"

He tweaked that nerve. "Deuce Tracy. Who's asking? And why?" I didn't feel hard-ass enough not to fish out my note from the Boss, though.

The Watchman considered exercising his right to be obnoxious. He accepted the note instead. He looked at it upside down, then passed it to the man who could pretend to read. After surveying Playmate and Saucerhead, the red tops opted for manners. For the moment.

They did have those tin whistles.

Playmate and Saucerhead are intimidating just standing around picking their noses. Especially Tharpe. He looks exactly like what he is, a professional bonebreaker of considerable skill. One who wouldn't scruple about busting the skull of a tin whistle if the mood took him.

The second Watchman said, "It do look like he's got business here, Git. This is from Weider himself."

I use Watch and Civil Guard interchangeably. There is a distinction, mainly of importance to Colonel Westman Block. The Civil Guard is supposed to be the new order of honest lawmen. The old Watch is supposed to wither away. When the new order gets as corrupt as the old, they'll hire some new thugs and change the name again.

Git rumbled, "Just trying to do the job, Bank."

"Sure. So. Mr. Chief Security Adviser. We still need to ask you a few."

"Fine by me. Right after you answer me just one. Wha-t're you doing here? John, you guys go ahead. Get after it."

Git answered for his partner. "There was a murder. We're supposed to find something out. If there's anything to be found."

That startled me. "A murder? Here?"

Bank said, "An old man named Brent Talanta. Usually called Handsome. You knew him?"

"I met him yesterday. I came over after getting the as-signment from Weider."

"About?"

"You read it in the pass. He thinks there's sabotage. I'm supposed to make it stop. What happened to Handsome?"

The Watchmen eyeballed Playmate and Tharpe. Not rec-ognizing them, except as seriously dangerous.

Git said, "He got dead."

Bank added, "Messily. How ain't clear. Something tried to eat him."

I lost my inclination to be disagreeable.

We watched the ratmen take cages into the World. I said, "That puts us on the same team. Did feral dogs get him?"

"That mean wild?" Git asked.

"Yeah."

Feral dogs are a problem. They'll hit a corpse but I've never heard of them killing anybody.

"Definitely not dogs," Bank said. "And what tried to eat him ain't what killed him. There wasn't no sign of a fight. But what tried to eat him could be in cahoots with what killed him. If he didn't die in his sleep. Or commit suicide."

We swapped questions for a while. Then Bank quizzed me on the financial side of being a freelancer. Grousing, "This racket ain't what it was in my father's day."

I couldn't help myself. "And that's the point of all the reform."

Neither Git nor Bank liked that. Which told me they were holdovers from the old regime. It also told me they must be reasonably honest guys or they'd be out looking for work in a bad postwar job market.

"Handsome dying the reason nobody's working?"

Bank said, "You'd have to ask the people who didn't show up."

Which made sense. I'd get an employee roster if the case dragged on.

It shouldn't. Though Handsome's death could be a complication.

Time passed. We talked about the war. Git had done his five in the Corps, too. He hadn't heard of me there—or here, either—but he'd heard of my outfit.

I did remember to ask what became of Handsome's remains. In case I wanted a look later. They had him over at the Al-Khar, for now.

Saucerhead grunted, "Singe is coming."

Playmate added, "She don't look happy, Garrett."

She didn't. Sufficient unto the moment the ferocity thereof. I said, "Over there on that pillar by where they found the dead guy. There's a mark the tin whistles missed. Take a look and tell me what you think."

# 14

"What's up?" I asked Singe.

"We need more rats."

"Huh? They must've brought a hundred."

"But not enough, John says. Not nearly enough. He needs some boxes, too."

"We can handle that. I saw some around here yesterday. What for?"

"To put the evidence in. So you will believe him when he tells you what he has found."

"All right. Let's see if those boxes are still where I saw them." Or if somebody creative had snagged them.

Saucerhead said, "Hang on, Garrett. You was right. Good eye. It's a gang symbol. I don't know what one. Whoever made it musta done it with a really dull knife. That had blood on it. You can see little specks where it dried. Come here."

I went. Playmate was down on his knees studying the pavement stones. Tharpe showed me the blood. I asked Singe, "What's your nose have to tell us?"

She sniffed for a few seconds. "Fear. I think they probably beat him before they stabbed him. There were several of them. Maybe as many as ten. Very unclean. But almost nothing more can be told because of the smell left by the bugs who came to eat him."

"You wouldn't be able to track the killers?"

"No. Because there are too many smells."

Often a problem for her in this city. "Head, Play, how about you guys tell the tin whistles while Singe and I get the boxes for John Stretch?"

We weren't twenty steps away when Singe murmured,

"They are talking about you." She meant my pals and the red tops.

"I'm sure they're deciding what a right guy I am for not holding back what we found. Around behind these pillars. There were six or eight boxes that building stuff came in. They were probably saving them to put other stuff in."

They were there, no longer neatly piled. "We might not . . . What is it?" Singe had stopped. Her whiskers were twitching.

"Call those Guards."

I got it. "Bank. Git. Come here. We've got another one."

They arrived. Bank asked, "What?"

"Singe is a tracker. A pro. She smells something under those boxes."

Behind was where it lay. A corpse. "Careful. Don't bust the boxes. We need them."

"You want them, you get them out of here."

I got in and got, passing the boxes back to Singe.

Git said, "This one's been here a while."

"Lucky it ain't summer," Bank said. "You. Garrett. Take a look. See if you know this guy."

I looked. Could've been anybody. The clothing was what every squatter in TunFaire wore. Rags.

It was not clear, even, that the corpse was male.

Half the flesh was missing. Chunks hadn't been carved out or torn off. It was more like bits the size of gravel had been snipped away. Thousands of bits. "Here." Git pushed something with his toe, out where we could all see.

A dead beetle. The little sister of the bug from the day before. Five inches long, black, with a horn and pincers on the business end.

"Holy shit," Saucerhead said from behind me, in soft awe. "Lookit the size of that sucker."

"Yeah. Wow," Playmate added.

"There are lots more inside," Singe told us. "That is why John wants the boxes."

"Yeah," Tharpe said. "You guys hand a couple of them back here. Me an' Play will carry them in."

I didn't talk him out of volunteering, but I did say, "When you're done with that, help Git and Bank look for gang sign. Though this don't look like what Handsome's thing was." Then I said, "I've seen something like this before." As Git and Bank dragged the body into the open. "In the islands. Soldier ants did it."

The Guards kicked more dead bugs around. Git said, "This guy was alive when they got him. He fought."

Bank grunted. "He crawled in here to get out of the weather. They hit him when he was sleeping."

I edged closer. Old Bones would want every detail. Including the stink. "Where's all the blood?" There should have been blood everywhere.

"Down some bug's gullet," Git said. "Bugs got gullets? How do they work?"

"Got me," Bank said. "Gonna need some big boots to squish these bastards."

Singe said, "Garrett, you need to come inside."

Saucerhead and Playmate had boxes and were waiting. I grabbed one myself, toddled after the band.

The ratmen had gathered about where I'd talked to the carpenters before. Wicker cages surrounded them. John Stretch's henchrats were scared. My dull human nose could smell it.

John Stretch said, "This is bigger than it looks, Garrett." Producing some odor himself. "We need many more rats than we brought."

"Why's that?"

"Because there are so many bugs. And because they are fighting back. No. That is not right. They do not think. Less so, even, than the beasts I am using to kill them. But they are not afraid. They are eating my rats. And each other, when the rats dispatch them."

Good word choice, Pound Humility. "Dispatch." Very neutral.

"There are a lot of bugs, then."

"Thousands. And the ones that have surfaced are the smallest."

"Ouch! That's not good."

"Very much not good. I would like to withdraw now, see what I can learn from the surviving rats, and develop a more definitive strategy."

And renegotiate, no doubt. After flinging around a few more big words borrowed from Singe.

Saucerhead squeaked, jumped, snarled, "Holy fucking camel snot!"

A bull rat who looked like the undisputed heavyweight champion barbarian hero of all ratkind had just dropped a gift at our feet, then collapsed from exhaustion.

The bug was some kind of tropical exotic beetle, all shimmering oily shine on a deep background of dark green, indigo, and black. A foot long. Still twitching. But it had been conquered by the hero.

Other rats began to arrive. Each brought a prize. John Stretch's buddies tossed bugs into boxes and pushed rats into cages. Even the heavyweight hero seemed happy to be locked up safe. All his savagery had been spent.

I said, "I'll see Old Man Weider before we take any next step. Singe. John Stretch. Go back to my place. Fill the Dead Man in. If he hasn't fallen asleep. Saucerhead. You're on the payroll. Retainer rate for now. Play. Keep a coach handy. It may take an even bigger . . ."

I looked to John Stretch. "You sort of know what the critters found down there. Right?"

"Yes."

"Is this method workable?"

"Probably. But it will be a strain. It will require many more rats. They burn out. Most of these will refuse to go down again."

"Singe. I smell a business opportunity."

"Again? I still have not worked out how to exploit the last one." She meant taking advantage of ratfolks' high tolerance for boredom by using them to copy books. Most had trouble developing the necessary fine motor skills. "What is it?"

"We could get ratpeople work clearing the rats out of places. Ratters are expensive."

She and John Stretch looked fiercely uncomfortable.

"I say something wrong?"

Singe shrugged. "John Stretch is the only one who can command the rats. And they have to be willing to listen."

I shrugged in turn. "If it can't be done, it can't. You guys get going."

I went back to where Git and Bank were managing the removal of the body. I dug a usable gunnysack out of the mess the dead man had used as bedding. Nobody found any gang sign. Nor any evidence that the derelict had suffered any violence other than the attack of the bugs.

# 15

Hector wasn't excited by my return. But he did let me in. "Wait here." He had a voice like a bucket of rocks being shaken. He went to announce my petition for an audience.

People from the back stairs popped out to get a look while I waited. Remarkable things had happened back there a while ago, with me deeply involved. These folks would have been hired since.

I suppressed my theatrical urge. I didn't do a buck and wing.

Manvil Gilbey came. "So you've done your usual marvelous job and have it wrapped up already?"

"Not quite. Actually, just the opposite."

"Ah. So. Your usual marvelous job."

"And you're gonna love it."

A minute later I dumped the gunnysack in front of Max and Gilbey. I was forthright about what I'd done. I even mentioned John Stretch's special talent without naming his name. "Also, we got a murder of a security guard, with gang sign. The way those things work, that'll be the source of your vandalism and theft. Setting you up for protection payoffs."

Max considered the bug corpses. He considered me. He said, "They told me they were big bugs. I was thinking woods roaches. Those flying cockroaches the size of your finger. Not something the size of your mutant feet."

"Even bigger ones down below, Boss. So I'm told."

"This ratman can command the rodents? He could get rich calling the rats out of places like the brewery."

"I suggested that. He wasn't interested."

"He'd see the problems better than we could. So what do you need?"

"I just want you to be aware. Ghosts may not be a real problem. Nobody I talked to admitted seeing any. There was some muttering about weird music. They all seemed to think somebody was faking in order to force a slowdown. Maybe as part of the coming shakedown."

"Not a surprise. What about the murder?"

"We actually found two bodies. The guard was an old guy called Handsome. The other was a squatter. It looked like he was attacked in his sleep by bugs. Bugs chewed Handsome up pretty bad, too. Singe couldn't get a track on the bad guys but he was definitely murdered."

"Not good, that. Did Handsome work for me?"

"He told me his boss was Lego Bunk when I saw him yesterday."

"Bunk works for me. He used to, anyway. He'll be looking for work after this. Find out what you can about Handsome. If he has people we'll have to do something for them. Take care of his funeral arrangements, for sure. Now that Lego Bunk is gone, what're you going to do about taking care of the World?"

He wasn't that interested, though. He'd delegated the work. His direct involvement ended there. Unless I screwed up and had to go the way of Lego Bunk.

"Escalate. Bring in more rats. A lot more, if my ratman is right. Do the stuff for Handsome that you said. And let the tin whistles take care of the murder. The killers really want to work protection, they'll turn up."

"Do what you have to," Max growled. "Don't come back here bothering me unless you get grief from somebody who thinks they're more important than they really are."

Never before had he so blatantly admitted how loudly wealth talks.

When you're the god of beer in a city the size of Tun-Faire, you've got more money than the King himself.

"Then I'm free to do whatever needs doing? And you'll back me up? I want to be clear on this."

"I'll back you one hundred percent as long as you keep your hot ham hands off the rest of my daughters."

I'd broken Morley's First Commandment, about messing with crazy women, and had a fling with Kittyjo Weider. She was marginally crazy then. She'd become a howling lunatic by the time she was murdered.

"No problem."

"I do believe in your good intentions. And I know Tinnie. But I know Alyx, too. She gets an idea in her head, she gets as damned single-minded as her old man."

"I've managed so far. She's all talk, anyway. She just wants the reaction. From you and me both."

That should give Max a chance to relax. And it might even be true.

Maybe I ought to call her bluff.

Only, Tinnie would slice off some of my favorite limbs. And Alyx would call *my* bluff. Guaranteed.

Then Max would hear.

"Manpower," I said.

"Excuse me?"

"If ratpower isn't enough to solve the trouble at the World . . . Never mind. I have resources." If I needed twenty swinging dicks to clear the World, I could round them up in a couple hours.

"Come back when they're after you for killing somebody."

Gilbey hadn't said anything for a while. He spoke up now. "Or when you find yourself in some demonstrable fiscal difficulty."

He was the practical one.

Max suggested, "How about you have something interesting to report next time you come around?"

I exchanged glances with Gilbey. Manvil said, "Some days Max isn't so enthusiastic about the new challenges. Even dead bodies don't fire him up."

It's nice to have the kind of friendship that lets you talk about your pal that way right in front of him.

# 16

Playmate's stable was quiet when I went by. I didn't stop in. His brother-in-law was covering for him while he was away. I'd only met the man once. That was once more than I'd needed.

Play was turning the other one like a self-flagellation machine with that villain. But he loves his baby sister.

We tolerate crap from family that we'd butcher strangers over.

I couldn't resist taking a turn past The Palms. I didn't drop in, though. I stayed across the street. Morley's henchman, Sarge, came out to dump a bucket of filthy water. He scowled my way. I waved and kept going. Sarge scowled a whole lot more.

Morley didn't run after me. Not that I expected he would. Sarge probably didn't mention that he'd seen me.

No problem. No pain. I'd decided to continue giving Morley Dotes a rest.

Then I saw Playmate, heading home from my place. He waved but didn't stop. His business and life were at the mercy of a brother-in-law who should've been drowned at birth.

The people of TunFaire were still out enjoying the weather. Several stopped me and wanted to talk, usually about something I couldn't have found less interesting.

We all have our quirks and special passions. Mine are beer and beautiful women. Lately, beer and beautiful woman, redheaded and blessed with a surfeit of attitude.

One of whom was waiting in ambush. She overran me when I got home.

When I got a chance to come up for air, I gasped, "Hunh! Hunh! Hunh!" When my heart slowed down and the rest of me stopped shaking, I just had to check the gift horse's teeth. "What're you doing here?"

"I thought I made that obvious."

"You know how my head works. If it looks too good to be true, I figure it is."

"Should I be flattered or offended?" Tinnie asked.

"You'll decide that no matter what I say. I'm in the camp that figures you're too good to be true."

"Ah. You sweet talker. Too bad you have all these other people around here."

Singe could not stay away. She turned up to ask, "What did the principal have to say?"

"He said do the job. Stop coming round getting underfoot. Come back when it's done. Go have a beer. I'm busy here."

"You have a room. You do not have to mate in the hallway."

Tinnie snickered into my neck.

The woman is shameless when it suits her.

My partner amazed me by favoring discretion. I heard nothing from him.

Dean did appear to offer us an evening meal.

Singe saw the lay of the land. Sullen, she went back to one of her private projects.

"What's her problem?" Tinnie asked. "She trying to seduce you again?"

"That was just a phase. Adolescent fantasy. She got over it. Now she thinks she's a storyteller. She says she's written a book about me. And now she needs some interesting stories to put in it."

"I should get together with her. I could tell her about you before you met."

"I'm sure you could. And I'm just as sure that she don't need any more ideas than what she's got."

A faint fragrance of amusement tainted the psychic air momentarily. Old Bones no doubt conceiving a wicked notion that could find life only at my expense.

There was no one in the hallway but Tinnie and me now. And she was having no trouble with the invisible eye that's always there when the Dead Man is awake.

It didn't take her long to make me forget, either.

She's got skills, that girl.

# 17

The brain trust had gathered. Singe. Playmate. Saucerhead. John Stretch. With Old Bones in the background, ready to kibitz. Tinnie was in the doorway. She leaned against its frame in an indifferent, sluttish pose wasted on everybody. Me included. She wasn't happy about that.

*Would you care to direct your thoughts in a less prurient direction?*

I said, "We need to brainstorm the situation at the World. Our efforts yesterday may not have done much more than stir up the bugs."

Saucerhead observed, "It's freaking hard to get the bugs out of anywhere. Mice and rats, same thing. You wipe out the mess you got, another one moves in."

*It is notoriously difficult to remove vermin and keep them removed. This instance will be no exception. But it should prove less difficult than the sort of general debugging you would find familiar. There will be a finite number of these mutant insects. Though that could be a large number. A sustained effort should destroy them faster than they can breed.*

He was giving this more thought than he pretended.

*You are correct, Garrett. Though not in the way you think.*

I glimpsed something I didn't have the mental capacity to grasp. A three-dimensional mind map of the universe in the earth around and under the World. Developed, with John Stretch's help, from the minds of rats that had gone down there and had brought back memories of sights and smells. Especially smells.

John Stretch assures me that regular rats count on their sense of smell more than dogs do. Thus the thing inside the Dead Man's mind was a visualized translation of information collected mainly by rat snoots.

Rats are crafty. But rats aren't much smarter than a sack of hammers. I wasn't ready to bet my life, fortune, and sacred honor on what my sidekick could put together from their mad, crippled rodent memories.

I said, "We could handle this whole thing fast if we could dump a million gallons of water into the warrens under the World."

Flooding the bug tunnels was an obvious move. Figuring out how to deliver the flood was not.

"How about poison gas?" Playmate asked. "Some kinds would sink down into the bug warrens the way water would."

"Like?"

"Fumes from burning sulfur."

John Stretch said, "I would like to try rats again. Using more of them."

The Dead Man touched me privately. *Allow John Stretch the effort. Insisting on a much larger effort. Ten thousand rats if that is what is needed. Test the strength of this absurd conjunction.*

"Huh?"

*There must be sorcery involved. To explain the size of the bugs. The absurdity arises in the mix of insects that have mutated.*

Someone was doing to bugs what had been done to rats in the last century?

*You are unlikely to lose much money betting that way.*

I announced, "Guys, this may be a worse problem than I thought."

*Engage brain before opening mouth,* the Dead Man snapped. *Think before you pop off.*

"Huh?"

*You are getting ahead of yourself. It is possible the problem can be solved by application of a large number of rats. If it cannot,* then *you have your worse problem.*

So I said, "Never mind. John Stretch. By all means, take another crack. But go for overwhelming numbers. All the rats you can round up. If you can't run them all at the same time, fine. Use them in shifts."

*I need to know the outer bounds of the insect infestation. In all dimensions.*

He didn't say it but I understood. He wanted to isolate the point of origin of the giant bugs.

That would be handy to know. We could toss one fire-bomb in there. . . .

*Garrett. The most obvious and direct approach may not be the best.*

"For who?"

*All concerned. You have to know what is going on before you blow things up and burn things down. You cannot approach all problems with the methods espoused by Mr. Dotes. It is possible that the bugs are an unfortunate by-blow of something positive happening in that area. The creator of the bugs may be unaware of the effect of his work on the insect population.*

"Evil spirits and psychotic demons are more likely."

*No doubt. Nevertheless, it is important to examine and eliminate other possibilities. Unless you trip over some villain casting spells on cockroaches.*

"While practicing his evil laugh. Yeah."

The rest of the crowd watched like they expected to be entertained any minute now. Except that fiscal traitoress, Pular Singe, who toddled in with fermented barley soup for all hands. On good old Garrett.

I wouldn't earn any kudos dancing with the truth. They'd just accuse me of being a skinflint. Again.

It's so easy to spend the other guy's dough.

# 18

The weather continued favorable. The surviving city trees were about to bud. To their sorrow. The snow and ice would return.

Word was out. Garrett had a case. He had money. The street out front looked like I was gathering a wagon train for a *volkswanderung*. All six wagons boasted human drivers. Which said that John Stretch's reach had gotten pretty long, pretty fast.

Playmate had brought the same coach round, too.

There were ratpeople everywhere, all of them armed with cages or baskets full of regular rats. The neighbors were out in force, being nosy. Among them would be tin whistles in disguise.

I had a mild hangover. Singe and her brother did, too. But Saucerhead and Playmate were bright and cheerful, ambling around with acres of teeth exposed to the breeze. Early birds. Let 'em eat worms.

What the hell became of all my old pals in the seize-the-night crowd?

The only positive was, Tinnie was there beside me. A morning person. A lightning rod for all those bleak disappointments that haunt the world before noon.

Saucerhead told me, "We need us some horse guys in tin suits with flags on their spears. And some halberdiers."

"How's your bugling? You could sound the charge."

"That's up to the rat king. This being all about him and his critters."

Saucerhead can be as literal as a hunk of granite.

John Stretch was thinking like my imagination-challenged friend. "We are ready, Garrett."

"I are ready, too. Just waiting on Singe." She'd had to duck inside. As usual.

The watching tin whistles were restless. This big a show by ratpeople made them nervous.

*They will not interfere. Unless you fail to stop dithering long enough for me to fall asleep again.*

The reason for his impatience was in plain sight.

Tinnie spotted her, too. "Hey. There's Penny. I'm going to—"

"No. She don't want anything to do with us anymore. Except for His Nibs. And Dean, because she can mooch a meal off him."

Tinnie didn't believe me. But she didn't argue. She'd had a premonition that Alyx would turn up during festivities at the World. She wasn't going to let her main guy go into danger that fierce without moral backup. The word "danger" being spelled "temptation."

My backup was about to get her back up. But Singe breezed out and helped herself to the next to last seat in Playmate's coach. It took my favorite redhead a hundredth of a second to assess the situation and make sure that the last seat didn't go to waste.

This early worm was going to get some unwanted exercise. "Story of my life," I grumbled.

Tinnie gave me a dark look, followed by one of her blinding smiles.

Lucky for me, the wagons didn't roll fast.

Unlucky for everyone else, the wagons didn't roll fast. We had time to acquire a patina of curious urchins. Saucerhead, trudging along beside me, grumbled, "You'd think we were some kind of circus, or something."

Or something. "Been a long winter."

Our entertainment value faded once we got to the World. The ratfolk took their cages and baskets and went inside. Then nothing happened.

An hour later, Singe reported, "It seems to be working."

It might be, but before I left the house I'd seen Joe Kerr and had gotten a backup plan running. Here it came now, in the form of a goat cart pulled by a pygmy troll named Rocky. Rocky's family were all midgets, the tallest not going more than six feet. They're unobtrusive, rock-solid, foundation-type royal subjects who specialize in chemical supplies for sorcerers, physicians, apothecaries, and anyone else whose coin has a shine on it. He was delivering twenty pounds of powdered sulfur that I meant to fire up as soon as John Stretch was done for the day.

Rocky presented a flour sack leaking whiffs of fine yellow powder. I gave him several pieces of silver. He grunted, "Good," in a voice so deep it seemed like part of an earthquake. He started moving again. Slowly.

Trolls don't need to hurry. They don't have to run away, they don't have to catch, they have no need to get anywhere right now.

Earlier during the wait I'd taken a turn around the World site. I hadn't seen a soul, workman or watchman, nor the city employees who had been there yesterday. No place ought to be that deserted. TunFaire abhors a vacuum. If no one else was around, thieves should've been trying to find something worth carting off.

Saucerhead had noticed. "They's something weird going on here, Garrett."

"No shit." I set the sack of sulfur down out of traffic.

"You hear music?"

"No."

"I thought I heard music a minute ago."

One of John Stretch's pals headed our way. Lugging a beetle as big as a lamb. He didn't editorialize; he just dropped the monster when I didn't offer to take it. He headed back to the wars.

Most of the gallery had wandered away. A few kids still hung around in hopes of finding a pocket to pick. But when that bug hit the cobblestones you could feel the shock start to radiate at the speed of rumor.

TunFaire would be in a panic before sunset.

"Yeah, right," Saucerhead said when I started to worry out loud. "Like the time you got into it with that clutch of weird gods. All anybody cared about was the snow."

He had a point. Strange stuff happens. People shrug it off unless it happens to them.

Rather than panicking, my fellow subjects would likely come bury the World in bodies, hoping to see something novel.

Playmate said, "Hey, Garrett, whack that thing with something. It ain't dead."

It lay on its back. Its legs were twitching. Its wings, ditto. Then it stopped struggling. It seemed to be assessing its situation.

"Garrett!"

It flipped. It faced me. Big brown jaw things clacked.

It charged.

I delivered a masterful spinning kick. After which I deposited the opposite side of my lap on the cobblestones. A snicker came from the coach, where my sweetie was evading the weather.

The bug smacked into the coach's big back wheel. The hub did some damage. The bug fell, shuddered, and expired.

"Maybe less dangerous than they look."

I'm not big on reasoning this stuff out, but I figure bugs naturally come the size that's best for them. Which meant the normal vermin crop are exactly the right size.

So, back to the mad sorcerer notion.

# 19

"Mr. Garrett?"

A kid had come up behind me. "Kip Prose! How are you?" I hadn't seen him for a while. He'd grown, though he was still barely a mouse breath more than five feet. His blond hair was longer and wilder, his eyes bluer and crazier. His waist was more substantial. His freckles were more numerous. He did a better job of holding still, but broke into sudden, brief fits of scratching and twitching. Wealth hadn't changed him inside.

Cypres Prose is the strangest kid I ever met. He has three redeeming qualities. Two any man can see at a glance. A gorgeous mother, Kayne Prose. And an older sister, Cassie Doap, who makes Mom look dowdy. The third quality is less obvious: the boy is a screaming genius. Of no special ambition, but with ideas that could make a lot of people rich. Maybe including me.

I have that small interest in the manufactory producing three-wheels, writing sticks, and other innovations sprung from Kip Prose's twisted brain. I have the points because I found the genius, kept him alive, and put him together with people who have the money and space to create a manufacturing concern. The Weiders and the Tates.

"I'm doing quite well, Mr. Garrett. And yourself?"

I was suspicious immediately. Be abidingly suspicious of any teenage male who is mannerly, respectful, and absent attitude.

That kid is up to something. Guaranteed.

Kip wasn't alone. Two friends, of a similarly weird appearance, had stayed across the street. They pretended no interest in what was going on.

Definitely suspicious.

Tinnie is a clever judge of people. When she bothers. Usually she deploys her skills against me alone. She made an exception here. "And how is your mother? And your sister, Cassie?" She turned on the flaming redheaded heat, guaranteed to send Kip into cardiac arrest, turn him to gelatin, and make him speak in tongues with vocabularies of one syllable.

Kip chirped like a frog. Once.

Tinnie got very close to him.

Kip knew who she was. One of those black widow fantasy women from the Tate tribe. He'd seen her around the manufactory. No doubt she'd imprinted herself on his libidinous consciousness.

It's bad enough when that wicked wench turns it on to an old jade like me. It's fish in a barrel, targeting a repressed boy Cypres Prose's age.

"Oh, that's good," I said. "You fried his brain. How do I get anything out of him now?" Kip's friends, I noted, were not pleased, either.

"What do you want to know? Maybe I'll ask."

"All right. But afterward I'm going to drive a stake through your heart."

"That's a straight line I could play with for . . . a minute or two."

"Promises, promises."

Kip resumed breathing.

Tinnie told me, "You don't want to know about his mother or sister. When I snap my fingers you will forget he has a mother or sister." *Snap!*

"Yes, master. I have no interest in the welfare of absent beautiful women. But now I know how you cast your spell on me."

That earned me a nasty look. I survived it and worse consequences because Kip's eyes rolled back down. He began speaking actual words.

I asked, "What the hell are you doing down here, Kip?"

I could guess. He was a teenage boy. With the financial means to indulge a teenage boy's fantasies. The Tenderloin was a stone's throw on down the street.

Not smart. You could get dead. A dozen different ways. Not all of them sudden.

Clever lad, he avoided answering by responding to what I'd asked earlier. "Mom is fine. Kind of doesn't know what to do with herself now that she doesn't have to work all the time."

He has a significant interest in the manufacturing concern. Between them, he, his mother, and sister control the biggest chunk. He'd insisted.

"You get her that house?"

"The one where she always lived. It's all hers, free and clear, now."

"That's good. What are you doing down here? Not wasting yourself in the Tenderloin, I hope."

Kip turned bright red. Brighter than when Tinnie worked her witchcraft. He sputtered. Then choked out, "I'm just hanging out with my friends." He indicated the impatient boys across the street. He and those two looked like one socially challenged pod. The friends were tense and irritated and eager to distance themselves from the World. "I just saw you and decided to say hi. What're you doing?"

"Killing bugs." I pointed at the beetle by the wheel of Playmate's coach.

Kip's eyes got big. "Wow! Well, I got to go."

"Good seeing you again," Tinnie told him.

He gurgled, waggled a hand feebly, and headed out. Tinnie blew him a kiss, just to amuse his sidekicks. Who started in on him as soon as they could without having me hear what they said.

"Having fun with the cruel and unusual, woman?"

"You ever make that mistake when you were a kid?"

"I didn't know any beautiful redheads then."

"Cute. Try again."

"What mistake?"

"Trying to distract an adult's curiosity with a preemptive move."

"I don't follow."

"And you a skilled detective. He was going by. He didn't want you wondering why he was down here. So he decided to establish his innocence ahead of time. Neither of us would've noticed him if he hadn't pointed himself out. But now you have noticed. And now you're curious."

"Got you. Yeah. I made that mistake a few times."

"Never worked, did it?"

"Nope. Turned around and bit me every time. I'm going to find Singe."

Kip and his friends left quickly, all talking at the same time, all of them angry.

The ratpeople inside the World weren't pleased to see me. They figured I was there to micromanage. Like Max, though, I'd rather tell somebody what needs doing, then get the hell out of the way. Most of the time. "Singe. I need you outside."

As we headed for the coach, she asked, "That's the same boy who was involved with the silver elves?"

"The same." She'd tracked Kip before.

"What do I need to do?"

"Find out where he goes. And what he's up to, if you can do that without getting caught."

"You aren't coming?"

"You aren't ready to operate on your own?"

"I am ready." Proudly.

"Excellent."

She picked up the trail right away.

Tinnie asked, "Is that smart? Sending her off by herself?"

"The kid has to grow up someday. She manages ordinary household business on her own."

"I suppose."

"What happened to Saucerhead and Playmate?"

"They went down that alley over there. To check with a man about a mule."

Together? That was a girlie thing to do.

"You heard from Alyx? Or the others?"

"Not lately. Why?" Eyes all narrow.

"You and Max should form a club. He's also sure Alyx is in dire peril from the dread Garrett beast."

"The beast isn't that bad. But it better not get caught fondling any blondes. Of any kind."

Kip's mother and sister were blondes, last time I saw them.

"Pretty draconian, wouldn't you say? What?"

Her face had drained. Even the freckles had gone.

She was staring over my shoulder.

Before I ever turned, I told her, "Get in the coach. Lock any locks you find. And don't come out till Play and Saucerhead get back. No matter what."

# 20

There were seven of them. Teens, with the youngest just over the border but a decade older in his empty heart. The tallest was maybe five feet six. They were all pale brown, black of hair, empty of eye, the sons of refugees. And stupid.

They were up to no good. Obviously. In broad daylight. In an area that attracted Watchmen, though none were evident at the moment. They didn't know who they meant to mess with and they weren't carrying weapons. Not openly.

The leader announced himself with a short guy swagger. We locked gazes. He was dead cold inside, this boy. How do they get that way so young?

"Help you with something?"

"You ready to come across with the insurance now?"

"I'll be damned." I couldn't help laughing. "There just ain't no limit to stupid in this burg."

That didn't sit well. "You calling us stupid?"

"Yeah. Do the math, kid. Did you bother to find out who you're messing with? Or where you're doing the messing? You're going to try to run a protection scam on the richest man in TunFaire? He can afford to pay a thousand dorks just like you to scatter pieces of you from the north side all the way down to the delta. And he will, just to make sure word gets out not to fuck with him."

The baby of the crew sneered. "This is Stompers' turf now, old man. Nobody does nothin' here without they get our permission first."

"This is the Tenderloin, baby boy. Combine territory. Folks a lot less forgiving than Max Weider. You boys go home to mama. Before you give her a reason to cry."

These kids weren't used to having somebody not melt in
terror. Their particular combination of ferocity, ignorance,
and don't care if I see tomorrow could only mean they
were children of the Bustee, TunFaire's foulest and most
dangerous slum.

The kid gangs of the Bustee all have names like "The
Stompers."

The seven spread out. Their captain was disappointed by
my attitude. He planned to show me why they'd chosen
their name.

Saucerhead and Playmate, back from haggling over a
mule, came round the coach. Tharpe read the situation in
a blink, snapped up two boys, and smacked them together
so hard I heard a bone break before one started wailing.
He threw the lighter kid up on top of the coach. Where
the boy failed to stick. He fell back down, landing in a way
that had to dislocate his shoulder.

Tharpe selected another victim.

Playmate, saddled as he is with a conscience, took time
to assess the situation before he stepped in. His score was
just one knockdown, plus dishing a second serving to one
of the ones I put down when the kid tried to get back up.

Tin whistles tooted.

The leader of the pack was the only one who produced
a weapon, a rusty kitchen knife probably stolen from home.
He didn't know how to use it. Yet.

He would, someday. If he survived.

The first Watchman arrived after the action. Four boys
were hurt too bad to run. Two tried but had no luck. The
littlest was the only one nimble enough to get away, crying
as he went.

The leader's knife hand was all crippled up. Somebody
stomped it. He didn't whine. His eyes didn't get any less
cold.

The first tin whistle to show was a guy I knew, Ingram
Grahm. "What happened, Garrett?"

I told it. Tinnie backed me up. Ingram considered ar-
resting me for having a disproportionately beautiful companion. Playmate and Saucerhead told what they knew.
Ingram echoed my own thinking. "There's no bottom to
the reservoir of stupid, is there? These guys the reason
you're down here?"

"Maybe. Somebody's been messing with Old Man Weider's construction crew. He told me to make it stop."

"Yeah? Take care. There's probably a shitload more of these little peckerneckers. Their mobs run in the hundreds, sometimes."

He didn't want the hassle of having to deal with a bunch of kid gangsters. He'd probably want to give them a lecture they wouldn't hear, then tell them to drag their sorry asses home. In the pre-Relway era style of dealing with juvenile crime.

I said, "We've had two bodies turn up here in the last two days. You know Git and Bank?"

"Sure. This's their beat. Today's their day off."

"They're the ones dealing with that."

"Kind of turns things around, don't it?" Ingram eyeballed the teens hard.

I said, "Take a check of the back of that left hand. Somebody scratched that same tattoo into that pillar over there. Where the security guy's body turned up. Whoever did it used a bloody knife. That kid there had him a knife. It's around here somewhere."

Saucerhead held it up and waggled it.

The gang leader showed the slightest strain. He knew enough about current events to understand that he didn't want to catch the eye of the Civil Guard when murder was involved. You for sure didn't want them thinking you was the one who done it.

I'd bet all my shiny new angels there was a nasty murder lurking in Deal Relway's early memories. Something that galled his sense of justice. Potential murderers don't fare well in Relway's keeping. Even thugs who swim deep in the reservoir of stupid are catching on. Bad shit is waiting on the other side of what might seem like a good idea at the time.

Tin whistles continued to arrive. Ingram said, "I'll take that knife, Tharpe. We got a new forensic sorcerer who'll match it up if it's the blade that killed the guard. Garrett. Any chance we could borrow a wagon? Some of these little bastards are too busted up to walk."

"They aren't mine to loan. You need to ask the teamsters."

Playmate said, "Let the living carry the dead," quoting

scripture. Then rounded up a pliant teamster who didn't mind hauling casualties to the Al-Khar. For a suitable tip.

"You do lead an interesting life, don't you?" Tinnie said as we watched the city employees clear off. I was about to get a dose of stop this nonsense and get a real job.

"As long as you're in it."

"Do you think those boys murdered the dead men?"

"Handsome, yeah. Not the other one. Relway will get them to confess everything they've ever gotten into. Then he'll fix it so they never hurt anybody again."

"Doesn't that bother you?"

"Less than it would if they hadn't planned to stomp the snot out of me."

"You think they would've tried?"

"Absolutely. And they would've done. There were too many of them. And at that age they don't know when to stop." Handsome had been stomped before he was murdered.

"Guess that wraps the job up, then. Doesn't it?"

"One angle. There's still the bugs and the ghosts and the mysterious music, none of which those shitheads were bright enough to fake."

"Here comes your first wife."

"Smart-ass."

"I'm not so smart. But I'm cute."

Oh yeah.

# 21

Singe approached slowly. She sniffed the air and looked around nervously. "Are you all right?"

"They never laid a hand on me. Thanks to good timing." I indicated Saucerhead and Playmate. I told it. That being the easiest way to calm her. Once she knew she wouldn't lose her meal ticket, I asked, "What did you come up with?"

"They went to a house about a block past the theater. Down to that first corner, then turn left. It looks abandoned. Only we know there aren't any abandoned buildings in TunFaire."

The contractions came fast and furious today.

It isn't strictly true that there are no abandoned buildings. But a place has to be nasty beyond belief not to accumulate squatters. "Same as what keeps them from sneaking into the World at night?"

"Could be."

"Something you're not telling me?"

"Only that I think there is a connection. The same smell is coming out there. But stronger."

"You didn't go inside?"

"Of course not. I am not that brave. The smell is that strong."

"Bug smell?"

"Yes. But something else, too. Powerful and frightening."

"Let me think about this."

Three teenage boys. On the brink of the Tenderloin. But interested in a derelict building instead.

If the others were like Kip, that might mean something.

Due to the overwhelming weight of shyness and fear of failure in front of friends.

On the other hand, if they were like Kip, they'd all be mad geniuses. Who didn't have a clue.

Kip would be seventeen or eighteen now. And still desperately in need of Mom's help to make himself presentable in public. He could come up with amazing things—like the three-wheel, the folding knife you carry in your pocket, and the drawing compass—but he hadn't yet caught on how to deal with real, live people. Especially those special, real, live people who come equipped with soft curves.

Singe said, "I remember what that smell is. We smelled it that time with the shape changers."

"I didn't want to hear that." That had been a rough time, chock-full of horrors, wonders, and amazements. Max had lost his wife and several children. I'd met Singe. The Dead Man had left the house for the first, last, and only time. And we'd all learned how nasty shape shifters could be. And how hard it is to kill them.

"Not the monsters. The smell around them. That yeasty, beer-making smell." She preened.

Tinnie observed in silence. Her having no opinion became distracting. Tinnie Tate always has an opinion. Whether she knows anything or not. All Tates come that way.

"Max makes good stuff at reasonable prices. So why would those boys try to make it when they can buy it ready made, cheaper? Boys their age think work is a curse word."

"I did not say they were brewing beer," Singe growled. "I said the smell suggests fermentation."

"There you go again."

"Can I ask a question?" Tinnie said.

"As long as you understand that I might not give you an honest answer."

"Why fuss about that creepy kid making beer when your mission is to make sure the World Theater is finished on time, in budget, so Alyx and Bobbi and me have a place to show ourselves off?"

I grinned.

"Oh gods!" she burbled. "Don't you dare even think what you're thinking."

I kept grinning. "But, darling! Light of my life. Why not

be generous and give you my second floor to strut your stuff?"

"Garrett." That was Playmate, distracting me by pointing out another bunch of teenagers. Unfortunately for them, the tin whistles were lurking. The little thugs got rounded up before they knew what hit them.

For Relway's mob probable cause can be as improbable as they like.

Impatient, Singe asked, "Do you plan to do anything but crack wise and take up space?"

Tinnie chimed in, "Here comes something about sharp snake's teeth, hen's teeth, frog fur, or some other folksy observation about how unfair we all are."

So. Once again it was teak on Tommie Tucker season with Mama Garrett's baby boy starring as poor, sad Tommie. The damned horses pulling Playmate's coach were ready to join in.

Horses are all out to get me. Some just fake innocence better than others.

Singe said, "Response please. Take up space? Crackwise? Or?"

"All right. Show me the damned house."

# 22

"Damned" wasn't far off the mark.

The place Singe showed me was one spring storm shy of collapse. Its upper-story windows were empty eyes. The wooden parts of its stoop were gone, taken for firewood. Bricks had begun falling off. There was no door in the doorway.

But the structure remained upright, for now, fifteen feet wide and three stories tall. A squatter's delight. But there was none of the trash or stench found where outsiders put down roots. There were no filthy toddlers underfoot.

"Sorcery," Saucerhead opined. Having tagged along uninvited, accompanied by Tinnie and Playmate.

"You could be right. I already think sorcery is the root of the bug problem."

"You smell it?" Singe asked.

"No. I'm human, sweetheart." I climbed the stone steps to the doorway. They wobbled underfoot. Why hadn't they been carried off? And the brickwork, too. Bricks are valuable.

There was an obvious line beyond which scavengers had not dared venture. Chips of decomposing brick lay on one side, close in. Nothing lay farther out.

Even small chips of brick are salable at the brickworks. The brick makers crush them and add them as tempering when they make new bricks.

I walked inside the line.

"Place looks empty," I said. I reached in with the tip of my left foot, testing the flooring. It creaked. But it was still there. Not yet plundered. Mostly. Without squatters to explain its preservation.

"Sorcery," I whispered to myself. In case myself had missed that point before.

Of my companions, only the natural-born coward, the ratgirl, joined me on the stoop.

"I smell something now," I told her. "Not fermenting beer, though."

"There are several odors. Combined. The wort smell is the loudest. The others are unfamiliar."

Something clattered down below. It sounded like a thin board falling onto a hard floor. Someone cursed, in a "He done a dumb thing" mode instead of "Damn it, I just hurt myself!" I waved Singe back, retreated myself, watched from a respectful distance.

Singe asked, "Why did we run away?"

"I don't know. Maybe me thinking about that dead line. Why didn't scavengers pick up chips on the other side?"

"Somebody took the wood from the stoop. And the door. And the door frame and the windows are all gone, too."

Maybe I was thinking at it the wrong way.

Singe said, "I saw three boys go in. The Prose boy would be the most dangerous. Right?"

I took her meaning. "I'm scaring myself, here."

Tinnie suggested, "There must be more to it than that. A few minutes ago you were all babbling about sorcery."

"That's the answer," I announced. "There's some kind of enchantment designed to scare people away." You could buy those over the counter. Install the fetish where you needed protection, then pull the pin. It would work on anybody who didn't carry a counterfetish.

Crooked hedge wizards would put some of those aside to sell to the people you bought the fetish to keep out. So you, knowing that and being clever, would subscribe to a coun07charm antidote.

"That's the answer," I said again. "Nothing to fear but fear itself. Here I go. Once more into the breach."

Playmate asked, "Your feet stuck to the ground?"

"You want to take a look over there? In the doorway?"

A praying mantis had appeared. A dull lime green, it stood three feet tall. It looked around vaguely, as though blinded by the light.

Saucerhead rumbled, "Damn! That's uglier than Winger's mother."

Tinnie said, "It's got a rat in its hands."

They weren't hands but she was right. It bit off a chunk as it looked around.

I asked, "What do you think?"

Saucerhead said, "I think I should've worn my big boy stomping boots."

A more thoughtful Playmate said, "You wasted your money on that sulfur. If the bugs can just pop out another hole."

Singe resigned her membership in the stand-around committee. She headed for the bug. She had, I noticed, produced a weighted oaken head thumper like the one I carry myself. She wore more clothing than her brother, less colorfully. She favored browns. She had places to hide stuff.

She was much more forceful and determined than I'd ever seen. Monster bugs didn't intimidate her.

"You might want to back her up," Tinnie said. "Just in case."

"Yeah." I hustled after Singe.

The wort stench had grown stronger. I caught it thirty feet from the derelict house.

Earlier there'd been just a handful of people keeping an eye on us. Adding that giant bug had a magical effect. The gallery cooked up into a crowd in two shakes.

Singe climbed the wobbly steps. The mantis ignored her till she took a swipe at its big ugly head.

It leaped straight forward. Singe missed. It tried to fly but didn't have wings enough for the job. They carried it only a few extra feet. It landed badly, smacked its ugly face into the cobblestones.

Singe jumped after it. Now she had a knife in her other hand. She severed the bug's neck. Stuff came out. I danced to keep from getting squirted.

A kid ran up to Singe. "Wow! Cool! Can I have that?" He wanted the head. The mantis's jaw things kept clicking and clacking.

"Oh no! What did you do?"

"I think I killed a tall bug."

Singe spoke to me but the question had come from behind me. From a kid in the doorway of the derelict house. I gawked at his mustache, the saddest display of thin, prickly lip hair I'd seen in ages.

He was a pear-shaped boy Kip Prose's age, or younger, as pale as a vampire. He wore posh but badly matched clothing. He didn't look like he could survive a quarter mile sprint. He wasn't one of the boys who'd been with Kip earlier.

He looked like he'd just watched his favorite puppy get murdered.

Playmate murmured, "Be careful, Garrett. If that's the guy who made the big bugs . . ."

Pear-shaped boy was young to be messing with sorceries nasty enough to give us giant killer bugs. But I haven't stayed aboveground by taking people at face value. They fool you all the time. Sometimes deliberately.

Saucerhead and Playmate sort of organically drifted away from me and Tinnie and Singe. Pear-shaped boy would be surrounded if he did anything dumb.

The crowd began to buzz.

A giant bug had appeared in an empty second-floor window. It had exotic beetles in its lineage. Scarlet and yellow made a bold statement.

It made noises like tin sheets rubbing, spread its wings. It flew. In a sixty-degree glide. It hit the cobblestones with enthusiasm enough to break limbs and antennae and cause leaking cracks in its body.

Saucerhead waxed philosophical. "Big ain't everything, seems like." That from a man for whom big is a way of life.

Pear-shaped boy burst into tears. He started down the steps. Then he noticed the crowd for the first time. Seventy witnesses. He froze.

Another boy appeared. This one had been with Kip. He saw the mob. His eyes got big. He started to shake. He was a stunted beanpole with a fashion sense worse than pear-shaped boy. Sputtering, he grabbed the first kid and started dragging him back.

Seconds later a dozen bugs came out, none nearly as big as the first two. Several were Luna moths with wingspans like peregrine falcons. The world outside overwhelmed them quickly. The onlookers climbed over each other, trying to grab a giant bug for personal use.

Tinnie beckoned me closer.

# 23

"There's a man watching us," my sweetums reported.

"More like about a hundred." Half of them more interested in her than monster bugs.

"I'm not talking about these morons. Over there, in the breezeway between the brown brick wreck and the yellow brick one."

Those colors were only vague approximations.

It took me a moment to spot him even knowing where to look. The redhead has sharp eyes.

He was a matte maple furniture shade, made to blend into shadows. I didn't see much of him. His face gave the impression of being wrinkled and leathery. The feel I got for the rest was that he was put together like something more accustomed to living in trees, being mostly long, skinny arms and legs.

"Hey, Head. You see the guy Tinnie is talking about?"

"Yeah, I got him. He must really be rattled to give himself away like this."

"What say? You know him?"

"I don't know him. Nobody does. I know of him. Them kids are gone now. You want to go in after them?"

"No. I want to know who that guy is who's watching us."

"He ain't watching you. You don't count for enough."

"Saucerhead!"

"That's Lurking Felhske, man. *The* Lurking Felhske."

I sighed. The people you have to work with sometimes! "*The* Lurking Felhske? What the hell is *any* Lurking Felhske?"

"You don't know? Man, you got to start getting out of the house more."

Something about the derelict house had changed. The

folks in the street weren't intimidated anymore. The young and the bold had begun testing the wobbly steps.

Singe had a clutch of fans. Kids more interested in the mantis head than her, though.

"Felhske is his name. His surname. His real first name might be Tribune. He's called Lurking Felhske because that's what he does. Better than anybody who isn't a shape changer or has them one a' them magic cloaks or rings that make them invisible."

"He's a spy?"

"Private contractor. Only works for the biggest bigs. Up on the Hill. Him being interested here worries me."

"How come?"

"Because it means one of the top hands up there must be interested in what's going on around here."

"Interested in giant-ass bugs? Who woulda thunk? What's this Lurking Felhske do, then?"

"I just told you. He watches. Then he reports back."

"That's it? He doesn't actually do anything?"

"That's all. Something needs doing, they send another specialist."

"So."

Tinnie asked, "Are we going to go in there and nose around?"

"No. There's a crowd." People were pouring into the empty building. "Their weight might knock the place down. Plus, we don't want to get caught in the stampede."

"Stampede? What stampede?"

The small gods heard me. They cracked the whip of coincidence.

The whole neighborhood shook. A bright light appeared inside the derelict house. Jets of dust or smoke blasted out, initially glowing an almost blinding salmon. There was a great surge of sound that sounded almost like a demonic orchestra tuning up.

People screamed and trampled each other getting out. Folks in the street yelled and ran in circles.

When the noise subsided, Tinnie demanded, "How did you know that would happen?"

"I didn't. But those kids were up to something they shouldn't be. Stands to reason they'd want to cover their tracks."

Chunks continued falling. Including sizable chunks of bug. People helped one another stagger out of the building. Amazingly, there were no fatalities.

"Where did Singe go?" Tinnie asked.

"She headed over that way," Playmate said.

Saucerhead opined, "Less'en you got some awful good reason to hang on around here, we ought to get moving. It's gonna be raining red tops in a few minutes."

"Singe . . . Never mind." She was headed our way. Still armed with her trophy. Which wasn't moving anymore.

She said, "I checked the watcher's scent. So I'd recognize him if we run into him again. He was not watching us. He had been there a long time. For days, off and on."

I marveled. She was really thinking. I asked, "Why do you keep carrying that head around?"

"Maybe the Dead Man can get something out of it. If we get it there before it goes bad."

Man, she was thinking. That hadn't occurred to me.

It was getting scary, being around TunFaire's first genius rat.

Saucerhead was right. If the Civil Guards found me anywhere near something that blew up, they'd ask me dumb questions into the middle of next week.

Back to the World. Hi-ho.

And just in time.

# 24

One of the teamsters told me, "The red tops all headed out. There was an explosion somewhere up that way." Red tops being another slang term for tin whistles. Because of the red flop hats the uniformed ones favor.

"We heard it. It's why we hurried back. I didn't want to spend time entertaining the Watch. Anything happen here?" Max wasn't exactly getting his money's worth out of these teamsters.

"That head rat's been looking for you."

Singe put her trophy into a rat basket and headed inside. I followed. Tinnie started after me but changed her mind. She wasn't eager to find herself hip deep in big bugs. Or even regular rats.

I glanced at the sky before I went in. We might be in for a change of weather. Back to what we'd been enjoying.

I found John Stretch leaning against a pillar, exhausted. "You all right?"

"I will sleep well tonight. I do not look forward to doing this again."

"I do appreciate—"

"We are being paid well. And this, surely, will win our people a great deal of respect."

I nodded, though I wasn't sure. Some people wouldn't like it much once they figured out that there had to be a psychic connection between John Stretch and the everyday vermin.

We'd have to create some tall tale to cover that.

I said, "The guys outside said you were looking for me."

"I wanted to tell you that something has changed down below. Suddenly. And big."

"Maybe twenty minutes ago?"

"Yes."

I told what we'd witnessed. Singe did a lot of nodding.

John Stretch said, "I am afraid the bugs that are left are about to get loose."

I tried my famous lifted eyebrow trick, ordinarily reserved for beautiful women. The ratman took it to be a request for more information.

He said, "Sudden as a slap in the face, the bugs just ran."

That was one for the Dead Man. "That mean the job is done?"

Too bad ratpeople can't laugh. John Stretch was in a mood for it. "Close, maybe. But you have not dealt with the ghost issue."

"Ghosts wouldn't be your problem. You're the bug man."

"The bug man might have to deal with ghosts in order to get his bug killers to the bugs."

"You had ghost trouble?"

"No. But I hear ghosts are why there are no workers here today."

"Uh . . . let's take that up after we get moving. We're done here. We need to get gone before the Watch comes back." And they would. That's the kind of guys they are.

They knew Mrs. Garrett's boy had been seen within a mile of some excitement. It would be his fault, somehow. Or he knew whose fault it was but he was likely to hold out on the good guys.

Given word that it was time, John Stretch and his gang scooted like scalded rats. I noted a definite lack of enthusiasm for rounding up and removing their hunting cousins. But none had failed to appropriate at least one big bug corpse.

"Those will be some good eating," Singe explained.

I'd crunched a few tropical bugs in my day, just to get by. It wasn't a gourmet experience. But tastes differ. Especially for different races. There are even species that think people are tasty.

"If we could find some grubs, that would be really fine."

"Yeah?"

# 25

I heaved a sigh of relief when Playmate pulled up in front of my house. He didn't stick around. He dumped us and headed out. Probably terrified of what he'd find when he got back home.

Or maybe somebody told him that Old Bones was awake and he didn't want it known that he'd been lusting in his heart. Or something.

People are strange.

Singe, Tinnie, Saucerhead, and I headed inside. John Stretch tagged along. He didn't want to but figured he needed to get the work part over with while the information was still fresh in his head.

Saucerhead had hopes of cadging a meal.

I'd begun to suspect that things weren't going well for Mr. Tharpe. But he'd never admit it.

Two minutes later there was no sign that my place was occupied, let alone the hub of intrigues designed to offend people whom the king's little brother Rupert wanted to afflict with a law-and-order geas.

I shut and bolted the door. I was confident that one of the roomers at Mrs. Cardonlos's house, up the street, had taken notes.

I did hurry it. Because there had been a buzz inside the wall, beside the door.

"What?" Tinnie asked.

"The pixies might be waking up." Then I wasted breath asking, "Anybody hungry?"

Singe had reached the kitchen already. Checking to see what Dean was cooking. Because there were food odors in the air. The Dead Man had alerted the old man to our

approach. Dean had a tray with mugs and a pitcher ready.
Singe brought that to the Dead Man's room. She reported,
"Ten minutes, soup is on."

Which turned out to be true. Almost. It was a bisque,
which Dean explained is a soup made with cream instead
of water.

John Stretch and the Dead Man communed. The king of
the ratmen downed a second mug, then went home.

Even Singe was surprised to see him walk away from
more free beer.

"What's the story?" I asked, working hard to avoid taking notice of Saucerhead being disappointed by the bisque.

*He suffered a great deal of stress today. And, being clever,
he suspects that more unhappiness lies ahead.*

"Say what?" Tinnie, I noted, didn't appreciate the bisque
much more than Saucerhead did. Dean would be
heartbroken.

The Dead Man ushered me into the reality he had found
inside John Stretch's mind. The dimensions of the world
beneath the World, and all that neighborhood, were clearer
this evening—as seen through the one ratman able to read
the tiny minds of unmodified rats who did not experience
reality through the same mix of senses as us allegedly intelligent upright apes.

Old Bones couldn't translate the information into anything my feeble human mind could grasp.

"So, where are we?" I asked the air. Off to the side,
muttering to himself, Saucerhead finished another mug. It
looked like he had no plans to go home. Had he lost his
place? Was he about to start mooching sleeping space off
his acquaintances?

Tinnie took the bowls and spoons to the kitchen. And
didn't return. I was too worn down to work out if that was
a hint or just her being too damned tired to stay up drinking and thinking.

*Lurking Felhske. The spy. From what I find in Mr.
Tharpe's mind it seems highly unlikely that anyone would
enlist his skills in an effort to keep track of your doings.*

I sighed. More disrespect. But true, if Singe was right.
"It would be the kids Kip Prose is running with. Somebody
on the Hill wants to keep track. Giant bugs, after all. That
could turn out as important as the creation of ratpeople."

*That I doubt. I cannot imagine an insect being made intelligent. You are correct. Felhske must be in the employ of someone interested in the sorcery involved in modifying the insects. So. We have reached the point where your best next step is to round up the Prose boy and bring him here.*

"I don't see him volunteering. But I have to visit the manufactory soon, anyway." I hadn't made a security check all winter.

*Try to restrain your business and social observations when you do.*

Yeah. That. Sometimes a problem. "What about the World?"

*Poll the tradesmen and contractors. Get their stories about why they are not working. If, indeed, they are not. After today's events. Then you might return to that abandoned house and see what is to be seen down below.*

"I can tell you right now, it has a cellar that's hooked into the underground world."

The Tenderloin has been in place for ages. And the kind of people who engage in the sorts of services provided there tend to have things to hide and a natural desire to have a secret way out ahead of angry competitors, customers, or the law. There are tunnels all over.

Tunnels and secret underground chambers are common in most neighborhoods, though. Hardly anybody trusts anybody very much.

*Quite likely a safe prediction.* With an edge of sarcasm.

He does know the city. In a historical context. Inasmuch as he's been here for most of its history. He won't be too clear on what it's like at any given moment, though. He doesn't get out much anymore.

Dean wandered in, looked around, shrugged fatalistically, collected the empty pitcher, and departed. He returned with the pitcher filled. "I'm turning in early tonight. I have a family obligation in the morning."

"Really?" That did not come up often.

"Really."

He didn't want to talk about it.

The Dead Man didn't clue me in.

Must not be any of my business.

# 26

Dean was long gone when Tinnie and I drifted downstairs. He'd left breakfast on the stove. Singe was hard at something bookish in her corner of the Dead Man's room. Saucerhead hadn't stopped snoring.

Tharpe had dedicated himself to getting outside all the free beer he could.

The Dead Man was awake but in a contemplative mood. He wasn't inclined to be social.

I told Singe, "When you have time, see what we need to do to turn the small front room into workspace for you. The smell is almost gone. And we ought to keep it cooler in here."

That brightened her morning.

I told the brightness in mine, "I'll walk you home. Then I'll duck over to the manufactory to see if I can lay hands on Kip Prose. Or get a line on where I can lay hands on him."

"No."

"No, what?"

"No, you don't want to do that. If he's there he'll duck out when he hears you showed up."

Probably true. "But won't he be a little nervous about you? I figure he knows you know me." Me smirking. But her being literal.

"Of course he does. It won't be me that sets him up."

"Then who?"

"Leave me in charge of the vamping."

"I generally do."

There was a hint of amusement in the air. His Nibs enjoying himself at my expense. I told him, "I'm not as dim as you think."

He didn't respond but he held a contrary opinion. Though if he peeked inside my head he knew I suspected that Tinnie wanted to keep me away from the manufactory.

They really don't want an untamed conscience roaming around over there. That just isn't best business practices.

Breakfast done, I readied myself for the world. Tinnie did the same. She needed to go home. She needed a change of clothing. Which observation you couldn't have tortured out of me. Nor could slivers under my nails get me to suggest she keep a change or two at my place. Not because she'd think I was hinting at some deeper commitment but because she'd consider me presumptuous, assuming there was more going on than she was ready to admit.

And we're both grown-ups.

*Be careful out there.*

"Always." I thought he meant to beware the weather, which had turned unpleasant during the night. Tinnie and I retreated to find winter coats, she helping herself to my best while I made do with a jacket I should've passed on to the street people early in the last century. My sweetie told me, "I'll give it back as soon as we get to the house."

Grumble, grumble.

We hit the street, headed west on Macunado, uphill. We made it as far as the Cardonlos homestead before the darkness closed in.

I told Tinnie, "Now you see why I'd rather not get up before the crack of noon."

Four men had appeared, boxing us in. They looked spiffy in the latest Civil Guard apparel. And altogether businesslike. Which meant they had checked their senses of humor and humanity when they got to work.

The guy in charge was an old acquaintance. "Mr. Scithe. You moved in with the Widow Cardonlos now?"

"My wife likes it that way. She said tell you thanks for getting her moved up the waiting list, next time I saw you. So, thanks."

"I promised. I delivered."

"Miss Tate. Haven't you outgrown this artifact yet?"

"It's a disease. Won't go away. Is that an officer's pip on your cap?"

"Yeah. I did too good a job back when your addiction was trying to engineer the downfall of Karentine civilization. So they gave me a fancier hat and made me work longer hours. Garrett. The Director wants to see you."

"Am I under arrest?"

"If you insist. If you don't come, we get to hit you with sticks, hog-tie you, and drag you through the slush."

I decided not to call his bluff. "All right. But one of your guys has to see Miss Tate home."

Scithe betrayed a momentary longing. And who could blame him? To know her is to yearn.

Scithe said, "Mistry. Accompany Miss Tate to the Tate compound." Making sure the Watchman knew which family claimed this flaming glory.

"Yes, sir." Not even a little disgruntled about being handed this tough assignment.

"The Al-Khar?" I asked. "Or am I lucky enough to find him hanging out with Ma Cardonlos?"

"You wish." Scithe glanced at the remaining two men. They'd positioned themselves so as to foil any escape attempt by the infamous desperado, Garrett. Scithe whispered, "He never leaves the Al-Khar anymore."

He lied. I know Deal Relway. He's a slinking weasel who's always somewhere in the shadows, watching. He's no desk-bound bureaucrat.

"This going to take long?" After giving Tinnie a quick parting kiss that left every guy in sight hating me for being so lucky. "I'm not dressed for the weather."

He was kind enough not to ask whose fault that was. "I don't know. Way I see it, that depends on you. If you're your normal self, weather might not be something you need to worry your pretty little head about. Much."

I sighed. Nobody in the law-and-order racket appreciates my wit.

I miss the old days. The original Watch was completely corrupt and totally incompetent. Efficiency was a word that hadn't yet been imported into TunFairen Karentine.

"I suppose we should get on with getting on, then, Brother Scithe." I glanced up the street. Tinnie had Mistry totally subverted already.

We talked about the weather as we walked. Scithe wasn't a big fan of winter. "On the other hand, summer is worse," he opined. "I spent my war in the deep desert of the Cantard. You went out in the sun in the afternoon there, your weapons started to melt."

Army types.

My war had been all that, with bugs, snakes, crocodiles, and incredible humidity. And command stupidity. I didn't one-up him. He'd just come back with scorpions, jumping spiders, more snakes, bigger snakes, and command authority fuckups so awful they'll be remembered throughout the ages. Those Army guys are like that. I just said, "Winter, you can always put something else on. Including another log on the fire."

"That's the way I see it."

"Can I ask a question? Professional courtesy kind of thing?"

He was alert and suspicious instantly. "Yeah?"

"Ever heard of a character called Lurking Felhske?"

He appeared to give that an honest think. After being startled because I hadn't asked something weightier. "Can't say that I have. No. Put the question to the Director. There aren't many actors in this burg he doesn't know."

I filed that usage of actor in my mental dictionary.

The Civil Guard had evolved to the point where it was deploying its own inside language.

"I'll do that. If I can get a word in edgewise."

"You've talked to him before."

"Listened. Several times."

"All right. Here's one for you. The people building that theater down there. The World. I hear they plan to put together a whole chain of theaters."

"Sure. Max Weider is behind it. He's thinking if he goes a little down-market compared to other theaters, and he's got a bunch of theaters, he's got him a fresh way to move a lot more of his product."

Scithe went off on a rant about how that was typical of Weider's class. I reminded him, "You don't like that kind of people, you shouldn't make deals with me. I should let natural forces work on your wife's place on the three-wheel waiting list."

What I'd said sounded weird. But Scithe sometimes spouts strange nonsense about class and social standing. He thought we all ought to be absolute equals because we're all born or hatched out naked.

One of Scithe's men said, "It's all envy. The subaltern forgets that some folks pick better parents than some others. And some people were behind the door drooling instead of being in line when the brains were passed out. And some people got talents when some others don't. And some got ambition when some others don't."

"That'll be enough, Teagarden!" Scithe snapped. He admitted, "I loathe myself for working the system so Vinga could get a better number."

"And she's getting close to the top." I didn't observe that he hadn't been reluctant when we made the deal. I didn't mention his having accepted a job where he was in charge of other men—and obviously proud that somebody thought well enough of him to put him there. I just nodded when Teagarden said, "Only way you're gonna have a world with universal equality is if you got one where there's only one guy left standing."

That is so blazingly obvious that I've never understood how some people can't see it.

Every nut notion that ever was is floating around Tun-Faire somewhere, keeping itself alive inside at least one human head. Most are like diseases. The benign ones spread slowly. The deadly ones spread fast. The more virulent they are, the more quickly they consume their carriers.

I'm no thinker. I never cared about much as long as there was beer and a pretty girl somewhere handy. Though I do have a hyperactive sense of right and wrong. Which irks my business associates. And sometimes makes me slap on the rusty armor to go tilt at windmills.

The Al-Khar isn't far outside my neighborhood. We got there before the discussion could get much deeper.

"The place hasn't gotten any prettier, I see." Which wasn't entirely true. Prisoners get exercise cleaning it some now.

The city prison is ancient. It is built of a soft, yellowish sandstone that absorbs dirt and flakes away with changes in the weather. It won't last another two hundred years—even assuming responsible upkeep and the absence of civil unrest or war.

Scithe admitted, "This *is* the house where Ugly was born."

# 27

It's another world inside the Al-Khar. Someone who hasn't been there can't begin to imagine it.

First, the place is a cathedral dedicated to the religion of bureaucracy. And always has been. Deal Relway and Westman Block have ground away, but even after sustained, relentless attention from Prince Rupert's hounds, whole departments still suck up funding in order to monitor the performance of departments devoted to keeping an eye on departments tasked to keep an eye on. Here and there, like a blind pilgrim caught in a maze, is somebody actually trying to accomplish something. And having big trouble getting there because of the friction of the Al-Khar culture.

Scithe turned me over to a Linton Suggs. Suggs is a dangerous little man. He could be standing right next to you and you'd never notice. He looks like nobody's idea of a tin whistle. He has a shock of wild hair mostly gone gray, watery gray eyes, a big red nose and sagging jowls. He'd attract attention nowhere but in a girls' public bath. He accepted my handshake politely. "Glad you could make it. Follow me," in a tone that belied his words.

He didn't care that I'd shown up, one way or another. I was a body in need of moving from hither to yon.

Following, I noted that Suggs was even shorter than he'd seemed when facing me. And heavier around the hips.

Short is common on Deal Relway's side of the law-and-order industry.

Partly, that's because people aren't as wary of short.

Suggs walked me a long, long way, up and down, right and left, through numerous cell blocks. There wasn't much room at the inn. I was supposed to be intimidated. And too confused to find my way to the Director's hideout on my own.

Scithe might be right about Relway turning into a recluse.

Suggs handed me off to an anonymous little man he didn't introduce. This one had less hair, slimmer hips, and wasn't interested in small talk. He didn't bother with the maze. We passed through only one cell block. I saw faces I recognized. They belonged to men who had been overly passionate in denouncing the selfless labors of the new police forces. Or overly loud as racialist enthusiasts.

Anonymous Small Man planted me on a hard wooden chair inside what used to be a cell. He had no reason to suspect it, but I knew where I was. I'd been there before. One weak clay lamp beat back the gloom. There was nothing to do but sit. Unless I was in a mood to practice my soft-shoe routine. He told me, "Wait here."

This was supposed to give me time to start sweating.

My dance routine had all the polish it needed. And I hadn't forgotten other skills, picked up during wartime.

I went to sleep.


The small man poked me. He was upset. He'd gone to a lot of trouble to make me uncomfortable.

And I was. I was thoroughly miserable just being there with him. But he didn't need to know. I asked, "You done fiddle-farting around?"

"The Director will see you now."

"Oh, goodie! This will be the high point of my young life. Better than shaking hands with the Crown Prince when he welcomed my company back from the Cantard."

He did not fail to take note of my sarcasm.

A big black checkmark was about to go into a ledger with my name on it.

Relway was two cells away from where I'd waited. He had removed the bars between two cells. The larger space was his living and work space.

Guys who don't need more than that scare me more than do the totally corrupt.

I'd visited him here before. I didn't remind him. Nor did I criticize the gamesmanship. This was like a visit to a physician. I'd do what it took to get it over with fast.

The Director felt no need to put his stamp on the space. It was no more colorful than it had been as a cage for bad people. An unmade cot, rather than a reed mat on a cold stone floor, was his concession to luxury. Dirty or discarded clothing lay in one corner.

Relway was absolutely profligate with the lighting. He had four lamps burning.

Deal Relway is a small man of mixed ancestry, ugly as original sin. Rumor says a dwarf might have swung through his family tree a couple of generations back. He started out as a volunteer informant and vigilante helping track and control the virulent human rights movement. Superiors liked his dedication. Especially Colonel Block, who gave the little man a job as soon as he was able to hire people. Now he's the number-two man.

"Still working the smart-ass angle, eh?" Relway asked. He had one of our writing sticks clutched in his crabbed little fingers. He used that to point, indicating a chair. This one had a thin pad, thus pretending to be more comfortable than the one down the corridor.

I planted myself. "A man does what a man needs to do."

He cut slack. "I understand."

I became doubly paranoid. Slack he offered was sure to get tossed over a handy tree branch. Better keep an eye out for the hangman's knot.

Relway grinned. He could guess my thoughts. He said, "I asked the boys to bring you by because I want to consult you. Professionally."

My eyes must have bugged.

"Really." He grinned again. His teeth were not attractive. "There's something afoot. You seem to have dipped your toe in it already. The reports say you've been reasonably cooperative for the last year or so."

"Couldn't tell that by the way your troops talk."

Yet another snaggled-tooth grin. "They have a manual to follow. How to deal with guys like you. And you don't make it easy for them to give you a break. You just keep on trying to poke them in the eye with a stick."

I didn't see it that way. But I'd heard something similar so often that it might be worth some thought. "I have challenged social skills."

"Don't we all? Some folks take the trouble to learn to

fake it, though. But none of that is why I want to see you. Tell me about what you're involved in now."

I'd thought it out. There was no need to hold much back. He'd know most of it, anyway. I started at the beginning and told it to date, editing only enough to cover John Stretch and Kip Prose.

"No significant deviation from what's been reported. How do the ratmen manage those rats?"

"I don't think they do. They just trap them and let them get hungry. They took them to the World and turned them loose. I could be wrong, though. I just have business arrangements with them, not a social relationship. My sidekick is as baffled as I am."

"The Dead Man can't read them?"

"He can. But all he gets is confused. That's not unusual, though. It's way less easy for him to read somebody than he pretends," I lied.

"Interesting. I suppose you haven't heard. There's been a development."

"Um?"

"Big bugs. All over, down there. In the Tenderloin, especially. Not a real problem, the way I see. People are having a good time trying to catch them. And the weather ought to finish any of them that get away."

"Um?" A leading question, this time.

"The numbers are surprising, considering how many rats you used. But your real problem may come up on the dark side of the legal divide."

"Meaning?"

"Meaning the bug problem has scared off folks who like to off-load their excess cash in the Tenderloin. Business was way down last night."

I shrugged. He needed to take that up with somebody who cared. Though I amused myself with thoughts of the local underbosses putting the button on giant bugs.

"We've had a discreet inquiry from the Hill. As to why a certain freelance agent was seen in a certain location before a certain blowup. There was an implication that stolen sorcery may have been involved. And, possibly, some illegal research. You know anything about that?"

I knew that about the only person likely to have mentioned me to a denizen of the Hill would be the mysterious Lurking

Felhske. I showed the Director my famous eyebrow trick. "Illegal? How? Those people decide what's legal."

"Exactly. If they agree something is too dangerous, anybody who goes ahead is making a rogue play. Then the rest come down like the proverbial ton. Wearing their hobnail boots."

"You don't sound distressed by the possibility."

"It's attractive on an intellectual level. Practically, I have to consider potential collateral damage. But that doesn't matter now. I'm just interested in hearing more from someone who was there."

And if I swallowed that whole he'd be around later with a bargain offer on a gold mine in a swamp somewhere.

He flashed his dirty teeth. "How about the spooks?"

"What spooks?"

"I hear part of your job is to work on some ghosts that are bothering the builders."

"I didn't see any. I didn't find anybody who admitted seeing any. I'm beginning to think somebody just heard the big bugs scratching around in the walls."

"That could be." He did not sound convinced.

He knew something I didn't.

It would be a waste of time to press.

Instead, I asked, "There some special reason you're interested in a construction project?"

"Only because illegal behaviors are going on around there. Those kid gangsters. Not going to be a problem anymore. No more theft or vandalism."

He did not explain. They must have connected that rusty knife to Handsome. I didn't want to know what next. It was sure to be harsh.

He did say, "I'm interested mostly because of a sudden interest on the Hill in what's happening in that neighborhood. Particularly because somebody wants to go low profile. When Block can't . . ." He stopped. It was against his religion to volunteer anything.

The problem would be Kip's friends. Some had to be from the high Hill country. Doing what kids do. Helping themselves to their parents' stuff when the old folks weren't watching. I did it with Mom's brandy. And got caught every time. Hard to cover up when you pass out with the bottle in your lap.

"Any names I know trying for the down low?"

Snaggled teeth again. I wouldn't get Deal Relway that easy.

"And you get all over me for holding back, even when I don't."

"And if you're not, even this time, I'm the world's first nine-foot-tall dwarf."

I zagged when I hoped he expected a zig. "What can you tell me about somebody they call Lurking Felhske?"

He started, then faded into neutral mode. Turning off anything that might be a tell. "Felhske?"

"Lurking Felhske. Actual first name possibly Tribune."

"Why? What do you know about Felhske?"

"Interesting. There something special about him?"

"What do you know about him?"

"What do you know?"

"I know you're sitting in my cell way down here in the heart of the Al-Khar. And it's a long way to the front door. What do you know about Lurking Felhske?"

He'd gone from friendly to neutral to hard-ass in seconds. "There was somebody watching us over at the World. Saucerhead Tharpe said he thought it might be somebody called Lurking Felhske."

"Tharpe knows Felhske?"

"No. Knew of him. I never heard of him before."

"Tell it."

I did so.

"Run that description again."

I did that.

"I might want to borrow your tracker."

"Excuse me?" I hadn't mentioned Singe getting a sniff of Felhske.

"We have a strong interest in arranging a direct interview with the Felhske person." Naturally, he didn't explain why. "You've given me more than I've been able to put together before."

"I can't tell Singe to do it. She probably would, though, in the interest of good relations. And making a little money. But you'd have to give her something to start with."

"Um?" He figured I was handing him a ration.

"She's the best damned tracker in town but you can't

just tell her to go find somebody. She's got to have a place to start, the right scent, reasonable weather, and has to get started pretty soon after the subject leaves the starting point. This burg has got a lot of stinks."

"And stinkers."

"Of which I'm one?"

"If the shoe fits. Listen. I'm *very* interested in having a conversation with Mr. Felhske. Who sounds like an orangutan in clothing. I'd be appreciative of anyone who made that conversation possible."

"Drop by the house, talk to Singe. She's always looking for ways to ingratiate herself."

The Director's tiny smile told me I'd find myself running between the flop drops of a swarm of flying pigs before he visited my house again.

He was one of those paranoids who was dead on the mark when he thought somebody was out to get him.

Old Bones would love to prowl the labyrinth of his lethal little mind.

He muttered, "This might change things. I need to . . . I appreciate you coming in, Garrett. I may want to see you again. Hell, it's a lead pipe cinch you'll make me want to see you again."

There were questions I wanted to ask. I got no chance. This wasn't about me and my wants. He yelled. A little man with some gnome in him materialized. "Cut him loose."

"Sir?" Spoken to me. "If you'll come with me?"

I'd been dismissed. I'd need to throw firebombs to get Relway's attention again. "Lead on, Studly."

No point telling them I could find my way out. I might want to surprise them someday.

# 28

It was only afternoon but it had gotten dark. Snow fell in big, soggy chunks that could knock you down if you weren't careful. I'd need to beware ambushes. It was great snowball snow. Every kid in TunFaire would be balling up and waiting for victims.

Ten steps from the Al-Khar doorway one wide load of a human slid into my path. I was about to break out my head thumper when I recognized him. "What's up, Sarge?"

"Morley was worried about you. Sent me ta fine out what the laws was doin' wit' you. Good timin', you. I jist got here. Now I don't got ta freeze my ass off all day."

That would take a long arctic winter. Which observation I reserved. "Yeah? How'd he know they picked me up?"

"Dat frail a' yours. Sent somebody over. On account of she was worried about you." He shook his head in disbelief. "I don' get dat. Somebody like you wit' her."

"Makes me wonder, too, Sarge. But I don't look too close at its teeth."

"I don't get it." When there were treasures like him to be had.

"The gods work in mysterious ways, I reckon. Tell Morley they turned me loose. Give him all my love for caring."

"Maybe you might oughta go tank him your own self, slick."

Maybe. Hell, why not? My day was shot. Too much time inside the second most terrible Crown structure in Tun-Faire. And The Palms was closer than home. Meaning a chance to get warm again that much sooner.

"Why not?" I told Sarge. "I don't even remember what I'm supposed to be doing."

"Dey can do dat ta you, dem guys in dere."

"You know about that?"

"Been dere, ace. Every mont' or so, dey pull me in. Dey git somebody from da crew most ever week."

I didn't know that. Morley never mentioned it.

Maybe it was something new. I hadn't gotten together with Dotes for a while.

I'd turned into a real stay-at-home. They'd probably held wakes for me at my old habitual hangouts.

I said, "Must be tough, trying to run a business when you can't count on your people coming in."

We were trudging along with the snowflakes bashing us from behind. Sarge stopped. He looked at me like he was trying to figure out something. Which he was, of course.

Puddle, Sarge, the rest of Morley's crew, they never did connect fully with my sense of humor.

Morley Dotes, well-known half-breed dark elf, runs a toney watering hole that used to be a dive. And something worse before that. As had he.

We've been friends so long that I don't recall how we became blood brothers. So long that there's never any question anymore about turning out to offer a helping paw.

Dotes had his troops assembled for inspection when Sarge and I entered The Palms. He told them, "This snow will keep the punters away. Again. I don't want to lay anybody off. But if I don't have money coming in, I can't pay wages."

The faces were familiar, though I couldn't put a name to several. None looked like the kinds of guys who consider food service their life's calling.

Sarge told me, "Sit your ass down somewhere an' keep your friggin' mout' shut. He'll get to you."

"I could be down to the World counting giant bugs."

Sarge gave me the boggled frown often shown when I talk to him.

He isn't the brightest member of Morley's crew.

Sometimes I think Morley picks his associates with an eye to shining sunny amongst them.

Dotes finished haranguing his troops. "Sarge, get that coat out of the kitchen." He settled across the table from me.

I observed, "You look worn down."

"I am. Business sucks. I'm dying, trying to keep my suppliers paid and my people employed."

"You got through last winter."

"Last winter The Palms was still fashionable. The place to see and be seen. The place to make a connection."

That would be one of the more honest things he'd ever said. Admitting that his place was more than just a feeding trough for swells.

"Maybe it's time to move on to the next format."

"No can do. The only option now is a fallback to something like the Safety Zone. I don't want that. I've had a taste of the high life."

In one prior incarnation The Palms was the Safety Zone, which was basically a place where denizens of the dark side, of all races, could gather and do business without fear of assassination or other inconvenience. The Safety Zone had been great when I was starting out. I could hang out, listen, make contacts, find out who was who.

Then I met Tinnie.

"Then change up just enough to make them want to come see what's new. Serve something besides eggplant, parsnips, and rutabaga wine."

"Thank you, Sarge," Morley said. "Your coat, Mr. Garrett. Your redheaded friend sent it over with word that you'd been dragged off to the Al-Khar." He eyed me expectantly. I paid no attention to the coat.

How do you lie to your best friend? "Relway wanted to enlist me as a consultant. About what, or why, he never made clear. But he's interested in something involving kids off the Hill."

"Word is, you're working for Max Weider. Something to do with oversize bugs."

"Yes. I've taken care of that. I hope. I'll go make sure after I leave here."

"There're lots of big bugs around, scaring the marks in the Tenderloin. You're not popular down there right now."

"Me? I'm not? I need that explained."

"You loosed the bugs."

"I did not." Stupid is more pervasive than air. Inability to reason comes in right behind. "I was down there to suppress them. And did a damned good job, thank you."

Morley just smiled.

I may have mentioned it. Apologies if I have. Mr. Dotes is poisonously handsome and overloaded on animal magnetism. · If you're a father or a husband, he's the guy who haunts your nightmares.

He's keyed into fashion, always dressed to the pointy ears in the latest. Even here, working, with no one to impress, after a harsh winter, he was overdressed and preening, showing an embarrassing quantity of pastel lace.

Puddle, who could be Sarge's ugly twin, brought a tea service. Morley poured. I sipped and relaxed in the warmth. The usual stress around the place was absent. I thanked Puddle, asked Morley, "What's really going on?"

"Nothing. Tinnie was worried. I made moves to find out how bad off you were. Lucky you, they cut you loose. Sarge brought you here so you could get your coat. Once you got here, I amused myself by giving you a hard time about your bugs."

"Not my bugs. Kids off the Hill. Tell me about Lurking Felhske."

His good mood vaporized. He stopped lounging. Stiffly erect in his chair, he snapped, "What do you know about him?"

"Two things. First, nothing. Which is why I asked. I never heard of him before yesterday. Second, every time I mention him, people get the stone face and, instead of answering me, they start trying to get me to turn him up. Why the hell is that?"

"Are you for real? You never heard of Lurking Felhske? In your racket?"

"Morley. Look at me. I'm getting exasperated here. My friend. I told you. I have no flipping idea who Lurking Felhske is. I never heard of him before Saucerhead said something. I'm pretty sure there might be three, maybe even four other people out there who've never heard of him, either. There might even be people who've never heard of you. So cut the crap."

Sarge was back, examining the coat he'd brought. He told Morley, "His adventure in da Al-Khar drove him mad."

"Certainly made him cranky."

Sarge told me, "Dere's maybe a problem here, Garrett.

Couple of da guys in back, dey t'ought dis coat was left behin' by some customer. Dey got in a squabble over it. Kinda tore it some."

"Ssss!" I hissed, making descending wiggle fingers. "I'm a lightning rod for petty disaster. Crap. What makes me real cranky is friends who won't believe me. Who think it's funny to play games when all I need is a splash of honest information."

Morley tickled his ghost of a mustache. "I'll pretend you're really as dim and ignorant as you want me to believe. In the interest of getting on with getting on."

"How gracious."

"Isn't it? Considering the bad things that have happened this year." Feral smile. He was still irked about me getting him back for saddling me with a talking parrot who could make a sailor blush.

"All the hills don't go up. Some have a down on the other side."

"You've been hanging around with the old folks again."

"Lurking Felhske."

"Yes. Lurking Felhske. A legend. The spy's spy. A man almost as unpopular as gumshoe Garrett. A man so good at sneaking and eavesdropping most of his targets never know. So good, in fact, that most people have never heard of him."

"Including the aforementioned gumshoe Garrett. What the hell is a gumshoe, anyhow?"

"It's a kind of soft sole for people who spend all their time on their feet. Check with your friends on the Guard. Meantime, take it from me, those who have suffered because of Lurking Felhske would love to have a sit-down with him."

I couldn't see Relway being upset about being exposed by this character. I could see him smelling a chance to find out where a lot of bodies were buried. "You got something to hide and it gets out, you can't hardly claim you being in trouble is somebody else's fault."

"Of course you can. Most people do. Don't be naive, Garrett."

"I understand that most people are too self-centered to blame themselves for their own troubles. That's human nature at work. Come on. Lurking Felhske. Give."

"Felhske. The wonder. I told you. Legendary sneak. The man you hire when you want to find out what somebody else doesn't want found."

"Damn! I thought that was Mama Garrett's ever-lovin' blue-eyed baby boy. How?"

"Uh . . . you got me, Garrett. How what?"

"How do you hire a Lurking Felhske if he's so legendary that nobody knows what he looks like or where to find him? I've always wondered about that when it comes to legendary assassins and professional thieves."

"Thieves?"

"The ones who steal the holy gem eyes or fangs out of demon idols or ancient grimoires from heavyweight sorcerers. You want that kind of people to do a job for you, how do you get hold of them? You can't hardly hang a sign out. And neither can they. Especially neither can they. Here's this poor Felhske clown, got people hunting him and all he does is watch people."

"But then he goes and tells somebody what he saw. That's what makes people mad."

"That's all you know?"

"That's all I know, Garrett. That and I could solve my financial problems if I had a Lurking Felhske to auction off."

I made a face, repelled.

Morley smiled. He'd gotten me. Again. "How much influence do you have on the three-wheel business?"

"Five percent. And I can have my own guy check the books. So far, nobody's screwed me. I put it all back in. Eventually, I'll own more of the company. Singe has the math worked out. Why?"

"I have a cousin who thinks it would be dandy to have her own three-wheel."

I was suspicious immediately. I've only ever met one family member of his. A nephew. Who should've been drowned at birth.

Morley said, "Don't give me that fish-eye, Garrett. I was thinking about buying her a spot near the head of the list."

What about those financial problems? "Does this cousin live in the city?" He might want a three-wheel to ship out where feral elves could get busy building knockoffs. Though that is more a dwarfish-style stunt.

It's company policy never to sell to dwarves.

We'd have to design a special dwarf model, anyway. They couldn't get their stubby legs down to the pedals on a normal three-wheel.

Dotes shrugged. "Forget about it. Five percent isn't juice enough. How long do you think the fad will last?"

"A long time if the Tates are as clever at promoting three-wheels as they were combat boots back when Tate shoes became the thing for the in-crowd." They'd been supposed to make those boots exclusively for the Army.

"Snob appeal."

"The worst you ever saw."

I took a moment to enjoy The Palms. Good smells wafted in from the kitchen. My long affair with an omnivorous diet prevented my saying so. My best pal is a born-again vegetarian.

"An interesting notion," Dotes mused, mind a hundred yards away. "Change the menu. Come up with something the punters won't get anywhere else. Then get out the word about how exclusive it is. You're not as dumb as you let on, Garrett."

"A thought for the ages." And, "Thanks for caring enough to send Sarge out. I'd better get moving. There was a bunch of stuff I was supposed to do today. I haven't done any of it yet. And I'm hungry."

There was a lot of garlic in the air. I do like a dish with ample garlic flavoring the meat.

"Don't forget your coat." Dotes ignored my gratitude. In his world, doing for friends wasn't something you talked about.

It was a real men thing.

I held the coat at arm's length. "This was my best coat."

I didn't hear an offer to make good, or even an apology for the damage. I didn't challenge Dotes. The clever little villain would turn it around to make the damage my fault because I'd been dumb enough to loan my best coat to a redheaded woman.

I dragged the remnants on over top of the tattered beast I wore already.

# 29

The snow had eased up. What had fallen was too wet to drift. The wind had weakened, too. Excellent, considering the state of my winter apparel.

I hit the World. Men were working. I approached the carpenter in-laws. "Any trouble today?"

"Nope." The surly one wasn't, this time. He pointed. "There's your only bug today. That sulfur brought them up good."

A dead roach, lacking a couple legs, lay fifteen feet away.

Interesting. "I didn't think it would do any good. But I paid for the stuff so I used it. So. I heard there were all kinds of bugs last night."

"Right after you burned that sulfur, eh?"

Yikes! It really was my fault the Tenderloin had gone into a recession? "The other thing. Ghosts. My boss says I got to ask about ghosts."

The in-laws traded glances. Their faces went blank. Formerly Sullen said, "I don't know where that came from. Except them bugs could make enough noise to get your imagination going. And this place gets plenty spooky if you're in here by yourself."

I gave him the hard fish-eye. No way he was being straight. But he didn't smell like a guy being maliciously evasive, either. There was something these guys didn't want to talk about. Like it might be embarrassing, not some heinous crime.

The carpenter who had done no talking got a sudden case of the big eyes. I turned around. The foreman was headed our way, past what looked like a momentary heat shimmer. Could have been. It was hot in there.

The foreman, Luther something, wanted to know if there wasn't some way I could do my job without keeping his people from doing theirs. "I got six guys showed up today. Outta thirty-two. I'm falling behind fast."

So I talked to him. Being management, he had nothing constructive to do.

He hadn't seen any ghosts. It was his considered opinion that the ghost stuff was all bullshit from workmen who wanted an excuse to lie out for a day or two. There were no days off on this project.

The weather continued to improve. I was almost comfortable walking over to the ruin where those kids had made their bugs.

The structure remained uninhabited. I'd thought its notoriety would draw squatters.

I climbed the wobbly steps. I went through the doorless doorway, triggering spells meant to discourage trespassers. The first was subtle but powerful. It made me think that I was about to lose control of my bowels. I didn't, but they churned. Another sliding step on the creaky floor and I started seeing shapes move in the corners of my eyes. Were the ghosts at the World a spillover? If ghosts indeed there were?

There were other spells, all with a similar feel. Meaning they'd been set by the same caster, someone powerful but not polished. A professional would have been less obvious. I shouldn't have noticed that I was being manipulated.

I strolled on. Carefully. That floor was treacherous.

The spells worsened. When had they been cast? Anything there the day before yesterday should have broken down when the mob rushed in.

The floor creaked and sank. Likewise, the steep stair down into a fresh set of discouragement spells, one of which added violent wind to my tummy troubles. Looked like the point was to make an intruder flee his own exhaust.

I discover a less rickety stair to a cellar below the cellar. The floor down there was wooden but camouflaged by dirt so it would be taken as the bottom level. I knew better. I hadn't seen anything interesting yet.

Not much natural light made it down there. There had

to be a handy source. Those kids wouldn't have come down blind.

It was easy. They trusted their spells too much. But Kip would be the only one of the crew who had ever stood chin to chin with somebody really bad.

I felt around till I got hold of something like cold cobwebs. I shuddered. Something went *ker-chunk!* A tiny flame, from a tiny lamp, fixed to a reservoir that would keep it burning for weeks, came alive in a little eye-high alcove. Its weak light revealed an iron ring only partly hidden in the dirt at my feet.

There were more cellars, three in all, below that. The lowest had to be below river level but was no more damp than those above it. It was a place where mildew would feel at home.

Curious. Not once did I see evidence of any actual explosion. Had that been an illusion? Or something that happened on the same psychic level as the Dead Man's communications? Or just some very clever fireworks, meant to scare off potential invaders?

Lighting was always the same, a weak little lamp fixed in an alcove. Enough once your eyes adapted but you wouldn't be reading many books.

So. No more down. The last steep stair ended in the middle of a stone floor. The overhead was just high enough that I didn't have to stoop. The whole was eight feet to a side. The weeping walls were stone. Each had a wooden door in the middle, none of those showing more use than the others. None of them looked new.

Everything seen so far had been there a long time. Excepting the spells.

How had the kids found the place?

When in doubt, trust your right hand. I went to the door to my right as I left the stair. It wasn't locked. The darkness beyond fled when I stepped forward.

A dozen lamps came alive. An interesting bit of witchcraft. Which could have lots of commercial applications.

The lamplight revealed a square room twenty feet to a side and just like what I'd expect a rich kids' hideout to look like. There was furniture, nice but slightly worn. There were carpets. There were games, a couple in progress. There were books. There were toys. There was a three-wheel in a corner. I got the serial number. Overall, the evidence suggested that there were more kids in the group than I'd thought.

There was even a keg of beer from one of those snooty boutiques that serve only the lords on the Hill. I'd never tasted it. I gave it a try.

I'll spare Max. But it was better than Weider Dark Select. I was tempted to enjoy another. And another. But dedicated operative Garrett resisted temptation.

Beer reminded me that Singe had mentioned a strong wort odor. I'd caught the edge of that myself. There was none of that now. Basic cellar smells, fairly light, and something remote that had a touch of animal den to it. But no birth of the beer.

I found a hand-painted bamboo fan. I snapped it open. Well. Kip Prose might not be wasting time and money in the Tenderloin, but somebody was. That fan had been shoplifted from one of the sporting houses.

In the best houses management leaves the fans where the marks can swipe them for souvenirs. A form of advertisement. And a cute gimmick since a guy—or occasional gal—who brings in ten fans not only gets amnesty for the thefts; he wins a free visit.

Free enterprise at its fiercest.

A detailed look round turned up more fans, no two from the same house. Each came from a high-end establishment.

Somebody had money to throw in the river.

The search for fans turned up the fact that the furnishings all came from the same source. Mungero Farkas. I knew the name, vaguely. Farkas was a secondhand man. An honest one, not a fence, specializing in quality merchandise. I'd seen the Farkas shop in passing. It was about a quarter mile away, in the better part of the Tenderloin.

Nothing else interesting turned up. But I did begin to get a creepy feeling. Like I wasn't alone and the person I couldn't see was distinctly unfriendly.

I figured I'd tripped another spell.

Back to the foot of the stair. The door behind the stair looked intriguing. I opened it and stepped inside. A single lamp came to life.

The room was six feet by eight. It featured an unmade

bed and a nightstand. Its purpose was obvious. The door could be locked from inside.

So. A little something going on between members of the group.

The feeling that I was being watched grew stronger. The air felt damper and heavier.

I tried the door facing the foot of the stair, expecting another small chamber like the trysting room. It might have been. Or it might have been the antechamber to infinite space. I wasn't about to go find out. The darkness in there was absolute and alive.

I slammed the door. My heart hammered. I panted like I'd run a mile.

One more door.

I stalled. Behind this one would be the place where the bugs had been created.

The feeling of presence was so strong I couldn't help looking over my shoulder. Must be some sort of scare spell that kept getting stronger if you ignored it. Definitely clever work.

I found the wort smell when I opened up. It wasn't strong. I didn't charge ahead. I didn't get the chance. A half dozen very large bugs raced past me, headed for the light. As something that felt like a dead, wet hand caressed the back of my neck.

My next clear thought came with me leaning against a wall across the street from the ruin, hacking and gasping as I fought for air. A handful of big bugs stumbled out behind me, into the chill world of their doom. I was pretty sure they were the last adult insects.

I caught my breath. I wouldn't be bragging about this one any time soon.

Garrett don't panic. Garrett don't run away from things he can't even see.

Four blocks to the Mungero Farkas establishment. I could get my courage back by bullying the secondhand man.

I caught a whiff of body odor from the spot where Tinnie had spied Lurking Felhske. Felhske wasn't there now, lurking or otherwise. But somebody had been, recently. Today's snow had been trampled.

Watching me? Or watching the place?

I seemed unlikely. But news of me visiting the place might be of interest. To someone.

                              *    *    *

Mungero Farkas was open. I got the impression he meant to stay open till the evening crowd faded from the Tenderloin. Business did not appear to be good.

Farkas was a basic, ordinary middle-aged white guy who spent way too much money on professional grooming. A human Morley twenty-five years down the road. He was cooperative. He wanted company.

He recalled every item I mentioned. "That was a good several days. I moved a lot of stuff." But he had sold it in a half dozen lots over four days, two lots to a young couple who seemed to be just starting out and the rest to a man he could not describe other than to say he looked like he belonged in servant's livery. "I really don't even remember the color of his hair."

"He did have hair?"

Frown. "Oh. I get it. Yes. A full head. Graying around the temples, now I think about it. So it must have been dark. I got the feeling his employer would be someone whose fortunes were in decline. He was a little evasive but his money was good. I thought it deserved a home with me. Oh. And that guy? He had one droopy eye." Farkas pulled the corner of his right eye down and sideways. "Like this."

I thanked him. I took a few minutes to examine his inventory. He had some intriguing pieces but I didn't need anything.

I considered backtracking the fans I'd found. But where was the point? The people from whom they had been collected wouldn't remember anything. And wouldn't tell me if they did.

Time to go home.

# 30

"Oh, is it getting treacherous out," I told Singe when she let me in.

"What happened to your coat?"

"Tinnie's good intentions. Dean back yet?"

"No. We're on our own for supper."

That meant Garrett would boil some sausages. He might even get experimental and toss in a couple potatoes.

She asked, "So how was your day?"

"Damn, we're getting domestic. I spent most of it in the Al-Khar. Then I got dragged over to The Palms, where Morley had a seizure when I mentioned Lurking Felhske. That after Director Relway nearly volunteered me for the rack when I mentioned the same name."

"That strange-smelling man who was watching us yesterday?"

"He was watching. But the consensus is, not us. The very one, though. Apparently unpopular with a lot of people."

We were in the kitchen, banging the pots and pans. Singe drew us a couple of beers.

"No wonder, stinking that way," she said.

"You didn't mention an unusual odor before."

"It is not unusual. It is just potent. Body odor."

In a city where most people consider bathing unhealthy or an effete affectation, full-bodied personal auras aren't exactly rare.

Singe said, "It is more than failure to bathe. It is unusual diet. Or disease."

Not uncommon, especially amongst old folks. But what disease leaves a man looking like an orangutan?

I told her about the rest of my day, including the whiff I'd caught heading over to see Farkas.

Singe refilled our mugs. "You must have just missed him. Odor wouldn't stay around strong enough for a human nose in weather this windy."

The pot was hot enough. I filled it with smoked sausages and two large potatoes, quartered. "How the hell did I survive before I bought this place and hired Dean?"

"You ate out."

"Pretty much. Yeah. I didn't amount to much then."

"You are fortunate that Dean is not here to hear you admit that."

"He'd get in a shot. Yeah. What's with Himself? I haven't heard a peep." Though I was sure he'd helped himself to my day's adventures already.

"That child priestess was here. She brought some puzzles. He has been playing with those."

"Grrr! Even when Dean's away. How much did she eat? What did she steal?"

"You are too young to be a cranky old man." She refilled our mugs. "Maybe you should go visit your uncle Medford. Remind yourself how pleasant it is to be around crabby old men."

Medford Shale is my only living relative. He's a miserable grouch. "No, thank you, thank you. Swear to all the gods, these potatoes are going to take forever."

"You want to get that, then?"

I took a long drink of beer, set my mug down where she could top it off. "Get what?"

"The door. Someone is knocking."

*It would behoove you to move swiftly, Garrett. The glamour on the boy's mind is fraying.*

With no idea what that meant, I headed up front, muttering, "Go behoove yourself." Brew in hand, I used the peephole.

An uncomfortable Cypres Prose, well decorated with giant snowflakes, shared my stoop with a lethal creature from the Tate clan, Kyra, a sixteen-year-old uncut version of Tinnie.

*Sometime tonight, Garrett.*

"Why don't you grab him by the brain and drag him on in there?" I didn't ask. Not out loud.

He didn't respond. Meaning he had a whole lot of head tied up doing something else.

I popped the door open.

Both kids jumped like they'd gotten caught doing something they shouldn't. Kip had some definite thoughts obvious on his face, too.

You couldn't blame the boy. Kyra Tate was Tinnie in the raw, before she'd gotten it under control. Tinnie without polish or restraint. But maybe she'd started to understand. She looked guilty about something.

How had she manipulated Kip to get him here?

"Kip. Kyra. Welcome. Singe. Find some refreshments." I led the young folks into the Dead Man's room.

Old Butterbutt had enough mind space free to be amused.

Kyra apparently found Kip interesting—despite himself.

*There is new meaning to my existence,* Old Bones sent me. Privately. *I will not leave this sorry vale before this plays out.*

I couldn't ask because he was intent on convincing the kids that he was asleep.

But visitors in the know *always* assume he's awake and prying.

Kyra's freckled cheeks seemed redder than could be explained by the cold outside. And she couldn't keep her eyes off Kip.

That was as weird as having bugs the size of tomcats underfoot.

Kip was for sure a catch, in the "someday he's gonna be filthy rich" sense. He wasn't the guy girls get involved with for the adventure. That guy goes by the name of Morley Dotes and has enjoyed a career of making me whine in envy.

The Dead Man read me as I speculated, observed, and felt sorry for myself. His amusement grew.

I helped them with their coats, hats, and whatnot. And asked Kip, "What happened to your hair?" There seemed to be about twice as much as there had been in front of the World and it was flying away everywhere.

Kyra said, "I like it that way. It gives him a rebel look."

There you go. Good enough.

Singe brought the tea service, along with my beer mug,

filled, and my share of the sausage and potatoes. I relaxed. I didn't have to be entertaining to teenagers. I was too busy eating. They relaxed, too, building and working their cups of tea.

Singe had found a cache of Dean's sugar cookies. He can't hide anything from her magic nose for long. He keeps trying, though. He doesn't want to believe in her kind of magic.

"Here we go, kids," around a big bite of sausage. "I need you to explain some things."

"Sir?"

"You know where you are, Kip. There's no point trying to fudge. You and some other boys have been doing something weird and probably illegal under that empty house down on the edge of the Tenderloin. I was down there because the Weiders have been having trouble with giant bugs at their construction site. And, lo! Right off I find you and your pals and some big boy bugs all snuggled up."

*He is concerned that his mother will find out what he has been doing.*

Leverage!

*Indeed. But reserve the fact that you have been into that house.*

"I'm not looking to hassle you guys. I just want my client to be able to build his theater. So his daughter and Kyra's aunt have a venue to show off their acting skills. Or lack thereof. But somebody's been breaking some Hill-type rules. I've got the Guard on me because they're getting grief from somebody on the Hill. What's going on?"

Kip gnawed a cookie, slurped tea, and avoided my gaze. Kyra lapsed into the traditional pout of a Tate woman who suspects she may be off the bull's-eye when it comes to being the center of attention.

"It's a club, Mr. Garrett. Kind of a gang. *The* Gang. Or, usually, the Faction. It's for kids smart enough to spell their own names. There were six of us down there when you were there. You saw Kevans and Slump with me. Both seriously weird."

Wow. If Kip Prose thought you were weird, it might be time to move yourself into the howling hall psycho ward at the Bledsoe.

"Berbach and Berbain weren't there. They're twins.

They've been kind of fading out. Their mother is a Stormwarden. She never wanted kids in the first place. Zardoz is the one who loves bugs. Him and Teddy. I think they're icky. But the rule is, we help each other with whatever excites our passion. Because nobody else will."

Old Bones damned near laughed out loud. And him in his condition.

I said, "I can't imagine why anybody would want to make giant bugs. And it does got to stop. It wasn't just the Guard who had me in today. It was Director Relway himself. Not only is somebody on the Hill ragging him; somebody is curious enough to hire people to follow you around. If you kids don't want your lives getting painfully complicated, find some new hobbies."

"It's just kids helping each other work things out, Mr. Garrett. We aren't hurting anybody."

I talked about the economic disruption already caused by giant bugs interfering with construction and scaring people away from the Tenderloin. "And that's making some people cranky enough to crack skulls."

Kip just sort of gaped.

I said, "It's what they call the law of unintended consequences. Unexpected things that happen because of something you do."

Kip stared at the floor, which wanted sweeping and mopping. Which reminded me that it had been bare earth when I bought the place.

Kip said, "I really should think about that. Shouldn't I? I've been through this before."

There were differences. The principle beneath was the same. "Yep. Do your pals know you're *that* Cypres Prose?"

Kyra took hold of Kip's right hand when he started his mea culpa. Even Singe was startled.

Amusement.

Something else going on here.

Kip said, "Yeah. They know. But it don't mean anything to them. That's ancient history."

"They're not intrigued by those smoking-hot sky elf women?"

Kip's cheeks reddened. Kyra gave his hand a reassuring squeeze.

Something remarkably weird was going on. Which

thought of mine stirred the Dead Man's amusement yet again.

I tossed an inquiring thought his way. Was there really any need to hold the boy? The old lump had had plenty of time to paw through the clutter inside Kip's head.

*No need to keep him. But it might be useful to gather his friends here.*

"All right, kids. I've heard what I needed to hear. Kip, really, you need to think about the impact of the stuff you do. You really didn't realize that there'd be a big-ass stink if a hundred thousand giant bugs got loose?"

Singe said, "Stop that, Garrett. You're not his father."

That startled me. Then, "You're right. And he is almost grown. He should be learning from his mistakes. And should see new ones coming."

The slump started to go out of the boy's shoulders.

We couldn't let that happen. "But he hasn't shown us he's able to do that. Kip. The only thing else I'll say is, if this gets as hairy as it did with the sky elves, I'll ask your mother to keep you in a cage."

"Garrett!" Singe said. "Stop that."

"Yes, ma'am. Go on, guys. Kyra, take him back where you found him. And be nice."

# 31

I shut the door behind the young people, not yet sure what we'd accomplished. I expected Old Bones would clue me in.

I settled into my chair. "Singe, you ready to take notes?"

She lowered her mug long enough to say, "I don' think I can write so good right now."

"Well, damn! What good are you, then?" I got back up to collect writing materials for myself.

"I have a cute tail. Dollar Dan Justice told me so."

"Huh? Who's Dollar Dan Justice?"

"One of John Stretch's henchrats."

"Oh. Listen to your father. Don't trust him. They're all out—"

"I trust him implicitly, Garrett. To be your basic standard-issue ratman. All dim-witted and wrong-headed, with bad attitude for spice."

The Dead Man indulged in the psychic equivalent of a cough for attention. *Those few minutes with the young people restored my faith in the nature of the human species.*

"Two kids just sitting here?"

*You saw only the obvious lack of confidence of the boy. And the brash mask of the female. Inside, both are confused, frightened, and hopeful. In different ways and for different reasons.*

I was a teenager once. Back when thunder lizards walked the earth. Which they still do, just not in weather like what we'd been having lately. I vaguely recollect those days. Especially what it was like trying not to turn into a drooling idiot in front of a beautiful girl. Whose slightest frown could devastate me worse than the most ferocious natural disaster.

"I get you. Sort of. Maybe."

*Not at all.*

"All . . . right, then. Show me where I'm wrong."

*Miss Kyra turned on the heat to baffle, confuse, and control the young man. By which means she got him here.*

"That's what they do. A tiger is gonna be a tiger. And a girl like Kyra is gonna be a girl like Kyra."

*Of course. She will lead Cypres Prose around like she has a ring in his nose. But Cypres Prose is Cypres Prose, too, and will be the Cypres Prose who invents things.*

You can't tell tone in Himself's communications, generally. There was enough overburden on this, though, to suggest that he thought he'd made an important point.

Yes, Kip invents things. Three-wheels. One-wheels. Writing sticks. Priers. All because those sky elves did something to his head, back when.

"I'm all ears."

Singe's are bigger than mine but she was shutting down. She must have put away a lot of beer when I wasn't looking. All she had to say was, "How come he was wearin' a wig?" Which question she couldn't or wouldn't explain.

*No time for straight lines tonight.*

*Kip and his friends, the Faction, came together accidentally, accreting through the gravitational force of common inadequacy.*

*They are all bright, talented children with limited social skills. And, in several cases, have no interest in acquiring them. The boy who loves insects is obsessed with insects. He cares about nothing else.*

"The point you're dawdling toward is what?"

*A question. What interests the normal teenage boy? Stipulating that normal is a set with extended boundaries. What are all boys interested in, whatever else grabs their fancy?*

"In my case it was teenage girls."

*Right neighborhood. Defined by your own youthful inadequacies.*

"Hey!"

*Most boys are less selective than you were. For the majority, it is enough that the female be breathing.*

An exaggeration, perhaps, but he got the spirit of the thing. "And?"

*So Cypres Prose, being Cypres Prose, assumed there*

*would be a technical answer to his shortcomings. Assisted by the rest of the Faction's boy geniuses, he has created a means by which it is possible to determine, then improve, a woman's level of interest. So to speak.*

"Oh my! Really? He's invented a make-horny device?"

*More or less. With help from the rest of the Faction.*

"Oh, heavens! You know what that would mean if he could mass-produce it? Besides making everybody who has anything to do with it richer than . . . Hell, I don't know. There isn't anything to compare richer than."

*Wealth untold, yes. But there is a fly in the ointment.*

"There'd have to be, wouldn't there? Something like that . . . it could shake things up worse than peace breaking out did."

*The boys of the Faction have discovered that while their magical device works, it does nothing to make them less inept or undesirable.*

"Ha! Meaning they retain the power to quench the hottest fire by sheer force of personality."

*Exactly.*

"They could still make millions. Hell, we've got a thousand god shouters raking in gelt by the hundredweight selling amulets, pendants, rosaries, statues, whatever, that nobody ever actually sees work. How much more useful is something like this? If it gave you an edge even part of the time?"

*Shelve your residual youth, Garrett. Be content. For you, now, it is as good as it will ever get.*

Right. Tinnie isn't a gift horse only when I'm talking to guys like Scithe. After one giddy moment, I conceded the point.

Bloody hell! Had I turned into a grown-up when I wasn't looking?

"I hate it when you're so right."

Singe began to snore.

*The Faction are not the sort who give up after one setback. Nor are all of them as all for one and one for all as Cypres Prose. Naive boy.*

"Meaning?"

*The boy has seen signs, which he refuses to recognize, that the twins are distancing themselves in order to go into business for themselves.*

"They mean to steal his idea?"

*Yes.*

"But, knowing Kip, he has a better idea."

*Essentially. From the consumer point of view.*

"And that would be?"

*A means of combining scents drawn from several insects—
partially explaining the interest there, along with upsizing in
order to produce larger quantities of the scent—sounds beyond ordinary hearing, and some small-time mind-fogging
sorcery, all accompanied by advice to the consumer to avoid
being his normal self.*

"He was working it here tonight. With Kyra."

Amusement. *He was. As a field experiment. Testing the
latest version. I doubt anything will come of it. He remains
Cypres Prose.*

Meaning he couldn't help messing himself up.

The beer was taking its toll even though I'd slowed down
before Singe had.

"So them having a secret hideout near the World, where
they were doing their experiments, was why I ended up
down there."

*Probably. I would guess there will be no more insect prob-
lem. In that area. Work can resume. Probably.*

"Probably? Why only probably?"

*You have not yet dealt with the ghosts.*

"The ghosts? What ghosts? I couldn't find anybody who
said he'd seen one. I think it's all urban legend stuff that
can be explained by big bugs sneaking around making
weird noises."

*Possibly. If you have not made sure, you have not fulfilled
your commitment to the Weiders. Additionally, I would like
to meet the rest of the Faction as soon as you can arrange
that.*

"Kyra has probably suffered as much of those types as
she can stand."

*We have other resources.*

With that he subsided into his reveries. I went back to
the kitchen, drew myself a fresh mug. Singe continued snoring. I snuffed the lamps but left the bug candle burning. I
went across to the small front room to get an idea what we
would need to make it over for Singe to use.

She'd been in there already, scrubbing and polishing.

Good old lye soap had been deployed liberally. Furnishings that hadn't vanished had gotten shoved into the corner farthest from where the Goddamn Parrot's perch used to stand.

The stench of that little monster was gone, leaving me nothing but sour memories.

# 32

Someone pounded on the front door. Dean must be too damned lazy to use his key. I went to answer.

There was no light in the hall so I wouldn't give myself away by blocking it when I used the peephole.

There wasn't much light outside, either, but there was enough. I didn't know the man but I knew the type. All muscle, no brain. And this one had hair like a wild man. There must be a nest where they turn them out like a queen ant turns out workers. This one did what they all do when they don't know about my partner.

He decided to let himself in. He hurled his right shoulder against the door.

He had a solid work ethic. He put everything into the effort. Twice.

The door is made to withstand a mature bull troll. It endured this bruno's best without creaking.

He said, "Ah, shit!" after the second impact. I heard him distinctly. He staggered back, slipped on the slick surface, hit the porch rail, went on over. He landed on his back and slid into a pool of slush. His luck was in. The cold water wakened him before he drowned. It made a nasty mess in all that hair, where it started to freeze.

*Bring him inside before the Guard's watchers send collectors after him.*

So. Chuckles wasn't completely out of it. "How come?"

*He may know something interesting. But his mind is too well shielded for casual exploration while he is being manhandled by the Guard.*

"He might object."

*Which, I assume, is why you maintain a store of lead-weighted oaken arguments.*

Well, maybe.

I keep a "store" because I lose them, forget where I left them, or have them taken away from me.

Trusting Old Bones to help, I took the headknocker hanging behind the door, opened up, went down after the man with the muscles. It had turned damned cold again. I really needed a new coat. As soon as it got warm enough to go looking. But then I wouldn't need one anymore, so where was the point? "Let's go, big boy. Somebody wants to see you."

The big man got his feet under him. He reached out for support, wincing because his shoulder hurt. He didn't grasp the actuality of his situation.

The Dead Man can do that to you.

Big Bruno and I were at the door when Dean's voice asked, "What in the world?"

"You're finally home?"

"I am. What's this?"

"There have been developments. How was your day?"

"Marginally unpleasant. I spent it at a wake with relatives I loathe. But it could have been worse. This gentleman looks like a professional thug. Why are you fishing him out of a wet gutter?"

"He fell in after he bounced off the front door."

"One of those." With no excitement.

Some days it rains those guys around our place.

"One of those. With the added spice of being difficult for His Nibs to read."

Dean must have sucked down some smart brew at that wake. He landed on it with both feet just as I got there myself. "Which would make him the running dog of someone on the Hill."

"Look at you, getting all tooled up and working things out."

"Nobody appreciates a smart-ass." He held the door while I guided the failed door mauler inside. Wondering if Director Relway's serfs had noted the occasion.

The thug was still dripping when we seated him in the Dead Man's room. I left him in his street apparel. He had begun to melt.

*Tomorrow I need you to find Mr. Tharpe. I should not have let him get away today.*

"Easier said than done."

Dean headed to the kitchen for a mop.

*You are a professional of substance. Finding people is what you do.*

Sarcastic old lump.

*Your ambition deficit begins to concern me, Garrett.*

He should talk.

Dean yelped in outrage. I heard him all the way from the kitchen. "What's his problem?"

*Did you and Singe clean up after yourselves?*

Not me. I was busy answering doors and wrangling teenagers.

"What did she do?" Any problem couldn't be my fault.

*Do you suppose you can focus on something more significant?*

"You're not that attractive. Neither is Bruno, here."

*But he has a beautiful mind. Once you penetrate the ugly surface.*

I thought he was bantering, playing the snaps. But he was serious.

*Indeed. This Barate Algarda is a mixture of contrasts.*

"He's big. He's ugly. Instead of one or the other." If it barks like a dog and bites like a dog, I'm gonna say "Woof!" when I talk to it. Even if it plays the violin while it rips my leg off.

*He is nearer being two people in one body than any I have yet seen.*

That would be significant. We're all two-faced, or more, and Chuckles has peeked behind a lot of masks. Still, he was amusing himself by trying to make me whine for details. "How about passing along a little substance?"

His already overstuffed ego puffed up like a bullfrog fixing to sing. *Barate Algarda is a fixer, in your vernacular. By dint of circumstance rather than choice. Circumstance sometimes compels us to choose options we would otherwise disdain.*

There had to be some subtle shot in that.

*He is employed by the Windwalker, Furious Tide of Light.*

"That's a new one."

*To maintain the cosmic balance, I would suspect she has not heard of you, either. Or, sadder still, even of me. Yet.*

*All that is likely to change.*

Again, no clear tone, but I got the impression he was uncomfortable.

*The Windwalker is newly elevated. And young for one of her kind. Nor is she the sort usually found on the Hill. Barate Algarda is more than her operative. He is also her father.*

"Whoa! Hang on a minute, Chuckles."

*You understood right, first time. This is an unusual family. Yet this is not an evil man. Nor stupid. He loves his children. He will do anything necessary to protect them.*

"Does that include busting my door down in a snowstorm in the middle of the night? To protect them from somebody who never heard of them?"

*Including that, and then doing you bodily harm with considerable enthusiasm once the door is out of the way. It is confusing. Several whys are missing or inaccessible.*

"You said children. Since I've never hear of Furious Tide of Light, it would have to be someone else. Have I come into contact with another Algarda?" I've stopped being surprised that people I never heard of want to pound on me.

*There is a name that seems to be Kevans. It is hard to reach.*

"You'll find a way to get to it, though. Right?"

*He has protection. It does not appear to have been put into place against me. So yes. I will get to it.*

No tone? That was smug. With a reek.

He does have a high opinion of himself.

The sour truth, though, is that it's justified.

Like they say, it ain't bragging if you can do it.

*You begin to acquire wisdom. At long last.*

I kept my opinion behind my lips. Though there wasn't much point. "Tell me more about this Bruno who's two guys in one corpse."

*He intended to make you discover in your charitable heart a need to leave his daughter alone.* If it wasn't for him being dead he'd fall down howling at his own stand-up routine.

"Do I even want to know what that's all about?" Of course I did. If I wanted to make even a little sense of this late night raid.

*The Windwalker is out to protect her son. Who is really a daughter that she has always pretended is a son.*

"And you figured this out how?" It made less sense the more he explained. And, to speak true, he sounded puzzled himself.

*The Windwalker failed to deceive her father.*

"Uh . . ." You run into weird stuff all the time. In my racket, weird becomes the routine.

*Nothing gets weirder than just plain human beings.*

*Strange, yes. Exceedingly, to a neutral observer looking in from outside.*

*Barate Algarda knows that his daughter has a daughter herself instead of the son she has always pretended the child to be. Details are difficult to ferret out. The man's protection is firstrate. It is reactive. The more vigorously I probe, the harder the surface around his thoughts becomes. In sum, though, it is my estimate that the Windwalker's child is one of the Faction and your work at the World has put those children at risk, from the public, from the Guard, and, most especially, from the kind of Hill predators who would love to have command of giant bugs. Or of the sorcery necessary to create them.*

After recovering from being struck numb and dumb, I said, "I've faced vampires and zombies. Man-eating unicorns. Insane gods. And crazier priests. Plus platoons of professional killers and career loonies. Hell, I've survived Tinnie Tate and Belinda Contague almost forever. So I don't get what's going on here. It seems like there ought to be more to it. Something really weird."

*Families are all weird, from outside. But one common feature, often found in even the most dysfunctional versions, is an overpowering need to protect offspring. In this case, perhaps, there has been an overreaction. There are layers of reasoning and motivation that I am not yet able to reach.*

His response to that seemed surprised and frustrated. Most thinking creatures are open books. Those with secrets keep them by staying away.

I considered Barate Algarda. He sat there like a big, numb zombie wannabe.

A loving father. And a thug. A bonebreaker for his child. Out to protect a grandchild strange enough to be one of Kip Prose's crew. "There is something missing, Old Bones.

I have a feeling our easy job is about to get a whole lot darker." Until Algarda I had seen a light edge to everything. Giant bugs were sort of . . .

*Those insects ate people, Garrett. There is nothing light about that. And I share with you the sense that there is a darkness gathering. But I cannot identify it. And if it exists in the mind of this man, it is hidden or disguised beyond my capacity to capture.*

That had to hurt. Admitting failure was something he did not do.

In retrospective the both of us would feel like fools. We had everything we needed to define the darkness and failed to see it. Because even a trained detective will fail to see what he deems impossible. The Dead Man was blind, too.

There was sorcery and a sorcerer in the thing. Therefore, we decided, it must all revolve around the sorcery.

But we kept after it. I got blisters banging my head against the wall.

"All right. How about we start over? What did Algarda want here?"

*We have determined that. He wanted to make you stop interfering with the Faction. By whatever means necessary. Because that is what the Windwalker wants.*

"Why?" That was nuts. "That doesn't make sense." But in my life nuts turns up all the time.

*I cannot extract that and relate it to you in any way that you will understand. This man lives in a universe defined by laws created within his own mind and those close off every avenue I find to get past his protection.*

"He's mad?"

*No. But he lives in his own reality, by his own code. We all do, but this one even more so than you.*

He was recovering. He had the needle out.

"I get it. It's sad. Instead of dealing with the child's behavior he wants to silence the child's critics. The child being incapable of doing wrong."

*I do not think so. Not this time.*

That kind of thinking is common on the Hill. And elsewhere, with other powerful families. Algarda's grandkid could be killing and eating ordinary folks, but the old folks would make excuses, cover up, and commit crimes to make her problems go away.

"I've got some more general questions. Like, what's a Windwalker? I know what a Windsinger is. Kind of a Stormwarden. I saw one call up a baby tornado one time. But I've never heard of a Windwalker."

*A Windwalker uses the wind to carry himself—or herself—through the air. Swiftly. To the point where she would employ her other talents.*

"They are real people? Not demons? Not godlings? Not sky elves?"

*Nor even talking parrots.*

"And the girl pretending to be a boy business?"

*Based on my long acquaintance with your tribe, this would be a form of hiding from herself. Just for spice, Barate Algarda believes that at least one of the girls running with the Faction is a boy who wishes he had been born a girl. And dresses accordingly.*

"And why not?"

*Be not judgmental.*

"What? You're all right with all that?"

*I am not involved. It is not my place to judge. Nor are you involved, except insofar as the concerned individuals may be involved in what you are supposed to untangle. And we do know that they are inasmuch as they are the creators of the oversize insects.*

Not judging. A stand we'd all do well to embrace—where adults are involved. There is nobody more obnoxious than the guy who tells you how to live your life. At sword's point if you persist in your inappropriate behavior.

*There is no need for you to stay awake and torture yourself for answers,* Old Bones sent. *I will entertain Mr. Algarda. And he will entertain me. He cannot keep everything from me indefinitely. And, being a lifelong resident of the Hill, he knows where some of the bodies are buried.*

"You're sure?" I didn't want to hit the sheets just yet. There was a fresh keg in the kitchen and I had an arm that needed some exercise.

# 33

Barate Algarda was gone in the morning. Sent away with memories adjusted. He should no longer see me as a threat. The Dead Man was surly. His romance with Algarda hadn't gone the way he wanted.

Old Bones filled me in during the interlude between breakfast and the start of my workday. He'd gotten some interesting stuff.

*The harder I worked the more difficult it became to get anything out of that man. I am compelled to express admiration for whoever prepared him.*

"So somebody did know what he would run into here."

*No. I do not believe that was the case.*

"But . . ."

*He was hiding from someone else. Yet he did know your name. I got that much. At some point this evening he heard you mentioned in the context of trespassing in that ruined building. He may have been spying on Lurking Felhske's employer when Felhske reported.*

"But . . ."

*That someone appears to have become upset when your name turned up. Which upset Algarda in turn, though he did not know anything about you.*

"That makes no sense. I haven't bothered anyone on the Hill for ages." But Relway did say there was a Hill interest. I don't think Max has enemies up there who would scuttle his theater. So that would have to be about the bugs.

*They consulted oracles and augurs. They were not pleased with the results. Using "They" as the indeterminate pronoun. You have the potential to cause considerable embarrassment.*

In normal circumstances there isn't much embarrassment left over once I've dealt me my own share.

*True. Time will tell us if there is any rational foundation for their dread. Answer the door.*

"I didn't hear anything."

*You will.*

He was right.

A peek through the peephole showed me a choice selection of the female species. Alyx Weider, Tinnie Tate, and friends, including a peppery blonde I'd never before seen.

*Be polite.*

"You're kidding, right?" Me, be impolite to beautiful women?

He meant that the new woman was somebody I shouldn't offend.

*You would disappoint Manvil Gilbey if you did.* And Gilbey, in his sly, quiet way, is as ferocious as Max Weider if you pop up on his shady side.

*You are maturing.*

Alyx came in huffing and puffing and spoiling for a fight. She shoved me aside. Heading up the hallway, she snarled, "What the hell am I paying you for, Garrett?"

"Zip, last time I checked." I winked at Tinnie. The redhead seemed subdued this morning. There was something on her mind.

"Huh? What?"

"Zilch. Zero. Nothing. Your daddy is paying me. And I've been doing pretty good. The theft and vandalism are over."

"You leave that crusted old son of a bitch out of this!"

I eyeballed the new woman. She had a few years on the others but carried them as though they were just another plus. "Manners, girl child. And respect for the man who keeps a roof over your head."

"I'll show that son of a bitch some respect!"

Alyx's companions got busy tutting and patting and generally trying to calm her down. Except Tinnie. Tinnie had witnessed Alyx's histrionics for most of Alyx's life. Tinnie worked her fish-eye on me because I'd dared eyeball the new woman.

I said, "Don't waste your time, ladies. Alyx is just practicing her acting." Overacting.

I'd been around Alyx before, too.

I flashed her my disarming boyish grin, then sealed the deal with my raised eyebrow trick.

"You bastard." With most of the energy gone.

"So you were in the neighborhood. And you just decided to stop by and complain. About what?"

"Our theater, Garrett. You were supposed to clean it up. So the tradesmen could finish their work."

"And? You might want to consult Director Relway. Who hasn't been that happy about me cleaning up those bugs. Likewise, the Outfit in the Tenderloin, because their business has been affected. And, especially, the parents of the kids who created the bugs."

"Screw the bugs, Garrett. Get rid of the ghosts. The ghosts are why the workmen won't work."

"Really? What ghosts would those be, Alyx? I didn't find anybody who said he'd seen a ghost. All I got was guesses that what somebody thought were ghosts was really the bugs making noise in the walls."

Alyx wasn't listening. "Ghosts, Garrett! Listen to me! There are ghosts! And the workmen are staying away because of them. I want them dealt with."

I made a couple of lazy warding signs, then asked the rest of the covey, "Did she have too much to drink last night? Or did she just get out on the wrong side of the bed this morning?"

Alyx sputtered. Fetchingly.

She's one of those women who can't do anything that doesn't instantly chunk my mind into a man's main track. I have to confess, I've been heroic in my struggle to maintain my good behavior.

All those witnesses helped, right then. Especially the quiet one.

*Garrett.*

And that witness, almost as much as the one with the copper hair.

The lovelies restrained themselves. Though it was clear that Bobbi and the new woman had reservations about Alyx's histrionics.

"Anyone like tea? Or a beer? Got some Arctic Moposko...."

Alyx sputtered again.

The new woman said, "Alyx, the Moposkos went out of

business before you were born. Control yourself." Her calm, emotionless voice reminded me of long-service NCOs in the Corps. And had the same effect.

The blond brat stopped her tantrum.

Hmm.

*Keep talking.*

"Alyx, sweetie, you need to give me information, not attitude. Why do *you* think there's a ghost problem when nobody else down at the World does?" The Dead Man would dig around inside her head while I distracted her. If there was anything in there, he'd find it. Which could be a straight line leading to a crack about a long search.

*Unkind thought, Garrett. I do not believe that Max Weider considers his youngest child empty-headed. Overindulged, certainly, however. A weakness on his part. He cannot help himself after all that happened to the rest of his children.*

Dean materialized. His appearance had a magical effect. The women turned convivial instantly, Alyx included. The geezer sped me a smug look. Unaware that Old Bones had taken the opportunity to indulge in a little emotional expurgation. Not to mention shameless snooping.

I remember when he bragged about never going where he wasn't invited. I remember believing him.

I said, "I'd really like to hear what you have to say, Alyx."

The newcomer said, "She's upset because the project is behind schedule."

Tinnie nodded. As though the contention needed special support.

"I understand that. But why ghosts? And you are? Since none of these fine ladies have bothered with an introduction? Me Garrett."

"Me Heather Soames. Manvil Gilbey's favorite niece."

Alyx snickered. Tinnie's face darkened. Niece must be a euphemism. Which gave me a whole new appreciation for Max's best pal.

Heather Soames stilled Alyx with a glance. She paid no attention to Tinnie. Tinnie was playing ghost here, herself. "I'm set to become TunFaire's first female theater manager."

"Wow."

"Yes. It'll be tough. But not as tough as if I didn't have Manvil and Max behind me."

No doubt. Not many folks buck Max Weider.

"You're honest. I like that."

"Don't go getting all droolly, Garrett. She's taken."

"So am I, Alyx." I didn't look but I hoped that played well. "Heather. You talk to me about ghosts."

"I haven't seen one. But something is going on. Most of the workmen refused to come in again this morning. And they know the bug problem has been solved."

*I have enough.*

Two minutes later, all looking like they couldn't remember why they had come by my place, Alyx and her henchwomen—the beautiful Miss Tate included—slipped back out into the weather. Which had improved during their visit. Macunado Street was busy.

# 34

When I got back to the Dead Man's room, I said, "You want to take a feel around the neighborhood? See if you can spot anything that might be a Lurking Felhske?" I'd caught something from the corner of my eye.

A moment later, *In the shadow of the stoop, across the street in the downhill direction. Where they always hide when they want to watch this house without being seen themselves.*

"That's the one." The one the neighbors all watch because a lurker means good family entertainment might be about to happen.

*There's a chaotic shimmering. I cannot penetrate it. But that is of minor import. You need to move forward. Find Mr. Tharpe.*

"How come?"

*We must take full charge of the security function at the World. Using people we trust.*

"Ah. I see." Not really. He isn't a managerial type. He wants to unravel puzzles, not to get tangled up in mundanity. "This based on what you learned from the ladies? And what was Tinnie's problem?" If she'd been any more remote, she'd have been invisible.

*Women talk about relationships. How they are working. How they are not. Miss Tate has been the butt of considerable pessimistic speculation concerning her most significant relationship.*

Uh-oh. Something more to worry about.

*I understand that the complications are as much her creation as yours. She recognizes that herself. But she cannot blame herself in front of her friends. They would say she is enabling you by making excuses for your bad behavior.*

Definitely not something I wanted nagging me right now. "Back to the subject. You learned things."

*Principally from Heather Soames. She has an organized, scholarly mind. She is slightly insane, as well. Miss Weider, on the other hand, is as empty-headed as she appears. Yes, I know. She has her positive attributes. From a young man's point of view. But you, as you declared earlier, are taken.*

"Taken. But not dead. Or blind."

*The other women, including Miss Tate, have no particular knowledge concerning the World's troubles. Only Miss Soames and Miss Weider do. Miss Soames is interested in the opportunity the World offers. Miss Weider despairs of it ever coming to fruition.*

"She isn't sabotaging things, is she?" I'd seen stranger things.

*No. But there seemed to be substance to her ghost story.*

"How could she be the only one who . . . ?"

*There have been others. Few with the regular sightings she has experienced, however. It would seem the sightings are of considerable emotional impact. Denying them might be easier than discussing them.*

"Hang on. How would Alyx see them? Max wouldn't let her go near the World."

*Max Weider knows only what Max Weider sees. And what Manvil Gilbey chooses to tell him.*

"Like that, eh? So. A targeted ghost?" In TunFaire most anything can happen. And eventually does.

*Based on anomalies in Miss Weider's memories, it could be that she was hypnotized and told that she saw ghosts. But that seems unlikely.*

"That would mean someone close to the Weiders, or who can get close, wants to sabotage the World. I'd agree. Improbable."

*That is all I can give you. Nothing inside her head looked like a thread begging to be tugged.*

"And Heather Soames?"

*Miss Soames is, truly, an interesting mix. Very nearly two people in one body.*

"Another one? Let's fix her up with Barate Algarda. They could be their own extended family."

*You find me in a charitable mood. I have been handed several worthy puzzles. So I will exercise my benevolence and stipulate that your observation included amusing elements.*

"Score one for Garrett. All right. Give me the gory details on Heather."

*Miss Soames is determined to develop the soul of a serpent. But she cannot get shot of a soft spot for Manvil Gilbey. Whom she seems to have met the week she started tricking, at a tender age. Who has always treated her with respect, as an equal, not as what she was determined to be.*

"So Gilbey is a good guy." No earth-rocking secret wriggling out of the sack, there. "And, hard as she tries, she can't help liking him. And can't make herself work evil on him."

*In essence.*

Because she needed one anchor in the world outside. She had to have somebody out there to care about. And who she could let care about her.

Been there. On the anchor end. For Belinda Contague, psychotic queen of TunFaire's underworld.

*He understands. He is clever in the ways he manipulates Miss Soames. Refusing to let her slide under by placing less destructive alternatives in her path. In such a manner that she cannot refuse without worsening her own concept of who she is.*

"I've known Gilbey a long time. He wouldn't waste the time if he didn't see something worth saving."

*Just so. And try as she may to trip herself into falling down the well of perdition, the thing Gilbey sees betrays the destructive urge. It compels the other Heather to respond and produce. She has found a passion for the idea of the World. She could be the finest theater manager working— if she steps off the road to hell long enough to give it an honest effort.*

Heather Soames would not be the first or even tenth person I'd met who came with a wounded personality, fitting a similar mold. There are droves of them. The cleverest and strongest have learned to hide it. "Why do so many people get that way?"

*In your species the most common cause is what the child must endure. Especially from their own families.*

"Huh?" More of that wit on the razor's edge.

*It is the cruelest secret of your race, Garrett. I have seen dozens of generations of your people. I have seen the bleakness and darkness and despair haunting ten thousand human minds. It would amaze and horrify you to discover how many of your young are maltreated, how often, and how terribly.*

"I'm not sure I can be amazed by human evil." He was right, though. The exploitation of children isn't uncommon. Nor is it illegal, except in the churchly, moral sense. For some faiths.

I have no direct experience but I've known plenty who do. And suspect there are more who just can't talk about it.

*That is true. You see only the surface reality. Exploitation is so common that your people shrug it off as part of growing up. Assuming the victims will forget. And many do, because so little is made of what was done to them. But the internal influence never ends.*

Now I was uncomfortable. I felt a crusader zeal beginning to bubble down deep inside him. And that was not a crusade I wanted to take on. The cure for that lay in the hands of fanatics like Deal Relway. People who saw in black and white exclusively and would act on what they saw. Change doesn't come through persuasion. Not in a single lifetime.

I could imagine numerous commonlaw and customary exceptions to any do-gooder law the Crown might hand down. Including the inarguable fact that before your thirteenth birthday you're legally the property of your parents. Unless you have the stones to run away.

There's a timeless conflict between what's right and what's legal. Laws, most times, get handed down with good intentions. And immediately become cobblestones in the highway to hell. The instant the grand good purpose thuds down, unintended consequences start bubbling up around the edges.

*You are a cynical beast.*

"It's the company I keep."

*Indeed.*

Amazing how much sarcasm can be loaded into one supposedly neutral message.

*The perverse foibles of your species need not concern you*

*now. Unless the children of the Faction turn out to be prod-ucts of abuse. Which could well explain their penchant for sneaking around. Ah! Interesting.*

"What now?"

*Another of the company you keep is about to pass across the stage.*

"Huh?" Master of witty repartee. That's Mom Garrett's ever-lovin' blue-eyed baby boy. "Tinnie came back?" I was in a mood for that. In a mood, lately, for having the red-head underfoot most of the time.

Pular Singe, in damp street clothes, stuck her snoot through the doorway briefly. She didn't say anything. She wore a chagrined look, near as a ratperson can. She went on, not in silence, raising an angry racket climbing the stairs.

"Did I miss something?"

*No doubt. That is another of your master-level skills.*

At least he was awake at a time when his minds might come in handy.

*She spent last night away from home.*

"Ouch!" I turned into a worried father in two seconds flat.

*Again, you need not be concerned. She did nothing to worry you. She did nothing but disappoint herself. And be forcefully reminded that she is not human. And, therefore, less prone to be victimized by the vagaries of romance.*

"I'll take your word." Provisionally. But that world out there is overrun with guys just like I used to be. Some might even be ratmen.

Lucky for Singe, ratmen aren't interested unless they're close to a ratwoman in season. And a determined rat-woman can avoid that through judicious use of pharmaceu-ticals.

Of course, a ratman of a mind also has the option of injudicious use of pharmaceuticals.

Me and my baby girl maybe ought to have a talk about the kind of guys she's going to run into now that she's almost growed.

Old Bones was over there trying not to laugh out loud.

"I'm not ready to be daddy to a litter of ratpeople pups, Chuckles. Not to mention, Dean would quit on us if we had ratbrats underfoot."

*But he does not mind cats.*
"No. The racialist. Well, species-ist, I guess."
I could feel him regretting being too dead to break out in belly-busting laughter.
I went to have a look outside. Sourly.
The weather had gone the direction opposite my mood. Good. I wouldn't freeze completely once I got out there.

# 35

First stop I visited Mr. Jan. My family have bought clothing from him for generations. Half each of two different generations, anyway. Mr. Jan might fix me up with a new coat.

I took my time getting there. People were watching. I didn't want to add any excitement to their days.

Mr. Jan had been issued to the tailoring trade from its First Chief Directorate of Stereotypes. He was a skinny little old guy whose war service must have happened in the first half of the last century. He shone on top, had bushy white on the sides, white mustaches but no beard. And a persistent accent that made me wonder if he might not have avoided the war altogether. Age hadn't blunted his mind. He recognized me although I hadn't been in since my move to Macunado Street.

He asked what I'd been doing while he laid out choices in coat styles. I gave him the high points, none of which sent an eyebrow up a fraction of an inch. Nothing outside Mr. Jan's world could be as dramatic as the tribulations of the tailoring trade. He did manage an occasional well-timed, unenthusiastic grunt to let me know he was listening.

I wasn't focused on old adventures, either. I was trying to figure out how to make my tails collide so I could watch the fur fly.

Seeing me underwhelmed by the choices, Mr. Jan said, "You're the man for a new kind of all-weather coat we're thinking about doing. My son Brande brought back a sample from a trading trip he made with friends from the war." The old man cast furtive glances around. Brande and his Army buddies must have had the good fortune to have a few tons of surplus weaponry fall into the hold of a ship that they then quickly took beyond the reach of Karentine law. Where they could enjoy the benefit of a profit margin with a tiny underside.

There's a lot of that going around. The markup between wholesale and retail is just too seductive.

Mr. Jan told me, "This example will be tight on a man with your shoulders. But you'll get the idea." The coat he brought out looked like light brown tent canvas. "This would be the summer weight. Waterproof. There's a button-in winter lining. They wear these in Kharé, where it rains all the time."

I recalled the name. Vaguely. From a long time ago. Stories about rain and fog.

He was right about the fit. But I liked the coat after I saw it in a mirror. "You've sold me, Mr. Jan. When you make it, pretend I'm some kind of street magician."

"You want hidden pockets?"

"Lots. Big and small. Put some in the liner, too."

"How long do you want it to hang? To the knee is the style in Kharé, but their weather isn't as fierce as ours."

"Mr. Jan, you're the coat maker. Use your own judgment."

"I'll need to take measurements."

"Do your worst, foul fiend. Oh, I need something temporary, too."

"I expect I'll have something used that will do," he said. Ignoring my jest. After numerous measurements, carefully noted on reusable vellum, he asked, "How is your mother?" In a cautious, tentative way. My answer meant more than he wanted me to guess.

"She's gone, Mr. Jan. Some time ago. She had no will to go on after Mikey died."

The war with Venageta had been on for generations. People just assumed they would lose some of their male kinsmen. My mother lost her father, her husband, and two brothers. And remained unbroken. But she gave up after Mikey went down.

That hurt. Secretly. I've never convinced myself that my death would have triggered as intense a response.

"Sorry I brought it up."

"You didn't know."

"Goes to show how long it's been."

"You make this coat as good as the last one . . ." I stopped. I didn't want to suggest that I expected his product to outlive him.

"I won't see you again after you pick it up. I understand the commercial implications. There are coats out there that my grandfather made. And Jan trousers even older. We're less about fashion than value and durability. There. That should do it."

"How's business been since the war ended?"

"We never depended on military sales. We have plenty of work."

"Good. Good. How long till the coat is ready?"

"Ten days? Probably sooner. Check in after the weekend." He went into the back, then brought out a hideous, multicolored rag I wouldn't have been caught dead in if it weren't for the weather. "This is the only thing I've got that's big enough. Try to bring it back in one piece."

"Every crook in town will want to take it away from me."

Mr. Jan just stared. The First Chief Directorate doesn't issue them with a sense of humor.

"Look, once I leave you'll likely be visited by somebody who wants to know what I wanted. Whatever they want to know, go ahead and tell them."

That made the old man frown. Had we been out of touch so long that he didn't know what I do?

He'd get the idea soon enough.

I left a generous deposit.

# 36

My whole life I've suffered from a compulsion to tug the king's beard. The temptation has gotten to me more times than I care to recall.

Natty as all hell, I left Mr. Jan's place fighting an impulse to go throw an arm across the shoulder of one of the guys following me. Just to mess with him. And with any other watchers.

I resisted. This time.

I moved out slowly so everybody could keep up. I headed for The Palms. Which would amaze no one.

I did not receive the usual hostile reception. I was suspicious immediately.

Sarge seated me in a comfortable chair. Puddle brought tea. Quickly. In a silver tea service. My suspicions deepened. "What's going on, Puddle?" It wasn't like them to ignore such a stylish coat.

"I told 'em your head wouldn't be turned by no tea."

"Nor by manners. That just makes me wonder where they've been for the last ten years."

Sarge said, "I don't know about Morley, Garrett. But I ain't known you dat long."

"The question stands. How come you're being nice?"

"Orders."

"I know Morley isn't suffering a conscience attack over the way you guys usually act. So what's the story?" I had a notion. Any time somebody is slimy nice to me it's because they want a name moved up the waiting list for the three-wheels.

"Da boss has got him a new girlfriend."

"Earthshaking news. What's it been, days and days since the last one?"

"A while, actually. Ever' time you turn around, here came another one a' dem sky elf women, wantin' some a' his special."

"They aren't bothering him anymore? That would be disappointing."

Sarge looked a little shifty. "Don't you figure you about got even by now?"

"Hey. You've had the Goddamn Parrot here all winter. What do you think? Is a hundred years long enough to get even for that?"

The big slob just laughed. "Dere ya go, overreactin' agin. You oughta sign up wit' one a' dem actin' companies. Ye're so big on da drama."

So I've heard from a few folks. Who are just fooling themselves.

Morley appeared. He had a big smile pasted on. Which just revealed the sharpness of his teeth.

"Gee! You guys must want something real bad."

"Garrett, you have to be the most cynical human being I know."

"The key phrase being human being, of course. I can think of a whole list of folks more cynical and manipulative than me. But they've all got a little nonhuman in them somewhere."

He did not stop smiling. "What did you want?" Implying that I wouldn't be seen around The Palms unless I wanted something.

"Just putting you on the spot with the guys following me around."

His smile vanished. "We could put a sign out. Invite them in. Help build the business."

"So we've pranced around. Now what?"

"You go first. What do you want?"

"Just to put my dogs up. On the way down to the World. To find out why Alyx Weider insists it's haunted when nobody else sees any ghosts."

"Going to bullshit a master bullshitter?"

"How's this, then? I want to leave a message for Saucerhead. He's never home anymore. You're likely to see him before I do." I don't know what it is with Tharpe. He's no born-again vegetarian but he likes The Palms. "The Dead Man has work for him. He's having trouble recalling who the senior partner is again."

"And?"

"Where can I find me a gypsy necromancer? I could settle the ghost business in a minute with a professional."

"Now we're getting somewhere."

"I thought that up on the spot. I was telling the truth about wanting to put my feet up. I haven't been getting enough exercise."

"You never did."

"Your turn. How come the nice show? Give it to me straight. I can take it."

"It isn't that big a thing."

It was that big a thing.

"We want to borrow Singe. For a tracking job."

Aha. "Singe is a free agent. Go over to the house and ask if she wants the work."

"We were hoping you could intercede on our behalf."

"Of course you were."

"You know she won't lift a paw if you don't give her the go-ahead."

"Then when you go see her be sure to tell her I said it's all right by me." I struggled to keep a straight face.

Morley gave me the fish-eye. Wondering if I realized that he didn't want to talk to Singe where the Dead Man might take a gander at the circus inside his head. He decided I was smart enough to see it.

I said, "Of course I am. It's my only joy in life."

"What?"

"I'm a major pain."

"You got that right."

"You thought of a gypsy necromancer?" He knows everybody on the underbelly of society. I know a few myself but am intellectually allergic to the region of the beast's belly where the parasites practice the sorcery trades.

"Belle Chimes."

I managed a credible impression of a bass out of water. Mouth moving but producing no sound till, "You're kidding."

"Probably not a real name."

"You think?"

"I've never met the guy. He's way on the down low. He has a reputation like yours. Straight arrow in a sleazy racket. Better dressed, though."

"Thank you. I think. The coat's a loaner."

"Of course it is. You're Mr. Style."

"You saw what your guys did to my good coat."

He couldn't argue with that. He said, "Go to a tavern called the Busted Dick." He offered an approximate location in the Tenderloin. "Buy yourself a beer. Talk to a barkeep named Horace. Tell him you need to talk to Bill about last week's D'Guni tournament. Buy yourself another beer. If they decide you don't look like a bonebreaker from the Hill or a ringer on the Director's payroll, they might hook you up."

"I'm not looking for a vampire."

"A vampire might be an easier find. They don't have Hill folks wanting to exterminate them."

"I'm out of here, then." Getting up and getting gone before he could nag me about Singe again.

If he was desperate enough he'd turn up at the house, Dead Man or no.

# 37

Manvil Gilbey was outside the World when I got there. "Don't see you roaming around much anymore."

His frown wasn't encouraging. "Your efforts haven't gotten things moving again."

"Bugs shouldn't be a problem anymore. Goofy teenagers, I don't know. I'm working on the ghosts nobody but Alyx believes in as we speak. How about you? Seen any? No? Hey, I met your niece, Heather. Seems to have a good head for business."

That didn't improve his mood.

"No worries. I'm a one-woman man these days."

"Getting ready to settle down?"

He meant to be sarcastic.

"Maybe. Not sure the other half of the equation is, though."

"And you'll never know if you don't come up with the guts to ask."

"Voice of experience?"

"Lots. Long time."

"So. Again. What's your take on the ghost business?"

"I think they're there. I think somebody besides Alyx has seen them. But they don't want to admit it. No telling why. I think ghosts are why the workmen have been staying away. In this town it could all be just business. Somebody who wants to keep us out of the theater game maybe hired a sorcerer. Because once we're serving our beers in our theaters we'll have a huge competitive advantage."

Meaning that the Weider brewing empire wouldn't supply competing theaters. And Weider is the main source of liquid refreshment in commercial quantities.

I didn't dismiss that, silly as it sounded when it plunked down in the light of day. Raw capitalism goes on all the time.

"There was anybody whose head had that kink, I'm sure you'd know his name, rank, and pay number."

"Guess what, Garrett? You got rung in because Max and I *can't* put a face on that somebody."

"I'll figure it out," I promised. "One way or another."

"Or die trying?"

"I don't love you guys that much. You found out anything useful here?"

"That it's possible the workmen are scared of something nastier than ghosts. Something about spooky music. Nobody wants to talk about that, either."

"Smells like a protection racket trying to move in. But I dealt with that already."

"And nobody is asking for anything. The purpose of a protection scheme is to extort money. Isn't it?"

"You'd think. You going to be around? I've got something to do. But I'll be right back."

"I'll be here. Though all I can do is look for proof that somebody lied."

"What *did* they tell you?" I hadn't yet seen anybody who looked like a workman.

"The ones who did show up are staying out of sight. They don't want to be seen."

"Gilbey, you, me, Max, and every idiot on the payroll here survived the war. That should've taught them how to deal with fear."

"These are construction guys, Garrett. They did their time in construction companies. If they got into fights it was because the combat battalions didn't do their job."

"Fire some of the people who aren't showing up. I'll find replacements. They might not be as skilled but they won't run away. Hire the real guys back later, after they've gotten intimate with the terrors of unemployment. For now, I'm going looking for a specialist who can help us with the ghost business."

I headed into the Tenderloin, pursuing Morley's instructions. I assumed I was being followed despite a lack of evidence.

I was concerned about Morley. He has a gambling problem. He'd had it controlled for a while. I hoped he still did. It isn't pretty when he weakens. The debts pile up, triggering ticks and irrational behaviors as he tries to get out from under.

He'd shown that style of anxiety during my visit. And was way too friendly.

Being a natural born paranoid cynic, I feared my best pal was betting on the water spider races again.

# 38

The Busted Dick wasn't hard to find. Though the sign out front didn't help. In timeworn paint it showed dice, domino tiles, and a tumble of noodles or sticks.

The tumble turned out to represent a game in which skinny sticks with writing on them are shaken in a jar, then tossed onto a tabletop. Not a game common in Karenta.

There's a kind of fortune-telling that uses little sticks. I'd never seen that, either.

I went inside. It was your standard low-end dive. Six small tables, each attended by several rickety chairs, lined the right-hand wall. None were occupied. The bar was to the left, with ten wobbly stools. It had been something special in an earlier century. Two stools were occupied. Three empties stood between them. Neither professional drinker seemed aware of the other. Both, however, took a moment to glance at me and be impressed by my borrowed coat.

I invited myself aboard the center of the 'tween stools. It had been polished by thousands of dissolute heinies. "Beer." I laid down a small silver piece. That would keep the cold barley soup coming. "Good beer."

They would have a special keg reserved.

A generous mug materialized. Its contents were drinkable.

My change reflected the quality of my purchase.

The Busted Dick must get a few up-class drop-ins, using it as a way station when sneaking toward or away from the Tenderloin.

I pushed a copper back to the barman. He nodded his appreciation. I doubt my companions ever tipped. I relaxed, enjoyed the barley nectar.

No local barman made anything that fine in a thirty-gallon tub in a room in back. The small guys don't have the patience to do the water right. They don't boil it long enough; then they don't fine all the chunks out. They don't have time. They can't store and age their product. They've got to turn it over.

I raised my mug. "I need a refill." Like a serious drinker.

My flanking competitors hadn't raised their mugs twice between them while I drained mine.

Having delivered the new trooper, made change, and pocketed his tip, the barman failed to go back to cleaning mugs, which seems compulsory whenever they're not separating a customer from his cash.

He leaned back and waited for my pitch.

It was obvious that I wasn't some derelict who had wandered in looking to build a quick buzz. My coat gave me away.

I enjoyed half my second mug before I asked, "You know Horace?"

"Why do you want to know?"

"Because I need to talk to a guy named Horace who works at the Busted Dick. A name I'd like explained almost as much as I'd like to connect with Horace."

"A busted dick is the worst possible throw of the sticks in the game of points. Like snake-eyes, shooting craps. Only worse. I take it you're not a points player."

"I never heard of it. From context, I'd guess it's a gambling game."

"You catch on quick. It came from Venageta. Prisoners of war brought it back. I've never figured it all out. The rules go on and on. There're thirty-six sticks. They have symbols on all four sides and the ends are colored. None of them are the same. You shake them in a jar, then dump them out. There's a million ways they can fall. Come in some night, there'll be games at every table. Used to be dominoes. Them that gets into the game get into it *seriously*. The only reason they aren't at it now is, we don't let them in till nighttime. On account of, everybody's got to get some sleep sometime."

"Horace?"

"There a reason?"

"Yeah. He can put me in touch with my old Army buddy, Belle Chimes."

The barman's eyes narrowed. He glanced past me, toward the door. He was caught in the forked stick of the underground economy. You're there, you need customers. But you can't know for sure who they are when they come round jingling silver. Sometimes not until it's too late.

I could be some guy sent out from the Al-Khar to fish for people looking to cut costs and corners by hiring uncertified specialists.

Same trap is right there waiting for the consumer.

"I can probably get you in touch with Horace. What would you want with this Bill?"

"Weider Brewing is building a theater a little ways from here. Some of the workmen say the site is haunted. I hear tell Belle can maybe help me find out if that's true."

The barman stared over my shoulder.

I finished my beer. "I could use a refill."

That stirred him. He took my mug to the quarter keg filled with the good stuff. He brought it back full. So distracted that he forgot to take my money. He said, "The loo? Back there. Through that door. Take your beer with you. Unless you want it to disappear while you're gone."

He did take my money then.

So much for him being rattled.

I took my beer.

The loo wasn't. As I'd expected. For places like the Busted Dick the jakes is just the alley out back.

The barman joined me. "Be quick. Those two will drain the taps." He kept a foot inside so the door wouldn't close all the way. He could duck back in and leave me holding my own if he wanted. Or he could see his clients if an impulse toward larceny brought them back to life.

"I told it. I've got a purported ghost problem. I need an expert without conflicting motives to check it out. To tell me if it's true. And how to cope with it if it is. And to tell me why people think it's true if it isn't. I'll pay a reasonable fee for the service."

I was impatient. But I knew the romance was necessary.

You don't find independently operating sorcerers hanging out on street corners. Folks on the Hill have no qualms about getting lethal while enforcing their monopoly. But they won't come out to back up your everyday kind of guy. Somebody like Mom Garrett's blue-eyed baby boy. For a freelance you have to find a winner in the birth lottery who got a load of talent but no ability whatsoever to play well with others.

I exaggerate, but we all know those people. Reeking with genius. Dripping talent. And completely incapable of sustaining a personal relationship. With almost as much trouble keeping a job.

Careful, Garrett. Sounds a little autobiographical.

"This ghost problem. Where would it be again?"

"Hop, skip, and a jump. The World. The theater the Weider Brewery is building."

"It's farther than that. But not much. Let's go back inside. You buy another beer. I'll ask my dad if he knows somebody who can help you." He pulled on the door.

We got back to the bar in time to save one of the professional drunks from suffering a severe moral lapse. He was just fixing to slide behind the bar, empty mug dreaming of a refill. Caught, he faked a stumble, then headed on back to the jakes.

The barman filled me up. "I'll be right back. Keep them honest." He hit what looked like a skinny pantry door at the back end of the bar. An equally narrow stairway lay behind that. He had to go up with his shoulders turned slightly sideways.

The width of the stairs dated the structure. There'd been a time, a hundred fifty years back, when TunFaire's dwarf and ogre populations were very restless. Neither species would be narrow enough to climb that stair.

I'd have real trouble myself.

If the barman ditched me by sneaking out a back way, I'd serve beer on the house.

A little old man pushed through the stairway door. He was maybe five feet tall. He'd been taller in the long ago, but the weight of time had bent him over and had shrunk him. He had what the old folks call a widow's hump. He was a shiny chestnut color. I saw nothing to suggest any actual kinship with the barman, who came out the stairway door a moment later.

The little old man shuffled over. "Who you looking for?"

"Belle Chimes. Friend of mine says he can give me advice about D'Guni racing."

He frowned. "Here's some, now. Don't do it." Hard to tell about that frown, though, looking downhill into that nest of wrinkles. "Who told you to see him about the bug races?"

I didn't want to give Morley up. But his name might be the password.

A freelance sorcerer might have a different name for every shill he had referring trade. "Morley Dotes. I don't know where he got the name."

"Who was you supposed to talk to when you got here?"

I told him what Morley told me.

The old man took a deep breath, stuck one shaky old hand back over the bar. The barman brought a brown briar walking stick up from somewhere down below. The old man took it. "Let's walk, boy."

"All right." I held the door for him, going out to the street.

The old man got more spry as soon as the door closed. He headed for the World. Not exactly smoking fast, but without the shuffle. "Talk to me about money, boy."

"Some could end up coming your way."

"No shit. I'll retire to my own vineyard on the slopes of Mount Kramas." He referenced the mythical mountain where the grapes are so perfect only the gods themselves are allowed to drink what comes of letting their juice rot.

My doubts about the man's credentials as a sorcerer faded before we got to the World. When we arrived he was twenty years younger and four inches taller. And moved with corresponding ease and grace. And was miffed because I didn't ooh and aah over his transformation.

I'd run into masters of illusion before. Hell, I'm halfway engaged to one particular redheaded mistress of illusion.

Tinnie got into the mix because she and Alyx Weider's girl gang had turned up while I was off recruiting. Alyx and Heather were harassing poor Manvil Gilbey.

My new friend became ten years younger, fast, while making little purring sounds of appreciation. "There might be a perk or two here, after all."

"Just stay away from the redhead."

"Dangerous?"

"And taken."

# 39

I told Gilbey, "There're some ragged potato sacks over there. One of the dead guys was using them to keep warm."

"Figuring on swapping them out for that coat? Where did you get that thing?"

"No. I thought you might help me stuff Alyx into one."

"I'm about ready." Gilbey was out of patience with Alyx.

I couldn't figure what her problem was. She was a long step past the usual. Maybe she was trying to impress old Belle. Now insisting on being called Bill.

Poor Alyx. Bill wrote her off two minutes after they met. Beauty can take a girl just so far—especially if she's only one of a posse of smoking-hot females and the rest all come equipped with manners.

Bill went to work. Or so he said. He ambled on inside the World.

I cut my sweetie out of the pack. "How come you guys are down here? And how come you're all the time running with this bunch instead of being over at the manufactory busting that sweet patootie to make me rich?"

"Why, Mr. Garrett! I do declare! You say the most romantical things. You in your fancy coat. You who could be over there making your own self rich."

"I just can't help being romantic when I'm around you. My brain turns to mush. I drool. And the most absurd things—"

"Quit while you're ahead, Malsquando." Referring to a legendary lover of ages past. He'd even seduced the queen. And her daughter. And her son, according to some. The king hadn't been pleased. It's not a good idea to piss off the king if you haven't seduced him, too.

"I quit." I'm no fast learner with some of this stuff. But pain is a fine teaching tool. Tinnie has been plying that one for a long time. She's almost got me broken in.

"Come here, Malsquando."

Good little doggie, I heeled and trotted after.

She turned on me as soon as we were safe from eyewitnesses.

I didn't even have to apologize for something I didn't know I did.

I came up for air about ten years later, panting and speaking in tongues. But feeling a certain pride of workmanship. My favorite redhead was thoroughly disheveled and fighting for breath herself. She gasped, "So where have you been lately?"

I'm so smart. I have skills I haven't even used yet. I made dead sure nothing left my mouth that even remotely sounded like words. Words are treacherous. They could clump together to offer some silly notion about me having been in exile because of the quirks of somebody who wore her hair big, long, and criminally red.

When you're the guy in the couple that includes one of those women, you're right there at the end of the rainbow. But you pay for it. You're always in the wrong.

"Will you kids quit snogging long enough to get something accomplished, here?"

Manvil Gilbey had found us. And was not happy to see us preoccupied by trivia.

Heather Soames was right behind Gilbey. And looked like she envied us our distraction.

Manvil told me, "If you can drag yourself away, Bill is back. He says he needs to talk to you. He seems rattled."

Uh-oh. That didn't sound like anything I wanted to hear.

Bill had reacquired most of the years he'd shed coming over from the Busted Dick. He radiated grim seriousness. He reached up and took me by the elbow, eased me away from the crowd. I steeled myself for a sales pitch.

"What's the story, Bill? And how much is it going to cost me?"

Naturally suspicious right down to my brittle little toenails, I even wondered if Bill might not be the one haunting the World. Just to provide himself some employment. Which wasn't rational thinking.

He said, "My profession brings out the cynic in clients like no other. They come crawling, desperate because they don't know where to turn. But then they can't trust me to do what they need to have done."

Had he been following me around, making notes?

"So, tell me the horrid news, Bill. How much special equipment and how many specialist sorcerers from the underground economy am I gonna need to deal with this?"

"Your cynicism spring is wound too tight, boy. Hear me out before you decide you're being scammed."

I have been known to accept good advice when I hear it. "My lips are sealed. For the moment."

"Excellent. Here goes. There's something down there." He wagged a finger. "Uh-uh. You'll learn more with your mouth shut."

More good advice. Given me on a regular basis by various associates. Especially the big guy at home. I'll get it someday. "Go."

"Excellent. Again. There's something down there. It's big. It's alien. And it's ugly. It's still a long way from being wide awake. It considers the world its nightmare. Your bug makers disturbed it. The bugs are still disturbing it. Bugs that it may have helped dream. Yes. There are a lot of bugs down there. Thousands. Still. Probably feeding on the thing. Something beyond my knowledge. Or maybe anyone else's."

Oh no! Hang on! This time was supposed to be simple. Deal with some bugs. Stop some sabotage. A couple days of easy work for a bucketful of gold.

"How would that tie into ghosts?"

"Susceptible minds might think they saw ghosts if their obsessions reflected off the dreams of the thing down below."

I grasped what he meant because I live with a dead Loghyr. I didn't like it. Nor did he convince me, really. "Any idea what it is?"

"No. But there's precedent for ancient horrors wakening."

"Of course. Suggestions?"

"Keep people away. Find experts. Do research. Look through ancient records."

I sighed as vistas of work expanded before me.

I beckoned Gilbey. "Come on over here. You need to hear this." I told Bill, "He does: He's the money." I told Gilbey, "You'll love this."

Gilbey listened. He didn't interrupt. Bill expanded on what he'd told me. Gilbey said, "First step, identify the threat. Determine the extent and magnitude."

"Right."

Gilbey looked at me. "I blame you for this."

"What?"

"If we'd sent anybody but you, it would've been over after those Bustee kids got rounded up."

He was joking. I didn't feel it. It did seem like this stuff happened to me all the time. "Yeah. Well, I did take care of them. I can follow up with the Guard and the Outfit, if you want."

"The Outfit?"

"The Chodo family enterprise. The Combine. The Syndicate."

"I know who you mean. Why bring them up?"

"They're very territorial. The World is at the edge of their territory. It ought to spin off a demand for secondary entertainment. Which would be why you haven't heard from them. Chodo and Belinda understand business better than most people."

"We're going to help them get better, too?"

"A fair dinkum, I'd bet. Anyway, they don't allow competition. And no freelancing on their patch. You're safer down here than you'd be anywhere but the Dream Quarter."

Gilbey grunted. "So there are several things going on."

"Yeah." Seems to be my fate. "Like this. Looks like. You decided to build a theater. To anchor a chain. But you picked a spot where something ancient and unpleasant is buried way down deep. The enterprise attracted wannabe gangsters from the Bustee."

"And the bugs?"

"Teenagers. Psychotically brilliant kids, mostly off the Hill. They found a secret place to indulge some strange hobbies. The bugs they made got loose. Besides getting up here to the surface, they went down and irritated whatever it is that's buried down there."

I was cooking. Who needed the Dead Man to work this stuff out?

Gilbey asked a trick question. It wasn't *the* trick question but it was a good one. At that point I had only a glimmer of the key question myself. "What are you going to do about it?"

"That's the big one. It'll take some thought. Right now, recruit a gang of thugs and take complete control here. Then find out why the workmen won't show up when jobs are so scarce. Maybe go down under to look around. If the sulfur I left burning hasn't made the air unbreathable down there."

"That'll take time."

"Everything takes time. Even taking time. The impossible especially takes a little longer. Here's what you can do. Tell your construction foremen I want their men here tomorrow. Or they can kiss their jobs good-bye."

"We don't operate that way, Garrett."

"Why not?"

"We'd rather look out for our people."

"They know that. Right? So, you talk this way, they know you're serious. Bill. Suggestions?"

Belle—Bill—was looking a little younger. "Before anything else, you need to tell me what you want to accomplish."

"We're building a theater. Shooting for an early spring opening date. We've had problems. Vandalism. Theft. Giant bugs. And the haunting I brought you over to check out. The theft and vandalism have been dealt with. I used to think we had the bug problem licked, too."

Using a slick redhead's slide, Tinnie eased in close, inside my left arm, while I was talking to Bill and Gilbey. "You were way too optimistic about that, Malsquando." She pointed.

Up where the roof sheathing should start going on soon, a brace of foot-long blue beetles decorated the World, glistening in the afternoon sun. Something the size of a small terrier perched up top, between naked rafters, wearing big

antennae. It sparkled in the sunlight, too. I couldn't make
out the color. Black or dark brown, and very shiny. "All
right. I got way ahead of myself."

The neighborhood had been quiet. Today. Enough for
me to make out the chatter of a sizable group headed my
way.

That turned out to consist of Morley Dotes, Singe, Saucerhead, and several of Morley's troops. I'd asked Morley
to find Tharpe. I told Manvil and Bill, "Let me talk to
these guys." Noting the wench pack starting to size Morley
up already.

How does he do that? Get them breathing faster just by
showing up.

"Saucerhead. Great. I need you to run security here.
Round yourself up five guys you trust, then keep everybody
who don't belong here out of the place."

Tharpe's mouth opened and closed several times before
he asked, "How will I know who belongs?"

"We'll work that out after you pull a crew together." He
knew where to find the right kind of people.

"Pay?"

"I've got the brewery behind me. As long as people drink
beer we'll get paid."

Saucerhead glanced around. He recognized Gilbey. That
made my case. "That'll do." He headed out without another word.

I faced Singe. "And what are you up to?"

"Freelancing. For Mr. Dotes."

"I see." I glanced at the sky. "Are you dressed warm
enough?" I had a notion what was up. That might take a
good, long time. If Singe could find a track at all after the
weather we'd been having.

She gave me the kind of look an adolescent does after
that kind of question. And added a big rat sneer at my coat.

"All right. You're a big girl." I told Morley, "Don't get
her into any tight places." And strained hard not to start
moralizing about bounty-hunting somebody who'd never
done anything to him personally.

"More bugs," Gilbey said. He pointed. A huge walking
stick had appeared up top. It was big enough for me to
make out its head rolling right and left, checking the blue
beetles. It decided they looked tasty. It charged. Something

I'd never, in my limited experience, seen a normal walking stick do. They usually move slow, or just wait for dinner to come to them.

The beetles scooted. One lost its grip on the wall. Down it went. The walking stick fell right behind it. The beetle pounded the air desperately with inadequate wings. It survived its collision with cobblestone. The walking stick did not.

Morley and Gilbey alike hustled over for a closer look. I said, "They just keep on hatching out. I should head over to the Tenderloin, find out if—"

Miss Tinnie Tate has mastered the secret of bilocation. She was beside me, gouging me in the ribs, before I could finish my thought. Belle gawked, amazed. Though he seemed more taken with Lindy Zhang. Whenever he looked at her he sloughed a half dozen years.

The years came back the moment he looked somewhere else. Somewhere behind me. I turned but didn't see what had turned him gray at the gills. He pretended nothing had happened. But he looked around some more, marking lines of retreat.

Morley returned. "You have an interesting one here, Garrett. Not as lethal as usual, but interesting. Good luck. Singe. Time to go."

Gilbey approached. He wore a weak smile. "Ditto, what your friend said. I understand why it's taking so long. Alyx! Let's go."

"Hang on. I need to talk to her. Alyx! Come here. Godsdamnit, Tinnie, turn it off for two minutes." There are rare moments when enough Tate is just about enough.

"What?" Alyx was pouting now.

"Cut the crap. Give me some straight answers. Why do you keep insisting on ghosts here when nobody else sees them?"

"*I* see them!"

"Seen any today?"

"No."

"Where do you see them when you do?"

She waved a hand behind her, indicating the World. "Inside."

"So. You've been coming down here despite your dad's instructions."

She stared at the pavements, for once unready to squabble.

"You have. Bad Alyx."

"I just wanted to see how things were going. I talked Daddy into building all this."

"The ghosts. You keep insisting."

"Damn it, Garrett! I saw them! Every time I ever went down into the part that's going to be under the stage. That's where everybody else saw them, too. And sometimes even up on the ground floor."

"Who else saw them? I can't find anybody."

"They all quit. Or lie because they don't want to talk about it."

I didn't get that. Ghosts aren't common but so much weird stuff happens around this burg that I couldn't see anybody getting rattled over a spook or two. Unless . . . "What did you see?"

"I don't know. It was just there. All kind of formless. And there was, like, music. Or something. Really faint."

Had I not had Bill's report I would've discounted everything Alyx said. As it was, I couldn't get anything more useful than her stubborn insistence that she *had* seen ghosts.

"All right. Go on home with Gilbey. Take the ladies with you." Bill, I noted, had managed to spark a conversation with Lindy. Which he was using to cover his moving continuously to survey the neighborhood.

I had a distinct feeling that Bill had seen a ghost of his own. One that made him extremely nervous. Which just added on to the pile.

I invited myself to interrupt. "Bill, talk to me some more about what's going on down there. I really don't understand."

# 40

"What now, Malsquando?" She was going to beat that dog hairless.

We were alone now. We had the World to ourselves. Discounting the presence of several Relway Runners driven by a need to keep an eye on what was happening. Tinnie had refused to leave with the other women. She insisted that she was smitten by my borrowed coat.

"You don't want to wear that Malsquando thing out the day you invented it." It irked me for no reason I could pin down.

"Why aren't you wearing your regular coat?"

Though she'd stared some, this was the first she'd commented. "The guys at Morley's place tore it up fighting over it."

"What?"

"They thought somebody left it behind. It looked halfway decent and didn't smell too bad."

"A found treasure. I meant well, Mal . . . All right. It's gotten really quiet, hasn't it?"

Yes. There was no one else in sight. Except Relway's guys, at rare moments.

"Why aren't we up to our ears in gawkers and opportunists?"

"You want to go inside and poke around?"

"When reinforcements arrive."

"You'd get a better look at everything in there."

And there wasn't much anyone could take from the outside. Not without prying pieces off.

Some word had to be out. Something to the effect that

whoever messed with the World could expect to come up missing useful bits.

It *was* the edge of the Tenderloin, where freelancing is seriously discouraged.

Seconds after we got inside I received proof that my redheaded friend was way too subtle for me. She had a good reason for getting in out of the weather.

I should have run for it. But I couldn't.

Tinnie said, "I'm getting a lot of pressure from the old folks, Garrett." She paced and twitched, her voice taut and pitched higher than usual.

This wasn't the Tinnie I was used to. That Tinnie is the personification of self-confidence. I'm the one who panics when personal talk gets personal.

I had a premonition. Here came a time to panic. "Oh? Yeah?" I squeaked, too.

"I'm out of excuses. For everybody. Including me." Her voice kept going higher.

"So . . . Uh . . . What do you think?" I shoved my hands into the back of my pants. She didn't need to see them shaking.

"Uh . . . I think . . ." Her voice was up there in mouse talk range. "We're grown-ups."

"So we ought to be able to act like grown-ups."

That didn't come out smoothly.

"Yeah."

"Grown-ups manage this stuff all the time."

"Every day."

Both of us could hear dozens of absent voices muttering that our behavior was worse than juvenile.

Tinnie went on. "And we are grown-ups. Aren't we?"

"Have been for years and years. Though some would argue."

"People years younger than us manage perfectly well."

"They do, don't they? And we're professionals. We've dealt with tough people and tougher situations."

Talking all around the central issue. Not getting to the heart but relaxing the defenses a little, here and there.

It went on. The consensus was, we couldn't just keep on keeping on. There were people in our lives. Something had to give. But the risks were huge.

"Am I interrupting?"

"Bill! I thought you went back to the tavern."

"I did. Then I had a thought. On the house. Because about a dozen of those giant bugs are running around out there, even in this weather. Which means the problem could get really awful when the weather turns warm. If everything isn't straightened out by then."

Tinnie seemed more relieved than aggravated by the interruption. Though the subject still had to be addressed. Soon.

I said, "You could give me more information about what's going on down there, then."

"I could. If I had anything. I can't without going down there to look."

I could arrange that. I didn't tell him out loud.

He might have read my mind. "Find yourself a real, legal expert. Not a necromancer, either."

I didn't press. I knew where to find Bill. He was thinking that, too. And regretting it, maybe.

He said, "That's what I wanted to tell you. That whatever is down there, it's so ugly that you need to get a really big stick onto it. Fast. Before it really wakes up."

He regretted having come back. But something wouldn't let him just cut me loose.

He wasn't shaking now. He had been when he'd first come back outside, earlier.

It might be a good idea to take the evidence to the self-proclaimed experts after all.

I glanced at Tinnie.

I could use some expert help over there, too.

Back to Bill. I got the impression there was more on his mind. A lot more. Some of it personal. His twitchiness seemed to be the sort that comes when you think somebody is stalking you. Then, too, there must be something he thought I ought to know but couldn't bring himself to say.

I said, "The brewery will send a nice fee along to the Busted Dick. With a retainer. So we can call on your expertise again."

"Retainer?"

"A fee you get for keeping yourself available. The brewery has several specialists on retainer. Me among them." My heels clicked hollowly on the floor planking. I heard scratching sounds. "There's what's been spooking our troops." I glanced behind me, past Tinnie, expecting to see a big-ass bug looking for a way to escape the underworld.

I saw a ghost instead, and very, very faintly heard some kind of music.

No other way to put it. I didn't want it to be, but that was a ghost. Someone I knew was dead. Someone who had been dead for a long time. Swaying to the music.

That was a ghost I'd seen before. As a ghost.

"Garrett? What is it?"

"Eleanor."

"What?"

"See? There? The woman in white?" Becoming more real by the second. Smiling. "The one in the magic painting in my office." The music grew louder by the second, too. And less melodic.

Tinnie wasn't happy. She didn't know the whole story about Eleanor, though. Lucky for me. She hadn't had as much claim on me then.

I was amazed and dismayed that so much emotion still lurked within me. That so much hurt still surrounded that beautiful dead lady.

She smiled as she came toward me, glad to see me, reaching with one delicate, pale hand. Backed by vague music that was turning into half-heard clanking.

"I don't see anything, Garrett." Just a little put out. Then, "Oh! Oh, gods! It's Denny!"

Bill said, "You're both seeing people who had a powerful emotional impact in the past."

Tinnie said, "Uncle Lester."

Two more females began to form behind Eleanor. For a moment I thought one was my mother. But she was too young. Kayanne Kronk. My first love, so long ago. The other was Maya, a street gang girl who had grown up to become a serious entanglement—till I ran her off by being the same way with her that I've always been with Tinnie. But Kayanne and Maya were both still alive, insofar as I knew. And they didn't go around accompanied by bad music so soft you had to strain to be irked by it.

Both women faded as soon as I thought that.

Tinnie was distraught. Bill grabbed hold and hustled her out of the theater. I stumbled along behind, ten percent of me clinging desperately to present reality. My brother

Mikey had begun to materialize behind Eleanor. Who looked real enough to bite now.

I saw Tinnie's ghosts, too, but they had no form to my eye.

The light outside helped. "Bill, that was all inside our heads, wasn't it?" I suspected that because of my long exposure to the Dead Man.

He shrugged. "You'd think. But I bet if you faced your ghosts long enough they'd come alive on their own."

I told Tinnie, "I begin to see why Alyx was upset. Her ghosts must've been her brother and sister. Maybe even her mother." All people whose deaths she'd have no trouble blaming on herself.

Tinnie had nothing to say. She'd gone missing inside herself.

# 41

Safely away from Eleanor and Mikey, I thought I understood why people refused to talk about the ghosts. Mine hadn't been awful. And I see weird all the time. But what would the impact be on people for whom ghosts were the hardware of scary stories? People who had skeletons or heavy guilt in their closets? Which so many do. "Hey, Bill. Did you see anything in there?"

"Not this time. I did before. It was hairy. And there was some kind of ghastly music in the distance."

"Garrett!" Tinnie was as pale as death. She pointed. I expected to see a street full of ghosts.

"Cypres Prose! Get your young ass over here! Now! Your friends, too."

Kip Prose had been sneaking along in the shadows on the other side of the street, between two of his Faction friends. One was the chunky kid from the abandoned house. The lover of bugs, Zardoz. The other had been with Kip last time he came past the World.

The youngsters hadn't expected anybody to come busting out of the theater. Especially not that fierce defender of order and propriety, Mama Garrett's boy.

All three kids thought about running. Kip decided there was no point. I'd tell his mother. He wouldn't like what came of that.

Kip came over staring at the ground a yard in front of his feet. His cronies tagged along. The thinner kid was a ringer for Barate Algarda, only younger.

"Kevans and Zardoz, I presume."

They weren't startled. Except Kip, who knew he hadn't given me information enough to give Kevans away.

"Kip. Why are you down here this time?"

He wouldn't meet my eye. "We left some stuff."

"Of course you did." Bugs still wandered around on the outside of the World. "Kip, I don't get it. You've got stuff to do at the manufactory that ought to keep you busy twenty hours a day." He had a million inventions inside his head. His job was to get them out and explained in a way the rest of us could understand. "So why the hell are you down here rooting around under a slum with a bunch of goofballs?"

The redhead jabbed me in the ribs. Just reminding me that I wasn't Kip's father.

And wasn't being smart, disrespecting his friends.

He stopped staring at the pavements. "What are you doing down here? You could have a real job at the manufactory *or* the Weider Brewery. But you're down here chasing insects and harassing kids."

Tinnie chuckled.

Wow. Up on his hind legs and barking back. Which left me speechless.

I do what I do because I don't want to be a wage slave. I'm doing what I want to do. Usually reluctantly. I've got a lot of dog in me. Like most hounds, I don't want to do anything more than the minimum needed to get by. I'm good at that.

I'm sure my mom and dad are spinning in their graves. Maybe Kip could come up with a clever way to tap that rotational energy.

I could hear my only surviving relative, antique Medford Shale, telling me my main problem is, I've never been hungry. If I'd ever been truly hungry, I wouldn't have all these pussy, wimp-out excuses for not nailing me down a real job.

"You score a couple points. But you're not exactly following your passion by helping social and emotional cripples off the Hill hammer society by creating a plague." I felt like an idiot as soon as I said that. It wasn't what I'd meant to say.

"And I'm nothing like them, am I, Mr. Garrett?"

"All right. I apologize. I was getting emotional. There was no need for that. Stipulated. Your friends aren't likely to be weirder than Cypres Prose. On the other hand, Cypres Prose doesn't have family on the Hill who want to get involved in my life. Or who hire people to follow you around."

"Huh?"

"Tinnie. Can you keep these two entertained while I show Kip what's going on inside the World?"

The redhead sneered. Two teenage boys? She'd turn them to jelly, then set them howling at the moon like werewolves lamenting the change.

She didn't know about Kevans.

I didn't plan on exposing Kip to the ghosts of the World. I just wanted to shed the audience so I could give him the word about Lurking Felhske. I'd forgotten how sensitive he was, back when we'd been involved with the sky elves who'd helped spark his mechanical genius.

I told him, "Most of your friends are from the Hill. Some have big personal problems. You've got a girl who pretends she's a boy. You've got a boy who wants to be a girl. You've got somebody who's so interested in you that they've hired the slickest assassin in TunFaire to follow you around." All right. I exaggerated. Lurking Felhske might not be a high-powered lifetaker. But I'd dealt with Kip before. You have to get his attention. "You've got somebody who's so interested in what you're doing that they've even tried leaning on Colonel Block. Any idea who that might be?"

He had none. Nor did he believe me.

He did show more than sullen interest, though. "I know about Kevans and Mutter." He shrugged. "We all do. Mutt is just a freak. But Kevans has got real problems. You'd understand if you knew her family."

"I do. Barate Algarda came by my house. He wanted to pound me till I changed my attitude toward you guys. He didn't have much luck, though."

"Your smugness tells me you didn't get much out of him, though. You won't. Not him. Not even with a Loghyr to paw through his head. He's a tough old man." I saw him wondering about his own brief visit to a Loghyr with Kyra. "You know about the compliance device?"

I confessed that I had no clue. "Unless you mean that thing that's supposed to get a woman ferociously interested."

The light was weak but Kip's blush was visible. "Actually, Kevans invented that. With help from Mutt. And that's not what it does."

"What, then?"

"It's pretty simple. You take some common, off-the-shelf spells and braid them so they have a heterodyning effect. The device isn't anything special. A spool wound with silver threads that anchor and store the spells. The spool is mounted in a wooden frame. You rotate till you get the right frequency and relative strength. That gives you an idea what somebody's chemistry is. Doesn't matter what sex they are. It's just more likely that males will use it to look at females. That's the way the culture is stacked."

"I'll take your word. Even if I don't know what the word means." I felt like I'd just sat through a lecture by somebody ten times smarter than me, who had tried to dumb it down. I did agree that guys would be more likely to deploy the gimmick. If it did what I thought. "Why would Kevans want to know if somebody was interested or aroused, or could be engineered into it?"

"Sometimes girls want to know the odds, too, Mr. Garrett."

I smelled the reek coming off that. "And being able to manipulate the other party?"

"Uh . . . The influence part was serendipity, Mr. Garrett. It wasn't planned that way. Not so guys can improve their chances. It doesn't do that very good, anyway. Kevans wanted to find a way to read people's emotions and intentions. The rest of us all went in on it because we thought we could use it to help us not do the usual inappropriate stuff that scares people off. You've seen me go around with a foot in my mouth like a hunchback goes around with his hump. And then you saw me with Kyra. *Kyra Tate!*"

"I was curious. But not too much. I didn't want to jinx myself with Tinnie."

"Yeah. Well, listen. I'm the gleaming social butterfly of the Faction. I'm the master of slick in that crew."

"All right. I won't disagree, based on what I've seen so far."

"Really, honestly, the compliance device was only supposed to warn us when we were doing dumb stuff. So we'd stop. Plus, Kevans hoped it would help her get along better at home. But we couldn't ever get the damned thing to do what we wanted it to do. It just let us figure out if somebody was in the mood. If you knew that, you could fiddle the spool a little and kind of tune them in."

Then he made a little squeaky noise. His eyes bugged. And I faced off with another invocation of the law of unintended consequences.

"Power up its ability to influence. Figure out how to mass-produce it. You'll get richer than Max Weider in a week. Call it the Shortcut. Something like that."

There might be holes in my reasoning but I knew I'd fingered the soul of it. I was sure, too, that even a superpower compliance device wouldn't make irresistible studs of the Faction.

I was sure because I was them when I was that age.

Still, these baby blues had actually seen Kyra Tate tagging along after Cypres Prose, apparently liking it.

Did any of the Faction have the slightest notion how disruptive a workable compliance device would be? Socially?

We might be about to find out. The device might be the reason these kids were in the sights of somebody who could deploy a Lurking Felhske.

Staring into infinity, Kip said, "Oh my God! Ohmigod! Ohmigod!" Over and over, faster and faster.

Some wisps of mist over yonder had him seeing the unfortunate dead from back when first we'd met.

My own ghosts began to form. The same as before. I was armored with a powerful cynicism. They troubled me not. I heard no music, either.

Still, Kayanne and Maya did achieve a reality that surpassed the phantom stage. I didn't doubt that I'd find them warm to the touch if I went over and fondled.

Eleanor did bother me. I still had issues there.

I dragged Kip toward the exit. Once out, I slapped his cheeks. It took three shots to shake him loose.

His eyes focused. He remained confused. "Listen!" I

told him. "What happened in there did because of what your bunch have been doing. There's something ancient and dreadful way down below here. Your bugs disturbed it. It's trying to wake up."

Kip had no defiance left. "I don't understand, Mr. Garrett."

"I don't, either." I had a notion Bill Chimes couldn't make it any clearer. Bill Chimes who had gone missing again. "All I can tell you is what I just did. That's all I've been told myself."

His eyes glazed over. But he wasn't going back to where he'd just been. He was doing what always boggles me when I witness it in a kid. He was thinking.

"It would have to be something that operates in a mental realm like the one your partner occupies."

My partner. It could be time to drop everything and hustle my sweet self back to Chuckles. "It might be useful to have the whole Faction sit down with him. He'd make connections none of the rest of us can."

"That won't happen, Mr. Garrett. Nobody wants somebody digging around inside their head."

"I understand that. I don't like it myself. But he won't do anything you don't let him do. He isn't some barbarian raider. Consider, though. He does have multiple minds. He can look at things from several viewpoints at once."

"I know. I've suffered him before. It isn't me you have to sell. Right now, despite everything you've told me, the Faction wouldn't see a problem that needs solving."

I could have argued on but where was the point? Pushing kids in a direction they don't want to go just makes them stubborn. Unless you've got a really big stick and don't mind using it.

Better to be more clever.

"I can't force you. But you've had a taste. You know there's something bad crawling out of the darkness."

"Bad? I don't—"

"Think about it, Kip. What do you know about ghosts? Why would the ghosts you saw wait for you here? Did any of them come anywhere near here when they were alive?"

"I'm young, Mr. Garrett. Not stupid. I see the implications."

Kip had had enough. He took off toward Tinnie and his

friends. He and the friends headed out. Fast. I didn't hear
what they said. Kevans glanced back once; then the three
rounded a dirty gray brick building, headed toward the
Tenderloin. Headed for their hidey-hole.

# 42

Tinnie said, "So you did your Mr. Sensitive, bull thunder-lizard in Aeleya's teagarden routine. And, lo! The kid didn't knuckle under."

"A gross exaggeration."

"I'm sure. Here comes Saucerhead. Give him the true facts and ask what he thinks you could've done better."

"I'm telling you this, Red. You keep picking and chipping . . . What the hell is she doing, tagging after Head?"

"She" would be Winger, stacked blonde slapped together on an epic scale. As tall as me. My friend, theoretically. But not a friend I want turning up anywhere where I'm the guy who'll be held accountable.

Winger is a female Saucerhead Tharpe. With more flexible ethics. You don't trust her around the family silver. Or anything else of value.

She does try. But she just can't resist temptation.

Distracted by the approach of big, beautiful blond trouble, I didn't immediately notice that she wasn't Tharpe's only companion.

He'd brought six people along. Well, five. The Remora, Jon Salvation, is just an extension of Winger, these days. He's not really a person.

The rest were serious thugs. I recognized three of them. They'd be men a man I trusted could trust.

Saucerhead's knack for selection was perfection in all particulars, excepting only family deserter Winger.

I cut Tharpe out of the crowd. "You're gonna be the guy, here, Head. Your job is, keep everybody out unless they bring you a pass signed by me. No exceptions. Not even Winger. There are some hungry ghosts in there."

Saucerhead stared with eyes grown large. He didn't want to believe me. But he couldn't shove aside the fact that he'd been there with me so many times when the weirdness squared itself on the freaky scale.

"Ghosts?"

"Something that looks like ghosts. It might be something else a whole lot worse. I'm hoping the Dead Man can figure it out."

He saw me give Winger the fish-eye. Again. "Don't worry about her, Garrett. The Remora hanging around has straightened her up. She's awed by the written word. It don't change, no matter how much you bluster and threaten and try to make it."

That was one long-winded homily for Saucerhead Tharpe. "I'll take your word. From what I hear tell, though, Jon Salvation isn't exactly an impartial observer."

"You think? Him mooning after her like she's the born-again avatar of Romassa?"

"Romassa?"

"Goddess of physical love. For one a' them tribes we worked with down in the Cantard. The Avatar was even bigger than Winger." He did cupped hands in front of his chest. "Her job was to teach the young men coming up about doing it."

"She was a real person?"

"Sure. She was the Avatar. Not the goddess herself but her stand-in. It was a big honor to be picked."

You hear everything at least once. After you've heard it all, you check out.

"Lot of happy boys around there, I guess."

"The Avatar smiled a lot, too."

Tinnie had been eavesdropping, off and on. Showing no happiness about the strange ways they have in far-off lands. "I should've gone with Alyx in the coach. Now I have to walk all the way back to midtown."

Saucerhead leaned in like he was about to pass along a juicy punch line about how they did things in the Cantard. "So, what's with the goofy coat?"

# 43

Tinnie Tate was short of temper by the time we got to my house. I kept my opinion of her choice of footwear closely guarded. No need to tempt the lightning.

I was digging for my key when the door opened.

Pular Singe stood there staring at me, sort of befuddled.

"What?" I asked.

"I could not track him."

"What?"

"That Lurking Felhske. That Mr. Dotes wanted to find. I could not track him." She was thoroughly unhappy. "That never happens."

"I'm sorry. Don't get all suicidal about it."

Tinnie punched me from behind. And I just knew that if Singe was a human girl she would've burst into tears right then.

"All right. How did he kill his back trail?" That would take it out of the realm of being her fault.

"How did you . . . ?" She looked back to the doorway to the Dead Man's room, inclined to blame him for giving her away before crediting me with the ability to work something out. "He went through areas where the stink overpowered every other smell. Even body odor as bad as his."

"He always came out somewhere besides where he went in. Right?" I've worked both sides of that gambit.

"Possibly. I think."

"What?"

"Sorry. I am not feeling good about myself right now."

"I understand. I've been there. Couldn't you circle the bad smell till you found where his spoor came out?"

"In theory. But not really. The bad smells were so strong

my nose went dead. And everybody coming out of there carried the stench with them." She had to be talking about the tannery district. There is nothing quite like that when it comes to overpowering smells. "I can only pick out individuals if they wear something like that awful stink-pretty Saucerhead Tharpe soaks in when he is feeling especially single."

The girl is an amazement. I couldn't restrain a guffaw. She had Tharpe nailed. When he works himself up to go on the prowl he splashes that stuff on like . . . There is no adequate simile. Nothing compares. He'll never get lost. Singe will find him underwater. Sometimes the stench is unbearable. And its results are entirely predictable. No score, unless he runs into a woman totally blind and deaf in the nose with no discernible sense of taste. Or one of those gals who has the same bad perfume habit. There are squadrons of those, though most are a tad long in the tooth for Mr. Tharpe.

*Garrett.*

"And that answers the big question. Himself is awake. Now, if Dean happened to be hard at work womping up a supper, in quantities adequate to fill me and my sweet patootie, life could be reclassified as perfect."

Tinnie growled, "Don't you ever turn it off?"

"Tight shoes," I told Singe. "And no lunch."

"Next time I come down here I'll wear my winter boots."

"Not the pretty ones. Bring the work ones."

"The midthigh tops? With a shovel?"

I disengaged from further discussion of shoes. "Singe, something that came up today got me wondering about the differences between ratpeople and humans."

"Yes?" Instantly defensive.

"We saw ghosts. All of us. Some of us heard music." I told her about it. I didn't scrimp on details. Old Bones was listening, too. "But you and your brother, and his guys, never saw anything."

Singe managed a facial tick that resembled a puzzled look. "I'll take your word for that."

Damn! It would be ridiculous if she started managing human facial expressions, too.

I'd have to head that off, for sure. She'd end up burned at the stake.

"Come help us mull it over with the Dead Man." Or

whatever you call the situation where His Nibs picks the brains of mere mortals, to help us discover the meaning of life.

*Your cynicism has migrated from the realm of the mildly amusing to the uglier principality of the irritating.*

"Oh, good. You're still awake."

So we communed, brainstormed, and schemed. The sad truth, though, was, we needed more information. My sidekick knew no more than I did about ancient, dramatically powerful things buried under TunFaire. He recalled no legends, fairy tales, or religious fancies that accounted for what was stirring.

The Tenderloin is a storied moral sink. It's been the bad part of town since the first nomad families pitched their tents on a hospitable riverbank and never got around to moving on.

I was particularly pleased. My sweetie, once she had some food in her, dropped the attitude and focused on the problem at hand.

We ate while we worked. And Dean's effort made the wait worthwhile.

Amazing what that old man can do with a capon, wine, mushrooms, and a few tubers that aren't supposed to be in season. All washed down by a fine, potent Weider winter wheat lager.

# 44

Tinnie went to bed. Likewise, Singe. And Dean beat them all to the friendly sheets. I stayed where I was, enjoying my beer. And persevering.

Old Bones had let me know he wanted a word in private. Whatever that meant to somebody who could carry on multiple silent, isolated conversations at once.

*I permitted myself a presumption this morning, once you were on your way. Penny came for a lesson. I hired her to check into a few things.*

Brilliant me, intellect puffed by the Weider brew, I asked, "Like what?"

*The histories of the properties involved in the World construction site. The background of the man you knew as Handsome, for Mr. Weider and Mr. Gilbey, because you have not found time for that. I also asked her to see what she could find out about members of the Faction for whom we have names. And about their families. And I tasked her to find out what she could about the history and ownership of the property the Faction turned into their clubhouse.*

"And I thought you made ridiculous demands on me. A grown man."

*Sneer.*

"All right. All right. Whatever you've got, go ahead and crow."

Some things you learn just being around him long enough. Like his need to show off how good he is. Or how good his protégé can be.

The experience was humiliating. During a single day Penny Dreadful, totally marginal teenage person who would play no other role in the case, had, as a favor to her pal the Dead Man, dug out almost all the information he wanted checked.

History of the ground where the World was going up? Bland. Nondescript. Nothing interesting had happened there as far back as available records went. The first several slumlords who sold to Max were convinced that they had hornswoggled the beer baron. The procession of ownership started with an uprising two hundred eighty years gone that had destroyed every older record.

Who owned the ruined property? Fellow name of Barate Algarda. He bought it off the wife of a once-famous smuggler who got put out of business permanently by Chodo Contague's predecessor, thirty years ago. Algarda's daughter had used it for a playhouse, growing up. It had had a reputation as a deadly place, back then. Old hands still steered clear.

Brent Talanta, also known as Handsome? No children. Wife deceased. Survived only by his mother. Handsome was her only source of support. A forensic sorcerer had connected the knife found in the hand of a Stomper known as Funboy to Handsome's wounds. Likewise, the shoes of several gang members to bruises on the corpse. Handsome's remains had been sent on for cremation at a contract crematorium. Funboy's body had been sold to a resurrection man. The rest of the Stompers were headed for a labor camp.

I told Old Bones, "I have to admit that I forgot all about Handsome. Even though I promised Max."

*Miss Pular wrote the report. Joe Kerr will take it to Mr. Weider in the morning. Mr. Weider will do the right thing. Now. For someone who keeps telling himself how amazed he is by his advancing maturity, you do seem to work with a solid teenage mind-set most of the time.*

Ouch. Possibly true. But doubly hurtful since the harvester of so much marvelous information barely qualified as a teen herself.

*But wait! There is more!*

There would be, wouldn't there?

The keg I'd found down under the ruin had been purchased from the Goteborg Enterprise by Riata Dungarth. Riata Dungarth was the personal servant of Elmet Starbot-

tle, a member of the Faction known to his crew as Slump,
who was a cousin of the twins, Berbach and Berbain, who
seemed to have walked away from the Faction. The keg
had been delivered to the ruin, wrestled downstairs, and
installed by Idris Brithgaern, who made all the deliveries
for the Goteborg Enterprise brewery. Mr. Brithgaern delivered a new keg the first day of each week, always prepaid
by Riata Dungarth. The ruin was outside Brithgaern's normal range, but he did not mind. He got to keep the beer
in the old keg. Sometimes that had not been touched. He
could sell that beer, legally, off the back of his wagon. But,
mostly, he took it home and enjoyed it himself. It was a
beer that deserved a man with a discerning palate.

By this point I was ready to whimper. The little tramp
obviously vamped. . . . I had a couple smart-ass questions in
inventory but reserved them because I was afraid the little
witch had reported what color socks Idris Brithgaern wore.

*Mismatched. Gray to the left, brown on the right.*

"Argh!"

*I jest. But there is a lesson in all this.*

"Yeah. And I don't need help from you figuring out what
it is, Laughing Boy." Simply, Penny Dreadful had no trouble with the concept of hard work. Given a task, she
whapped it in the schnoz with both fists and pounded it
into instant submission.

I could fake that kind of youthful enthusiasm. For a few
minutes. Sometimes. "So, who does this Brithgaern creature work for?"

*The Goteborg Enterprise craft brewery.*

"All right. My mistake. Let me get focused." Weider
Dark Select might not match up with Goteborg, but it's
pretty damned good. "Make that Riata Dungarth. Who's
he work for?"

*Elmet Starbottle. Where Elmet Starbottle would seem to
be a name chosen by the person wearing it. There are no
Starbottle families amongst the elites in this city.*

I could have told him that. Silly-ass name. Starbottle. Ha.
"What you're doing now is prancing around the fact that
you don't know which one of the Faction uses the name
Starbottle."

*Pretty much, there. Yes. Pretty much. Unless it might be
the boy they call Slump, as I might have mentioned earlier.*

He's so smug.

*I expect all that will be cleared up for sure next time I see Penny.*

"You mean next time she decides to mooch a meal?"

*I believe she has earned a few.*

And I did feel petty even before he chastised me. So I punished myself by draining another mug of beer. Then I trundled on upstairs, clambered into bed behind my favorite gal in the whole wide world, and fell asleep in about seven seconds.

# 45

Tinnie didn't put away as much holy elixir as her favorite man. But she had less experience handling it. She woke up with a pounding head an hour before the early birds took wing. She turned into the beautiful woman who never heard of mercy.

"Rise and shine, Malsquando. For the first time in your life you're going to do an honest day's work."

"Ow!" Not good news. Not good news at all. I'm no Morley Dotes but I am acquainted with the comfort of a dishonest day's work. A day with as little real work in it as I can arrange.

I was over last night already.

"This may be why we can't get to a grown-up solution to our grown-up problems," I grumbled. "Here you come, six hours too early for even thinking, let alone working."

No argument. No snide commentary. Just another stiff finger and sharp nail between a couple of my favorite ribs.

I almost said something I couldn't take back. Lucky me, though. I have a resident guardian angel.

*Do not! open your idiot mouth!*

I clung to that advice for the dozen seconds my sweetie needed to lose focus and fall asleep again.

I went back to sleep, too. Wondering, for the first time, about the discrepancies between my partner's report on the compliance device and Kip's. Kip isn't real good about making up plausible stories.

Next time I woke up it was time to set the beer free. That took a while. Then I poured a little in to replace what had gone away. Tinnie snorted and snored worse than Saucerhead or Playmate, both true champions. The racket didn't bother me. I climbed back into bed and, after a few random thoughts, got down to business making it through to the crack of noon.

Old Bones—or maybe the gods themselves—did something to the redhead while she slept. She woke up in a sunny mood. Unfortunately still convinced that Ma Garrett's boy ought to haul out and become an important ingredient in her wonderful day. "Don't you got some books to balance? Or maybe some bribe sheets to update?"

Tinnie has some big generational differences with the elder Tates. But none having to do with milking maximum cash from folks interested in our manufactory's products. Her number-one mission is to maintain the waiting list of three-wheel buyers.

Bribes paid to move names on the waiting list generate more cash flow than sales of the units themselves.

Every entrepreneur and financier in this burg hates us.

I don't get it, myself. I really don't. People are nuts over the three-wheels. I've ridden them. They're fun. They make getting around a little faster. But not much. Not when you have to deal with everyday traffic in twisty, narrow streets. And, more especially, not when you have to deal with the upsides of hills. Not to overlook the ride on cobblestones. And the even harder pull where there are no pavements at all.

And then there are thieves. Though my senior partners had been smart about that.

Every three-wheel has a unique signature spell applied, traceable by the company Charmstalker. Should your three-wheel be commandeered by a freelance socialist, it can be located, and justice can be delivered, with dramatic quickness. It happens often enough to discourage all but the terminally stupid.

If only there were some way to deal with those people before they breed.

Deal Relway may be on to something. He's clearing the raging idiots out of the criminal class.

There are people out there in definite need of disappearing. Problem is, once you start, how do you confine yourself to the "right" bad guys? And do we want our only surviving criminals to be people too smart to get caught?

*Garrett. It is past time you dragged your self-deluded posterior out of bed.*

Everybody has an opinion. And, as my old platoon sergeant explained, they all reek like the waste sphincter everyone also has.

*Garrett.*

The sending was gentle. Like the soft voice of your father just before he lets you have it upside the head.

Old Bones wasn't in a patient mood.

*Truth on a silver tray. Get dressed. Eat. Then get in here.*

While I endured attitude from my sidekick, my favorite redhead vanished. She dressed, headed downstairs, ate, and was gone before I tied into my own sausages with biscuits and gravy. A country-style breakfast Dean uses as a hammer when he thinks I need reminding that I'm not nobility.

"You're losing it, old man. Or maybe you've just gone loony."

He was ahead of me. Knowing I'd think the menu was a statement. "The thing in there expects you to work a long day. What little is left. I wanted you to eat something that will stay with you."

"Dean, you need to test the job market. See what's available for a man your age, with your skills. After that, come give me another ration of shit."

Oh. I was feeling it now. My head throbbed. My patience was short. I couldn't work up a good goddamn's worth of care about anything. Faced with the worst atrocity in all history—*or* its all-time best moment—my response would have been an indifferent, "Ain't that some shit?" While I felt around for my beer mug.

"I hope your attitude improves before you have to deal with people who might not suffer in silence."

I grumbled some. Fortified by breakfast and armed with a fresh round of honeyed tea, I trudged off to play dueling sullens with my business partner.

# 46

Singe came out of the Dead Man's room. She glowed like fresh-minted sunshine. Her arms were full. I didn't volunteer to help. She chirped a bright greeting. It's hard to be nasty toward Singe, however bleak I feel. The guilt afterward is poisonous.

She explained, "I'm moving my business stuff. The furnishings are supposed to come today."

Even a mention of frittering my money didn't set me off. I grumbled politely. Though not politely enough to suit. She got huffy.

I settled into my chair. I drank tea. As he sometimes does, Dean had spiked the pot with something to ease my headache and stomach.

The biscuits and greasy gravy were lying heavy already.

I said, "I never learn. Is it possible that I can't?"

His Nibs was feeling less confrontational. *That is not quite the case. Your people, despite their gifts of memory and senses of history and mortality, despite their being able to foresee the consequences of actions taken, seldom bother.*

"Huh?"

*You people cannot shed your animalistic tendency to live life in the moment. Even the most brilliant of you ignore tomorrow's certain pain in order to enjoy today's fleeting pleasure. The hangover is Nature's perfect metaphor.*

"All right."

He did have that right. Dumb as it sounds when you have your reason kicked in. You tipple of an evening, you don't think about how you'll feel in the morning. No matter how often you've been disinclined to wake up and suffer the consequences.

*And you for damned sure do not want anyone to remind you.*

"Hey!"

Singe was back. She made a startled squeak.

"Sorry. I was barking at him, not you."

She loaded up, went away.

*Are you ready? There is work to do.*

He seemed eager. That was disturbing. He is more allergic to real productivity than I am.

*We face a mighty challenge! You cannot imagine how much I am enjoying myself, winkling out the hidden meanings of everything going on with all that you have stumbled into or over.*

He was going to be cheerful? Sickening. Just sickening.

"I do hope you enjoy yourself. Big time. Because it just occurred to me that my boy genius, Cypres Prose, on whose freaky brain the company depends for product ideas, is a serious candidate for Mr. Deal Relway's special justice."

Pursuant to his bad habits, which keep getting badder, Old Bones took a look inside my head without asking.

*Oh my! That had not occurred to me, either.*

Two bodies had been found at the World, both mutilated by bugs. One was still breathing when the vermin started chewing. The law could lay that death on whoever created the bugs.

Kip Prose might be facing a manslaughter rap. Him and the Faction.

I regained confidence quickly. Kip's pals came off the Hill. Their mommies and daddies would cover them. They'd cover Kip. And my cut of the ingenious ideas would keep right on coming.

After his moment of self-disgust—he was supposed to see things I didn't, and had lapsed several times lately— Old Bones moved on. *None of that is germane at this point. We are being paid to end the problems at the World. Anything else would be incidental and serendipitous. Not so?*

"So." He was right. He always is about business responsibility.

*But it is all still a hugely exciting puzzle.*

What the hell was he thinking? I was getting worried.

*We are going to do two things immediately. And a few things more once the right people have passed through my sphere of influence.*

Naturally, he did not explain his thinking.

*You are too easily distracted. Though, admittedly, less so now that your involvement with Miss Tate is progressing beyond the adolescent.*

That involvement ought to concern him. If it gets much more serious, him and Dean and Singe will have to find new digs.

Diffuse amusement. Cause not explained.

*Your immediate task is to visit the Royal Library. See if you can find anything that sheds light on our situation.*

"And then what?" Because I wouldn't be at the library long. They weren't going to let me in. I was in deep, bad odor with my friend there because of all my hanging out with Tinnie. I hadn't been round to see Lindalee in ages. And Lindalee's boss has me on her all-time shit list.

Bad memories. Last time I went to the library I'd been ambushed by a guy who was mostly troll or ogre. I wasn't sure which. I was too busy getting away.

Fond recollections of Lindalee, though. Fond recollections.

*Stop that.*

"Sorry. Didn't mean to kick your prude-sparking trip wire."

*You are wasting time. You must visit the library. You must see Mr. Tharpe at the World. You must organize an expedition into the hidden places beneath that abandoned house. We need more information.*

"Hey! There are only so many hours . . ."

*And you have wasted a significant fraction lying in bed. You continue to waste it on argument. The truth you refuse to acknowledge is that neither wickedness nor good fortune willingly conform to your preferred schedule.*

Ouch! How do you come back hard once you've been slapped in the chops with a brass-bound Truth? "When I'm King of the World—"

*Go to the library. Now. I do wish Miss Winger were available. I could use her literate shadow. We could get a great deal more accomplished much more quickly.*

Were he among the breathing I would've wondered what he was chewing.

*Get going.* Patience exhausted. Cranky again.

Nagged unto death, I donned my loaner coat and went. A Singe all thrilled because she had her own office now, bigger than mine, all to herself alone, shut the door behind me.

I saw all kinds of unhappy truths during my descent to the pavements of Macunado Street. In *that* direction Little Miss High Priestess in Exile, Penny Dreadful, waited for me to disappear so she could cadge a meal and, probably, make me look even badder. In *this* direction lurked a guy I couldn't see who radiated a cosmically bad odor. *Yonder*, a clutch of nonchalant loiterers in mufti, with tin whistles under their shirts, looked forward to getting some exercise trudging around TunFaire behind the city's most lovable former Marine.

Barate Algarda was in the gallery, too. Lurking with less success than Felhske. Could I lure him close enough for the Dead Man to snap up?

*Head east. Turn south on Wizard's Reach. Then take the alley. Try not to frighten Penny.*

A pear-shaped, bug-loving teen sat on the steps to Mrs. Cardonlos' establishment, uphill. He had fallen asleep. Thereby failing to note the magnitude of his folly. The Relway Runners avoided disturbing him as they came and went. I wondered what the hell he was doing but did not want to put him on the spot by stopping to ask.

I followed the Dead Man's suggestion. Except for the part about not scaring Penny Dreadful. I couldn't resist.

Round the block I went, in a direction I seldom travel. And came back into Macunado nose to nose with the Cardonlos place. I was tempted to drop in unannounced. Or maybe play a game of wild goose with the widow's houseguests, leading them around till the spring thaw came.

I would have done it, too. A few years ago. Deal Relway be damned.

That old devil maturity had a hold on me.

Absent Barate Algarda, I toddled onward, onward, into TunFaire's black bureaucratic heart. To the Chancellery, where I took time to enjoy the ranting of the hardy lunatics spouting paranoid conspiracy theories and political absurdities on the building's steps. A last taste while I could get it. This tradition wouldn't last. Some raving conspiracy theorists lack the sense to leave Deal Relway out of their formulae.

A sizable percentage of the city's population waited impatiently while I indulged. All those potential witnesses wanted me to get on along and do something interesting.

In ages past, in the long ago, when I'd wanted to get into the Royal Library—which is *not* for the use of any hairy Tom Dick who claims he's Karentine—I'd shown up at a particular side door. A small cash transfer blinded the guard there. The unstated rule being, I'd start no fires and wouldn't pee in the corners while I was inside.

No tip, however, ever sheltered me from the wrath of sweet Lindalee's superiors. Who were sure thumbscrews and branding irons were too good for someone who actually wanted to look inside their books. Or maybe wanted to get close to a particular young librarian.

No reasonable man expected exemption from betrayal under the circumstances obtaining at the Royal Library. A smart man handled his business fast.

And here, now, with the weak half of an army tracking me, where was the point of expecting privacy?

## 47

I went to my special side door. No way a lowlife like me could walk in through the front. There are maybe fifteen Royals who enjoy that privilege.

Snootiness doesn't keep us lesser beings out. If we're armed with the silver key.

The old soldier watching the door was new. He didn't know me, either. But he liked my coat. I could tell. And he was old pals with the dead king on the chunk of silver I passed him. He didn't even speak. He just closed his eyes as a stray gust whiffed into the library. Probably planning an outing with his old pal, King Whoever.

I headed for the rare books, not sneaking. Hardly anyone visited them, though Lindalee always enjoyed their company.

For a moment I feared I might feel guilty about how I'd treated Lindalee. Maybe even about how I'd treat her now, considering I was fenced in by Tinnie.

Curses! This was worse than the hives. I was breaking out all over in a *bad* case of growing up. And wasn't worried about finding a cure.

I took a wrong turn. In the sense that I rounded a stack and buried my beautiful honker in the brown sweater armoring the belly of a familiar ogre. Wool on an ogre? Yes. This big boy looked like the male equivalent of the librarian stereotype. He even wore reading glasses, which are expensive. Even when their lens don't have to be custom-ground.

The ogre didn't move. There was no way around him. He had an acre of foot at the end of each tree trunk of a leg. The outsides of those lapped against the bases of the stacks to either hand.

In the real world ogre expressions are easily read. There is snarling while they sleep. And there's snarling as they try to rip bits off of you. They don't stand around looking at you like the unexpected rat dropping that just surfaced in the porridge.

That's what this one did. He stared. Then he stared some more, upper lip rising in a sneer. He did nothing else but breathe. And take up space.

I apologized for my clumsiness and stepped back.

With my nose in brown wool I was too close to handle easily. I did him a favor by opening the range. He took advantage, latching on to various limbs. In seconds I was back in the weather, floundering in nasty slush, my spiffy borrowed coat all wet, filthy, and torn. Poindexter the literary ogre was back inside. Through the open doorway I heard him suffer harpy shrieks because he had been too gentle.

That wasn't Lindalee being shrill. That was her boss. A lovable spinster—for whom they invented the word "harridan" because nothing already out of the forge was harsh enough to fit. She never did like me.

The man I'd reunited with his dead pal stuck his head outside, curious to see how far I had flown before splashdown. He looked guilty round the edges. Like he might have operated some kind of silent alarm.

So much for a cerebral line of investigation.

What now?

# 48

The Dead Man opened with an oblique, snide observation about pigeons coming home to roost. Singe helped me out of my wet things. She hustled the loaner coat into the kitchen for a drying session. Meanwhile, I nearly panicked, thinking Old Bones had found him a way to get the Goddamn Parrot back.

He was just being a pain.

*We will access the library another way. Do we know a respected member of the community who owes us a favor?*

"And can read? No. People like that try to stay away from people like us."

*Unless they go into business with us. Surely, there are those who might be induced.* He offered suggestions, including Max Weider, Manvil Gilbey, even Tinnie Tate.

"Tinnie? You looking to start a war?"

*I doubt there would be problems. What competition there may have been is over. I expect Miss Tate and the other woman would spend an afternoon amusing themselves by trading war stories. Or horror stories, as the mood demanded.*

That was worth being nervous about.

*Go to the World. See what Mr. Tharpe has to report. Ask Miss Winger to come see me.*

"What do you want with her?"

*Nothing. As I mentioned recently, I can use her shadow. Who will not come if he knows he is the object of my interest.*

"The Remora?" I'd thought he was just making mental bathroom noises. Jon Salvation was a standout among the dozen most useless human beings I'd ever met.

*Indeed.*

I shook my head. No more questions. He might give me answers I didn't want to hear.

*I will want Cypres Prose, too.*

Had he mentioned that before? Maybe when I was more focused on beer? My mind wasn't at peak today.

*Or most any other day, inasmuch as you refuse to exercise it.*

"Use it or lose it." See. Mind at half speed. Handing him a straight line like that.

Of late, he's made a habit of ignoring these opportunities. Leaving me to stew in my own humiliation.

*I did not mention Kip Prose before. Perhaps your undermind is engaged even while the rest lies fallow.*

It could happen. "If I run into him. If he's willing to come back." I reminded him, "He has been here before."

*Yes. And I may have missed something important.*

Oh, it pained him to confess. Especially when I observed, "Hubris."

*Close.*

He was irked with himself. He had gotten sloppy. Too full of himself, and sloppy.

*Garrett!*

Though you could not have pried it out of him with a giant's crowbar.

I heard the front door open and shut. "Where is Singe going?"

*Miss Pular is on a mission.*

"And Penny Dreadful? I saw her hanging around out there."

*She had a report. And hoped I would have more work for her. Likewise, Joe Kerr and his countless siblings.*

Uh-oh. It's not good when he starts playing general and king spider tugging strings from the heart of his web. He has too much fun. And I get scared. And too soon penniless.

*Web-spinners are, generally, female. And the brewery is underwriting expenses.*

"There are limits, even for Max Weider. Who has a nose for financial bullshit better than Singe's for a track. What about Barate Algarda? Did you get anything out of him?"

Embarrassed pause. *No. I was unable to gain control. His protection was stronger than before.*

"That's kind of scary." I told him about seeing the pear-shaped boy asleep on the steps of the Cardonlos mansion.

*That is odd.*

"For a while I was thinking he might be on Relway's payroll. But that wouldn't make sense. If he was he wouldn't be out where people could see him. So I figure he didn't know where he was when he sat down."

Dean appeared. He brought a fine meal. I know that because Dean cooked it. But I was too distracted to enjoy it. I don't recall what it was. He told me, "I've packed something for you to take along. Since you'll be out late. Your coat is almost dry."

I suffered a fleeting inclination to visit my old-time haunts. Get a take on the pulse of the city today. Very fleeting. I ate. I listened to the Dead Man wax eloquent on the possibilities inherent in a rumor that Dean had stumbled over during a shopping run he hade made while I was off enjoying a lesson in humility.

*Glory Mooncalled may be back.*

That would have nothing to do with what we were into today. That was excitement from the past. Interesting to the fans of Glory Mooncalled, but, no way. "Anyone who claims he's Glory Mooncalled is an impostor."

*You think so? Is he really gone? He is a folk hero. A lovable rogue. The man who steals from everybody and gives to himself, but the poor and weak just see him thumbing his nose at the rich and powerful.*

"Dean's imagination is overwrought. I'll believe it when I see it. Whatever the story is. What does it have to do with what we're into?"

*Nothing. As you reflected, just a bit of news that might someday prove interesting to his many aficionados.*

Not just women but whole societies sometimes love the bad boys.

# 49

It was getting on toward evening. Despite the chill nothing was coming down, chunk-style or liquid. People were out enjoying themselves, without fear. I watched excited young people take turns ferociously racing three-wheels. Not once did I see one of those once common, sinister characters who had a stretch of his side of the street all to himself.

The why was plain. Wherever you looked you saw a guy in blue, sporting a red flop hat. Where was Colonel Block getting the money to pay them? He poor-mouthed constantly whenever I saw him.

When you thought about it, though, the Crown could use money it once spent making war. Were it so inclined. Cynical me, I couldn't see the Royal crowd giving a rat's ass. Excepting Prince Rupert.

The prince is a special nut. A Deal Relway fan at the highest altitude.

People followed me. Not so many as before. They had decided I wasn't going to do anything interesting.

I hoped. I'd had about enough interesting times.

I found Saucerhead in a state of excitement, roaming around the outside of the World. Some work had gotten done today. A brace of roofers were still on the job.

Gilbey had taken my advice about offering discharges.

Tharpe practically exploded. "Sekmat on a broomstick, Garrett! What the hell is wrong with this place?"

"Excuse me?" And, "What the hell is that?"

I did know what "that" was, not being blind. It was a flying thunder lizard. There are a dozen species out in the wilds of Karenta. Here in town they're usually small and pick on pigeons. But we don't see them during the cold winter.

The beast that had snatched a cat-size beetle off the unfinished roof had a ten-foot wingspan. The roofers saw that as God's way of telling them it was time to knock off for the day.

Tharpe said, "That kinda shit's been going on all day. Along with ghosts roaming around inside, and weird music playing. Two of my toughest guys quit. Couldn't take it. The ones that stuck, none a' them will go inside no more. What did you get me into, Garrett?"

"You wanted a job."

"Yeah, but . . ."

"I don't know what's going on. Finding out and making it stop is why we're here. Here's a fact for you, though. Only one guy has gotten hurt so far. A drunk who passed out behind those pillars. The bugs got him."

"Oh. That helps. When the carpenters say it's way spookier now than it was before they walked out."

"What happened?"

"Besides what I done told you?"

"Yes. Besides the exciting stuff." A pair of flying thunder lizards banked overhead.

"Some guys—eight, altogether—showed up for work. Two tried inside. Four went up on the roof. One did some base coat painting by that far doorway. The last guy went around yelling at all the rest. Reminding me why I got a such hard time holding that kind a job. I keep thumping guys like him. Anyways, he said more guys will show up tomorrow. And he'd sincerely appreciate it if *somebody* would do *something* about the goddamn *bugs*."

The flyers up top tipped over, one after the other. They streaked down at the roof of a nearby building. And climbed away with wiggling giant bugs in claw. "Looks like that problem could solve itself."

"I find myself sympathetic to the foreman's viewpoint." Which wasn't something Saucerhead Tharpe would normally say.

"Where did you hear that?"

"What?"

"What you just said."

"About sympathy? This old-timer came by this afternoon. Bill something. Said he works for you, too. He said that about sympathy on account of, the foreman couldn't stop whining about the bugs."

Bill, eh? What was he up to? Looking to profit from the situation, no doubt. Any red-blooded Karentine would. It's the nature of the beast.

"Where's Winger? Old Bones has got a mission for her."

Tharpe was suspicious immediately.

"I was against it. He wouldn't listen. Just said there're some jobs for which Winger is ideal."

"She's over yonder. Hanging out. Not getting too much underfoot. Since she ain't getting paid. The Remora's been bitching all afternoon. He's delicate. He don't like the cold. And he can't work on his new play if he's out here." Tharpe grinned yellow and green. A sight to behold. I can't figure out why his teeth haven't rotted down to the bone. He pinched the sleeve of my loaner coat. "I can see where you ain't never gonna be cold again."

"Blame Tinnie. That way?"

He grunted.

"I'll be back."

# 50

I found Winger in an alcove fifty feet away, snuggled up with Jon Salvation, smoking a pipe. "Gods, woman! What are you incinerating in that thing?"

She passed the pipe to her biographer. "What's up, G?"

"Gee?"

"Whatever. You're cool running. What's the beef?"

Must have picked up a new dialect. "Looking for work? Old Bones has something for you. He wouldn't tell me what."

A winged lizard whiffed overhead. Winger observed, "I hope them bastards never figure out how to shit on the fly. Get up, little man. I found us a job."

The stuff in the pipe had worked its magic on Jon Salvation. He was limp. Winger hoisted him with one hand.

"Whatever he has you do, try not to kill anybody. And don't do anything to make the brewery look bad."

"Yeah. Yeah. I know the drill. Hey. You got some weird shit going on around here, Garrett. I been thinking about it."

"There's a scary notion." Really. Winger gets to thinking, she comes up with ideas.

"Smart-ass. Everybody that goes in there, they see ghosts. Right?"

"Seems like. Sooner or later."

"Sooner and sooner, the way them carpenters tell. Only two of them had the stones to go inside and work."

"And? So?"

"They seen stuff. But they didn't let it scare them."

"Got a point?"

"Yeah. Them two was breeds. But not very. They was brothers with maybe one half-breed grandparent between them. So I was thinking maybe some of the Other Races wouldn't react the same as people do."

An interesting notion. The ratmen hadn't had much ghost trouble. I'd have to experiment. Exercising great caution. Because the human rights thugs would be all over me if I replaced a cowardly workforce with nonhumans.

Winger said, "See you in the morning, sweetheart."

I told Saucerhead, "I officially declare Winger only half as dumb as she acts."

"How come?" Tharpe stared at the entrance to the World like a mouse watching a snake it hopes will overlook it.

"She came up with what might be a useful idea. What're you watching for?"

"Spooks."

"Just remember that they're not real. Whatever you see, it's really all inside your head."

"And I declare you officially batshit, Garrett. Officially a walking, talking blivit."

"I've been in there. I've seen my own ghosts."

"Yeah? Like who?"

"Maya. You remember Maya."

"Yeah. And that girl ain't dead. I seen her last week. Her an' her old man. That guy's even older than you. But she definitely married up, 'stead of down."

Meaning me, of course. Maya used to insist she was going to marry me. "Good for her." Through clenched teeth.

One problem for me had been our age difference. Maya was a decade younger. Physically. It was the other way round on the maturity scale.

"Who else?" Tharpe asked.

"Kayanne. Eleanor. And my brother Mikey."

"All right. I'll cut you a cubit of slack. Your ghosts don't count much. Excepting your brother. Did they sing? I hear tell some a'them sing."

"I'm grateful. No. No songs. Who did you see?"

"Not gonna talk about that." Absolute. Final.

Other people seemed to see ghosts connected with guilt.

I never feel guilty. Much. Despite my mama's effort to raise me in the faith. Other people feel guilty about all kinds of crap, all the time.

"I have the perfect experiment," I said. "You guys will be fine as long as you don't go inside."

"It gets a lot hairier after dark, Garrett. And we don't got no place to get in out of the weather. Not to mention, no food."

"It's not so bad out here."

"You spend the night with us, then."

"I'll get some kind of guard shack put up. Tomorrow. Look. I got to go. I need to see Morley."

"Tell him we need some takeout. This is hungry work. And ain't none of us seen the color of no money yet."

I was getting so trusting of the Civil Guard I actually had money in my pocket. I handed it over. "Sorry, brother. I should've thought about that." I made a mental note to let Gilbey know there was no place to get a meal anywhere near the World.

Hold on.

Did I know anybody in the restaurant racket? Somebody maybe having business difficulties but who was skilled at mingling with punters from all up and down the social scale?

Sure I did.

"Garrett, you got that starry look. You just figure things out?"

"No. I just got a great idea. A new business opportunity."

"I hope it's better than the ones Singe says you been coming up with."

"Ha! What does she know?"

"From what I hear, enough to keep you from going down for the third time, financially."

"Humbug. I'd be rich if it wasn't for her, Dean, and the Dead Man spending all my money. Look. I'll get some food headed your way. I promise."

I headed out without looking the World over any more closely. I nearly jogged.

The Dead Man would be irritated.

# 51

There's a rule in heaven called Garrett's Law. It says things can't go simple and straightforward for me. If I decide to walk from the World to The Palms as night falls, the interesting times have got to be stirred up.

I slowed down after a few eager blocks. Huffing and puffing. I really had to consider getting back into shape. Fat and slow aren't healthy in my line.

That reminded me that a true survivor has to be engaged with his surroundings. All the time. I've suffered more than a few knocks because I got too busy thinking to notice somebody sneaking up.

The thought surfaced at exactly the right moment. As interesting times were about to commence in the form of young folks that Director Relway had assured me would be no problem ever again.

Stompers. A whole school of the little pustules. With the crying runt leading the way, pointing and yelling, "That's him! That's the one!"

Not good. My future had fallen into the mitts of folks who had no interest in seeing me enjoy one.

Where were the red tops when I needed them?

I staked out a nice piece of wall and got my back to it. I readied my oaken headknocker. The Stompers spread out in the gloaming. I wished I'd gotten a tin whistle for my birthday.

The little guy kept yelling, "That's him! That's the one!"

Three bigger kids closed in. One carried a rusty kitchen knife maybe four inches long. Another had a piece of broken board. The third brandished a short sword that had spent at least a hundred years underground somewhere.

A half dozen more kids hung back in reserve. The mob was awfully tentative for having so big an advantage.

The kid with the antique sword worried me most. He was on my weak side. When he got where I wanted him I struck like lightning.

Which lightning was a little short on grease. I didn't get close enough to touch him. But I did whack his sword hard enough to bend it.

While he straightened his blade I worked on his companions. The one with the board took off. The kid with the knife took a couple bops on the noggin and folded up.

I focused on the daring swordsman. As his blade broke right where it had bent. A judicious whack took him out of the game.

"Ouch!" quoth I.

The rest of the little bastards had begun throwing rocks. They weren't much good at it. Not one in a dozen missiles came close. I charged. They scattered. I headed for The Palms. They regrouped and kept pegging stones. Though there weren't a lot lying around loose.

At this point I concluded that anyone shadowing me was not deeply invested in my continued good health. Proof was, no assistance of any sort had materialized.

I engaged the Stompers in a running fight. Failing a rock to my head, they would break up as we neared The Palms. Morley's neighborhood isn't one where kid gangs are even a little welcome. The night could turn lethal if they got themselves noticed by Sarge or Puddle.

Just to encourage other kids.

Sound strategy, me fighting on the run. But life didn't roll on the way I'd calculated.

It never does.

I walked into an ambush. Eyes wide open. But I was looking back at the bad baby wolves who just couldn't figure out how to bring the huffing old stag to bay.

The ambush wasn't meant for me.

I did have the honor of being the Judas goat.

The bushwhackers were Morley and his crew. A show tossed together, in haste, in hopes of laying hands on one Lurking Felhske.

The Stompers enjoyed an opportunity to regret not waiting for their revenge to be served cold.

I got a chance to be cursed vigorously for springing the trap with the wrong springees.

I didn't care. Though I did spare a black look for Singe, whose fault the makeshift ambush was.

"Too clever for your own good," I told Morley.

"So it would seem. Or just not clever enough." We were approaching his place. His was the sourness he shows only when he owes money. "Felhske is out there lurking and smirking. Having slipped the noose again. It's becoming a challenge."

I had an epiphany.

Director Relway might not be interested so much in what Lurking Felhske knew as he was in showing off his power where he had had no effect before. It could be an ego thing.

Power was more important to Relway than whatever good he might do with it. Though he would chant a mantra to himself about how he had to have the power before he could do the good.

Belatedly, Morley asked, "You all right?"

"They never laid a hand on me."

"Looks like they got you with a rock or two, though."

"I'll have a few bruises in the morning. Lucky me, they only hit me in the head."

"You'll have to replace another coat, too."

True. The loaner was in worse shape than the coat that had visited Morley's kitchen.

We entered The Palms through the front door. I was surprised. The place was less than half-filled. No wonder Morley was sour. They used to line up outside and wait. If business was this bad, he didn't have to bet on the water spiders to be hurting.

I said, "I had a couple reasons for coming up here. The main one was, I think I've found a chance for an experienced restaurant man to set himself up good." We settled at one of the empty tables, ignoring dark looks sent Singe's way. Things had gone so bad Morley didn't care if he offended the customers he did have.

I explained. "And you wouldn't be walking on Weider's toes. He's only interested in moving more beer."

"You might be on to something," Dotes conceded. "You just might."

The clockwork inside his gourd clacked and clunked. It picked up speed and gathered momentum. My good pal broke out in a grin filled with sharp white teeth. "You really had an original idea, Garrett."

Thank you very much. It does happen.

Singe started to defend me. I stopped her. "Don't waste the emotion."

Morley had discovered some implication in my idea that I'd overlooked. Nothing less would have him so excited.

Morley Dotes doesn't get excited. Not obviously. Not where someone might see it.

I might want to figure it out. In case it fell in on my head. "Don't forget. You've been appointed official caterer for Saucerhead's crew. Until they get sick of eggplant and acorns."

"That's being dealt with."

I turned to Singe. "What's this? How come you're out here with him?"

"I went to visit John Stretch. I had had all the Dean and Dead Man I could take. But I caught a whiff of that strong personal odor on your back trail. So I came here. I suggested that Mr. Dotes establish an ambush along your most likely route from the World to The Palms. You being a creature of habit."

Really? I had to work on that. "Why?"

"No arrangements had been made to support Mr. Tharpe. You don't think of those things ahead of time. It was reasonable to assume that you would come here once you decided to feed them."

I gave her the heavy-duty fish-eye. That was entirely too much reasoning for anyone of the rattish persuasion, even stipulating her relative genius.

Morley observed, "Them Other Races is gettin' more uppity all the time." Then dropped the ignorant accent. "Next thing you know, humans will be obsolete."

"Not likely. We've got one big advantage on you Lesser Races. We breed like rats."

Singe managed a credible snicker.

Morley contented himself with a gentle smile. "Eyes wide shut," he said. "Count on Garrett to step in it with both boots, then shove the entire pair into his mouth."

The notion I'd offered wasn't original with me, though I hadn't repeated it intentionally. It hailed from a speech I'd heard at a human rights rally during a former adventure.

Being almost as clever as a rat, I changed the subject. "How come you want Lurking Felhske so bad, Morley?"

I know. I asked before. I was hoping he'd give me a straight answer this time.

It could happen.

"Because he has a fat bounty on his head. And I need money. Business is bad."

"You couldn't stay away from the bug races?"

"I'm staying away just fine. What I can't escape is the curse of family."

"I'll bet that makes sense to a guy with the inside poop."

"You know I've got obligations to family outside the city."

"That arranged engagement. And your idiot nephew. Whatever happened to him?" A slow, cruel death if there was any justice. That psycho was responsible for me having had to suffer through a century-long affliction known as the Goddamn Parrot.

"He's fine. And not the problem. The problem is the side of the family that thinks I ought to be getting married now."

"A pressure not unknown at our house," Singe observed. With another rattish smirk.

I asked, "The arranged marriage?" Country elfin folk betroth their offspring while the kids are still trying to figure out how to walk without holding on. Morley had one of those connections. He'd mentioned her name a couple times but I couldn't remember it. The family made noises occasionally—the boy wasn't getting any younger—but the dark elf maiden involved had no more interest than he did.

"That one. Yes."

"I thought nobody was really behind that. And wouldn't her family have to cover the costs? Or do you have some dumb custom like our nobility where you have to come up with a bride price?" The one thing the Venageti have right, to my way of thinking, is the dowry business. Where the bride's family, in essence, pays the groom to take her off their hands. Sort of.

"Most of us weren't. Except for her people. Even so, it wasn't a real problem till she took an interest herself. Out of the blue. Evidently thinking I'm rich."

"Joke's on her, eh? Here's what you do. Don't tell her till after the honeymoon."

Morley made ugly, inarticulate noises. He turned red. His face puffed up.

"Whoa!" I gaped. I'd never seen him like this.

Sarge and Puddle closed in, looking anxious. If Morley suffered a massive fit of apoplexy and assumed room temperature, they'd have to start thinking for themselves. They were just marginally bright enough to recognize what a disaster that would be.

Man by man, quick as an evil rumor, the rest of Morley's troops came from whatever they'd dropped, expecting their boss to implode or explode.

Contrary as ever, Morley did neither.

He grinned his wicked, hundred-sharp-teeth grin. "You almost got me. How about that?"

"Almost, nothing. But getting you wasn't the game. I was just asking. Because I care."

"Sure. I know."

A little sarcasm? I wondered.

I asked, "What's money got to do with it? Do you have to be rich when she shows up for the wedding?"

"No. I need to buy my way out. Money is why she started pushing. She's pressing so I'll come up with more money to get out."

That made sense. To someone raised in this place and time. "Call her bluff."

"I could cut my own throat, too. But it isn't going to happen. I wish I knew where she got the idea that I'm rich. Whoever told her that would end up cursing his mother for not having gotten the abortion."

Singe couldn't restrain her whickering snicker.

Morley leaned back, shut his eyes, went to a happy place for a few seconds. He returned a changed man. "Garrett, I'm going to crawl out on a limb. I'm going to make a wild guess. You're not supposed to be here. The Dead Man is awake. And he's interested in what you're doing. Which means he's using you to find out what he needs to know before he figures it all out for you. Not so?"

I confessed with a small nod.

"So what should you be doing now? Instead of socializing?"

Singe and I went home. The Dead Man took a peek inside my skull. He had no comment. But his disappointment reeked like a psychic wet dog. I began to think it might be a good idea to move out if Tinnie and I set up housekeeping.

It was still early by my standards. I went to bed anyway. After just one sweet sample of Weider Select.

I might have had a touch of something.

# 52

"I forgot to ask last night. Did Winger show up?"

*You were distracted. She did. She and her biographer are on the payroll. I offered each a challenge suited to his or her pride.*

What did that mean? "You split them up? How clever are you?"

*An appeal to pride and ego, presented with sufficient subtlety, ofttimes will do where even bribery is futile.*

"You did split them up." Word was, that hadn't happened for months. Even when Winger herself wished it would. It was why Jon Salvation was called the Remora by those who played his game. Those who just saw an obnoxious little geek still called him by his real name, Pilsuds Vilchik.

*Both were motivated at the time but that may not last.*

"What are they supposed to do?"

*Jon Salvation will execute the library search you were unable to complete, assisted by Penny Dreadful.*

"Definitely wouldn't want Winger along on that." That woman loose in a building full of rare books? She'd burn them to keep warm.

*Miss Winger will round up persons I wish to interview, inasmuch as you are unable to find time.*

Ouch! But he was right. "Oh, for those slower, lazier days of yesteryear." And, "But I'm up irrationally early today."

I ate while we talked. Multitasking, Tinnie calls it. Didn't matter if I talked with my mouth full. Old Bones knew what I wanted to say before I said it.

I wondered what Tinnie was up to. I hadn't seen her for hours and hours.

Himself disdained the opportunity for a disparaging remark, offering instead an observation about my unnatural wakefulness. *Which affords you the opportunity to pursue some basic work at and around the World.*

He filled my head with chores, the most immediate of which was to have the construction workers build a shack so Saucerhead and his troops could get in out of the weather without having to be haunted. He thought I ought to add a stove so they could keep warm, make tea, and cook a little something.

"You expecting winter to last forever?" I was thinking, if I gave them someplace warm, then they wouldn't go out where it was cold.

*You will see.* Then: *Fuel. They will need fuel to heat the shack. You may have to go to the waterfront to arrange a delivery.* Because all of TunFaire's fuels have to be barged in from up or down the river.

Yet one more chore. And one I didn't know how to execute. That's Dean's area of expertise. We're profligate with fuels here. We're too prosperous. Except in the Dead Man's room, of course. Wood, coal, and charcoal all are delivered. At some expense. The delivery folk have to travel with armed guards.

Not many villains will go for a load of firewood accompanied by guys with crossbows. That's a quick way for a dimwit to commit suicide. Though stupid is as plentiful as air.

*Make good use of the time available to you today.*

That sounded portentous.

*Tomorrow will be your turn at the shovels.*

"Oh, don't tell me!"

*It is about to come down. It could go on for days.*

A professional storyteller once clued me that the way to drag your audience along is to hit them with One Damned Thing After Another. And that's my life. The malevolent, sniggering, buggering toadlet gods tugging on the threads of my tale plot it by that very method.

The older religions—we're afflicted with several hundred—generally assign three vindictive crones to work the warp and woof of individual destinies. But that all goes on in a side room. The main stage features a team of fifteen working Poor Garrett's Ever More Miserable Homespun.

Singe says I overdramatize. Which only proves that she hasn't been paying attention.

*Do you suppose this might be a good time to roll out your equally absurd tendency toward equine hysterics?*

"What?" Then I got it. He was needling me.

Horses.

Because I have a rational, reasoned attitude toward those fiends.

People mock me when I report anything about the innate wickedness of horses. Those monstrous beasts have most people so fooled that every damned idiot out there thinks they're man's best friend. Big old cute pals who carry civilization itself on their backs. But the truth is, the beasts just lie in the weeds, waiting for a kill shot they can score while leaving nobody the wiser.

You don't want to be alone with a horse.

Never, ever, under any circumstance, do you want to be alone with a whole bunch of horses.

Amusement tainted the psychic atmosphere.

There seemed to be a lot of that lately.

But what does he know? Even when he was breathing and waddling around on his hind legs he couldn't have ridden anything smaller than a woolly mammoth.

*You know what needs doing today. And you have finished eating. I suggest you earn some of the buckets of money the Weider interest has thrown your way.*

Buckets? I hadn't asked Singe how much more money Gilbey had sent over. Old Bones made it sound like it would be worth finding out.

*Time to go, Garrett. It cannot be long before Miss Winger begins delivering persons of interest who may not wish to be seen by you.*

"Harsh." But what I was really thinking was, who could that possibly be? Which tossed up an "Uh-oh!" as I caught a whiff of something maybe called plausible deniability.

He wanted me away from the house, stumbling around, making myself a fat, solid alibi.

Time to go.

I took care of personal business, pulled myself together,

dressed for winter, and stepped outside. And ducked right back inside for a sock cap and muffler to add to what I had going already.

The cold had hit me like a punch in the snoot. That meant Dean and Singe were keeping the house too damned hot. They were turning silver into smoke.

# 53

This wasn't my first time out before the sun hit the meridian. Mine is a life of sorrow and misfortune. More often than I like I've had to be out with the early worms. Back when I was one of the Universe's Elect, a Marine, I had to be up before the sun dragged its sorry ass over the horizon every freaking morning. So, though it was unnatural, I could take it.

I didn't like the looks of the snow in Macunado Street. The slackers on the crew before mine wouldn't do anything but make a show. Tomorrow would be hell. As in the realms of the cruelly used dead in religions where the abode of the fallen is an icy waste and the souls there do hard labor for having been too milquetoast in life.

I gave it all a second look, shrugged, sucked it up, and headed out.

It was time for an off-season New Year's resolution. I spend too much time grumbling and anticipating all the ways that life will jump up and bite me. I should become more positive. And more active. I should drink less and get up earlier.

I've told myself the same thing at least once a week for the last five years. Along with, I need to get more exercise and to shed ten pounds. Or maybe twenty, these days.

So far it only takes for a few days at a time before the relapse sets in.

"I ain't seen you out this early in years," Saucerhead told me.

"A gross exaggeration, sir."

"Possibly an exaggeration. But not gross. What's all this stuff? What's going on?"

"I'm doing a two birder. These guys are going to build you a guardhouse. Complete with a charcoal stove and a garderobe. They'll do it fast and efficient, right here, in broad daylight, while Weider's contractors watch." My workmen were breeds who were eager to work. "How many showed up today?"

"Almost all a' them, what Luther says. They're getting scared a' being outta work."

"This ought to give them a little extra incentive, then."

"Or start a riot."

"I see four Relway tin whistles without even trying. Anything starts, there'll be a bunch of guys donating skilled labor to the Crown."

Desultory work continues round the seasons on the Marcosca aqueduct. Someday—maybe even during my lifetime—it will improve dramatically the quality and quantity of water available to the city. The system is a long, slow project because the labor is almost entirely convict.

Saucerhead watched the breeds unload carts and a lumber wagon. I suggested, "Show them where you want the shack put up. That one with the growth on his face is the top kick. Goes by Rockpile."

There was a story behind that name but Saucerhead wouldn't care. A guy called Saucerhead all his life don't much care how somebody else got hung with an oddball nickname. Unless they hit it off and decided to go get drunk together.

Tharpe had definite ideas about the optimum size for his guardhouse. He and Rockpile began jabbering.

Bill appeared. So suddenly I jumped. "What the hell?"

"You ought to keep one eye open."

I'd started thinking about Tinnie and where my life was headed. "Maybe I ought to. What's on your mind?"

"I spent part of the night here with your thugs, last night. Mr. Tharpe mention that?"

"Not yet."

"Well, whatever is down there is getting stronger. Putting an end to the damned bugs would probably turn that around. They weren't all the time chewing on it, it could go back to sleep. But they just keep hatching out."

"And?"

"Just saying. Do something about the bugs. The rest could follow."

"We'll see some action on that today."

My partner had plans afoot. Numerous plans. Some of them he'd let me in on. Plans were why he'd recruited so many messengers.

"That's good. Me, I don't mind the bugs. But the music could drive me nuts."

"Music?" I hadn't pursued that. I hadn't dismissed it, either. I'd heard something myself, though calling it music would be a stretch.

"They're bad melodies," Bill said. "Very bad melodies. In several senses of bad. But mostly just awful as music."

I waited. Bill was one of those guys who has to fill a silence. And had a gift for making himself understood.

"This'll be hard to explain, Garrett." We were old pals now. Brothers of the sword. "You'll understand after you hear the music. Which you'll do for sure if you hang around here after dark."

"All right." How would a thing buried down deep know when it was dark? "Give it a shot. Sometimes I can figure things out. Wow. Look at those guys go."

Rockpile and his gang had a frame going up. Workers from the contract crew were watching. They didn't look happy.

"All right. But I need to digress. When I got back from my five in the Cantard, the first job I got was working for my uncle. He was a specialty founder. A small operation. We made custom alloys, especially latten and electrum. Exotic stuff, but useful to people who can't afford solid gold and silver. And to some specialist operators on the Hill."

"Latten? Electrum?"

"Electrum doesn't matter here. Nor does latten, either, really. Except that I used to help make it. It's an alloy of nickel, copper, tin, and zinc that takes gilding well. It isn't easy to make. The zinc part is where I was headed with the metals and music notion."

"You were moving too fast and light for me, Bill. You lost me way back."

"Which explains why I live in a loft over top of a third-rate tavern. Lack of polish in my communications skills."

"I'll buy you a jar of the finest. Do your best to make me understand now."

"All right. Metals make music. They ring. Like wind chimes? You use strips or tubes of copper. Or silver, if you're too rich to be allowed to live."

"Sure. I've seen them made out of glass and ceramics, too."

"Good on you, boy. But let's stick to metal. Zinc. When you mix up latten you feed in small, flat strips of zinc, after your other metals have melted. Strips like you could use to make wind chimes. If you made one out of zinc, though, all you'd get is a lot of clink-clunk. Zinc don't sing."

We were getting somewhere. On a long road winding up a tall hill. "Are we getting somewhere?"

"Considering your slick-talking ways, it's a wonder you're still alive, let alone successful."

"So I've heard. My social skills get the best of me sometimes. Zinc wind chimes."

"Exactly. The music is like the sound of the world's biggest zinc wind chime."

Really? I stood there trying to trap random snowflakes with my open mouth.

"Let me take that back, Garrett. I thought of something it's more like than wind chime music. Only I don't know what you call it. One of those music things where you hit little pieces of metal, all different sizes, with little wooden hammers."

"Chimes," I said.

"That's the kind that hang off a rail. Yeah. But I mean the kind where they're laid out on a little table."

I could picture what he meant. Only place I ever saw one was in the orchestra pit of one of the World's competitors. "I don't know, either. But I know what you mean."

"Good. Because the music is like from a band of those, all with zinc chimes."

"If the racket is that bad, how come you think it's music?"

"You have to hear it to get it."

"If I must, I must."

# 54

Saucerhead and Rockpile worked well together. The guardhouse went up quickly. Saucerhead's henchmen glowed with anticipation. I reminded Tharpe that the job was more than just hanging out in a warm place.

His guys were on the job, though. Men called Sparrow and Figgie Joe Crabb brought in a prowler they said was up to no good around back of the World. He wasn't big. He wasn't well dressed. He stank. Not as much as Lurking Felhske, but enough to stand out in a city where most people are allergic to soap. He could've stood to eat a meal, too. His limbs were like spider legs. He needed to stand straighter, too. His hair was a tangled mess of greasy strings. He wouldn't look anyone in the eye. He knew who I was. He was hoping I wouldn't remember him.

Life had been one disappointment after another. His luck wouldn't change today.

"Snoots Gitto. It's been a while. Little out of your normal range, aren't you? What's your story?"

Snoots mumbled something about he was looking for a job. That changed under the press of a battery of sneers. My companions didn't know Snoots but they knew the breed.

Snoots then whined about trying to find something he could sell so he could buy something to eat. Snoots has a talent. He can mumble and whine at the same time.

He might be telling the truth. If information was what he wanted to find.

I told Saucerhead, "Let's don't start pounding him yet. Snoots is more than he seems."

"Seems like a bum to me."

"Exactly. But he's really a spy for Marengo North English and that crowd."

Tharpe, Sparrow, Crabb, and a couple others considered Snoots. And didn't believe me.

"Behold the master race," I told them. Then, "Snoots, you've stumbled into the gooey poo. Only one way out. You tell the truth."

Snoots stared at the pavements and made whiny noises. They didn't add up to words.

"What're you doing here? I'm listening. If you deal off the top of the deck, I won't give you to Rockpile, there. You do mess with me, I'll have these guys break stuff and pull bits off till you do convince me. Then I'll turn you over to Rockpile anyway. He can drag you over to the Al-Khar. Where, I'm pretty sure, your name is still on the list of people Director Relway wants to meet bad enough to pay a finder's fee for an introduction."

Snoots became cooperation itself. If Cooperation were a goddess, Snoots would be a kitten purring in her lap and butter wouldn't melt in his mouth. He said, "There was a rumor that some nonhuman labor might be about to be used around here." He cast a worried glance at Rockpile.

"A rumor? Who did you hear it from?"

Snoots Gitto wasn't a complete craven. But he was a realist and a pragmatist. He knew he would give up everything. Given time. Time was of no value to him. So he wasn't principled enough to make us hurt him for a while before he accepted the inevitable.

"Couple of the tradesmen on this project. We have a party place over yonder a couple blocks. They passed the word. Sounded like they were just pissed off at their foreman. But I wasn't doing nothing. So the sector chairman sent me to check it out. I was trying to find the snitches when these guys started hassling me."

"And what snitches were you looking for?"

Snoots dragged his feet a while. Naming names would make him unpopular.

He figured six seconds was an honorable effort. "Myndra Merkel and Bambi Fardanse."

"Bambi?" Saucerhead gasped. "Really? You're serious?"

I beckoned. "Luther." The foreman had been hanging around, trying to catch the conversation. I told him,

"Bambi Fardanse and Myndra Merkel. Tell them to pick up their tools and go home. They don't work here anymore."

That set him off. "Who the fuck do you think you are? You don't fire people. They don't work for you. They work for— Yah!"

The shriek started when Saucerhead laid hands on. Saucerhead has a knack for wringing inarticulate noises out of uncooperative people.

"That should do it. I think we have his attention. Luther. Those men are gone. See to it. Snoots, tell your boss to mind his own business. Your bunch messed with Max Weider once before. He went easy because he had friends involved. That won't happen again. Understand? Considering the current political climate?"

That weather was fickle but the people in charge, and, notably, the master of the secret police, enjoyed an antagonistic attitude toward the human rights movement. There were those—notably, the head of the secret police—who were overjoyed whenever evidence of rightsist misbehavior fell into their laps.

Snoots bobbed his head. He made inarticulate, whining sounds. I spun him around, slapped him on the seat of the pants. "Off you go. And I hope I don't see you again in this life."

"You maybe shouldn't've said that, Garrett," Tharpe opined a moment later. "Now you got him thinking about options he never saw before."

"He won't think too hard. Look over there. A man Snoots is sure to recognize. And recall that we have a special relationship."

Morley Dotes, Puddle, Sarge, and somebody I didn't know were ambling along the far side of the street. Paying the World no heed. Morley and the stranger were engaged in an animated conversation. Sarge and Puddle seemed bored.

I muttered, "That son of a bitch is looking for a place to put a restaurant."

"What?"

"Huh? Oh. Just being startled by seeing somebody actually take my advice."

"Is that unusual?"

"It is in this case."

Puddle noticing me staring. He said something. Morley looked over, waved, showed me a rack of needle teeth, then went on about his business.

Nearer to hand, Rockpile's crew started roofing the guardhouse.

# 55

The thing below must have burped. Or something. We all
felt the psychic wave. I gasped. Everyone made some kind
of noise.

Workmen poured out of the World like rats fleeing fire.
A horde of a dozen, at least. Across the way, Morley and
his crew stopped to watch.

Flying lizards flapped up off the roof. They wobbled
away clumsily, hurling indignant shrieks behind. Bugs burst
out of hiding and raced off in every direction. There were
only a few but they were all the biggest I'd seen yet.

Saucerhead murmured, "Damn, I'm glad they didn't
make no spiders! I hate spiders."

I looked around nervously. When somebody says something like that it's certain I'll be up to my hips in tarantulas
the size of sled dogs within minutes.

No spiders materialized. Saucerhead Tharpe was at peace
with the gods.

They love some of us more than others. They are quite
mad. And their favoritism is completely unreasonable.

The psychic wave passed.

Several workmen refused to go back inside. I told the
foreman, "They don't go, Luther, it's a voluntary quit."

I noted that those of Rockpile's crew who were most
obviously breeds had shown the least reaction to the psychic shock. A few hadn't responded at all.

Luther consulted his troops. They were sullen and rebel-
lious. I joined the group. Saucerhead followed. Just in case.
I said, "Before you guys make a decision that could shape
the rest of your lives, answer me this. Have any of you
gotten hurt by what's going on in there? You? You? You?

No? And you don't know anyone who got hurt, either. Do you? So what it adds up to is, you're running away from your own imaginations. Your own guilty consciences. Eh?"

Every word I spoke was true. Every man listening knew it.

Fear squeezed them, even so.

Part of the human pattern predisposes us to bend the knee to a supernatural power, however improbable. Or even ridiculous, to an outsider or atheist.

"So what will it be? Go looking for work? Or suck it up and carry on? I'll be working on making the spooky stuff stop."

It was easy to pick out the single guys. They were the ones who thought twice before clenching their jaws and heading back to work.

# 56

"Here comes Winger," Tharpe told me.

Conditioned by an age of disappointments involving that woman, I turned, expecting a whole new set of problems.

Well . . .

Winger had a family of dwarves in tow. Mom and Pop, adolescent son and prepubescent daughter. All readable only because they'd all gone native.

In the normal scheme sexing a dwarf is something only a dwarf can manage without getting closer than I want to imagine. Male and female, they come with immense crops of hair, arsenals sure to include at least one huge ax and an amazing variety of supplemental cutlery, and a lot of attitude. In general, dress consists of a chain-mail shirt not tucked in, an iron hat, and a leather apron something like a kilt. The more pockets on the apron, the higher the status of the dwarf.

Got to be a joke in there somewhere.

The mom in this crew wore a paisley apron that started life as a carpet. Her helmet was a feminine little pillbox in blackened steel, without horns or other appurtenance. Dad wore a stylish pullover made from burlap bags, hiding most of his mail.

The younger dwarves, almost human in apparel, seemed painfully embarrassed to be seen in the company of parents. Definitely a custom borrowed from humans.

Winger boomed, "This here is Garrett. Runs things at this end. Garrett, this is Rindt Grinblatt."

Papa Dwarf offered the slightest of bows. It was the kind dwarves deploy when confronted by lesser beings in superior numbers.

"Good to meet you," I lied. And turned to Winger for an explanation.

"The Dead Man hired them to poke around under that abandoned house. They have all the information they need."

The little one whined, "Daddy made me go in the house with the creepy thing! It messed around inside my head."

Rindt Grinblatt—a name either made up or adopted because it wasn't traditional dwarfish—admitted it. "I wasn't gonna go in dere wit' dat t'ing. I don't need my mind swept. Mindie don't got no secrets to give away."

Fathers. You got to love them.

Generally, dwarves are inscrutable. Mindie was not. Her expression said her father didn't have a clue what he was blathering about.

Winger told me, "The Dead Man said to tell you he put a map of the underground into her head."

Dwarves being folks who live in caves and tunnels in the wild, this bunch should have no trouble if the map they'd gotten was the one Old Bones based on my recollections of those cellars.

"My partner told you what he wanted done?" Since this was all a surprise to me.

"We got it," Rindt Grinblatt grumbled.

"The Dead Man told me. I explained," Winger said. "In case Mindie gets distracted."

Rindt grumbled, "You just show us where the house is."

Grinblatt was not in a bad temper. He was being upbeat. For a dwarf. He had a paying job.

I looked to Winger for further illumination. She told me, "You take them to the abandoned house. And turn them loose."

"Follow me," I grumbled, cheerful as an employed dwarf. Snowflakes had begun to swirl. I wasn't looking forward to manning a shovel. I wondered if Max and Gilbey would notice the charge if I hired a stand-in shoveler.

I led. Grinblatts followed, none with any enthusiasm. They were working only in response to the supreme motivator, hunger.

Very upbeat. For dwarves.

Winger brought up the rear.

We hadn't gone half a block before a brace of flying

thunder lizards wheeled through the random snowflakes overhead, hitting something on the roof of the World. The lead flyer flapped back up with a pair of struggling beetles, one neatly mounted atop the other. The bottom bug fell. It crunched into the cobblestones a dozen yards away, the fall instantly fatal.

The dwarves surrounded the beetle. Its limbs continued to twitch. Rindt Grinblatt said, "I didn't believe it. But dere it is. You cain't argue wit' dat."

I explained, "They're big but not dangerous. They haven't—"

"I know dat. We're supposed ta find out where dey're comin' from. An' git rid a' any a' dem we runs inta."

Looking at those four, with all the mail and armament, I decided the Dead Man had been very clever indeed. Dwarves were perfect exterminators for these vermin. They were used to tight places, underground. And they were unlikely to be hurt by the bugs. The darkness, smells, and spells wouldn't bother them, either.

I visited Dwarf Fort once, a long time ago, warrens where dwarves who won't acculturate live once they come to the big city. The perfume of countless never-washed dwarf bodies, in tight quarters, while potent enough to water the eyes of a maggot, go unremarked by the denizens of the place.

"Here we are," I said when we arrived. The abandoned house looked bleaker than ever. "I can't tell you much. I went in there once myself but I didn't get very far. Be careful on the stairs."

Grinblatt rumbled, "We'll let you know what we find." He and his tribe had gone native, but he wasn't going to let some mere human get too friendly.

"I'll be back at the World when you want me."

Clan Grinblatt unlimbered axes and tromped up the shaky steps. They vanished into the abandoned house.

Winger and I headed for the theater. I observed, "Joyful bunch."

She responded with a Grinblatt grunt, then asked, "You got any idea what Pilsuds is up to?"

"Who?" It took a moment. "Oh. The Remora. I forgot that was his real name. No. I don't." I dared not tell her that the Dead Man was more interested in enlisting Jon Salvation than her.

"Why can't you just call him by the name that he wants, Garrett?"

"Because Jon Salvation is ridiculous. And you just called him Pilsuds."

Winger is no addict of consistency. She ignored me. "Jon Salvation is gonna be famous. He already finished his second play. He read it to me. It's really good."

Winger is no fan of the arts. Nor has ever been. Unless she can find someone willing to buy it, off the books.

She said, "The little shit drives me nuts when he's around. He's so damned clingy. And needy. And horny. But now that he hasn't been underfoot for a few hours, I'm missing him."

She'd be nervous about the constituents of the crowd who meant to perform Jon Salvation's plays. Alyx. Bobbi. Lindy. Cassie Doap, who had yet to show her primo self. Even Heather Soames. Every one definitely worth considering a threat.

I was nervous about the redhead of the set. Though not that a wannabe playwright would carry her off. I was afraid that someday she'd go away because old Garrett couldn't help going right on being Garrett.

There have been rare moments when I haven't been the most lovable guy roaming these mean streets.

# 57

A train of wagons had appeared outside the World. Saucerhead was directing traffic, moving them on to park farther along once they unloaded.

Curious bystanders had begun to turn out. We had giant bugs, flying thunder lizards, and now, ratpeople by the wagonload. That's entertainment.

Morley and his crew continued working rentable buildings nearby.

The wagons spilled ratmen and cages full of cranky rats. More than ever before. I spotted John Stretch. He must have been preparing for the callback for days. I headed his way. "Thought you'd had enough of this place."

"I do not like it, Mr. Garrett. It is a bad place. But it could make me rich."

"And me poor. The Dead Man hired you?"

"Yes. He wants one more offensive against the bugs from down below."

"They're so big now, your best rats may not be able to hold their own."

"This could be the last time this approach is possible. Rats are not smart. They are cunning. But they do learn. And they pass their learning along. By the time today's game is played out, it may be impossible to gather any significant number of feral rats willing to be used here."

"Ratpeople could take over."

"You are mad."

"It's completely safe. Hell, there's a family of dwarves down there poking around right now."

"There are ghosts."

"That only bother humans."

"Till now."

John Stretch was well on into an extended graphic description of what I could do with my idea about sending ratmen down when an unexpected visitor interrupted.

"Rocky? Hey!" It was the midget troll who made deliveries for a living. "What're you up to?"

Rocky is a blazing fast talker. For a troll. He's had too much exposure to human beings. It took him only ten seconds to get going on an answer. "It is my day off. Playmate told me you might could use some help. I could use a little extra money."

"Playmate had a good idea." I sure could use Rocky. Nothing much will dent a troll, let alone do serious damage. Plus, Rocky was small enough to get around in the same kinds of places dwarves can go. While being a dozen times stronger.

Hell, this was an idea so great it was embarrassing that it took a preacher man to think it up.

There was a problem, though. Trolls and dwarves are not an inert mix. No way could I send Rocky down to help Rindt Grinblatt. The Grinblatts would, almost certainly, attempt to test to destruction Rocky's natural invulnerability.

"Here's what you do to start. John Stretch!" I beckoned the ratman. "John Stretch, this is Rocky. He's going to go inside with you. He'll handle any physical challenges that come up." I told Rocky what we were up against and how he could protect the ratmen.

He said, "I hope it's warmer inside there, Garrett. This cold really slows me down."

"Warm won't be a problem." John Stretch's people were complaining about the heat. And ratfolk like it hot.

Rocky went off with John Stretch.

Luther planted himself in front of me. Before he started, I said, "Work around them."

"There's ghosts already. They don't usually come out this early."

"We're trying to deal with that. Remember, they're harmless. They just manipulate your emotions."

"Yeah. I know. But knowing and believing are two whole different buckets of monkey piss."

That was hard to argue. I'd seen it too often. Fear has its own logic. Too often, there isn't a dread of physical harm driving it. "All right. If you must, take breaks. That's all right. As long as I see everybody challenging their courage." I leaned in, whispered, "We don't want no ratmen making us look bad, do we?"

During Snoots' visit I'd gotten the notion that Luther didn't disdain rightsist ideals.

Luther was surprised. For an instant. Then puzzled. Then satisfied enough to smile. "Right. Got you."

Which left me feeling unclean. But not a lot. That's management. Tell them what they need to hear to get them through the day. Tomorrow can take care of itself.

I screwed up my courage, went inside to see how the ratfolk were doing. Wondering why Singe hadn't come to stick her nose in.

The heat was amazing. I ordered every doorway propped open. Why hadn't anybody done that? And there were vents up top, there to let the heat out when the World filled up with playgoers. Those were shut, too.

Might the thing down below be like a snake or thunder lizard? Or troll? Would a good chill slow it down?

The ratmen were staying out of the way of the workmen. Who weren't being too unpleasant to them. John Stretch had set up down on the cellar level. That helped.

Ghosts wandered everywhere. At least a dozen of them, all just milky shimmers. The ratmen saw them but weren't impressed. The tradesmen weren't bothered, either. None coalesced into anything anyone found frightening. Too many minds, too many ghosts, too many distractions.

A lot of people doing a lot of stuff might just be the perfect workaround.

Luther, making a circuit of his troops, paused to shoot me a thumbs-up.

# 58

Morley Dotes invited himself in to tour the monster destined to be the talk of high society. My first hint of his presence was him saying, "I'm impressed, Garrett."

Startled, I stopped watching Rocky crunch bugs. The midget troll wasn't fast but didn't have to be. He'd found the hole that the biggest insects used to get into the cellar. He let them come to him. The rats had gone down by lesser ways and were driving the bugs toward him.

Morley twitched as I turned. A ghost had bumped him from behind. He looked back, didn't see anything, but twitched again when the ghost touched him again.

Interesting. I hadn't seen a ghost touch anyone before.

"What the devil?" Morley said. "You have practical joke spells floating around in here?"

"No joke." I explained. "You really don't see anything?"

"No. But I feel it. It's like being touched by cold, wet hands." He twitched, turned quickly. Several times.

"We need to get you out of here. You're drawing them like you might be good to eat." Six were in touching distance. The rest were drifting our way.

The Dead Man should find that interesting.

We ran into Belle Chimes at the door. He didn't recognize Morley. Nor Morley, him, either. I didn't bother with introductions. I told Bill my best friend seemed to attract ghosts but couldn't see them.

"He might be psychic," Bill suggested. "Which would make him more obvious to them than the rest of you are."

"Why can't he see them?"

Bill shrugged. "Garrett, I'm just a guy who lives over top of a third-rate bar."

"But . . ."

"Not my field of expertise. What's his problem?" He pointed.

I looked.

Morley hadn't stopped twitching just because we'd gone outside.

"The spooks came out with him. A couple of them." By squinting, cocking my head, and looking slightly to one side, I could detect them. But they were fading. "Morley. Scoot your ass on across the street. See if they can stay with you."

My best pal said unflattering things. He wasn't sure what was happening. He didn't like it. But he did what I said.

"Try getting into shadows," I told him. "The spooks are easier to spot when they're not in the light."

"They're gone." He'd moved only a few steps into the street.

"You sure? How do you know?"

"I know because there's nobody painting me with cold porridge fingers anymore." He came toward me, a step at a time. And defined the range of the spooks in seconds. "Three steps make all the difference."

I wasn't happy. I'd just found out that the ghosts could come outside a good ten yards. Would their range increase again tomorrow?

About the time Saucerhead was set to christen his sudden new guard shack, we discovered that Morley's escape marked a supernatural high water. The ghosts' range dwindled fast, afterward. Possibly because of the chill winter air flooding the World.

John Stretch told me, "We do not like this cold. But the rats definitely like what it is doing to the bugs down under."

"Good?"

"Good. This time we may get them all."

"You'll need to find their eggs," Belle Chimes told us. "Otherwise they'll just keep coming."

"That's true," I said. And thought about the Grinblatts. I'd heard nothing from the dwarves.

I worried. There should've been something, if only a

"Screw you very much!" "Hey, Rocky. I've got a mission for you."

"More fun than squashing bugs?" His outside was covered with insect insides.

"I can't tell you a lie. No. It could even turn unpleasant. I've got some dwarves that might've got themselves into a tight spot."

Troll faces aren't especially expressive. But Rocky managed to betray his thoughts without saying that tight spots are right where dwarves belong. The tighter the better. A pine box, eight feet down, being ideal. Or maybe farther than that, just to be sure they didn't claw their way out.

"They love you, too. We'll make it a compromise. You go check, see if they're all right. That's all you got to do. Just come back and tell me. Anything that needs doing I'll take care of myself."

Rocky glowered. Volcanic rumbles started up inside him. Digestive distress? I hoped.

"And all this will pay exactly the same as having fun. Right?"

"Exactly." I wasn't going to hand out a bonus because an employee did what he was told. "Come on."

I took Rocky to the abandoned house. I explained again. Rocky grunted, muttered something about if a man wanted a job done he ought to have the stones—*snicker*—to get in there and do it his own self.

He didn't understand. I was management. Management don't get its hands dirty. Management concentrates on making conflicting decisions and issuing orders with no obvious rationale behind them.

I'd make a fine manager. I had the example of my partner to emulate.

Rocky was gone long enough to get me worrying. But he did turn up eventually.

"Your dwarves ain't lost. You're wasting your time worrying about them."

"Why's that? And what took so long?"

"It takes a troll time to sneak, Garrett. And I didn't want them to know I was listening."

"Tell me." I sensed a disappointment coming on.

"They were talking about how to fix things up after they move in. And how to clean out the mess. And where they could sell some of the stuff that's lying around down there."

"What kind of stuff?" Evidently they'd had no trouble with the stuff that had frightened me. But, then, Kip and the kids had had plenty of time to change the whole lay of the underground land.

"Glassware. All kinds. And funny tools. And stuff."

I muttered. I grumbled. I groaned. That would be the Faction's laboratory stuff.

Belle or Saucerhead or somebody had suggested, in passing, flooding the down below. I spent a few seconds wondering about how I could get the water.

There would be difficulties. The neighbors would be disgruntled. And wouldn't be understanding. Unless they had unwanted big-ass bugs in their own secret basements.

Reassured about the Grinblatts, I went back inside the World. Rocky filled me in on what he'd overheard as we walked.

Rindt Grinblatt had talked himself into thinking that he'd stumbled across the pot at the end.

Friend Rindt was due some disappointment.

# 59

I snapped, "I swear by all the gods that ever infested this damned city, you people just flat refuse to be satisfied."

John Stretch's henchrats and Luther's workmen alike complained constantly about the cold. "Anybody see any ghosts?"

Headshakes.

"And there you go. Stop whining. Get back to work."

Shivering, John Stretch told me, "We have seen no bugs for a while, either, Garrett."

"Excellent! Wow! Look at me. Making good things happen." I turned slightly. "So what do you want?"

Morley looked offended. He said, "I hope your bark is worse than your bite."

"Sorry. Getting tired of people who whine all the time."

He flashed a mocking smile. "I came to say we found a perfect venue. Thanks for the idea. When the new place is up, dinner is on the house. Whenever you want."

"Wow." I smacked the crankiness down, tied it up wiggling and squealing in a mental bag that wouldn't hold it long. I pasted on a smile that probably looked like I'd borrowed it off a corpse. "Great. Good for you. Did you catch Lurking Felhske and turn him in for the reward?"

"No." Puzzled.

"Then how can you finance a new shop?" He'd been desperate as recently as yesterday.

"I found an angel who likes the idea better than I do."

Interesting. I tossed up an inquisitorial eyebrow.

Which he ignored like a pregnant girlfriend.

The question had to be answered sometime.

John Stretch coughed. He wanted my attention back. He said, "The bugs are sluggish down there now."

"You just told me—"

"Meaning they are not attacking anymore. The rats tell of a steady wind bringing hot air up and pulling cold air in behind. They have found many kinds of grubs and pupae. The grubs have distracted them. They keep stopping to eat."

"That's not bad. Let them get fat."

"Trouble," Morley whispered, looking over my shoulder. I turned.

Barate Algarda had invited himself into the World. And he'd brought a date. She was a pale wisp of a woman, five feet ten, thin as a starveling elf, going maybe a hundred pounds with gear and hair included.

That hung to her waist in streamers and fanciful braids. It was blond, so pale that in the available light it looked white. Her eyes were implausibly large and blue.

So heavily was she bundled that I feared she might be even more insubstantial than I first thought.

Furious Tide of Light. Sorceress of the most dangerous sort.

Had to be.

But such a forlorn waif . . .

I couldn't take my eyes off her.

I was not unique. Every man in the place felt it. Morley's breathing became labored, like he had run a long way to get here in time to embarrass himself.

Despite the magnetism, at first I figured she couldn't be more than thirteen. She had no apparent figure.

But she had a daughter older than that. I needed to remember that.

I lost the color of her eyes as she considered the chaos inside the World. But I felt them. Like I'd felt the eyes of great, deadly snakes when I was in the islands. When I caught it again they seemed to be green.

Saucerhead and several of his thugs materialized behind the couple. He gave me an inquiring look. I had no answer. I just shrugged.

Algarda headed my way after a pause for effect. Arrogantly confident. His companion followed a step behind and one to his left, letting him shield her. Despite his breathing difficulties Morley managed to drift away so he could get a clear line of sight. Carefully, not knowing who these people were but recognizing what.

Whatever their physical appearance, they have a distinctive smell, our Lords off the Hill.

I gulped some air. Then glanced aside. That gave my mind an opportunity to reengage.

I turned back. The frail frail had aged precipitously. Now she was a woman my age fighting a desperate rearguard action against conquering time. Her eyes were violet and my hunger wasn't any less wicked.

There's a puzzle for the great minds. How come one woman can inspire ferocious, unreasoning desire while another, virtually identical . . .

Never mind. That's a mug's game. If, by some wild chance, the boffins did find an answer, women would change the question.

The Dead Man would, no doubt, go on about unconscious cues presented by the personalities inside. Meaning that the same body, occupied by different souls, would conjure different responses.

Furious Tide of Light absolutely reeked of "Come and get it like you've only ever imagined getting it before." She could fog the minds of those statues of forgotten Karentine heroes that infest the government part of town. She might even make Max Weider glad that he'd lived long enough to meet her.

What caused an insecurity so deep that a girl needed to wrap herself up in an aura that powerful?

Strategically positioned between the Windwalker and me, Algarda looked around. He learned what he wanted to know in an instant. He told me, "The Windwalker promised your partner she'd help undo the mischief Kevans loosed down here."

"Really?" My recollection was, Kevans was behind the compliance device, not the robust bugs. With drool dripping as I tried to ignore the Windwalker.

For once the gods were not cruel. Tinnie was somewhere else.

A damned good thing there were witnesses. None of them more smitten than I.

Not even my best pal.

Furious Tide of Light had a characteristic I'd noted before in women who have that smack-in-the-chops impact. She didn't know what she was doing, which meant she didn't pay attention. I had a feeling she really didn't know much about the interplay between men and women. Maybe because she'd never had time for anything but what helped her become Furious Tide of Light.

Tinnie might ask, if she was so damned naive, why did she dress like that? Pointing out that the woman was bundled against the weather would be a waste. The argument would become something about her using witchcraft to inspire the response she did. At which point I would meticulously fail to declare that the entire female subspecies practices that same black magic. Some just get blessed with a bigger ration. Some were maybe behind the door when it got passed out. Or didn't get in line. But it's there in most of them, making sure there'll be future generations.

Which thinking didn't get on with finding out why the Dead Man had sent these people to join me. "Let's step aside so we can talk."

The Windwalker appeared to be considering the World as though it was something she was dreaming. She reached out to touch a curious ghost.

# 60

Distracted, I'd let the spooks slide out of awareness. Now I noted that all the nearer shapeless glimmers were moving in on the Windwalker.

Curious.

The woman said something so softly I couldn't catch it.

Barate Algarda didn't seem concerned. "Your partner being what he is, I'm sure you know the situation in our household. Try not to let your prejudices get in the way."

What the hell did that mean? I started to ask. His expression stopped me. We weren't going to talk about it. Over my dead body, if necessary.

I've had plenty of practice not judging my clients. The people I have to work with, or for! "I can do that."

"Good. We understand that Kevans is involved in . . ." He lost focus. A ghost had captured his attention. The Windwalker fixed on that same apparition. A pseudopod of shimmer reached toward her.

The Windwalker looked up at Barate Algarda with a big, glowing smile. She eased over against him, slipped an arm around his waist, hugged. He responded in kind.

They saw the same thing. And it made them happy.

The Windwalker shed a decade, or more, becoming the adolescent I'd thought I saw when she showed up. She could give Belle Chimes lessons. She bounced with youthful excitement. Algarda grinned, pleased. She extended her hand to the ghost. Algarda reached out, too.

For more than a minute father and daughter looked as content and happy as two human beings can be.

Their happiness conjured its object ever more clearly.

The ghost assumed a form that I could make out, a woman who looked a lot like the Windwalker.

I struggled to disbelieve. I couldn't let them pull me into their fantasy.

Work stopped. Everyone stared at the odd couple and their ghost, which had acquired substance. It joined hands with Algarda and his daughter. Those two acted like they had hold of something real.

Talking to myself, I muttered something about it might just be possible that my own personal freelance necromancer ought to commence to begin to explain what the hell was going on. Unfortunately, Belle Chimes was too far away to hear me croak.

Weirdness squared. The Algardas had themselves a happy ghost. Unlike all us morally upright twits who ran away from what our secret hearts conjured.

All right. They'd called up his wife and her mother. For both it was a reunion so sweet they welcomed the world to join them.

As their special ghost gained life and definition, the other shimmers faded.

Their ghost began to lose color. In a single minute it diminished till it was just another misty shimmer.

Neither Algarda nor his daughter seemed disappointed. The woman, in fact, had come to life. She was attentive and interested but had nothing to say.

Algarda said, "That was intriguing. Kevans really was involved in raising these create-your-own-specter things?"

"Presumably. If you visited my partner you should know as much as I do. Or more. He doesn't share his speculations with me."

Algarda told me what they knew. That didn't include the compliance device.

I explained what I was up to today. My goal being to get construction back on schedule. Said schedule having suffered ferociously because of the Faction.

Unintended consequences.

I didn't mention the compliance device, either. We had excitement enough.

The Windwalker touched Algarda's arm. He bent so she could whisper. Was she crippled by shyness? That would make her unique. Hill people aren't bashful. Most have ego enough for a clutch of kings.

I filed her timidity under "Be wary!"

There would be a lot of power there. Otherwise, she'd never have been invited into the senior caste.

I wasn't yet clear on what made a Windwalker special. I did know that what you don't know can kill you quicker than the devil you go to bed with every night.

Algarda said, "Having unskilled people down there might be counterproductive."

"Meaning?"

"You sent dwarves down."

"I did. To explore. Not to do anything else. Except get rid of any giant bugs they run into. Seemed like the sort of work dwarves are made for."

"Underground? Indeed. But what damage are they likely to do? In their ignorance and arrogance."

"We're all going to do some damage. In our ignorance. Because nobody knows what's down there. Which is why some people accustomed to living underground are doing the poking around."

"My point, sir. We don't know. Best guess would be, the thing down there is just stirring in its sleep."

"Sure." My sources all agreed.

"So suppose you wake it all the way up? And it's as cranky as you are when they make you roll out before you're ready."

Who had been poking around inside whose head, back at the house? "I'm open to suggestions. Remembering that my job is to get this place slapped together with as little trouble as I can manage."

New trouble, however, had arrived already. In the form of that frail blonde. All work had stopped. The roofers had come inside to check her out. Most of the men didn't pretend to do anything but drool.

"Hang on a minute." I moved over to Belle Chimes. Another stricken zombie. "Bill, wake up. Pull your eyes in. Pass this word. She's off the Hill. Out of the inner circle." I didn't know that but it sounded good. And it for sure got his attention. He got those eyes they say are big as saucers. "Goes by Furious Tide of Light." All making the point that she was someone you didn't want to irritate. Which Belle seemed to have gotten in spades. He flat-out turned scared.

Interesting.

The effect was salutary once Belle started whispering. Though the workmen did not deny themselves the occasional hungry look.

Saucerhead proved himself smarter than he looked. "I got a fire going in the shack now, Garrett. You might take these folks out there. Be easier on everybody."

# 61

We decided that Barate Algarda and his daughter should follow the trail blazed by Rocky and the dwarves. They would go poke around the Faction clubhouse. They would evict the dwarves unless Rindt Grinblatt could show that he had done something especially useful.

They headed for the abandoned house, needing no guide. I stood around enjoying the fact that the snowfall consisted of fat, random globs that were not accumulating. If this kept up I shouldn't have to do any shoveling.

Most excellent.

"You have no idea how lucky you are," Morley Dotes told me. As I considered Furious Tide of Light through the aforementioned random flakes.

"Sir?"

"If Tinnie saw you come out of that shack, with that woman, with that look on your face . . ."

"That woman, with her father right there?"

"You honestly think that would make a difference?"

"Maybe." If a brace of nuns had been in there, too. "She's growing up. We both are." Me whistling past the graveyard.

He gazed the direction I did. "Pity I'm single. Pity you're not."

He must not have gotten the word. "You know who she is?"

"I'm sure you're going to scare me off by telling me."

"She goes by Furious Tide of Light."

It took a second. People off the Hill seldom cross his path as objects of amorous intent.

Him turning off the interest was like a lantern damping down. "You had to tell me."

"You're my bestest pal. I don't want to see you turned into a big old hairy-ass hoppy toad."

"You had to tell me. So. Why is a Hill-type bundle of heat getting heads-together with you?"

"She has a daughter. A teenager. One of the kids whose experiments blessed us with the giant bugs." There weren't any of those around right then. "She wants to make sure the kid is covered."

"Typical." He frowned at something behind me. I heard the measured clop-clop of a team approaching, along with the rattle of iron rims on cobblestones.

I turned mainly because Morley looked like he dearly hoped I wouldn't.

I knew that big black coach. I'd ridden in it. I recognized the men up there on the driver's seat. I didn't know the footmen running at the corners but I knew their type. "Now, what would she be doing here?"

"She," being Belinda Contague.

Belinda was not a complication I needed. Ever, anymore.

Belinda didn't necessarily share my attitude.

It can be tough to argue with Miss Contague.

Morley isn't often at a loss for words. He made an exception now. He stumbled around, hunting for a plausible answer. Failed. Decided to try the truth. "She's my angel. She's providing my financing."

"You know what you're doing?" Getting involved with the Contagues wouldn't bolster his reputation. His places have always been neutral territory. Whoever you are, whatever your associations or alliances, you don't have to worry about your back. Morley will watch it.

"I hope so, Garrett. It's supposed to be a straight-up deal. Front money for forty percent of the net. If word doesn't get around I can keep it the way it's always been."

He wasn't convinced, though. He could see what I saw. Right here, right now, there were nine people who knew something was up. I could trust me not to speculate with my friends. But how about those footmen and the guys up on the coach? What about the dark lady herself?

How many times had Belinda tried to make it look like I'd sold out and was on the Outfit's payroll?

Only plus I could see was, Belinda had no reason to cut Morley down. She saw a chance to get a piece of a lucrative business.

Hell, I could see a whole row of small businesses popping up if the World itself took off.

If, maybe, Heather Soames came up with some stage talent that wasn't all amateur wannabe.

No point me going on at Morley about it. He'd still be busy debating with himself.

I couldn't fathom his reasoning. Unless he was in truly bad odor with his debts everywhere else. He'd explain. Someday. Maybe.

Belinda Contague descended from the coach. She was beautiful, her skin pale as death, her lips painted scarlet, her hair uncovered, black and glossy as a raven's wing. The rest couldn't be cataloged because she was in winter dress. But, believe me, it was outstanding. I'd seen it all. And still regretted my weakness.

It gave her the idea she had a claim.

She beckoned.

I looked around to see who might watch me talking to the daughter of death.

Morley said, "You don't have to tag along."

"That summons included both of us. I'm on thin ice with her already. I'm not going to set her off. If she's in one of her moods."

Belinda is crazy. Psycho killer crazy. Masking it with intelligence and beauty. In a rational world they'd keep her in a cage without a door. Instead, she's the overlord of the syndicate that manages organized crime. She has at her disposal any tool needful to indulge any whim her madness tosses up.

"What have I told you about avoiding women crazier than you are?"

"Hard to remember in the heat of the moment, sometimes."

"But you're unafraid. Fearless Garrett, champion of the disenfranchised and downtrodden."

"That's me. Absolutely. Lately having developed enough bruises to suspect there's no need to push for another unnecessary round of hurt." When it only takes a touch of manners to avoid the pain.

Morley gave me a look that told me I was so full of it my baby blues had just turned brown. But he didn't pursue it. For now. We were too near the dire woman.

He was out in the wild and woolly himself, setting himself up to grab what might be the stinky end of a deal with the Outfit.

Belinda smiled. There might even have been some warmth behind the surface pretense. She's always had a feeling for me. I've saved her from herself several times. Unfortunately, she isn't the sort to let sentiment get in the way at throat-cutting time.

That's part of what makes the woman scary. The fact that the machinery inside her noggin doesn't work like anybody else's. You never know what might set her off.

She uses that, of course. Like a sledgehammer.

And she has a few fears of her own. Especially Deal Relway. The Outfit has traditionally shaped law enforcement with carrot and stick. An incorruptible like the Director is one man. He could be removed if he became too obnoxious.

But Relway won't let that happen.

Several dim candle baddies have gotten the Director stuck in their craws already. They all choked on him when they tried to swallow.

They overlooked the fact that he has a bigger gang and is as ruthless as any of them.

Civil and conversational, I asked, "What brings you to the wicked part of town?"

"Bad boys. You know how I love them." She sneered at my queasy look. "Not to worry. You're not on the spot. I came to look at my new investment." She touched my arm in an intimate way. I managed not to flinch. "I'm looking for legitimate ventures." Big smile. "This will be my first."

I didn't disagree. But the Combine does have interests in a lot of legitimate businesses. They force their way into some. On the other hand, whatever he pretends to the world at large, Morley is not entirely legit. He wouldn't keep the company he does if he were.

Belinda made me sweat with her too-friendly gestures on a public street. While Morley pointed out the place he had chosen and explained why it was perfect for serving the theater crowd. Then Belinda let me off the hook. "Just messing with you, sweetheart. I know Tinnie won the race."

"Uh . . ." All right. That would work. For now.

"I couldn't live with myself if it turned out to be my fault all that planning went to waste."

"Huh?" Conscience? Didn't know she knew the word. Decided not to ask if she knew its meaning.

"Not to worry, buddy. All you have to do is show up, on time, sober enough to stand, without a date."

My best pal looked at me like I'd sprouted a facial toadstool. A psychedelic toadstool, from the magnitude of his double take.

The beautiful woman unacquainted with mercy laughed. She headed for the place Morley had indicated. I retreated to the theater side of the street. Where I found Puddle and Morley's other man considering their boss nervously. Puddle said, "I don't like dis, Garrett. I don' like it a'tall."

"Got me a little less than excited, too, Puddle. Makes me wonder what's happening inside his head." But that wasn't my problem. The World was. I needed to concentrate on that. I was making some headway. At last.

# 62

I didn't get back in out of the snow. Pular Singe materialized, breathless. "I know where he is! I know how to
catch him!"

"Great! Good for you, girl. Go! What're you talking
about? What're you doing down here?" Since she hadn't
had anything to do with her brother's latest efforts.

"Oh. I had some stuff I needed to do. But I finished. I
can help you here now. Oh. There's Mr. Dotes. I'd better
tell him right away."

"Tell him what?"

But she was gone. And Puddle was looking at me like
he was trying to figure something out. He asked, "Dis ain't
gonna turn rotten on us, is it, Garrett?"

Uncertain what his "this" might be, I went for reassurance. "I don't think so. Though I don't really know what
Morley is thinking, any more than you do. Nothing to do
with me, I'm pretty sure."

That part seemed to be what Puddle wanted to hear.
Better his boss was hobnobbing with the queen of crime
than getting into something with that Garrett guy.

I'm never quite sure what the problem is for those people. Like women, they think I ought to know without
being told.

I went inside.

Despite the open doorways it was much warmer in there
than out front.

John Stretch spotted me, beckoned. He looked smugly
pleased. I went to find out why.

The lord of the ratmen indicated the under-stage pit.

It was filthy with bug scraps. The Rocker himself had returned to his station. He no longer had anything to do.

"All right. It's a mess. But that isn't it. Is it?"

"No. It is that there are no more bugs coming. The rats are finding very few down below now, too. Just grubs. The burned-out rats come up carrying them. Carrying food back to the nest."

"Good. That's good."

"It is an instinct thing."

"That's good."

"I have enough of them back out now to get a feel for the way it is down there. I am going to examine them."

"By all means. That's excellent." Then, fearing he might think I was being patronizing, "Maybe that'll give us enough to get this part wrapped up."

So, then, the ghosts. Once the spooks were settled my job would be done.

I could hope. I could pray. Knowing prayer would set them to howling in the heavenly jakes. Nothing could work out that well. Hell, this had been going on for days. I hadn't gotten my head kicked in once—though the Stompers did have that on their agenda. I'd received no death threats meant to scare me off. I'd run into no villainy that couldn't be explained by simple stupidity. There'd been a corpse, or two—one barely qualifying as negligent homicide.

I did my damnedest not to invite recompense for hubris.

Pular Singe scooted in, all flustered, whiskers flaring, ears folded back. "You have to stop them!"

All right. Maybe I could do that. Given something to go on.

Singe took a moment out of her excitement to greet her brother, who waved vaguely because he was communing with some of his unmodified cousins.

Sort of ironic. The sorcerous by-blow of a prior century trying to exterminate those of the present.

Singe reclaimed the frenzy. "I am afraid one of them will do something neither will be able to take back."

I thought I got that. "Ease up, girl. Who? What? Where? Basic stuff like that."

"Oh. Yes. That. All right. Mr. Dotes. Miss Contague. They are having a huge fight. It started after I told Mr. Dotes that the stinking man is out there watching and I think I know how to catch him."

One eyebrow up and the other eye squinting because she isn't usually so formal, I wondered, "Why would they argue? Does Lurking Felhske work for Belinda?"

"Oh. No. Mr. Dotes decided he would not need Miss Contague's financial assistance after all. Since he was about to come into a large sum by selling the stinking man."

"And, naturally, he didn't have Lurking Felhske in the bag when he decided that."

"Correct."

Counting chickens. I couldn't do anything but shake my head. That was so unlike Morley, the born-again pragmatic realist. Had he caught something from Winger? Or maybe a Saucerhead with a hangover having an especially feeble-minded morning after one of his periodic breakups? No way. Not the count of cool, Morley Dotes.

"Stay with John Stretch. See if he reports anything we can use right now." I headed out fast, worried that I had made a lethal mistake by not staying with Morley and Belinda. How could Morley have abandoned basic common sense? Nobody gets into a pissing contest with Belinda Contague. She'll whack your pisser off and make you feed it to the hogs.

Puddle and the unnamed henchman were still shuffling around in the cold out front, feeling much put upon by their captain. Puddle had the look of a lost four-year-old. As I passed them I said, "Come on. Sounds like Morley has done something stupid. We might have to bail him out."

Right. If it came to knuckles and head-bashing, Belinda only had her big, healthy six to our seriously-out-of-shape three.

Belinda's bunch were standing around sharing hot tea and bullshit with Saucerhead's crew like they were old pals. Which they might be. It's a big city but guys in similar rackets tend to know each other.

I slowed to what I hoped would appear to be a disinterested pace as I went by. I exchanged good-natured insults with Belinda's chief driver, who hated me for the luck I'd had. The four footmen didn't bother to check me out. But the final villain, probably officially Belinda's bodyguard, tried fixing me with the hard stare. I considered giving it right back. But that's an invitation to butt heads until somebody can't crawl away. I didn't find him scary, unlike some who had gone before him. Who were no longer above ambient temperature. Or ground.

I winked and got on with tracking Morley.

"That one guy is coming after us, Mr. Garrett," unnamed henchman reported nervously.

"All right. If it gets exciting, you and Puddle sit on him while I crack some heads."

The storm had passed. Though they still eyed one another sullenly, Morley and Belinda had not come to blows. They were talking business.

Belinda snapped, "What the hell are you doing here?"

"Came over to protect my investment."

"Investment? In what? You aren't part of this."

"In friendship. There was a rumor that you two were behaving badly. Thought I'd make sure nobody did anything stupid."

Miss Contague glowered. She manages that with a furious impact. It's the blood. You look at her and forget the cold beauty. You just remember that she's Chodo Contague's daughter, old Death on the Hoof himself. You recall times when she made her pop look like a pansy dance instructor.

She said nothing now. Nor did Morley. "Have you worked it out? Morley? You letting a deal float on your skill at predicting the outcome of a water spider race?" I tried giving him a meaningful look. No doubt he thought I was constipated.

Puddle, Unnamed, and Belinda's bodyguard hung out around the doorway, bewildered.

Morley told me, "I've got it under control. Just had a minute when wishful thinking got the upper hand on common sense."

Deadly calm, Belinda said, "He thought he could do business the way he plays at romance. He found me less pliable than his preferred women."

"Kind of the way the rumor ran, too, best buddy. Don't

go betting to a pair in the bush that you haven't even seen yet. When you've already agreed to play a different hand."

"Your metaphors are as feeble as ever, Garrett. But you are sniffing the right trail. I did let reality get away for a second. It's slippery, some days. I got a little overheated. Being an adult, I recognized the futility and got it under control. The tempest is over. You had palpitations for nothing."

He glanced at the group by the door. The boggled boys. Who really had no part in things. Useless.

Belinda nodded. Agreeing with Morley and, likely, with what I was thinking. For a moment I got lost in those incredible blue eyes. Then managed to mutter, "Gods damn! It's hard to be a grown-up."

Morley looked disappointed. But I'd gotten the point of his odd little speech. All was not as well as he was saying.

What more could I do? He'd made his bed. I'd made sure the sheets weren't bloody.

"All right. If all is well, I'm going back to work. But you two better behave. I don't want my best friends quarreling like street urchins."

That fooled nobody. Except maybe the witnesses by the door. But it let Belinda know where I stood. And my opinion, for some reason, does carry weight with her.

That had been explained to me, including by the man at risk here, but I still don't, down in my liver, completely understand. But I found out long since that understanding isn't nearly as important as acceptance with some things.

Morley said, "I'll come over after I finish showing Belinda what we're going to do here. Ask Singe to wait for me."

It was the kind of straight line Morley doesn't give up often. But I let it go. More of that belated growing up, I guess. Why go for a joke that belittles one friend in order to score a point on another?

Puddle and the others followed me. Puddle said, "Hey, Garrett. All dat mean evert'ing is gonna be all right?"

"I hope so, Puddle. I for sure never want to get on the wrong side of that woman."

"You said it. Anybody be dat damn foolish oughta get whatever he gets."

"Yeah." His remark brought back unpleasant memories. "Hang in."

# 63

I went back to the World. Losing my cadence for half a step, en route, when the breeze hit me with a whiff of incredible body odor. From someone I couldn't see.

The day, I noted, was getting on. Time flies, fun, like that, I guess. I spied Rindt Grinblatt and pack in the distance, headed my way. Brother Grinblatt looked to be in a foul mood. Though how you tell with a dwarf is subject to debate.

I went inside and found Singe. And hardly anybody else. A whole herd, excepting ratfolk, had skipped. "Darling, when you all do catch the stinking man, ask him why he's interested in me. Or the World."

"I can do that. Though maybe the Dead Man already knows. He had hold of the stinking man for a while. I think. But not for very long if he did."

"I'll ask." And Old Bones would withhold the answer, most likely. He'd tell me I needed to figure these things out for myself. Or the like.

I went to look into the basement. "Hey, Rocky. I'm going to need your backup in a minute. Come on up." Saucerhead and his thugs are good at what they do, but some jobs just howl out for a specialist.

Singe needs to get reconnected with her own culture. She has become too human. She was suspicious. "What are you up to, Garrett?"

"Nothing. But in about a minute a mightily pissed off dwarf is going to stomp in here. I'd like somebody handy who isn't intimidated by all those axes and chopping swords and maces. Somebody with a natural-born knack for making hairy folk stand still and listen to reason."

Good old Rindt, I suspected, had talked himself into thinking he'd established squatter's rights over yonder just by virtue of his presence. The sort of magical thinking that makes us think we "deserve," and "have a right to," something we didn't earn, just because we're breathing and happen to be passing through life. It's a plague on all intelligent species. I was born. Therefore, I have the right to pick your pocket so I can buy the bottle of rotgut red I want to curl up with tonight.

Lately, I've been seeing a new species of graffiti. Traditional Karentine graffiti is human rightsist crap. Or kid gang crap. Or "Ferdie Pins wants to get into Minnie Tong's cootch" crap. But the new stuff rides the premise that being required to produce, to work, if one would rather not, amounts to an egregious social injustice, inhumane involuntary servitude, and economic terrorism.

Really.

You got to wonder about the magnitude of the brass ones on a guy who could come out in public and, with a straight face, say that. I'd be inclined to give the man what he wants. But not feed him. Loaf on, brother! We'll dump you in a skinny little grave.

That from a guy who is almost allergic to work himself. A guy with a moral imperative to avoid work as much as possible. But a guy who accepts the consequences of his inactions.

Well. There went a parenthetical diversion from the everyday.

Rocky stamped up, providing the closing ellipsis. "What's up, Garrett? Better not take long. I'm gonna gotta get out of here in another hour."

"Those dwarves I had you check on earlier? They're going to be here in a minute. On account of getting evicted from under that empty house. Property owners can be such pricks. And dwarves can be so presumptuous." Rocky would grasp that better than a detailed explanation. "I need you to stand around looking like you're thinking about dwarf goulash for supper."

Rocky grinned. "I can do that."

Where were the Grinblatts, anyway? Dwarves aren't famous for getting in a rush but Rindt and family should have arrived by now.

And here they came.

I'd just started wondering if cold weather effected dwarves the way it does trolls. But that was silly. The hairy folk hail from wild mountains where it's chilly during the summer and there are recorded instances of snow falling during Midsummer's Night.

If this crew got slowed down it was because their hob-nailed boots couldn't get much purchase on icy cobblestones. And it was, for sure, cooling down out there. The slush had begun to firm up.

The Grinblatts entered, all hair, clatter, and attitude. Which began to change after one look at Rocky. Rindt shed surly with every step. Had he had a few miles to warm up he might have mustered a passable diplomatic smile.

"We kind of got distracted over there, boss. Sorry." He was awash in remorse. But Rindt Grinblatt just being aware of the concept was more proof that he had gone native. "Some people showed up and run us out."

"Those would be the owners," I exaggerated. "You weren't rude to them, were you? They're off the Hill. The skinny one is Prime Circle, though you'd never guess to look at her."

Dwarves can't manage the color changes we see in the paler breeds of human. Otherwise, Rindt Grinblatt and his lady would have gone white as death.

There was an event somewhere deep in dwarfish history that marked them with a dread of sorcerers that had gotten into the blood itself.

"Rindt, they aren't looking for trouble. They just want to know what's been going on behind their backs."

"You knew that when you sent us down there?"

"I did not. No. They turned up. They asked questions. I answered. That's how it's done." He knew. He'd gone native. "Now. Your job was to go down under and scout around. So tell me what you found."

I noted several people sliding our way, meaning to eavesdrop.

Then came Morley. Through the front door, looking like he'd barely survived a heavy date with a vampire.

Rindt Grinblatt was calm enough to earn his pay now. He began a detailed report. His family felt free to jump in wherever a point needed clarification.

It took a while. As I'd suspected, Kip and his friends had done a good deal of housekeeping.

Before the Grinblatts wrapped it up Belinda wandered in, curious. At which point I noted that I was now the only other one hundred percent pure member of the master race in the whole damned place. Most everyone else had gone off without saying good night. "Singe, you want to take Rindt back to the house so you can pay him?"

"Sorry, Garrett." She had been muttering with my best pal. "Previous obligation."

"Damn! Rindt, you go on back out to my house, my man Dean will see that you get what you've got coming. Damn! Poor choice of words, that." They were accurate but that lineup usually rolls out only where vengeance is about to be done.

Grinblatt was distinctly unhappy. He had a few things to say about my ancestry, incestry, and sexual proclivities. But Rocky was standing by. And Rindt was hungry. He went. Leading his family gang and grumbling all the way.

I hoped the Dead Man drained him dry.

Belinda screamed.

# 64

I'd forgotten the ghosts. They hadn't been much of a nuisance since the dwarves showed up. They'd faded, maybe because they were kind of used up. Or maybe the cold getting down under had begun to have an impact.

But now they were back and there were only two human targets, one already immunized by knowledge.

Belinda screamed. Her behavior baffled the nonhumans.

The shade troubling her was, to me, an indistinct, pus-colored shimmer.

She screamed again. Why didn't she just run away? That would solve it. Though the racket sounded more horrified than terrified. A distinction sometimes difficult to see. Stipulated.

I shed my marvelous loaner coat, stepped over, wrapped Belinda's head so she couldn't see. I don't know where that came from. Maybe from having seen a tinker do it to his cart dog when the mutt had a seizure.

It worked.

The shimmer faded right away. It tried to assume several familiar shapes. I showed it my back and hung on to Belinda till she stopped struggling.

Saucerhead appeared in the doorway. "Hey, Garrett. The drivers are here to get your ratpeople."

I turned to look for John Stretch. The ratman nodded my way. He'd heard. He went to gather his henchrats.

Belinda let me know she was ready to come out. I turned her loose.

"Wash that damned thing, Garrett. It's ripe." She looked around nervously.

"What did you see?"

Her honesty surprised me. "My mother. Looking exactly the way she did when I found her the day she died." Her voice turned chill. Her mother had been murdered. By her father, Chodo, the world assumed. For fooling around. A sport in which Chodo himself had indulged, regularly. Belinda asked, "What happened? And will it happen again?"

I tried to explain. Without being sure myself. "I don't know why people see what they see. Most get something bad. But I've seen my mother, my brother, and a couple people who aren't dead yet. You saw your mother. Some Hill types who were here earlier shared one ghost and brought it into focus so good that I'd recognize the woman in the street."

Aside, I said, "Good night, Rocky. Thanks for helping." Morley and Singe had vanished.

Belinda maneuvered to keep the ghost behind her.

Did it mean anything that there was only one, now? Why not one for me?

There had been a platoon of the damned things before the Windwalker and her dad showed up.

John Stretch's people moved out. Soon I'd be alone with Belinda. Not an eventuality to which I aspired. "Where did your thugs get to?"

It was absodamnlutely guaranteed that if she maneuvered me into any position where temptation could be laid on, I'd be drowning in furious redheads before the smoke cleared away.

Belinda mused, "I hadn't thought about that. Yet. It's a question I'll need to explore."

Really. She should have had six guys all over her the second she screamed.

She was herself again. "I'd better go. We don't want Tinnie frosted about us being alone together with only twenty ratpeople and a few thousand rats for chaperones."

"You surprise me sometimes."

"I surprise myself. I have these impulsive moments when I turn human."

She was a sociopath fully aware of her psychosis.

I meet sociopaths in my line. Most know their heads don't work like regular people's. None of them consider that a handicap.

We went outside. Belinda's men were gathered around

the new guard shack, trying to keep their bits and pieces warm. To a man, supported by Tharpe's crew, they hadn't heard anything from inside the World.

Curious.

I saw Belinda off, then John Stretch and the last of his mob, with their harvest of succulent grubs. It was twilight, the sky now cloudless, the night coming up indigo. Shivering flying lizards perched high above, disappointed by the absence of game.

"Don't got much use for them things," Saucerhead said. "Though their skin makes a damned good bootlace. But they help keep down the vermin."

"Really? How so?"

"How many pigeons you see?" Tharpe isn't fond of pigeons. Something to do with a strategically placed load at a critical juncture during a pickup game of outdoor passion at some point in the past. He won't talk about it.

"There is that."

"Silver linings, brother. Silver linings."

# 65

I went back inside. It was lonely in there. A couple of ghosts floated aimlessly. They weren't interested in me. They were too feeble to be scary.

I shut down most of the lamps. Thoughtful Garrett, trying to save the boss a bit of silver.

It was freezing in there now. I closed vents and exits that I couldn't watch directly. Saucerhead and his guys were good, if they bothered, but there are some slick operators in this burg. I didn't want any of those faced with too much temptation.

I had no real plan. My hanging around belonged to the category "Seemed like a good idea at the time."

I settled against a wall not far from the main entrance and thought about clunky music.

I dozed.

Somebody called, "Garrett? You in here?" Then, in a softer voice, "You're sure he didn't go home, Tharpe?"

"No, sir, Mr. Gilbey. No, sir. He never would've gone off and left the doors unlocked."

"Over here." I went to work getting my feet under me. It was hard. I'd stiffened up. "I fell asleep."

Hand on the wall, I looked around. I saw three ghosts, little stronger than heat shimmers, uninterested in the newcomers. The air was warmer now.

Gilbey and his niece stood just inside the main entrance. A nervous Saucerhead Tharpe filled the doorway behind, reluctant to come any farther. Gilbey said, "I stopped by to see what headway you made today. Looks like some work did get done."

"There'll be a full crew tomorrow. They don't show, they

lose their jobs to the breeds who tossed up that guard shack out front."

"We had a complaint about you pushing the workmen around."

"And?"

"I see some work got done today."

I took time out to be smug.

Gilbey asked, "What about the other problems? I see some things that might be ghosts."

I explained that we did seem to have dealt with the giant bugs. "For now. I'll be amazed if more don't hatch out. You know how hard it is to get rid of roaches."

"And the ghosts?"

I talked about that, too.

"Interesting. Answer me this. How do we make it so cold down there that we don't hear from this thing anymore?"

Heather Soames drifted off in pursuit of a shimmer that appeared to prefer to avoid her.

"I think we just need to keep the bugs off. It's been content to hibernate for the gods know how long. I figure, keep the bugs away and the cold run down, it'll fall asleep for another thousand years."

"No idea what it is yet?"

"My partner took over that research. I had a couple Hill types in here earlier. They weren't excited so it can't be something sorcerers whisper about or shop for behind our backs."

Heather caught up with a ghost. She poked it with a silver hat pin.

I swear, vague, pus-colored shimmer that it was, it began to sweat. Fine drops rained down on the floor planking, speckling briefly before evaporating. The ghost fled.

Then the music started. The zinc orchestral maneuvers. Bill had done a good job describing that clunky sound. What he had failed to capture was the ferocious volume.

It was *loud!* this time. The building shook. Despite the fact that the World was so new that it was still only half-finished, dust and dirt drifted down from overhead.

Saucerhead called from the doorway, "What's up, Garrett?"

"I think it's under control." I had to yell.

Meantime, Gilbey caught Heather and told her, "Maybe you shouldn't do that."

"You think?" Though she was stalking a second ghost at the time.

The music changed. A children's game song became pounding jungle rhythm. And got louder.

Its mood I could not discern.

I'd started to sweat. The place was heating up.

I got busy opening things up again.

Outside temperatures had plunged since sundown. The barking wind was bitter.

The music did not falter.

Finished opening up, I rejoined Gilbey and his niece. Beautiful woman, Heather Soames. Bright. But solidly equipped with a taste for self-destruction.

Saucerhead remained in the doorway. He wouldn't come inside but he wanted to keep track. He had his hands over his ears. For what good that did.

Then he moved, pushed aside. Barate Algarda and Furious Tide of Light had returned.

# 66

Algarda looked drained. The Windwalker could not have gotten paler without going albino. There was no guessing her mental state. She moved like she was ready to collapse.

The beat of the music picked up. I'm not a religious sort, except maybe in the trenches, but I spun off a poorly remembered childhood singsong prayer. By the time I finished Algarda and daughter were up close. Algarda made a megaphone of his hands. "What happened?"

I explained. He scowled at Heather but didn't put much power behind it. Beautiful women always get that extra edge.

The Windwalker poked him exactly the way Tinnie would have poked me.

There are a hundred thousand stories in the city. Most of them will boggle or baffle the shit out of you. That one boggled me. I saw what I saw but rejected it after a moment's reflection. Some things you just don't want to believe.

Algarda shouted, "Let's move outside!"

"Sure couldn't hurt."

Everybody headed toward Saucerhead, still standing in for the angel with the sword blocking the gateway to heaven.

Several ghosts wanted to stay close to Furious Tide of Light. But they couldn't get past her big ugly protector.

It was cooler outside. Also less noisy.

The music remained, hammering away without a touch

of silver to it. Yet with my new advantage against loud I was able to pick out a few nuances and chords.

It really was music, from a genius whose natural instrument was rocks.

Xylophone. That was the thing Belle Chimes and I hadn't been able to remember. A lot of that racket did sound like a big old clunky pot metal xylophone.

Barate Algarda said, "We can hear ourselves think now."

"But do we have to?" I asked. Twenty minutes ago I was planning to spend the night in order to live the whole experience.

My weariness was not unique. Exhaustion had a hold on everyone. Algarda and the Windwalker in particular, since they had started already worn out.

"Possibly not, in your case. However, I rather enjoy my thoughts."

"So. What did you learn from your adventure today?"

The Windwalker startled me, her voice strong for someone so slight. This wasn't the squeaky little girl voice from before. "We learned that nearly adult children require closer supervision than we thought."

I hoisted an inquiring eyebrow.

Algarda said, "They were up to all kinds of mischief down there." He shrugged. "When I was that age girls were the only experiments that interested me."

"And he hasn't changed much since. Which is why he's a running footman instead of a Man of Standing." Which was someone considered an insider by the community of sorcerers.

Algarda looked like he'd bitten into an alum-crusted lemon. This would be an old argument being dealt up fresh.

He swallowed. And let it go. "The oversize insects are a product of their experiments. There may have been other experiments potentially as embarrassing. We may have to twist their arms. They've done a lot to clean up and cover up."

The Windwalker said, "I blame the Prose boy. He's filled their heads with crazy ideas."

Kip wasn't my kid but I defended him. Obliquely. "To understand the Faction you need to consult my associate. He discovered some interesting facts about those kids."

The Windwalker didn't listen. She was too tired. Algarda would have to carry her home if they stayed much longer.

He told me, "We wore ourselves out over there, making sure their experiments don't create any more trouble. Tomorrow, we'll come help with the thing they wakened."

The clunky music shifted tempo, coincidentally but disconcertingly.

"Are they likely to go back down there?"

"They might," he said. "It's perfect. It's a good place for young people to get together."

"You want to keep them out? I could bring back Rindt Grinblatt."

"There's no need to banish them. So long as they aren't doing things that they shouldn't."

The Windwalker nodded emphatic agreement. Her eyes, I noted, were an intimidating shade of steel gray.

Algarda added, "No. We'll do some research in the morning. *She* can maybe consult a few of her . . ." He stopped. He'd been about to take a bite of the same sour apple his daughter had chomped a moment ago. "I doubt that it's some forgotten god who dozed off a thousand years ago and got buried in the mud when the river changed course." That was more sniping, but subtler.

The Windwalker may have presented that hypothesis.

Gilbey liked the notion. "It couldn't be a human god. The river wandered, back when, but its course hasn't run through here in human history."

In recent centuries TunFairens have taken care to keep the big muddy confined to the same channel. It'll flood a couple times a century, but . . .

Furious Tide of Light collapsed. It wasn't a faint for effect, as practiced by some young ladies of spoiled and self-centered status. Algarda caught her before she hit the planks.

Heather Soames said, "I'm about to pass out myself, Manvil." She sounded puzzled, though. Like she thought she shouldn't be so tired.

I suggested, "Let's all get some shut-eye." Which clever turn of phrase earned me several vaguely worried looks. But nobody had the energy to comment.

Saucerhead took hold and steered me toward his guard shack. He should've been more worn out than anybody, having been awake a lot longer. But he hadn't spent much time inside the World.

New problem rising, then, maybe.

A theater that naturally puts people to sleep. Not so good for people in the entertainment racket.

Not so good at all.

# 67

In the Corps they told us you can get used to anything. Which they proceeded to prove by sending us to the islands, where everything, from bugs no bigger than a pinprick to forty-foot crocodiles, and the snakes who ate the crocs, had people on the menu. While we hunted and were hunted by the Venageti who sometimes had the same taste. So a little remote midnight mood music from down in the ground didn't keep me awake longer than about eight seconds.

I had some remarkable dreams. I remember that. But I don't recall what they were. Not even the Dead Man could winkle them out later. Which he found more irksome than troubling.

Sunshine was sneaking through cracks in the guard shack's wall when Saucerhead shook me awake. Bent-nose types snored around me. The place was crowded. But that wasn't keeping Figgie Joe from cooking breakfast. "How you like your eggs, Mr. Garrett?"

"Just scramble them up. It's iron rations time. Something up, Saucerhead?"

"Me. The sun. And now you. You got work to do. I figured you might ought to get on it."

I listened. I heard hammering, sawing, cussing, and a lot more hammering. What I didn't hear was any indignant heavy metal music from way down deep in the ground. "I take it the whole crew showed up today."

Saucerhead grunted. He sipped from a mug of tea so potent I could smell it over the stinks of cooking and sleeping thugs. "You got your bluff in on them, Garrett."

I asked, "You guys have any dreams?"

"Everybody has dreams," Figgie Joe said as he splatted my eggs onto a tin plate. "You're gonna wanna eat fast. We only got four plates and four mugs."

"I mean really weird dreams. I had some classics but I can't remember them now."

"I get them kind all the time."

"Me too," Tharpe said. "But I'd say, it feels like last night they was more potent than usual."

I ate scrambled eggs that hadn't come out half bad. "You got a new girlfriend, Head?"

"When would I have found time for that?"

"Graziella, then?" Wasn't that the name that Singe mentioned? Something like that? "Somebody's been civilizing you. Figgie Joe. Decent job on the eggs, brother."

"My short hitch I was a cook. Division headquarters."

I raised an eyebrow. Figgie Joe didn't look like a lifer. And wasn't, of course. Not old enough.

The "short hitch" was your first voluntary re-up after you survived your obligated five. It lasted two more years. You gained all kinds of perks on account of you were there by choice now. It was a mutual tryout. If you completed your short hitch and still favored the soldier's life, then you re-upped for the long hitch. Twenty years. For the rest of your life, in effect. Troopers who survived the long hitch are only slightly more common than frog fur coats.

I never figured it out but definitely don't recall any shortage of lifer noncoms during my five. Of course, all the stupid and stubborn guys got weeded out by the Invincible early on. After that it was plain dumb bad luck that ended an individual story. That or getting too close to, or caring too much about, the new fish in your keeping.

I asked, "How'd you get into this racket?"

"You take work where you find it, slick. Ain't a lot of jobs for mess cooks."

Ain't a lot of jobs. Period. It will take years for the Karentine economy to adjust to the sudden outbreak of peace.

The Venageti, having lost the war, have it worse than we do here. The battles that settled it all gobbled up most of their nobles and sorcerers. The peace dividend down there has produced a crop of "flayers," unemployed soldiers who survive by plunder and rapine practiced on their own people.

I told Figgie Joe, "You surprised me. You like cooking?"

He went all shifty-eyed.

"I'll take that as a yes."

He didn't think his pals would consider cooking fit work for a manly man. I told him, "I know a restaurant guy who'll be looking for cooks pretty soon. I'll drop your name. Hey, Head. Are you on a mission for Dean Creech or my athletically challenged sidekick?"

"I don't follow."

"It's awful early to drag me out."

"Tough. I told you. There's work to do. Sooner you get on it, the sooner it gets done. And the sooner I got me a spot for one of my night guys to lie down."

I began to retail some routine protest. He cut me off. "Don't matter if you are the guy what handles the payroll. There's stuff that's got to be done. Sharing my guard shack with management ain't one of them. It's just a courtesy."

I started to hand my plate and utensils back to brother Figgie Joe. He gave me a hard look. "There's a couple barrels outside. The one with the yellow paint splash is for washing. Don't use the other one. That's for drinking."

Being management didn't get me a whole lot from these guys.

They were my kind. But maybe I wasn't theirs anymore.

# 68

"You all right?" Luther the foreman asked. "You look all blurry-eyed. Like you got the hay fever, or something."

"It's this place. You think it's bad when you're here working, try staying overnight."

He composed himself, conveying the unspoken idea that he wasn't interested in my whining. He had troubles of his own. He did stipulate, "It's quiet today. The ghosts ain't been taking shape. It's like they ain't got the oomph. Not one of these superstitious shits has gone bug-fuck and run out."

"Good to hear. Lets me know I'm doing my job. Remind everybody that those spooks haven't actually hurt anybody."

"Not yet. Not physically."

Luther would find a way to contradict you, whatever you said. I hoped he was a better carpenter and foreman than he was a conversationalist.

"Yeah. There's always hope. Isn't there?"

Luther developed a puzzled look that turned suspicious immediately. He'd been mocked before.

My tone must have given me away.

I spent the next five hours prowling the World and its environs, attracting unfriendly looks and unflattering compliments on my choice of outerwear. I hoped Mr. Jan's loaner coat wasn't some priceless sartorial treasure handed down from antiquity. Because I was going to have to buy it. There wasn't much left but rags.

Around the five-hour mark I noted that the dirty looks and unkind fashion reviews had become less frequent. And the men were working slower.

I felt a lassitude myself.

Curious.

Something was going on. But what?

One damned thing after another. One way of telling a story. And pretty much the plot for my life. I call it the barroom method. Starts out, "So there I was . . ." and you get on with it by inflating the facts geometrically. A trip across town turns into a high quest through the heart of darkness to put paid to the foul schemes of the Wicked Witch.

"What the hell are you doing, Malsquando?"

A principal subspecies of ODTAA is, somebody busts through the doorway swinging a blade, screaming someone else's name. Or, as in this instance, just heating the place up because of natural-born talent. "She had gams that ran from here to there, all the way to the floor, and a voice like juniper smoke. She was the kind of gal that could get a dead bishop to kick the lid off his coffin." That kind of thing.

But this redhead was only the forerunner of an invasion. They were all there. Alyx with the glint in her eye. Bobbi, breathing heavy. Lindy Zhang, in a cloud of smoke. Heather Soames, just exactly the wrong lady to be den mother. Then, tagging along behind, not attached, but looking every bit like she ought to be part of the wrecking crew, Furious Tide of Light. Looking especially delectable outside the shade cast by Barate Algarda.

"Hallucinating, apparently. Because I can't have died and gone to heaven," I grumbled.

"No kidding?" the redhead asked.

"Because they ain't gonna let your crew in there."

"I'm thinking of converting."

"Uhn?" said the quick-witted detective type.

"I could get on as one of the seventy-two renewable virgins."

The survival instincts that got me through the war had kick enough left to stop me making any noise. I gave Tinnie a one-armed hug and a pat on the fanny, then slid forward to express my undying devotion to Furious Tide of Light.

Alyx blocked my path. "I have to admit you're finally getting something done here, Garrett."

"I've got the tradesmen doing their ever-lovin' best just

for sweet little ol' you, Alyx." I eased around her to get at the Windwalker. Which whapped Miss Tate right on the knob of her jealousy bone.

Quick calculation. Did I dare ignore the Windwalker while I tried to hammer information through Tinnie's default stubborn disbelief? How long before Furious Tide of Light slapped me for the slight?

Inspiration!

It was my lucky day.

"Ma'am. Windwalker. Welcome back. Might I introduce my fiancée, Tinnie Tate, of the manufacturing Tates? Tinnie, the Windwalker, Furious Tide of Light."

That left the fair Miss Tate with her mouth agape.

It didn't stop the gasps and giggles of her henchwomen.

The Windwalker never focused on us. She murmured, "Pleased to meet you," vaguely, and drifted toward where the floor planking was being installed. The workmen tried hard not to pay attention. Right now she wasn't firing their animal instincts. But they definitely remembered her from before.

Miss Tate remained tongue-tied.

The unexpected complication now coming through the main doorway might have explained that.

Furious Tide of Light had not come alone. I'd just gotten fixed on her having shown up without Barate Algarda to hover menacingly.

A representative selection of our most dread, dire, Hill-dwelling types had followed the pitiful waif. A half dozen alert, glowering, ready-for-anything secret masters. I recognized a couple. The interior of the World went quiet as the workmen recognized some of them, too.

That whole mob belonged to a class that no rational person wants to offend, whatever the circumstances.

The refugee-looking hot thing was traveling with some of Karenta's more dread names.

Why? What could possibly interest them here?

Did it mean anything? Anything at all?

An amazing thing happened. A thing wilder than seeing people walk through the sky or seeing actual gods getting on about their venal sacred business. Both of which I have done.

Miss Tinnie Tate deferred to another woman after that

other woman had dared show an interest in Mama Garrett's ever-lovin' blue-eyed baby boy.

Furious Tide of Light planted herself in front of me. Because she was slight she seemed younger than she was. But there was steel in that wisp of a frame.

This apparent child was nothing of the sort. She could be a lot more harsh than could the quiet little girl who traveled with Barate Algarda.

Big blue eyes locked on mine. "Tell me everything. From the beginning." The Hill folk began to form a circle around me, laying to rest the concept of Mr. Garrett hastily relocating somewhere more congenial.

Not even totally self-focused Alyx Weider managed a word of comment.

No need to be difficult with these people. That could only cause me unnecessary encounters with pain.

I did exactly what Furious Tide of Light said. Kind of.

From the beginning. Editing cautiously. Just enough to shield a few most precious souls. Especially my favorite. Me.

John Stretch wouldn't end up having to explain his connection with ordinary rats, nor his control of the rattish horde that had, effectively and efficiently, finally gotten rid of the giant bugs.

I found it intriguing, having these folks on hand. In their presence the ever-opinionated Miss Tate actually held her tongue. Likewise, all her pack. But it was plain that the Tate woman couldn't hold off forever.

Tinnie had something on her mind. It took everything she had to hold it while I dealt with the Windwalker. But it would come. Not even the end of the world would stop that.

I was comfortable enough with the sorceress. She was an attractive woman smack in the middle of my favorite age range: alive. And those amber eyes to die for . . . I let manly appreciation override the nerves that come when I have to deal with Hill types who have no doubts that they're living demigods. Breathe a little heavy and those lethal attributes just sort of fade away.

Despite the volcanic potential on the Tate horizon, I leaned into the little bit with the delicious green eyes. "Who are those people?"

"People worried about their children." She didn't name names or offer to make introductions. Just as well, say I.

I gulped air. I eyed those people. Those were the parents of the Faction? No wonder Kip's friends were screaming freaks. Just standing downwind of some of these grotesques was enough to turn you strange.

I murmured, "I'm wondering who goes with who but I'll save that till later."

The weird people mumbled amongst themselves. Tinnie overheard something uncomfortable. She turned pale and started oozing away. That clued her whole crew that this might be a most excellent time not to be noticed.

She told me later that she had recognized a couple of names when they were mentioned.

Me, I recognized faces.

Some of the Windwalker's companions had crossed my path before, in little ways. I hoped they wouldn't remember me as a serious annoyance.

There was nowhere to run.

They began to pepper me with questions. At a glacial pace, with long, thoughtful silences between queries. I answered so honestly it hurt.

One was an old guy who looked like somebody had shrunk a big brown giant down to five feet tall without taking away any of the skin or subcutaneous fat. He asked an elliptical maze of a question I gave up trying to follow. Behind him, the main entrance stood open to the weather. Everybody would've been bitching about the cold breeze had it not been for the sorcerers. Then Belle Chimes popped in, looking his youngest, boldly headed for the visiting firewomen. He was four steps in and still under full sail when he recognized the situation. He made a strong U-turn without missing a beat and stepped out briskly, headed for parts anywhere but here.

A lump of indeterminate sex and execrable fashion sense, built along the lines of Rocky the midget troll, somehow left my besiegers and became an immovable fixture in the doorway before Bill got there.

Bill halted, heaved an audible sigh, slumped. The nemesis lump wheezed, "Look what Dierber found, Avery."

Dierber? Link Dierber? Firebringer? Frontrunner in the pack competing for the title of foulest of all the wick-

ednesses infesting the Hill? Not good. Not good at all.
Rumor said nobody knew what Link Dierber looked like.
And he kept it that way.

Avery, then, would be Schnook Avery. Dierber's companion. His partner in life and evil. His accomplice. Said
to delight in torture.

How could they be the parents of a Faction child?

I glared at the Windwalker, silently demanding, "What
hast thou wrought?" Because this situation had become
fraught with scriptural foreboding in a scant few seconds.

A tall, black-clad, pallid thing resembling the oversize
praying mantises of yesterday already tainted with the nostalgia of blissful ignorance, husked out, "O Frubious Serendipity! Years and years spent in the hunt, then we just go
and stub our toes on him. Ring-a-ding-ding Hello, Bellman.
Doesn't look like you're dead, after all." He used "Bellman" as a title, like Stormwarden, Windwalker, or his own
Night Whisperer.

Belle Chimes said, "I blame you for this, Garrett. It
wouldn't have come to this if you hadn't surrounded yourself with irresistible women."

A sentiment I've heard from the Dead Man, Dean, and
others.

Would that it were true.

"Get to work!" I hollered at the tradesmen. "You aren't
getting paid to gawk at this freak show."

Tinnie, behind Furious Tide of Light, shook her head
like she could not believe I'd just said that.

Kind of like the cat that just fell out of the tree I put on
my best "I meant to do that!" expression. And told my sweet,
violet-eyed Windwalker, "My turn. What're you doing? I've
got a theater to build. And we're way behind already."

"We all want to know what our children have been
doing." She seemed indifferent to the drama unfolding between Belle, Dierber, and Avery. "Tell me more about the
Felhske person. I find his interest troubling." Her eyes were
a businesslike steel gray.

I told her what I knew. It was close to a compulsion to
give her whatever she wanted. It was necessary to please
her. She might give something back.

And Tinnie wasn't there to thump on me, to keep me
focused. Then I exploded, "Oh, damn it!"

Behind Furious Tide of Light, behind Tinnie, behind the rest of the women, Heather Soames had become distracted by another opportunity to do something self-destructive. She was stalking a ghostly shimmer with her silver hat pin.

"Heather! Stop that!"

Too late.

# 69

The sound was like the low of the great mother cow in the origin myths of several primitive religions, complaining because she needed milking. Then the zinc wind chimes started. New ghosts formed all round. I saw bland shimmering pillars but, obviously, they presented intimate detail to everyone else.

One Hill type murmured, "Oh, excellent!"

The music grew loud enough to rattle skulls. As more ghosts materialized.

And the place began heating up.

All of which thrilled the Hill pack.

Belle Chimes made a swift departure while Link Dierber and Schnook Avery were distracted. Quick as he went, though, he came close to getting trampled by Luther and his crew. Not to mention Bobbi, Lindy, and Alyx.

I made hand gestures advising Tinnie to keep up with her friends. She replied, "You don't get shut of me that easily, Malsquando." She glared at my hazel-eyed friend. She was shaking all over but she meant to stand her ground.

Sometimes the girl doesn't have sense enough to add up to a penny.

Heather kept stalking ghosts.

That great planetary bray sounded again as she skewered another apparition. The zinc xylophone hammered out an even louder, more energetic tune. There was a tremor in the earth.

Dust and dirt fell again. There must be an infinite supply. Maybe there's universal continuous creation when it comes to dirt and dust.

The wonder folk from the Hill commenced to begin to fix

to get ready to start considering the possibility that they ought to get the hell out because none of them had a clue about how to stop the racket. Several, like Schnook Avery and his good buddy, definitely decided that the wisest sorcerer would contemplate future events from outside the World.

Where they got distracted by a row over who had lost track of the Bellman.

Then there were just four of us left inside. Me, Furious Tide of Light, loony Heather, and Tinnie Tate. Tinnie was not going to leave me unchaperoned, be the final trumps of doom themselves a-braying.

Which she paid for in good old-fashioned wet-your-pants terror.

I was having no courage crisis. I was too damned dim to be scared.

Furious Tide of Light snapped, "Stop that woman!" Meaning Heather. Her eyes rolled up. She went away somewhere, the way her sort sometimes do.

"Tinnie. Help me get Heather out of here."

Green eyes big, freckles standing out against skin gone dead white, Tinnie got herself going. My gal. Never panics. She had enough clever still engaged to get in Heather's way while I sneaked up behind.

I held on tight and managed not to lose focus because of the hottie wiggling. Tinnie pried the hat pin loose, flung it through the doorway. All the while snarling, "What in the *hell* were you *doing,* telling these people that I'm your *fiancée?*"

Uh-oh.

Did I do that?

"I don't remem . . ."

My survival instincts kicked in.

I was caught in a cleft stick. Nothing I said would be the right answer. And silence would be a loser, too. Again.

"Ow!" I let go of Manvil's favorite niece. "She stomped on my foot!"

"Which is what you're supposed to do when a bad guy grabs you, Malsquando." She stayed put.

To do anything, stupid or otherwise, Heather had to go through Tinnie first.

Oh, I'm so clever! Oh, I'm so smart! That saved me having to answer for minutes and minutes.

Heather was in no mood to be moved. Or subdued.

The two of us had just enough push to get the job done.

I helped herd Heather through the doorway, gave Tinnie an encouraging swat on the behind, then went back to give the Windwalker a hand.

Not quite the same hand. Though it was a cruel strain, keeping my favorite pair to myself. With her magic engaged that beanpole radiated sexual compulsion more potently than the wildest elfin girl. And elf girls are the lodestars of sex. They define the irresistible, compulsive attraction. In fact, the Windwalker so resembled an elfin woman that I was sure elf sap ran in her family tree. Not far back, either.

The ghosts were all over her now, tight as a gang of constrictors. And that didn't bother her.

I guess she knew they weren't dangerous.

To her.

Curious.

Furious Tide of Light had no guilt. Or understood the ghosts so well that she wasn't vulnerable.

I fought an urge to throw her down and make her squeal. I did go grab hold and begin tugging her toward the exit. Gently.

The ghosts felt the same attraction, I suppose. And they didn't need to show any self-control.

"Whoa! Hey!"

The Windwalker had begun making little noises. Suspiciously sensual sounding. While the zinc racket took on an urgent rhythm.

Then silence as we reached the doorway.

The Windwalker collapsed.

Outside, in a voice loud enough to be heard for blocks, Tinnie said, "You still got some explaining to do, Malsquando!"

# 70

Next thing I heard was "Mom? Are you all right? What happened?"

And, right there, right in front of me, closer than the stormy-browed pyrotechnical redhead, were most of my least favorite teenagers. The backbone of the Faction, including Kevans and Kip Prose. I couldn't tell immediately which of the others were connected with the visitors.

Excitement across the street told me that the escape of the Bellman rated beside the end of the world with Link Dierber, who showed no interest in the kids at all. Schnook Avery, on the other hand, wasn't much invested. He was talking to the kid they called Slump.

Somebody mentioned Felhske in conjunction with a failure to locate the Bellman. But that sounded like something that had happened years ago.

Odd juxtapositions arise because people with special skills are so uncommon. I needed an under the table necromancer? How many were there likely to be? Why would he be in hiding? Given his calling, Belle's reason would be a desire not to be found by someone off the Hill. So this would be a less fierce coincidence than it appeared at first glance.

I wondered what Belle had done to make Link Dierber go all bubbly when they ran into one another again.

What would Deal Relway think? Might be interesting to find that out, too.

Relway was likely to know the real story.

"Young Mr. Prose. So not good to see you. Your timing is impeccably awful. See the freaks squabbling over there?

You do? You know them? Kevans' mom brought them. To see what the Faction accomplished here."

Kip Prose had been through a previous quarrel with smack-you-in-the-mouth reality, as a more central player. He had one set of toes stained by a dip into the real world. He knew he wasn't invulnerable, immortal, or immune from the humors of beasts like Link Dierber, Schnook Avery, and whoever the rest of those people were.

Meanwhile, Kevans whined because somebody had gotten into their clubhouse and wrecked it. She had no idea of the real situation. None of the youngsters understood the impact they had had because of what they had been doing. They were playing around. The world saw the foundations of civilization shifting.

And everybody exaggerated.

"Kip, go inside, cut through, go out one of the back doors, then haul ass to my house. Take your friends. Stay there till the grown-ups sort things out."

"I can't. . . . I have a date with Kyra to go three-wheeling."

"Kip! Kid. You aren't listening. Look over there. With Slump. Those two doing all the fussing. The stubby one is Link Dierber. Even you have to know that name. The long, tall mortician is Schnook Avery." That pair were famous for their devotion to torture, to cruelty as personal amusement. They used their real names and didn't care if everyone knew them. They considered themselves their own law.

Director Relway would have them on a special list.

"The fat woman must be Shadowslinger. She kills people, eats them, and enslaves their spirits. The only one of this whole mob likely to give a rat's ass about you is Kevans' mom. And I wouldn't bet a wooden Venageti denario on her."

"Uh . . . you're wrong, Mr. Garrett. I know all of them. I've been to all of their houses. They aren't any different than my mom."

"Just go, will you?"

"But—"

"Kip! Shadowslinger is checking us out. Getting interested."

And still he didn't want to listen.

His friends were even less inclined. They hadn't listened at all. They saw no need to be afraid.

Furious Tide of Light backed me up. "Kevans, Kip, do what the man says, please." Over the youngsters, to me, she said, "It could be that I miscalculated when I brought the other parents. But I couldn't know that we'd run into that man, could I? Kevans. Sweetheart. Seriously. Do go, just so I feel more comfortable."

And still the girl wanted to argue. Of course.

And yet, so many do survive to become disgruntled old farts like me.

I had, for sure, begun to understand Medford Shale, my crabby antique of an only living relative.

Scary.

Life was turning around on me, big time.

Shadowslinger started toward the World.

"Get your ass moving *now*!" I told Kip. Adding a hearty slap upside the head.

You do have to get their attention.

I asked the Windwalker, "Who comes with this one?"

"Hard to imagine her as a parent?"

"Yes."

"She's actually the grandmother. Of Strake Welco. The kids call him Smokeman. And she isn't a tenth as bad as the stories claim. I'm pretty sure she's never actually eaten anyone."

"Smokeman? I haven't run into that one."

From a little bit of over yonder a disgruntled Miss Tate watched me and my hazel-eyed friend. I felt her nurturing her need to have Malsquando do some explaining.

Furious Tide of Light said, "This is the last time I'm going to tell you, Kevans." In the tone that tells a kid there ain't gonna be no more slack cut. Doom is a-comin' to town.

Kip and Kevans banged into each other getting through the doorway into the World. Two others—Teddy and Mutter—decided to keep up. They were embarrassed instead of afraid. I got no chance to work out which freakish adults were embarrassing them.

Shadowslinger kept gathering speed. I asked the Windwalker, "How did those people get down here? Two of them can hardly move."

"Coaches. In her case, a purpose-built wagon with the body low-slung between the wheel sets."

"Are you all right now?" I'd been amazed how light she was.

"I'm recovered. I had a dizzy spell." She didn't want to rehash. She picked up the silver hat pin Tinnie had taken away from Heather. "This might be useful." As an afterthought, she said, "Thank you for not leaving me."

"You're welcome."

The owner-operator of the hat pin was being harried into the coach that Alyx used, twenty yards east of where Dierber and Avery were burning out on blame-gaming the Bellman's escape.

The workmen who had fled had collected in two locations, each about a hundred feet from the door. The inside guys were with Luther, to the west. The outside guys were to the east, out beyond the Weider coach. They missed no opportunity to get some joy out of that.

Tinnie, especially, suffered a plague of eye tracks, top to bottom, and lingering. She definitely didn't want to leave while I was stuck back by the door, within snatching range of an intriguing, exotic woman. She stopped fifteen feet from Alyx's coach and glared my way till Miss Weider herself dismounted, came, grabbed a handful of red curls, started marching.

Such caterwauling!

Shadowslinger had covered half the distance from there to here and was still gaining speed. She bulled through Saucerhead's crew, indifferent to their presence. I had to admire her self-confidence.

The Windwalker kept making "Not to worry" noises.

Saucerhead appealed for guidance, by gesture. Though, plainly, he didn't want to be noticed by the Hill bunch. He knew what they were but would act if he was told to. He had taken my money.

In a manner of speaking.

We hadn't had an actual payday yet.

Tinnie vanished into the Weider coach.

A couple more Hill types got a notion to come chat with me and my new pal. Or maybe they just got caught in Shadowslinger's wake and pulled along.

I signaled Tharpe to let it play.

I wondered what Director Relway would think when he heard.

As always, his Runners and red tops would be watching.

Most likely he'd have me dragged in for a few intimate moments.

Furious Tide of Light suggested, "Let's go inside where it's warm."

"Yeah. And where we can enjoy the romantic music."

That got me a look. Not quite "What's this I stepped in?" More like "What language is this cretin speaking?"

"I can't help myself sometimes. Lead on."

Shadowslinger and the rest formed a scattered parade coming after.

# 71

We were near the edge of the installed floor planking. I considered Rocky's mess, down below. "Need to get that cleaned up."

The Windwalker told me, "This is a good spot. Keep me between you and the old witch until we find out where you stand. And remember, none of us are as bad as our reputations make out."

I had reservations.

Ghosts drifted our way, drawn by Furious Tide of Light. I couldn't quite get my mind around the differences between this woman and the Windwalker who tagged along after Barate Algarda. "You aren't twins, are you?" Her eyes had remained a steely shade for several minutes now.

"No. I'm a role player. Like these ghosts. Only I try to be what the beholder does want to see."

Did that mean I was in need of a kick-ass blonde who looked like a starved teenage elf girl in ferocious heat?

Clammy fingers brushed the back of my neck. The very sensation Morley had reported. Meanwhile, that creepy thing called Shadowslinger made an ugly silhouette coming through the doorway. Outside, unseen but heard, Link and Schnook argued genially about what news of the Bellman they ought to squeeze out of me first. Once they laid hands on, of course.

I decided never to forgive Morley for having sent me to the Busted Dick.

Furious Tide of Light giggled. She started breathing heavy.

Hopefully a reaction unique to her, here, and only when

Barate Algarda wasn't around. There'd been no panting or sighing when she visited with him.

What else might she do when her old man wasn't there to kibitz?

The clammy tentacle-touches kept delivering the creepy chills. Those ghosts loved me today.

In truth, they touched me only because I was between them and Furious Tide of Light.

What a woman. Even the dead wanted to make her groan.

The dead? Well, not really. Something else. If these were actual shades, Shadowslinger would be the one making happy noises.

I wasn't sure Short, Broad, and Hideous saw the spooks. She just kept coming, muttering something about her granddaughter. The Windwalker said something in one of the gobbledygook dead languages her class use to impress the marks. Shadowslinger barked something back.

Commenced a bit of back and forth, the old and wide sounding like a granny reprimanding people pups whose behavior failed to meet her exacting but ever-shifting standards. The Windwalker not only didn't back down; she showed no evidence of being intimidated.

I was.

The Windwalker was, however, unhappy. In an aside, she told me, "She's my father's mother. Berbach and Berbain are her grandchildren, too. She just can't understand why we won't do things her way all the time, whatever she says." Her eyes were an angry green.

"I thought she was the grandmother of—"

"Teddy lives with her. Teddy is Kevans' second cousin. She's Kevans' grandmother, too." And that was all the time she had to explain which of the Faction were related to who, and how, because the rest of the parents' club began to form up between us and the doorway. Link Dierber continued evaluating ways of getting me to tell him all about Belle Chimes.

Furious Tide of Light growled, "Knock that crap off, Link. We aren't here because of something that happened between you and the Bellman fifteen years ago. Which, from what the rest of the family says, was your fault, anyway."

That little lump actually shut up. The others did, too.

Amazing. Some of the ugliest pustules on the body politic ever. Walking nightmares to us down on the mundane streets. Apparently mostly related and all just worried parents.

Dierber sputtered suddenly, unable to control something that had to get out. The gist being that the disrespect shown him by the Bellman had been so egregious that the only possible response had to be orchestrated atrocities.

Schnook Avery tried to calm him down.

So Dierber had asked for trouble, had gotten it, had gotten the worst of it, and had carried a murderous grudge ever since. He wasn't the sort to sleep in a bed of his own making without complaining.

His spite had been such that the Bellman faked his own death and went underground.

I asked the Windwalker, "Who is Belle Chimes?"

"Link's brother. Half brother, actually. Link hates him because their mother always favored Belle. Link's father didn't ask permission before he got her with child."

More family nutso stuff. I'd fallen into the weirdest dream ever.

I was premature when I concluded that the ghosts weren't interested in Shadowslinger. It just took them a while to find her and connect with her secret self.

A phantom laid hands on. It took plain form once it did. Not a human form, but close. It had a face like an ape, but less dark. Its eyes rolled up in ecstasy.

Link Dierber shut up. Aghast. He stared at the creature enjoying Shadowslinger. Which changed slightly, I presume to resemble what he thought his father looked like.

I tried to ask Furious Tide of Light.

She made a whimpering noise. A couple of ghosts were snuggling her up again.

Shadowslinger suddenly cackled like she was auditioning for wicked witch.

Furious Tide of Light reclaimed her self-control. She shoved one of her ectoplasmic suitors away. She had that spook so blue-balled it didn't care who it mated. It clamped on to Shadowslinger, too. The witch loosed a startled, long groan filled with undertones of abiding amazement.

Schnook Avery, beset by ghosts of his own and definitely not in an erotic zone, began to ooze around Shadowslinger's left flank. I don't know what he thought he saw but he had blood in his eye. He didn't have family matters on his mind. He looked like he expected to have a whole lot of fun playing games in which the Windwalker or I would do a lot of screaming.

"Not good. The monster has taken over." Furious Tide of Light startled me by wrapping her right arm firmly around my waist. Then she skewered her remaining randy specter with Heather Soames's silver hat pin.

That got results. Loud results. The rattle and volume were overwhelming. The ghosts on Shadowslinger didn't fade, though. They didn't stop. They didn't give up. And they didn't run away.

Distracted by that horror show, I didn't notice that I was dancing on air until I realized that I was looking down at a troop of panicking sorcerers.

"Stop wiggling," the Windwalker told me. "You don't want to fall."

No. I for sure didn't want to do that.

"Don't tense up, either. Just relax."

Easy for her to say. This was what she did.

"If you don't relax it's harder for me to lift you."

We reached the high balcony used for managing the upper vents. The Windwalker released a long sigh. "That was hard work. You're big."

She didn't turn loose right away.

Me being me, I didn't get it till after the fact. Till after we'd both had a good look at what was happening forty-some feet below, where everybody but us was getting a great big "Love you long time." To thunderous, chaotic metal music.

The show changed. It became the horror fest I would expect to see with people like those down there. With Furious Tide of Light off the floor the ghosts lost interest in love play. Shadowslinger howled in the clutches of things that filled her with terror. Blood and gobbets of flesh flew but didn't discolor the floor or pile up the way Rocky's bug scraps had. Nor did any real damage accrue to the ugly people inside the scarlet whirlwind.

The sorcerers fought back. Against creatures of their own consciences. They danced with their nightmares. More or less.

To do the wicked things they do, Hill folk have to have their consciences and souls pretty well tamed.

Furious Tide of Light whispered, "Can you climb through this window?" Her eyes were a warm, inviting brown.

Two or three of her could do so at the same time. Easily. "Yeah. But why?"

"We're making our getaway." With eyes gone an amused, very pale blue. "Schnook has lost it. You're an outsider. You don't want to be where he can see you for the next several minutes."

I became aware of how crowded we were. And of the effect she was having on me. Which was too reminiscent of her impact on everyone else who got close to her, living or ghost.

Her green eyes offered an invitation. For after we were safe.

No cold bath being handy, I practiced my multiplication tables. Eight times seven is what? I can't ever remember. What's seven times eight?

I swear, that chit could read my mind. "I don't get many chances to be on my own."

Danger! Danger, Garrett! Deadly danger!

Disappointment. Abiding disappointment. I got no chance to test my ability to resist a temptation so fierce.

"Damn!" she swore, as I was worming my way out onto the roof. "How did he get done so fast?"

I didn't spot Barate Algarda right away. I was busy surviving a barrage of furious looks from my special redhead, who had escaped the custody of the honey pack and had returned.

"Some other time," the Windwalker told me. With promise like a forest fire.

"Yeah. Like you said. Damn!"

And thus I saved me the fury of a Furious Tide of Light scorned.

Still, she gave me a look that would haunt me.

And said, "Stand up. We're going to jump."

I didn't want to stand up. The World was shaking like it was warming up to star in an earthquake. And the roof slates were slick. But I did as I was told. Ever pliable me.

The Windwalker wrapped an arm around me. "This

would be easier if I wrapped everything around you." We floated off the roof, began a slow descent. "Think about the possibilities in that."

That would haunt me, too.

I've got a pretty good imagination.

How come I got to grow up?

# 72

"You got a guilty look on you, Malsquando."

"Because you're determined to make me feel guilty about something. Including getting away from bad people."

"I saw the way she was hanging on to you."

"Because I'd fall like a rock if she didn't. And I don't have the spring in my legs that I did when I was a Marine." Then, for no reason that I can recall, I added, "She's left-handed."

"Well, of course she is. Her kind always are." Tinnie didn't expand on that.

Elsewhere, though nothing but the music had happened, the human population had gotten thin. The workmen were gone. Saucerhead's team had decided they'd better keep an eye on the workmen. Tharpe hadn't gone along. But he wanted to. Badly.

Barate Algarda was having a discussion with the Wind-walker much like mine with Tinnie. But less intense, and, like Tinnie, reserving all the suspicion for me.

Furious Tide of Light had turned into the deathly shy wallflower. She kept trying to change the subject to the Bellman and bad behavior by cousin Link, and Schnook Avery getting "taken over by the beast."

It didn't take her long to get Algarda focused on business.

"Tinnie, godsdamnit, enough! This shit isn't about you!"

Miss Tate looked like some zombie horror had just come prancing out of an awful night. And he was me. And I felt like one. Almost.

The redhead is nothing if not flexible. She adapted quick

as a snap, with an absolute unspoken reservation. If Garrett was blowing smoke! . . .

The racket from inside the World took on a sudden new, darker note. Everything capable of flying took sudden wing, getting the flock out of the neighborhood. I was amazed by how many sparrows there were.

Panic even flushed a brace of giant beetles. They should've stayed hunkered down. They didn't make thirty yards horizontally before they enjoyed a fatal encounter with the cobblestones.

"And that's that," I said. "I hope."

The chaos inside tumbled into public. In the form of half a dozen high and mighties clearly stunned stupid and humbled, and all the worse for wear. Even from where I stood, poised to set a record in the quarter-mile dash to safety, it was clear that Shadowslinger had been bitten off by something that hadn't seen her as more than it could chew. She was all torn up, at least on the outside.

Link Dierber owed his pal Schnook a big kiss in a special place for having dragged his wicked ass outside. Schnook was sane again.

The rest crawled and dragged one another into the weather, not a one grinning over a prank well played.

What the hell? They had suffered a serious, collective ass-kicking. How? "I can't claim those ghosts never hurt anybody anymore."

After half a minute of silence the zinc melody pounded out a few bars of a sinister-sounding march that faded into dark echoes.

What appeared to be a young ghost, defined to the point where warts, freckles, and zits were individually obvious, leaped out of the World. It lugged a six-foot length of floor planking, six inches wide and two inches thick. It applied that to Link Dierber, then went after Schnook Avery— while bashing any of the others who got in its way. It stayed only a matter of seconds, then abandoned the board and fled into the World.

Odd behavior for one of those ghosts. Who seemed vaguely familiar, on reflection. But it all happened so fast. . . .

Total silence. No talk. No music. The concert had ended. The fat lady had nothing more to say.

Shadowslinger kept trying to get to her feet, kept falling back down. She had taken a truly hearty whack because she'd shown the bad judgment to be between the ghost and Schnook Avery.

Those of us stupidly still in range just plain refused to believe our eyes. This couldn't be real. This couldn't have happened. Those people were among the most dreadful of the dire, drear potentates of the Hill. Of all Karenta. Of the whole damned world. They were people who, collectively, the gods ought to fear. But Dierber was down, Avery was on his hands and knees and bleeding, and Shadowslinger looked like she might have lost the use of one arm.

"Oh, Malsquando!" Tinnie gasped. "This just turned into some serious shit." She doesn't use that kind of language often. "We'll never get the World finished now!"

That had begun to worry me, too. Max was going to be pissed off. He'd be in no mood to be confused by facts if Hill types started getting themselves dead on his property. That's never good for business.

Tin whistles tooted. Red tops came out of the woodwork. A few went chasing into the theater but the rest just rolled up, stopped, and stared at the battered sorcerers, unable to believe their own eyes. Not a one had any idea what to do now.

Not good.

They were likely to start hitting and breaking if they couldn't think of anything more practical.

Barate Algarda and I suffered the same mad impulse at the same moment. We shoved through the crowd, Furious Tide of Light moving in his wake.

For me, the sensible thing would've been to stand back, lean on a handy wall, and hope I wouldn't be noticed. Then maybe drift off somewhere, take an hour to enjoy some artificial courage. Instead, I just had to charge in there to try saving lives. Knowing the fallen, the injured, and the just plain confused, all deserved to be put down like mad dogs. And knowing Mrs. Garrett's boy would get blamed no matter what.

So here are Garrett, Algarda, and the Windwalker, trying to restore breath to the kind of people I always hoped the lightning would slip loose from heaven and find.

A couple of red tops got into the act, too.

It took only a moment to see that Link Dierber was beyond mundane help. The rest were all breathing. The uninjured three stood around drooling like the smarts bandit had picked their brains clean.

That old black magic.

Schnook Avery would need some repairs but he would live. He needed something for the pain and swelling, plus a few dozen stitches. No bones poked through his skin. Nothing was obviously broken. He offered no work for the bone setters or cast makers.

Shadowslinger still hadn't been able to get onto her feet. She might be hurt worse than I first thought.

Algarda said, "We need a healer. Fast." He grabbed a red cap. "You. Take this—"

Furious Tide of Light interrupted. "I'll go. I'll be faster."

Father considered daughter. "Are you sure?"

"I can do it."

"All right. Be careful."

"I promise."

She floated up. Her soles cleared our heads. She drifted eastward, rising, gathering speed. Her legs worked, taking giant strides. She vanished in half a minute.

I'd seen something similar before. But I remained as slack-jawed as everyone else.

Algarda muttered, "Where did she find the nerve?" Then he looked at me, oddly. "She's been acting strange all day."

Tinnie pushed through the crowd. She had an odd expression of her own. But she wasn't watching the Windwalker. Or me. She was fixed on the bloody two-by-six, lying between Shadowslinger and what was left of Link Dierber. The watermills of her mind were turning.

I began shivering. The excitement had worn off. And a breeze had come up. It swirled and shifted, playing among the buildings. It brought a whiff of potent body odor. As always, I saw nothing when I looked for the source.

Barate Algarda observed, "Let's not move anybody before the healer gets here. We might do more damage. Schnook. That means you should stay in one place and don't move."

Poor kid Slump. He was the only member of the Faction who hadn't run for it. He couldn't make up his mind what to do now. Hang with Avery? Cry over Dierber? Schnook made up his mind by grabbing hold and not letting him get near Dierber.

Dierber was alive, after all. But he wasn't going to last.

I nodded, told Algarda, "Good thinking." I'd seen that often enough during the war. "Where did you do your five?"

# 73

Furious Tide of Light returned in less than fifteen minutes. Like a proper witch, riding a broomstick.

But I was wrong about the broomstick. It was a coat tree. She had somebody behind her, a Hill type big on visual drama. This one loved black, starting with a vast hooded cloak that fluttered and flapped as the Windwalker hurtled toward us. Inside the hood was a bleached-bone mask holed for eyes, nose, and mouth.

What did it take to bring someone like this out, with complete kit? Black bags dangled from the foot of the coat tree.

The newcomer dismounted stylishly. He, or she, took the black bags off the coat tree. Furious Tide of Light settled to the pavements, dismounted, set the coat tree upright. It wobbled on uneven cobblestones.

The newcomer considered the injured. Triage with non-medical judgments included. Who got helped first would be whoever had offended the healer least.

The Windwalker floated over to her father. She studied our surroundings intensely. She was looking for someone.

Tinnie slipped in under my right arm. She was shaking. After a moment to just snuggle she began nudging me out of the press.

I thought that might be because she'd noticed Colonel Block among the onlookers. Block seemed only vaguely interested in me. Like it was only to be expected that Garrett would be part of the furniture at a particularly grotesque crime scene.

Satisfied that she could do so without being overheard, Tinnie whispered, "Garrett, it wasn't a ghost that did that.

What happened out here. I don't know about what happened inside."

"I don't follow."

"It wasn't the thing under the theater that attacked those people."

"I'm listening." She had an interesting theory. And I had nothing.

"It was that man you brought around. The one with the hots for Lindy."

"Bill? Belle Chimes?"

"Whatever. Somebody called him the Bellman, too."

"You have my interest, Miss Tate. On more than the usual level."

"That's refreshing. Finding out you can be something more than my boy toy."

"Can't have you getting distracted from that, though."

She wasn't in the mood for banter. I wasn't, myself, except as a distraction from disaster.

She said, "I'll bet everybody saw the same ghost come out after those people. What did you see?"

I described it. And recalled thinking the ghost looked familiar.

"Same here," she said. "That was Chimes. If he was twenty."

"Damn! Sweetheart, you are on to something. Dierber and Avery were out to get him. He turned the tables."

Maybe Belle Chimes wasn't the feeble bush necromancer he pretended. Maybe, when he was really stressed, he could regress his apparent age by decades, long enough to smash heads, crack bones, and get gone before anyone reacted.

I replayed events in my head. They didn't come together seamlessly but I convinced myself that Tinnie was right.

Could we prove it?

Should we care? Or even bother?

Belle's squabble with the Hill was a private matter.

I had troubles of my own.

I had to do some stuff, fast. Before Max and Gilbey decided that employing me created more problems than it cured.

I took my case to Colonel Block.

The good colonel grunted, with admirable timing. He was

both curious and sympathetic. Until I finished. Then he asked, "And you expect me to care, why?"

"What?" Startled. "That's what you do."

"It's hard for me to get excited about helping you do your job when you're always determined to complicate mine."

Tinnie chuckled. "You know what they say about paybacks."

Ever-maturing me, I stifled a query as to whether she might not be a payback herself. I told Block, "I thought you'd be interested. Hill folk are involved."

"I'm disinterested on account of those folk. They're all the time telling me to stay out of their business. This looks like an opportunity to give them what they want."

"Did I mention characters called the Bellman and Lurking Felhske?" I had, of course. "The Director hauled me in the other day because he thought I might tell him something about Felhske." Just a little fib, for effect.

"Deal has his own priorities."

Block was having fun. A twinkle in the corner of one eye betrayed him.

Or maybe that twinkle was about him having gotten a good look at Furious Tide of Light. Who was sparking a few speculative twinkles, despite the situation.

I told him, "If you sniff the breeze you can catch an occasional Felhske whiff."

While Block mused, "I've heard so much about her. First time I've seen her. Looks just like her mother."

Um, a little charge of nostalgia? Was there a history?

Could be. Barate Algarda had a hard face on him all of a sudden and he was looking our way.

Tinnie turned on some heat. Just enough to get Block's attention. He knew what was going on but he couldn't help himself. None of us can.

It's sorcery. It's the blackest black magic.

My gal. She's got the magic in spades but doesn't want to rule the world. Lucky world. She's content to cloud men's minds one mewling sack of sludge at a time.

The good colonel seemed fascinated by Miss Tate's hypothesis. The very hypothesis that I'd put forward just moments before.

Tinnie closed with a fetching pout. Block set tin whistle to lips and tootled.

Red caps came out of the brickwork. They sprang out of the ground. They dropped from the sky. Westman Block allowed himself a smirk of satisfaction over my discombobulation.

A few quick instructions and the Watchmen scattered. Except for the handful directly working the matter of the fallen and strewn sorcerers.

I suggested, "You might want them to know that the Bellman can change his apparent age."

"Timely, Garrett. Very timely."

"Huh? What's that mean?"

"I didn't stammer, stutter, or speak in tongues. As is your habit, you sat on a critical point till it was well past ripe."

Man, you hold out the teensiest bit on behalf of a client, once way back in the dawn of time, they hammer you about it till the sun goes cold. "Tit for tat, my old friend. I've got the scars and bruises to back my argument, too."

More than once the good folks at the Al-Khar had just plunked me into the deep soup to see how the broth flew.

"As you say, old buddy. That was then. This is now." Block worked his whistle magic again, using a different musical phrase. He was a bit more talented than the thing down under.

Red caps materialized.

Ah. Most were the same ones as before. So Block hadn't thrown the entire herd into the stampede.

After a few quick words the troops got busy pushing the neighborhood rubberneckers back.

# 74

I beckoned Saucerhead. And told one of Block's thugs, "Let him through. He's my chief security guy. Head. Round up your troops. You need to lock the place down before somebody gets a bright idea and tries to sneak in the back door."

Some of TunFaire's bad boys are fast on the uptake, swift to seize the day, and stupid enough to go for a quick hit on a Weider property.

Some did beat Tharpe into the World. Where, unfortunately, they ran into angry ghosts. Or the Bellman making his getaway.

Three freelance socialists were scattered over a quarter acre of floor, physically undamaged. Two were hard at work babbling, one in tongues and the other talking to his dead mama. The third was in a coma. But there was no evidence of any big fight between the sorcerers and the ghosts.

The thing down underground seemed content. I saw only a few indeterminate shimmers, uninterested in us. Saucerhead hadn't minded coming inside.

"Garrett. Hey. You got to see this." Saucerhead pointed into the cellar.

"What?"

"Couple guys who must have been in a blind rush to get away."

I joined him. Colonel Block joined us. The lighting was feeble down there. Most of the lamps had burned out. But I could make out two men who did appear to have fallen, possibly while running blindly.

One had hit down where Rocky's leavings were piled.

He still twitched. He cut loose a long moan that might have been a cry for help.

Furious Tide of Light joined us. Barate Algarda was close behind. She used her timid little voice to ask us to get the inside lamps burning again.

"Good idea," I said. Wondering where the hell the lamp oil was hidden. I hadn't seen any during my prowls. "There's got to be a better way to light a place this size." Then I jumped, startled.

A glowering Tinnie Tate had turned up. Evidently, I'd had some sort of glint in my eye while talking to the Windwalker.

I was too distracted to appreciate either lady. I'd been stricken by a fit of genius.

Need a better way to light a place as big as the World? I had the answer.

Go tell Kip Prose he needed to figure out how to do it.

That kid can figure out how to do anything. If you hand him the challenge in the right way.

"You're getting a look on you that I don't like, Malsquando."

All because I had my eyes pointed at a skinny little blonde while my genius was perking. I wasn't seeing the Windwalker, let alone appreciating the view. I was trying to recall Kip's comments about something we'd discussed in the once upon a time, long ago, while we were getting in a few minutes of time killing, hiding from some bad guys.

It wouldn't come. But I knew it was there. All I had to do was take it up with Kip, next time our paths crossed.

Where the hell was the boy now? Had he paid attention when I'd told him to go see the Dead Man?

"If he didn't, I'll go see his mother," I muttered. Reviewing some fond memories.

"Whose mother? What are you—"

"Tinnie. Darling. Sweetheart. Light of my heaven whom I love more than life itself. If you don't stop this shit . . . Do I come around, sticking my oar in and getting underfoot when you're trying to work?"

That woman is a multiple personality. Ninety percent of the time she is the absolute center of her own universe. But once in a while, if you crack her between the eyes with a big enough stick, she'll step back from all-about-Tinnie long enough to look at something differently. Plus, I got to admit, the personality she shows me is one I pretty much handcrafted for myself.

"I got it, Garrett," she said. "I'm pretty sure."

"Pretty, anyway." She might have a clue, after all. She sounded serious. And she didn't call me Malsquando. "So, thank you, Light of My Life. Now let me get on with my work."

A core problem was, despite her having known me for ages, from days when my chosen profession pulled both of us into far harsher, deadlier, and spiritually more dangerous places, Tinnie can't see what I do as real work.

She doesn't need to know, but I feel the same way, sometimes.

I do what I do mostly because it's better than working for somebody else.

"Hey! Saucerhead."

Tharpe gave up looking into the pit. He came alongside, courageously inserting himself between me and the redhead, apparently under the misapprehension that I needed help. "What you got, Garrett?"

"What I got is, I'm thinking I want to bail on this whole adventure for today. I want to head on home, talk it over with my motion-challenged sidekick, then get myself twelve hours in a real bed. Not to mention some of Dean's home cooking."

"I could go for some a' all that my own self. But my boss is a prick. Ain't no way I can get loose long enough to get some a' that for me."

I disdained any reply. I couldn't win.

He was laying the groundwork for some kind of extortion.

"Attitude, Garrett," Colonel Block said from behind me. "Everything depends on how people respond to a man's attitude."

Everybody I know, given the ghost of a chance, piles it on, higher and deeper. Fanatically determined to make the world's ills all my fault.

Sometimes you just have to walk away.

That's what I told me as I headed west, leaving the World and its miserable environs to stew.

No one else walked away—excepting Tinnie, who stuck tight. The rest all kept on keeping on, doing what needed to be done.

I was going to hear it from the Dead Man. I was going to hear it from Max Weider and Manvil Gilbey, too. I might hear it from Alyx and her smoking crew. I might hear a little something from Colonel Westman Block and Director Relway, later. I might get the random admonitions from Dean, Tinnie, Tinnie's niece Kyra, and even lovable, quiet Kip Prose. Hell, I might even hear it from my great-uncle Medford Shale before the final word got spoken. My acquaintances are a chatty bunch.

Let them bark. I had to step outside of events for a while. I had to have some time out to see if I couldn't get something to add up.

The appearance of the freaky families of the Faction might have put a new spin on everything.

# 75

Singe opened the front door as I was about to let myself in. I told her, "Look what followed me home. You think I should keep her?"

Tinnie shoved the back of her left hand under Singe's nose like she expected the ratgirl to kiss it.

An air of abiding amusement suffused the house.

So did voices.

"Do we have company?" Feeling stupid the instant I asked.

"Yes. Mostly to do with business." Getting in a dig, "You just missed Penny Dreadful."

No doubt because Old Bones told her I was coming. What had he had her doing now?

Tinnie observed, "You've really put the fear of Garrett into that little girl, Malsquando."

"I can't help entertaining a mild suspicion that Tate women are somewhere behind that."

Speaking of: A semihysterical peel of laughter came from the Dead Man's room. That couldn't be anybody but Kyra, Tinnie's apprentice in the arts and sciences of heart-breaking. What was she doing here?

I asked, "What?"

Singe told me, "Go on in. I'll let Dean know you're home."

The big, wicked grin Tinnie had worn while showing Singe the landscape of the back of her hand vanished. Dread replaced it. She was worried about her niece.

My Miss Tate was scared walleyed that the other Miss Tate might be just like her favorite auntie.

"Ha-ha-ha," I said, softly. "What goes around." I stepped into the Dead Man's room.

My arrival sparked a marked lack of hosannas.

I stopped so suddenly that my sweetie plowed into me from behind.

I was right. The airhead noises, still bubbling, came from Kyra Tate. Who had such a hold on Kip Prose that it looked like he'd never get away. Also on hand were Winger and the Remora. They seemed to be having a good time, too. There was a taint of beer in the air and an empty pitcher near every couple.

And Winger was letting her little man be himself.

Usually it's like she has her hand up his behind, using him for a sock puppet. I mumbled, "Must be the wonderful compliance device at work."

*Not so. These people are just happy. Good things have been happening while you were away.*

"Good to know not everything will head for hell in a handbasket if I'm not there to manage it."

Old Bones sent, *You have not had a good past few days.*

"There's the understatement of the decade, Chuckles. Take a peek in here and see how they went."

He helped himself to a big dollop of Brother Garrett's days of misery, sorting bits for processing in various minds. *The man is becoming melodramatic as he approaches his elder years. Garrett, these past few days have been interesting but do not qualify for a place in your worst one hundred.*

Melodramatic? Me?

Meantime, Tinnie worked the crowd, making sure everybody got a good look at the backside of her left hand. I snapped, "What the hell are you doing, Red?"

Dean forestalled her by bustling in with a huge tray way overloaded with finger food. Singe was right behind with a teapot and a pitcher of beer. My mouth watered. I forgot Tinnie's strange behavior.

My right hand was headed for my mouth, loaded with something made of meat and cheese tangled up around a sliver of sour pickle. Miss Tate managed a left-handed interception. I growled, "Hey! I'm trying to eat here. I'm starving."

"What is it that you don't see?"

"Huh?"

That aura of psychic—or psychotic—amusement spread through the house again. Sour old Dean managed a full-bodied chuckle.

"My hand, Malsquando. Right there in your face. What is it that you don't see?"

I felt the abyss opening under my feet but I couldn't help myself. I said, "I don't see why you keep waving it in everybody's face."

The girl has a little more tolerance for my density than I usually admit. She took a couple of deep breaths and counted to ten thousand before she told me, "That's because there's something missing, dear heart."

I grunted. That seemed safe enough.

"There's this man who's going around telling people I'm his fiancée. But here I am, totally naked of any of the paraphernalia. Not to mention, he never bothered to ask my opinion on the subject."

The abyss has no bottom. It goes right on down, all the way, right out of this world into others where men blissfully shove their feet down their throats. Would I run into some blind fool falling the other way?

I would've expected a little more moral support from my dependents. They *do* depend on me to keep a roof over their heads.

I began to shake.

The full flavor had begun to take hold.

"Look out, there!" Jon Salvation said. "He's going to have a seizure. Or maybe he's going into cardiac arrest."

Winger said, "He's gonna try to skate out on a bad health excuse."

I met Tinnie's eyes. I opened my mouth. Nothing came out. I tried. Hard. Though I don't know what I wanted to say.

Anything coherent would have been useful.

She was merciful. She pushed my hand on toward my mouth. Food entered the gaping maw. "Chew, Malsquando. Chew. We'll talk when we don't have an idiot's gallery kibitzing."

It took only a little of Tinnie having her own neck stuck out for her to back off. Some. For a while.

A reckoning was coming.

# 76

*Now that the entertainment portion of the evening has ended, suppose we consider business?*

I hadn't come home to do anything but stuff my face, brood about getting snakebit, and hit the sack. But, yeah, oh yeah, now. Anything to distract me from "Where would we live?" and "What about babies?" and "Just how much responsibility does a man have to endure?" Not to mention "Why did you bail on everybody down there just when they were beginning to pick up the pieces?"

There was a chance that these things were somehow related.

*A picture is coming together. Thanks to Miss Winger, Mr. . . . Salvation, Barate Algarda, and Garrett's observations. With invaluable contributions from Miss Penny Dreadful.*

"What? Come on, Chuckles. That street kid can't have anything to do with this."

*In fact, she can. As an indefatigable foot soldier in the campaign to collect information. That she was not there beside you, flashing ax in hand, when the World came apart around you, does not lessen her contribution. Nor does that lessen the contributions of Miss Winger and Mr. Salvation, both of whom have done yeoman work.*

"Mrs.," I said without thinking. "She's a Mrs." Winger had kids and a husband somewhere, just not in TunFaire.

*Refrain from retailing trivia. And it is too late for regrets about having walked away when there was still much to be done and seen.*

He had me there. Even trudging home, with Tinnie getting burned because of my sullen silence, I'd felt increasingly guilty about shoving off in the middle of everything.

And that just after I'd begun worrying about what Max and Gilbey would do.

"I had to catch my breath." Feeble, of course.

*Amusement. Perhaps. About Miss Dreadful. She is a reservoir of little-known myth and legend. Which I will share if you will relax. What is done is done. And there is nothing you can do about the other thing, either. Let us move on.*

I grunted. And considered my company. Was Kyra under the influence of something besides the Weider elixer? Why was Kip's hair such a mess?

*The compliance device does not appear to be operating. I can only suppose that the younger Miss Tate shares a genetic flaw with her aunt.*

A shot. "That's lovely." I shuffled in place. I had to do something. I had nerves so bad sparks should've been crackling off me. Tinnie just sitting there . . .

Singe chimed in with a total non sequitur. "Garrett, there was a message from a Mr. Jan. He says you need to come in for a fitting."

"Ha!" A grand new distraction. I'd focus on worrying about how the old tailor would react to what had become of his loaner coat.

It didn't work.

*Miss Dreadful had no direct—or indirect—knowledge of the entity beneath the theater. But she has suggested a possible legendary creature that fits the body of data that we have developed.*

"Which would be what?" He was playing to the full gallery, setting himself up for plaudits.

Startled, I realized that I'd only thought that question. The scary elder Miss Tate, looking rattled herself, had offered the verbal version.

Inspiration. "Keep an eye on Kyra, sweetheart. She's doing her damnedest to lead that boy into temptation." The kid was too young to get caught in the kind of cleft stick that had me squeezed.

Tinnie puffed up like a big old toadie-frog, turned red— then exhaled. What Kyra was doing to Kip was hard to defend even employing the most acrobatic, convoluted female logic. If there was malice. Though I promise you, the boy wasn't going to complain, either way.

Of course, he might be working a little magic of his own.

*No, Garrett. I told you. The compliance device is silent. And the girl is not deliberately teasing. Both are acting their age. Can we get to business? Please?*

"Go. Talk to us. Legendary creatures." I got to work on food and beer. Concentrating on the latter.

*We may have found a dragon.*

I sprayed pig-in-a-blanket. Dean barked at me. I ignored him. "No! You're shitting me."

*Not necessarily a dragon of legend. Not necessarily one of the absolute, lord of the scaly ones, slippery monsters of story. But an entity that fits the traditions, unseen.*

When I think dragon I picture a big-ass flying thunder lizard tearing stuff up and starting fires. Big fires. Kind of like an oversize, reptilian Marine.

*Not probable.*

"There ain't no dragons," Winger kicked in, supporting her boggled old campaigning buddy, Garrett. "They're whatcha-macallums, arch types. Symbols for thoughts. Externalized."

Jon Salvation beamed.

Damned if the runt wasn't having an influence.

*I said I do not necessarily mean dragon in the literal, mythic, fire-breathing sense. That creature almost certainly never existed. Put storybook dragons out of your mind.*

*Consider the concept of the deathmaiden instead.*

"Now you're getting way out there in the tall weeds, Old Bones," I said around a gobbet of soft white cheese. Pungent stuff. "What's a deathmaiden?"

*Also called a cairnmaiden. A custom your peoples have abandoned in recent centuries. To the joy of young girls everywhere.*

"Cairnmaiden. Rings a bell, sort of. But it's so far off I can barely hear the tinkle."

*Some of your more remote ancestors thought it was a good idea to murder girl children and bury them under the gates to graveyards, or at the corners, or in the entranceways to burial mounds, or on top of a treasure that someone wanted left undisturbed. The theory being that the spirit of the deathmaiden would be so traumatized and outraged that she would stay around and savage anyone who disturbed her grave. The reasoning may be elusive to us today, but the*

*fact is, everyone involved, including the murdered children,
credited the concept absolutely.*

The fad today is to bury a vampire on top of your
treasure.

"Kind of a waste," I observed. "Inasmuch as, traditionally, little girls grow up to be big girls. Why not use
mothers-in-law? You'd get more attitude, you'd conserve a
valuable resource, and you'd perform a public service."

Tinnie poked me. She was too busy eating to fight. But
she wanted to remind me that she had a mother.

If this relationship was going to go anywhere, we needed
that finger turned into a deathmaiden.

Winger asked, "What're you snickering about, Garrett?
This's some grim shit."

"Lady fingers," I said. "And that wasn't no lady, that
was my wife."

Winger told the Remora, "He's lost it. It's having that
thing get inside his head all the time that done it."

*Having that thing get inside his head all the time is what
keeps him as sane as he is. Garrett. Set aside your panic
over potential nuptials. The Weider establishment is paying
us a fortune. We have to deliver.*

A fierce glower came over my true love's face. But she
had a full mouth and couldn't comment. I pulled down a
long draft of Weider's finest. Which did little to ease my
nerves. "Could you share the reasoning that brought you to
such an unsettling conclusion? About the dragon, I mean."

Attitude for attitude. *I do enjoy a challenge.*

He had no trouble making himself clear. Where he fell
down was, because he was so proud of having pulled it all
together, he insisted on identifying every little connective
detail that only he had been in a position to jiggle into
place.

Bottom line was, according to him, in a time immemorial,
before humanity wandered into this region, possibly before
here was here at all—indeed, perhaps even before the arrival of the elder races—somebody buried something valuable way down deep in the silt, then plopped a sleeping
guardian on top. More silt piled up. Everything remained
undisturbed till the Faction started building bigger, badder,
hungrier bugs that found their way down to it. The ghosts

were the dragon's sleepy thought projections, tools it used to frighten threats away.

Bugs don't worry about ghosts. Their frights are more basic, animated by two drives. To eat. To reproduce.

I kept an eye on Kip while the Dead Man patted himself on the back.

The kid ate the story up. All Kyra's mystic powers weren't enough to extinguish his intellect completely.

You've got to admire a kid who can keep his head, even a little, under pressure from a female Tate. He said, "There's a hole in your reasoning. The ghosts only bother humans."

The Dead Man had an answer. He usually does. *Humans are the only sentient species to have gotten down deep enough for the dragon to reach and unravel the secrets of their minds.*

Nobody argued. Chances are, nobody understood. Singe snorted. I was sure she'd say something about all the rats that John Stretch had sent down. Then His Nibs would come back with something to the effect that he had said "Sentient."

"I'll get it," Singe said.

What?

I said, "Kip, I need to talk to you about a better way to light a place the size of the World."

But he was preoccupied. No way could he remain focused long.

I remember days like that. Some of them not that long ago.

# 77

We had company. More company. Only Singe had heard the knock.

Barate Algarda and his marvelous daughter, both with hair gone wilder than Kip's, added themselves to the mix. Which meant that they had to be brought up to date. And that they had to fill me in on whatever had happened after I'd left the World. I suggested, "You guys go first. Anything you tell us won't be half as hard to swallow as what's being served up here."

Algarda did their talking. "Link couldn't be saved. Slump and Schnook are distraught. Schnook will be out of action a long time. Broken bones and internal injuries. Shadowslinger has a broken arm and a crop of bruises, too. The rest suffered minor injuries. Belle caught them preoccupied with getting Schnook's beast under control. He led with a combo of stun and panic spells. Only what happened to Link was deliberate. The rest was collateral damage. Link has been after Belle for a long time. Belle must've had enough fear. Finally. It took forever but, like Schnook, the beast came out."

I glanced at the Windwalker. She seemed almost a zombie, interested only in scratching her head. She showed no expression and had nothing to say. Nor did she radiate any sensuality.

I asked, "Did Kevans get home all right?" Of the room in general. Since she wasn't present. But Kip's attention was elsewhere.

Algarda responded. "We hope so. We haven't been home yet. It'll be a while, too. I have to check on my mother, then make the rounds of the parents who couldn't get down there today. That tragedy needn't have happened. But Link had to start something. And now he's dead. Belle is going to wind up dead. The Guard are after him hard. He'll overreact again when they close in. And they will because they won't have Schnook sabotaging the search the way Link did."

He didn't sound happy. Who would in the circumstances? But he didn't sound like he blamed me for anything. And that was the most important thing. Right?

"He wasn't using Lurking Felhske? Link, I mean."

Algarda went thoughtful. He scratched his head. "He did try that, years ago. It didn't do him any good. I think Schnook bribed him to fail. Why?"

"Because we've had a Lurking Felhske in the shadows since my first visit to the ruin where the kids had their clubhouse. He was watching them."

"Curious. That would've been before we realized the kids were doing something dangerous. Felhske costs. None of us would have taken on the expense before we knew there was a crisis." Algarda went after his scalp like he had a toad in there instead of a flea.

Why was my sidekick leaving the talking to me, never so much as suggesting a line of attack?

"So. Parents wouldn't be running Felhske."

"It doesn't seem likely."

"The twins. Berbach and Berbain. They left the group. Possibly to market something the Faction developed." I glanced at Kip, expecting a comment. I could go right on expecting. He hadn't heard a word.

"I know there was a parting. It wasn't explained. With kids that usually means bad behavior. If they did create something with potential, Felhske could have to do with that. People on the twins' side of the Hill are a little strange and shifty."

He said that with a straight face. Then he grimaced.

His toads were getting frisky.

"Could Felhske have been hired to watch for a chance for the twins to get into the clubhouse and swipe secrets?"

"No. They could come and go. If they wanted. The other kids weren't down there most of the time. The twins knew the code spells to get past the wards. We gave Kevans a lot of room but she didn't go out much. Her friends hung

out at our house more than anywhere else. Somebody was
always underfoot."

Was that irritation? "Then somebody else who wanted
to know how to make giant bugs?"

"Possibly. Though I think you're feeding your suspicions
off your prejudice against our class. Even the sociopaths
among us don't want another disaster like the rat and thunder lizard experiments that blessed us with the ratpeople.
That kind of research is banned. No adult with a sound
knowledge of that period would plunge into that abyss
again. It was a close-run thing. But kids might. Their knowledge of history runs all the way back to breakfast. And
then they don't care."

Another peep into the Algarda family dynamic?
I wanted to pursue his remark about thunder lizard experiments. The Dead Man proved he was with us by nudging me away. He passed me his recollections of an era he
had witnessed firsthand.

The Hill folk of the time had done an ingenious job
covering up something far more horrible than their ratman
experiments, despite a rash of nasty deaths. Letting the
ratmen survive had been part of the cover-up, somehow.

I said, "I'll catch Felhske and ask why he's lurking. If I
need to know. Look. We've been kicking something
around. About what the kids stirred up."

I retailed the dragon hypothesis.

Amazing. During our entire exchange there hadn't been
one interruption. Kip and Kyra, Winger and the Remora,
Tinnie and Singe, the Windwalker and Dean when he appeared with fresh supplies, nobody said a word. Nor even
moved much, except to scratch.

I had an idea who to blame for that.

Algarda opined, "I find it plausible. In fact, it ricochets
off a theory I proposed in this very room, less than ten
hours ago. And got put down."

He'd visited earlier? And nobody bothered to tell me?

*It was but a rudiment of a notion at the time, unsupported
by evidence. It had to be developed. It had to be researched.*

Ah. Defensive. After only an oblique challenge.

It did tell me what he had had Penny Dreadful doing
today.

"Add this," Algarda said. "I talked with the family on

the way to the theater today. We have a collective memory that goes back several centuries. They recalled two similar occurrences, neither inside the Karentine sphere."

Wow! My problem at the World had turned geopolitical. And historical.

"I discovered four incidents," Jon Salvation said, with that snotty tone always adopted by the guy who corrects whatever you've just offered.

Winger knocked some of the brass off. "You and the girl. Penny."

"Yes. Well. Everything is in the *Proceedings*. If you can access them." Smugness aimed my way. The *Proceedings* must be something they kept at the library. "Though the most dramatic incident may be apocryphal."

I asked Winger, "You going to let him use language like that?"

Algarda considered a suite of responses. He settled on not letting his ego get in the way. "The two I know of happened in Oatman Hwy in 1434 and in Florissant about a century before that. Date uncertain. Florissant isn't a principality blessed with an excess of literacy even today."

I couldn't say. I'm not possessed of an excess familiarity with exotic geography.

The Remora preened. "The other incidents happened inside Venageta. The Venageti tried to cover them up. Both were huge disasters. The more recent happened on the boundary between their part of the Cantard and ours about two hundred years ago. This is the one that might be apocryphal. Local tribesmen were supposed to have caused it."

I grumbled something about Pilsuds Vilchik being worse than the Dead Man at inflating a story in order to focus attention on himself.

I'd later find out that he'd gotten into the library by confessing to be a playwright to Lindalee's boss. That harpy was addicted to historical dramas. Salvation promised her a complementary first-class seat the night his play opened.

He sneered. "You heard of the Great Roll-Up, Garrett?"

"Of course. It brought all that silver to the surface. Where it could be fought over for most of two hundred years."

"That was the dragon."

I confessed, "That *would* explain some things about how

the war got started." Better than any of the propaganda. But only marginally.

Algarda agreed. "That could be true." He joined me in awarding Jon Salvation an abiding look of suspicion, though.

I'm always suspicious when some dimwit shows off knowledge he has no business having. Or demonstrates skills at charming people that don't fit my prejudices.

What happened to the dragon? Or dragons?

*Do not push it, Garrett. The little man is possessed of several illusions that make him more useful deluded than ever he could be if exposed.*

That was a private message. An explanation would have to wait. I asked, "So, what's really down there?" The Venageti had blamed "the Great Roll-Up" on ferocious earthquakes. I'd never doubted them. "We don't want something busting out in the middle of the city."

"Dragons," Jon Salvation said.

"Dragons," Barate Algarda agreed.

Furious Tide of Light, positioned so neither Tinnie nor her father could see, nodded—then smoked off a violet-eyed promissory wink before snapping back into gray-eyed zombiedom, dully picking at her scalp.

"Come on! Dragons?" I glared at the Remora. "I don't buy it. It's a dragon, how has it stayed alive? How come it hasn't starved?"

"There are dragons and dragons, Garrett. Stop thinking big green scaly mean things with breath so bad it's flammable. There's no evidence that anything like that exists. But there must be a reason for the legends. And we see living proof of other legends every day. Hell, your place here is infested with living legends."

You might say, since I have a dead Loghyr, a ratgirl, a murder of pixies (pleasantly unobtrusive of late), and a natural-born redhead in inventory. Not to mention the world's greatest detective.

"So this thing down under isn't really a dragon. It just looks like a dragon, smells like a dragon, acts like a dragon, and thinks like a dragon. And might be what made people come up with the idea of the dragon."

"Exactly. Right first go. Darling, you haven't been giving Garrett nearly enough credit."

And they wonder why regular folk look askance at intellectuals.

Winger showed him a clenched fist. "I've got something I'm gonna give you. And it's a long way from what you want."

*Children!*

"Yeah," I chimed in. Despite both beer and exhaustion I was wide awake now. One sneaky wink from the Windwalker. That woman would never need a compliance device. "So. Not a dragon. But a dragon. One that doesn't need to eat for ten thousand years. Wow. Mystery solved."

Everybody stared. Even Old Bones, in his unique way.

"I'm fishing for suggestions on how to lay the ghosts to rest," I said. "I'm not the supergenius everybody thinks."

Those who had known me more than a week succeeded in restraining an impulse to disagree. So did the other two.

No other response, either. "All right. It's a dragon. How do we talk to it?"

The Windwalker startled us by asking, "Why make it more aware of us by trying to communicate? If the historical awakenings were all worse than any natural disaster?"

Did anybody mention that? I never heard that. Except by implication.

People still knew things they hadn't told me.

Something passed between the Windwalker and her father. A silent argument, the bottom line of which was that she was *not* going to be quiet.

Another bizarre angle to that relationship. Silent communication.

*Not the same as us. They are just close.* And, after a reflective pause, *But a gap seems to be opening. I caution you, urgently, not to yield to temptation.*

I glanced at Tinnie. "I don't think you need to worry."

*I must. I am at the mercy of human nature. Of which you demonstrate an abundant excess.*

Algarda got right back on his horse. "She has a point. The best thing that could happen would be for this dragon to go back to sleep. It would seem that they do sleep for geological ages."

Tinnie said, "Maybe they're waiting for something. Maybe they have a whole different sense of time and ten thousand years is like a few hours to us. Or maybe they're booby traps. Like for gods, or something. But once in a while some idiot finds a way to trip into their trigger line."

That's my gal. Escalating the whole damned thing into the realm of the divine. Me, being me, I wound up to spout something about the immorality of us passing our troubles to generations not yet born.

A dozen staring eyes brought the urge under control.

Me making the argument would be weak, anyway. The great philosophical thread tying my life together is, put off till tomorrow whatever doesn't absolutely have to be done today.

*The best course, indeed, based on the evidence available. Assuming we want to return to the situation that obtained a month ago. So we must do what we have been doing. Only more effectively. Mr. Prose.*

The formal address tumbled off into limbo.

*Kip!*

The boy yelped. And flinched away from Kyra. Betraying a guilty conscience simply by thinking he needed to open some space. "What?" In a breathless panic.

*You do understand that primary responsibility for events in the theater and its environs lies with the Faction? That it was your ill-considered experimentation that caused this dragon to stir?*

Being a teen, Kip was inclined to argue. But the pressure of the eyes was too much for him, too. "Yeah. I guess." He scratched his noggin.

*Then you and the Faction are obligated to make sure nothing you may have left lying around, or, more particularly, anything you might have sneaked out and squirreled away, in any way exacerbates the situation.*

When you're dead and don't have to pause for breath, you can reel off sentences like that.

*Do I make myself plain? Do you understand?*

That is what the gallery overheard. I was sure there was more communication on a private level.

Kip's surrender was meek and complete. I half expected the ancient formula "It shall be done."

*Excellent. Going forward from this moment Miss Winger and her associate will accompany you everywhere. For your protection.*

Winger received instructions on a private level.

*Kevans is partially responsible for this problem, too.*

I grumbled, "We already established that we can blame everything on the Faction."

Barate Algarda responded on behalf of Family Algarda. "Kevans will cooperate. Cypres. I believe Zardoz is the one who'll have to make this all right."

"Yes, sir. Zardoz and Teddy. And Mutter. And Slump and Heck and Spiffy."

I said, "We might see if John Stretch can find a few more rats to put down there. Just to ferret out any dead-ender bugs. Or any recent hatchlings."

*You might consider speaking more carefully in this company, Garrett. Miss Winger being no less dangerous than the Algardas.*

I might, indeed. I'd been focused on what John Stretch had said about the rats likely being unwilling to go under again. I should have been thinking about guarding his secret. Winger has a huge mouth. And no telling what Hill types would try if they got control of somebody who can master rats.

## 78

They were all gone, including Tinnie, who insisted she couldn't trust Winger and the Remora to properly chaperone two reekingly hormonal teens. Which made sense. The part about not trusting Winger.

I didn't remind her that she hadn't been much older than Kyra when we'd met. Of course, nothing more than a bad case of bugged eyes on my part came of that. Tinnie Tate was my good buddy Denny's tasty young cousin. Practically family. She and his sister Rose were both off-limits. At the time.

Times changed. Tinnie and Rose grew up. Rose turned wicked. Denny got himself killed, accidentally. Tinnie and I locked horns during the cleanup and got something going that neither of us has shaken since. No matter what distractions turned up.

I drew me a pitcher of Weider's most potent dark and retreated to the solitude of my little office. Which I share with the memory of one of my most potent distractions, Eleanor.

I filled my mug. I turned my chair. I stared at the magical painting. "What do you think, sweetheart? Is it time Tinnie and I go to the next page?"

The artist who painted Eleanor was an insane genius, slave to a powerful inner sorcery. All his work had been charged to crackling with magic. His portrait of Eleanor fleeing the horror of her past was his ultimate masterpiece. He poured bottomless love and hatred on top of everything else that made his works objects of such power and dread.

He's long gone. The magic in his work began to bleed

away the night of his murder. But its connection to the soul of long-lost Eleanor will never fade to nil.

The painting is never quite the same when I come to it.

Eleanor is my moral and emotional coach, crutch, and mirror. More so than the big lump in the other room. Who had troubles of his own tonight.

He'd had almost no luck picking brains. The most interesting people all had the split personality thing going. What he could read made no sense. The heads that were open contained nothing of interest. So now he was sulking and trying to work out what had happened.

Everybody, including my self-proclaimed demigod of a partner, insists that Eleanor doesn't exist outside my imagination. I'm content with that. It's even true, in its way.

Their truth or mine, Eleanor does exist. We communicate.

Reflection set some thoughts in motion. Like some multiple-minded Loghyr I fiddled with those while Eleanor helped me weigh the pros and cons of what looked likely to be Garrett's next big adventure.

I asked, "How come I always turn melancholy when we get together?"

She made me understand that melancholy was the price I paid, here, because the only person I could share my inner truths with comfortably was on the other shore.

I couldn't argue with that. Everybody on this side has the power to judge and down-thumbs me. Even Singe, who comes near being as comfortable as Eleanor.

Note that with me outside his little fiefdom the Dead Man didn't horn in. Not once. Might not even be eavesdropping.

Probably wasn't.

Almost certainly wasn't.

I've known Old Bones longer than Tinnie and almost as long as Morley. I live with him. I drown in him, sometimes. Yet I know him less well than my best friend or the light of my life.

Somebody came pounding on the door. I didn't respond. Singe and Dean had gone to bed. After a while the Dead Man paused in his ruminations long enough to send *Our would-be visitor was Colonel Block. He had business rea-*

*sons for being here, but his principal motive was a need for contact with persons not one hundred percent vile. A lonely man, the colonel.*

I had no wiseass response. In my mood of the moment I could only empathize with Westman Block, a good man doing his best in dreadful circumstances. "So what business reason did he have for an excuse?" He'd as much as admitted having rifled the good man's mind.

No doubt Block had expected that.

*The colonel foresees another twist. A further complication, from a direction we haven't considered.*

"And that would be? Details, please."

*None available. It is an idea he developed during a meeting with Director Relway where today's events were the topic of discussion. Evidently those Hill folk who were disinclined to have anyone poke around where their children were playing have taken a ninety-degree turn and now insist that the Civil Guard deal with Belle Chimes. Whose real name would be Belle Dierber. They also want Lurking Felhske found. Felhske is not involved with any of them. They want to know who set him on their children. And, of course, why.*

"The compliance device. Somebody wants it."

*Forget the compliance device. It is a red herring. I am certain. The secret of creating giant bugs would be far more valuable.*

"What's got you so cranky?"

*This explosion in the population of people whose minds I cannot access. All of whom, even Kip now, seem to have multiple personalities. None of which give up anything of interest.*

I could see where that would irk him. He was used to having his way with anybody who came in range. Now his confidence was threatened.

*I cannot get a handle on what is happening.*

I glanced at my painting. Eleanor seemed more amused than I was.

Old Bones had no humor in him at all. He betrayed the depth of his emotional despond with his suggestion that I take my painting down to the World and let the dragon build me a new Eleanor. Then I could . . .

There'd been a time, not that long ago, when I would've

considered it, off the wall as it was. Eleanor had been a strong distraction indeed. But now, not so much. Not that much.

Time to back off. I'd never known him to be so juvenile.

The moment passed. He apologized. And reminded me that Block thought we were headed for a surprise.

I hoped it would be revelatory rather than deadly.

Old Bones went away, his despair gently lightened.

After a while longer with Eleanor, because I didn't want to face the night alone, I did drag me upstairs and put me to bed. Alone.

I tossed and turned and worried about a world in which the landscape of Tinnie's left hand had changed.

# 79

I don't know why. The world seemed remade in the morning. Maybe because I had slept ten hours. I felt totally positive. This would be a good day. There'd be no more problems at the World. Max would be thrilled. He'd give me a bonus instead of firing me.

I should've had a hangover. I should've been worried about the fallout from the carnage yesterday. I should've been uncomfortable about the Algardas, worried about Kip, worried about the Faction cleaning up after themselves. I should've been worried about demons named Deal Relway, Belle Chimes, and Lurking Felhske. Most of all, I should've lost control of my functions because of the complications developing with Tinnie.

But I wore a smile when I joined Dean in the kitchen.

The doom and gloom were haunting him. Starting the sausages, he said, "I need some reassurance, Mr. Garrett."

He had a problem for sure if he was going to be polite. "I'll do what I can, Mr. Creech."

"Give me an honest assessment of our current case. I've caught snippets, naturally, but no context. Only enough to scare me. And you know fright tends to fatten up on ignorance."

This was out of character. He worries about whether or not I'll give the job enough attention, with enough ambition, to get myself paid.

I told the story to date, not in detail. "And you don't share that with anybody outside the house. Understand?"

"That's not nearly as bad as I thought."

"Good. I refuse to look on the dark side today."

"I'll do my part."

"Thanks." Puzzled. That didn't fit, either. He keeps house, cooks, handles most of the shopping. He isn't involved in operations, even in his own mind. He'll behave like a father, a mother, even a wife, sometimes, but never like a business associate.

I shrugged it off. So the Hill made him nervous. It does that. I was *positive*. First thing out, I'd see Mr. Jan. I'd have my fitting and make my peace in the matter of the crippled loaner coat. Then I'd get on back to the theater. "Is Singe with us this morning?"

"Very much so. I took her a bowl of stewed apples before you came down. She's working on our accounts. And finding no joy in them."

I headed up to see her, armed with a big mug of honeyed black tea. "I hear you're unhappy about something."

Instead of having acquired a normal writing desk Singe had brought in a six-foot-wide wooden easel. It was set at an angle halfway between vertical and horizontal. She had paperwork pinned all over it. Two chests of drawers the height of a normal table stood at either end. Those were piled with stuff, too. Important stuff, I'm sure. That's all I pile on my desk.

"Look at this place. Already. What's it going to be like in a year?"

"By then I'll be organized."

"Right." As the words "rat's nest" came to mind.

"I have been studying shareholder statements from the manufactory. I am not the best accountant. I'm still learning the sorcery of numbers. But most of the partners, us among them, are getting screwed."

"What? That doesn't make sense. By who? And where's the point? We don't have a big cut to begin."

"If I steal a fraction of a point from every shareholder, I could siphon off a big chunk of money that none of the individuals would miss." She rattled numbers. She convinced me.

"I see it."

"I didn't want to worry you. You have all that stuff about the World on your mind already. Forget that Miss Tinnie is part of that management team."

Right. We'll do that. She's just the person in charge of

fiddling the company numbers. Which was why her name had been mentioned.

Singe said, "Tell Mr. Weider next time you see him. Even the managing partners are getting shorted."

Not good. This could come down on Tinnie. "You scare the shit out of me when you talk like that."

"There are dishonest people everywhere, Garrett. If there weren't you would have to get a job."

"I'll pass it along." One more thing to brighten Max's week. "You saw John Stretch?"

"He can come up with a few rats. Dozens instead of hundreds, but some."

"How much do we owe him? How much do we have in the kitty? I want to pay Saucerhead and his crew."

"We owe John Stretch nothing. I allowed no arrears to develop." Looking smug. "We have no past due debts. We do owe Playmate for the coaches. He has not come for the money. I have it set aside. The Weiders were extremely generous with our advances. I have taken pains to record and annotate every expense on their behalf."

Absolutely terrifying, Singe is.

I lost track then because somebody hammered on the front door.

*Ignore that. We cannot afford further intrusions on our time.*

So I didn't go. Old Bones would let me know if it mattered.

Singe might not have heard anything. She kept on talking numbers.

I had to get moving. "I need to go to work. Singe. You didn't tell me if we have cash enough to ease the pain for Saucerhead and his guys."

Singe did not want to discuss our cash reserves.

*Miss Pular, provide specie sufficient to mollify Mr. Tharpe and his crew.*

Which she did, making sure I didn't get a look inside the cash box. Probably scared that if I knew how much was in there I'd run out and buy something shiny. Me. The only one around here who doesn't throw money away.

The girl came from a harsh environment. You couldn't blame her for making sure she didn't have to go back.

*Move it!*

"All right! I'm going. Hey! The other day Singe said she thought you'd gotten hold of Lurking Felhske. Did you?"

*She erred. It was Barate Algarda. Someone who might have been Felhske has come within touching range twice. I could not take advantage. He was much too well shielded.*

"Why would a Lurking Felhske be protected from you? This is a one-Loghyr town and almost nobody knows that. In general, why are we running into so many protected minds?" Kip, Algarda, Felhske, the Windwalker. Maybe even the whole Faction and Hill crew.

Thinking that triggered what seemed an unrelated conjunction down in the deeps of my mind. "The compliance device. It might not be the red herring you thought."

He watched the gears mesh. His own clunked and ground, sparking a burst of anger, of embarrassment, of temptation to claim he had known all along and was just waiting for me to find the truth on my own.

*So, even I fail to see what I do not expect or would find repulsive. Incest. The clues were all there.*

"I'd say they don't try to hide it."

*The incest still does not make the compliance device central. But it becomes more interesting.*

Whether or not Furious Tide of Light tried to hide Kevans' sex, for whatever motive, we knew that Barate knew the truth. We heard him say so. We also heard that Shadowslinger was grandmother to both the Windwalker and Kevans. Could've happened more than one way but only one seemed likely. Which was not big in this family, apparently.

*The Windwalker being the exception. Who would not want her daughter following after her.*

"Here's a kicker for your don't-see-what-you-don't-expect file. The Windwalker might be more jealous than protective."

He pulled the relevant incidents from my recollections. *You could be right.* A pause of a half minute for some heavy-duty multiple-mind cogitation.

*Kevans would be the one repelled by the idea. No doubt having had direct experience. Which would explain her initial interest in creating what would turn into the compliance device. She wanted a way to know when her father was interested. To give her time to get out of his way.*

"Then all for one and one for all, and the kids all hung out at her house."

*Indeed. Young Mr. Prose did tell us that the object of the Faction is mutual support. Assuming Kevans had the strength to ask for their help. . . .*

"That little shit lied to us. He came up with the compliance device. For her. All that stuff about trying to find a way to avoid social mistakes. . . . Smoke screen. Pure bullshit. The little asshole has been leading us around by our prejudices!" I got as wound up as the Dead Man had been a minute earlier.

I had no trouble imagining Kip and Kevans down in their bunker snickering over how they had snookered us. And their own old folks besides.

*If he comes up with any ambition at all, that kid will wind up king of the world.*

*This would be a side trail we can take up, on our own behalf, after we have made the World safe for play production. Our wounds are grievous deep but not fatal. We have a dragon to slay and ghosts to lay.*

True. The kitty had to be fed first.

But I was so stung I figured I'd be seeing Kip's mom by the end of the week. Tinnie willing.

*You really must get going, Garrett.*

"All right. All right. I'm on it." But, of course, I had one more thing to do before I could plunge into the cold.

I visited Dean, turned him into a temporary operative by giving him instructions involving Joe Kerr, Playmate, John Stretch, Saucerhead's wages, and Playmate's fees.

I stopped off and gave Eleanor a big wink before I hit the street.

# 80

I opened the front door. An arctic breeze handed me a full body swat, shoved me back. "There's a freaking blizzard going on out there!" I heaved the door shut before the abominable snowmen invaded.

*Time to layer up.*

Dean was at the far end of the hall, wearing a smirk. He'd come out to watch. Likewise, Singe, right there almost within smacking distance. Looking less smug because she hadn't yet mastered that human trick.

"Funny people. Somebody could've warned me. Came on kind of sudden, didn't it?"

*Not really.*

He was right. The signs had been there. I'd had other things on my mind. Still did, in fact.

I wondered what other things was doing right now. Showing her hand at home?

I did layer up, best I could. Then I went out into that mess, operating on the theory that I couldn't get lost in a city where I'd lived all my life, and driven by a need to show somebody something. Who knows what.

It ought to be a good day to get stuff done. Shouldn't be many people underfoot. I didn't notice anyone watching. I didn't smell anyone, either.

Mr. Jan was not distraught about his loaner coat. "No need to worry, Mr. Garrett. No need. It was crap, though I made it myself. I kept it because the man who ordered it never picked it up." This while he was fitting my new coat. Which I just plain loved. "You satisfy his marker and I'll say nothing."

"How much?"

He named a figure that disabused me of any suspicion that he might be a nice, honest, fair little old tailor. I protested. He told me, "I'm sorry you feel that way. Very well. I'll put it back on the peg. Jokes may redeem it yet."

Can't be many people who go by Jokes. There's only one Saucerhead Tharpe. Probably only one Lurking Felhske. And couldn't be more than one Jokes Leastor. Who expired of a surfeit of blood loss a couple years ago, after someone he didn't know as well as he thought objected to one of his pranks.

Jokes Leastor was exactly the guy who would've had that clown coat made.

"I'd better have mercy on you, Mr. Jan. Jokes won't be coming back. Or, if he does, he won't be needing a coat. Quite the opposite."

"Has something happened to him?"

"He played one joke too many. He ended up room temperature. A while back, now."

"I feared as much. He was slow but he did always get around to paying."

Face saved all round, we finished the fitting, I gave him his blood money, donned the remnants of Jokes' sartorial declaration, then pointed my nose toward the big cold.

Mr. Jan said, "This should be done in two to three days. I'll have a courier take it round to your place. Unless I need you to come back for some final measurements."

"Excellent."

I returned to the white reflecting on the fact that in just days an old tailor had managed to find out where I lived.

I made a big mistake. I headed for The Palms. It was the nearest place where I could both get warm and be welcome. I should've headed for Playmate's stable instead. That was almost as close. But Playmate is all boring and honest. Morley Dotes is crooked as a dog's hind leg. And he's involved in stuff that keeps me barking with curiosity.

# 81

Abominable men came out of the snowstorm, summoned by the dread melodies of silver whistles. They wore neither blue shirts nor red flop hats. And, as noted, their whistles weren't made of tin.

So I never made it to The Palms, where my best pal could've told me all about his hopes and plans and schemes.

Nobody said a word. We all knew our roles. Somebody at the Al-Khar wanted to see me. Somebody at the Al-Khar knew how to find me in the middle of a snowstorm. So I was going to put my life on hold till I'd enjoyed a chat with that somebody.

One particular somebody was more likely than any other. He didn't have his runners declare themselves with their headgear.

The runaround at the Al-Khar was abbreviated. That minikin Linton Suggs got me to Director Relway in jig time.

The Director was waiting. He wasn't alone.

Colonel Block was there to assist. I didn't know the third man. The deference he received suggested that he was Prince Rupert. *The* law and order fanatic in the royal household. He had a definite Relway-like gleam in his hard gray eyes.

Prince Rupert was just two failed hearts away from Karenta's throne. And he might get there. Which might be good for the kingdom. He had strength. Karenta needs a strong ruler.

In this pecking order the low man was Deal Relway.

Barring lower-than-gravel Garrett, of course, and the gawkers wandering past.

Relway started by asking questions obviously not his own.

He was no more happy than I, at the moment.

He is the most absolute realist I've ever met. He knows reality more intimately than he knows his own suite of perversions. He knows he can get anything he wants, and more, if he's just patient and pliable when the right people are around. He knows that most people who matter agree with the Director of the Unpublished Committee for the Security of the Crown, whatever they offer for public consumption.

Deal Relway is what he needs to be. Patient. Clever. Deadly. Unacquainted with pity, conscience, or remorse. He may be TunFaire's future. Nine of ten of the king's subjects will be thrilled with the future Deal Relway wants to create.

And there I was. Before much got said, bemoaning—in all privacy, of course—the tyranny sure to come. The tyranny certain to make life more safe, secure, and comfortable for the nine of ten.

Inarguably, in a TunFaire run by Deal Relway, the only frightened people should be crooks. But the crook class would include anybody who didn't like the way Deal Relway operated.

Relway stopped after a half hour of random questions, all of which I answered honestly. And which, frankly, left me puzzled because they didn't have that much to do with what was going on. Then he and the prince became observers. Along with the ever-changing gallery. Colonel Block said, "You put us in a tight place this time, Garrett."

"I'm gonna confess right up front, Colonel. I haven't got any idea what you're talking about."

"Some Hill people got hurt bad at your place yesterday. Two dead, on scene. Another died right after. Two more could still go."

"That's bullshit. Link Dierber died. Shadowslinger and Schnook Avery had some broken bones. The other three maybe got a couple bruises apiece. You want me to be honest with you, you maybe oughta not bullshit me."

"You—"

"Hold on. You guys want to run the world a whole new way. You want to make everybody responsible for their own behavior. Well, get your heads around that this time. Furious Tide of Light brought those people to the World. They were all family of the kids who created the bugs. I had nothing to do with them showing up. Neither did the ownership. If I'd known they were coming I would've tried to keep them away. They were sure to interfere with work. And they did. With all the tact their kind usually show. There was bad blood between one of them and one of my consultants. They were half brothers. They had an old feud none of those people would explain. I don't think it matters, really. The feud caught fire. If I was you slugs I'd worry about Schnook Avery instead of harassing that harmless old fuzz ball, Garrett. Who had nothing to do with any of it."

Block responded, "Fact is, we can harass you as much as we want. Nobody will care. Hill folk, on the other hand . . ."

"I'll care. A lot. One or two others might, too."

Prince Rupert made a calming gesture. Saying nothing. He was kind of a goofy-looking guy, tall and lean.

Block nodded. "No point in getting in a pissing contest because the man rubs me the wrong way." That for the benefit of his audience. "Particularly since he's connected with TunFaire's top financiers, magnates, industrial doyens, and criminal masterminds."

Block made the point gently and obliquely but in a way that wouldn't be misunderstood. Ma Garrett's boy is tight with some major players. Who might take mortal offense for no reason a true blue blood would understand.

Senior folk at the social poles, like Relway and the prince, have to nurture the happiness of the stinking-rich merchant classes. They don't like it. But they have to honor the power of the money.

Another face of the future.

I gained respect for Prince Rupert during the prolonged consultation. He said little. He listened. And he heard. When he did speak he avoided stupid with disarming ease, though he never had much to say. I found myself hoping he would have the misfortune to ascend the ladder of succession. Karentine monarchs are ephemeral, crowned and often murdered before we get used to seeing their profiles on the coinage. I didn't know anyone I'd rather see cursed with the Crown.

Eventually, I asked, "Can you tell me the point to all this?" I gestured at the red top parade. "Why do those guys need to come gawk at me?"

Prince Rupert was interested in my coat. The fifth time he asked about it, I said, "I'd give it to you if I had anything else to wear." I sang the sad song of the demise of my own coat, thanks to the good Director. I added several verses about Mr. Jan taking forever to finish the replacement, thanks to the good Director.

The good Director ground his teeth.

Colonel Block took me to the exit personally. "You did good in there, Garrett. You didn't let us rattle you. You even almost convinced me that you were telling the truth."

I had a creepy feeling that I'd survived some kind of test.

"I was. There's no reason to hide anything. Especially since the Hill people got involved." There had been mention of those folks, off and on, but I'd gotten the impression that the prince didn't care. He was more interested in the kids. And me. "Mr. Weider and I are better off having you know the truth. We might find ourselves needing the friendship of the Crown's men. Besides, isn't it every subject's duty—"

"Don't lay it on with a trowel, Garrett. Your cooperation has its boundaries."

Well, yeah. I'd withheld a few trivialities. But he didn't need to know about John Stretch's talents. And it wouldn't do to mention an improbable dragon, of potentially sundarkening magnitude, snoozing on a treasure way down deep beneath the World.

"I look out for my clients. Sometimes having you in the know is what's best." He had to get that into his head. That was a truth as solid as stone.

"Right." He winked. "Stay warm out there, Garrett."

# 82

"Hey, Garrett! Nice coat," Saucerhead said when I slipped in through the front door at the World. "What kind of fur is that?"

"Beaver, I think." It was obvious why Tharpe and his crew were huddled up inside. The ghosts weren't active and it was almost warm. Water remained liquid. "Prince Rupert traded it to me for the one I've been wearing. The ghosts on a holiday?"

Derisive laughter from all hands.

"Truth, Head. He wanted it so he could get one like it made." I needed to move on. But I couldn't. "Relway had me dragged in. The Prince was at the Al-Khar. He saw that coat and fell in love."

I don't know why I expected him to believe that. Dumbass street thieves made up better stories. "What's been happening? Have you seen Playmate?"

"Yeah." Tharpe wanted to go on giving me a hard time, but he did take time out for business. "He came by. He brung them two black cases over there. He said tell you the ratpeople can't make it today. Maybe tomorrow, if the weather is better."

I got busy with the cases, the little one first. It could win me friends.

I dragged out a heavy doeskin sack as Tharpe wound up to get back to my fabrications about an obviously stolen beaver coat.

The atmosphere changed. Saucerhead purred. "Garrett. My main man. What do you have in that sack, my brother?" He heard the music of the metal.

I showed him my precious metal trumps.

I had friends.

They stayed friends even after they hid their money in their purses and pockets.

I said, "It's too warm in here, guys. Whatever you think."

Saucerhead said, "You keep trying to freeze the place out. How come?"

I told him.

In moments it was obvious the dragon would go over worse than my beaver coat story. Had to be pure, unadulterated, nine ninety-nine fine, one ninety proof, Garrett-style bullshit. Which I shouldn't have been retailing, anyway.

My ego kicked in. I started getting hot. Then I recalled an incident from boot camp, nine days in.

We'd had only a couple hours of sleep. The drill gods were breaking us down. They rolled us out for some pre-dawn recreation. I got my undershirt on backward in my haste to avoid being last man out, which would guarantee the descent of the wrath of Sergeant God. I didn't yet understand that the wrath would find a way, no matter how hard I tried.

When my error was pointed out, in a friendly way, by a fellow recruit, I snapped. I insisted that *this* shirt was made that way and I had made no error.

I knew I was being stupid while I said it. But I couldn't stop.

That haunted me the rest of boot camp. The guys never looked at me the same. I never regained their complete trust and respect. Luckily, I wasn't posted to the same outfit when we went to the fleet.

The drill gods are all-seeing. All-knowing. And pretty wise.

I did good after that one stumble.

If I let the red beast grab hold of me here, these guys would look at me the way those guys in my training company had. They knew I wasn't right. It wouldn't matter if this shirt really was made that way.

"You're too smart for me. They thought I could sell it." I named no names, nor revealed why "they" wanted the suggestion of a dragon planted. "Gods be damned!"

"Garrett? What?" Saucerhead looked like he was wondering if he ought to be scared. Garrett was acting weird today. Weirder.

"I just realized. I got jobbed."

What I'd realized was that having people think there was a treasure-brooding dragon down there guaranteed disaster. Dozens of story cycles include a "hero" who separates a dragon from its treasure nest. That should be harder in practice than in fable. A dragon's hoard could become a total metropolitan obsession, worse than an unreasoning lust to be one of the earliest to own a custom-built Prose Flyer three-wheel. Greed would drive this obsession, not mere envy.

This truth had to be guarded. And shaped. Else this dragon would be nudged awake. And then? Disaster.

I told Saucerhead, "I don't know what the grift is. I do know I'm not half as smart as I thought."

He grunted.

"This is where you're supposed to jump in and give me some positive reinforcement."

He grunted again. Probably trying to figure out what those big words meant.

"All right. Be that way." I sulked. Selling that. Hoping word would now go out that Max Weider, ever clever, was salting a gold mine by having his cat's-paw Garrett go round spreading bullshit about a dragon. Just, coincidentally, a dragon, and hoard, buried under a Weider theater due to open in a couple of months.

People would figure the giant bugs were part of the publicity scheme, too. And if they did, we'd get the Faction kids out of trouble easy.

Which, no doubt, would happen anyway. They were related to the right people.

I chugged around the circle of speculation. My own occasional special cynical conviction that there are secret masters got me wondering if the ghost problem hadn't really been orchestrated by Max and Manvil.

Sounded dramatic enough. Ah! What a wonderfully psychotic reality that would be. But the notion failed two critical tests.

First, Simplest Explanation.

The simplest and most obvious explanation of any phenomenon is usually the correct one.

Second, the Stupidity Test.

It's unnecessary to invoke complex, convoluted conspiracy theories where plain old human stupidity suffices as an explanation.

"I'm getting old, Head. The inside of my melon is starting to fill up with the kind of stuff old Medford is always spouting."

Saucerhead knows my grand-uncle. He chuckled. "There's a lot of that going around, Garrett. And not just because we're getting old. The world is changing. On account of, peace broke out. And that means things can't stay the same. Nobody likes it but it's so plain even dummies like you and me get to thinking about it."

I do believe my jaw dropped. That was the deepest I'd ever heard Saucerhead get.

If you hang around long enough, and pay attention, you see that even the dim people can work through to some amazing conclusions. It's all a matter of speed.

My inclination was to pretend that I hadn't caught any of this. Following trails well blazed by brigades of my social betters before me.

But Saucerhead Tharpe was standing right there, looking me in the eye, waiting. Smugly confident that I would disdain real reality for the preferred, officially predecided reality.

"You don't know me as well as you think, big guy." But we weren't getting paid to save any slice of the realm other than this pimple of a theater. "So let's look at what we've got. Quickly, because the money guys are going to ask me some tough questions real soon. We'll all be out of work if they don't like the answers."

"You're nervous, aren't you? You're chattering."

"Yeah." Max was indulgent in the extreme. I'd done him a lot of good the last few years. But mine is a "What have you done for me lately?" line of work. Putting the Weider Empire out in front of the Hill mob might be a straw that Max would refuse to carry. "So, tell me what's going on here."

"A whole lot of nothing. It's totally quiet. No bugs. No ghosts. No bad guys. No freaks. That I noticed." Possibly implying that current company was questionable.

"No workmen?"

"Not so much their fault. Take that up with the tin whistles. They're all worried about if they let those guys in they'll mess up the evidence."

"What evidence? What happened in here was mostly illusion. The real shit went down outside. In front of witnesses." Few of whom had produced reliable statements, I was sure.

Saucerhead shrugged. "I'm just reporting."

"Yeah. I got that." I went back outside.

The red tops were holed up in Saucerhead's guard shack, concentrating on not freezing to death. They were a lot colder than the men they had dispossessed. They had used up all the fuel. I wasn't going to buy any more. They had one candle burning, providing weak light and a futile defense against the cold.

"You guys need to come inside the big place. It's warmer." And I could give them their due ration of shit without freezing my own favorite bits off.

Some didn't want to go. But it was seriously cold. Their one candle was all that stood for the memory of summer. They quickly found the limits of their motivation.

We all sat around the floor of the World, telling tall tales and outright lies. I'd been tempted to close a few vents to raise the temperature. That temptation I could resist more easily than the one involving a tall, smoldering, apparently willing blonde sorceress. Who could well just want to use me for something less exciting.

Of all unlikely creatures on the gods' frozen earth, Pular Singe wandered in. Only she wasn't wandering. She was in a damned big hurry, despite being bundled up till she could barely move.

This couldn't be good. Disaster was about to sweep me up and chunk me into the dustbin of misery.

Singe cut me out of the crowd. Another bad sign. "What's up?" I had to force the words.

She made sure we were too far away to hear, and that my back was to anybody who might read lips. "A man came from that Mr. Jan."

"The tailor?"

"I don't know that. Presumably, since you went to him for a fitting. The man said get word to you that Mr. Jan needs you back as soon as possible. That it's urgent. He will refund the price of that thing you were wearing if you get there before the bells toll four."

"What's going on, Singe?"

"I don't know. The messenger said it was urgent. The Dead Man told me to get you, fast as I could. He would not tell me what he saw inside the messenger's head."

"Why send you out? Why not that Joe Kerr kid?"

"Because you would not take the boy seriously."

Probably not.

The fact that Old Bones wanted me to take this seriously meant I ought to do exactly that. Despite the comforts of the World. Such as they were.

"And that's really all you can tell me?"

"That's all. Except for the sense of urgency. Speaking of. I have an urgency of my own. Where can I?"

Excellent question. "The construction guys use the honey buckets behind those screens. Or they take it into the alley out back. Saucerhead has a garderobe attached to his shack."

Damn! I'd just found Max a whole new problem. I'd been over the World top to bottom. The architects hadn't provided any personal relief facilities. Something would have to be done. The high-end punters weren't going to have their wives or mistresses go squat in the alley during intermission.

Hey. This might be another business opportunity. I could take over one of those places across the way and turn it into a pay-per-pee facility.

Singe told me, "Never mind. I have to get back home. They need me there."

"Huh?"

"Nothing to concern you. Go find out why your tailor needs to see you." Trailing a huge, put-upon sigh, she headed for the front door. Starting to develop a little attitude, that girl. I might lose her to the Faction.

"What was that?" Saucerhead asked when I came back over.

"One of those 'got to do it right now, this minute, I don't care if hell *is* freezing over' missions from the Dead Man. I've got to go, guys."

Tharpe's people all smiled and waved. They'd just gotten paid.

Before I hit the big cold white I opened the other, larger case so its contents could breathe.

# 83

The blizzard had worsened. In the falling snow parameter. You couldn't see twenty feet. It was warmer and less windy. The snow came down in big, sloppy, slow flakes. The walk to Mr. Jan's place was less miserable than I'd anticipated, though my calf muscles did ache from having to slog through snow in places already a foot deep. I gave a lot of mind time to a hope that it would melt before my turn at the shovels came again.

I thought it might. This blizzard had the feel of Winter's last forlorn effort.

I didn't proceed with battlefield caution. It was a storm. Bad people would be scarce. The reason most of them are bad is, they can't stand the stress and structure of honest work. Or they're too stupid.

Stupid were the kind who would be out looking for victims in this.

Still, my pace slackened ever more as I neared the tailor shop.

Something was off.

That old thing about it being quiet. Too quiet.

Even for the middle of a snowstorm, where it's always quiet.

The quiet was the wrong sort.

I saw nothing. But there was something. I felt it.

I sniffed. And sniffed. And sniffed some more.

There was nothing in this air but heavy, resinous smoke. Every working stove and fireplace was trying to hold off the cold, mostly by burning cheap dangerous softwoods.

Maybe I was overly sensitive.

I crept up to Mr. Jan's door without having anything

creep up on me. Wondering if this was one of those deals where the genius bad guy tells you all your questions will be answered if you show up at some remote place, all alone, and don't tell anybody.

That must have worked at some point, once upon a time. Else why would villains keep trying the blatantly stupid and transparent?

Inside. The bell jangling. Still nothing suspicious. But I had my weighted oaken headknocker deployed. My left hand, in my coat pocket, had fitted itself to brass knuckles cast in our own manufactory from a design suggested by Kip Prose. Just twelve had been produced before I enjoyed one of my few successes as self-appointed company conscience.

There really is no legitimate use for brass knucks.

Mr. Jan popped through the curtains closing off the back of his shop. He carried Jokes Leastor's special coat. "Ah. You're here. I didn't expect you for a while yet."

"My associates are fast. And have been known to be lethal."

That went over his head. Musingly, he observed, "They would be, wouldn't they? Come on back here."

I leapt and caught him. Not only my associates are fast. He yelped, startled. "Tell me, Mr. Jan. Where did you get that coat? It's only been a few hours since I traded it for what I'm wearing now."

The little man gasped, "Back there. In back."

He wanted me to go to the back. Into shadowy tight places where his fabrics were stored. Where villains by the dozen might be lurking.

"I'll be right behind you." I poked him with the end of my stick. Thoroughly put out, he pushed through the curtains. I stayed close enough to grab and use him as a shield.

The back of the shop was a surprise. It was spacious and lighted. Mr. Jan's fabric bolts hung on wall brackets where the cloth could be unrolled as needed. The floor was given over to cutting tables and manikins of varying size, most wearing apparel in some stage of construction.

"Ah. Sergeant Garrett. You have me at a disadvantage for the moment. I hadn't entertained the ghost of a hope that you would arrive so soon."

The other thing gracing Mr. Jan's back room was His

Royal Highness, Prince Rupert, Lord of This, Count of That, Duke of Something or Other Else. Hell. There I went. So up on my Royals that I didn't know which titles Rupert preferred. A failing unlikely to garner positive reviews from His Grace. Though not that unusual down on the street, where who is what doesn't make a lick of difference, day to day.

I tried to recall the rituals you're expected to pursue when entering the presence of someone so exalted. "I apologize, Your Grace. I've never been taught the appropriate obsequies."

"Never mind. There's no one here to see."

There was Mr. Jan. But he had recovered his aplomb and was back at work on a larger, gaudier, new and improved version of the coat he had built for Jokes Leastor.

I had a sinking feeling.

Clown coats would be all the rage by the time winter rolled around again. Had to be if it was what the most popular Royal was wearing.

Mr. Jan hummed softly as he cut and pinned.

He could see that future.

He'd be a made man this time next year. He'd have squadrons of employees. After all those years in the trenches he'd be an overnight success.

The reason the prince felt at a disadvantage was, he was in his underwear. The tailor was using his exquisitely made outerwear to get the refined measurements needed to make sure the new coat was a perfect fit.

# 84

"Take a seat, Sergeant Garrett. Forget everything else. We have business to attend." He had a jerky way of speaking that was unsettling.

Prince Rupert conjured a couple of chairs, placed them beside an empty cutting table. I didn't protest his use of a rank I no longer wore. I avoid contradicting princes whenever I can.

I sat myself down, wishing I'd had the foresight to strap on my chastity belt this morning.

You need one when nobility invites you to come be one of the boys.

"You're skeptical and suspicious," the prince said. "And nervous. Good. Your mind doesn't freeze up when presented with sudden, unusual circumstances. But relax. Let's talk like professionals, here away from everyone else."

Damn! He'd used the clown coat to create a way to meet without Block and Relway looking over his shoulders.

I peered around.

"I'm alone, Sergeant. My bodyguards are somewhere warm. They don't know I'm out prowling the stews again, alone."

He fibbed. A little, maybe. Their presence, behind the white, would be what I'd felt earlier, with senses honed in a more deadly place and time.

"All right. You've got me here. Your Highness." There were situations when he was supposed to be a "Your Highness," and situations where he was supposed to be a "Your Grace." I didn't know the rules. I should've chosen my parents more carefully.

"Neither Westman Block nor Deal Relway will be listening in. Neither will hear of this meeting unless you tell them."

I wouldn't bet on Relway missing anything. Some of those guys out there shivering probably reported to him. Unless Rupert really understood that and did leave his people behind. In which case I'd been imagining what I'd felt out there.

I waited.

"The situation at the World. The one involving Shadowslinger, Link Dierber, and the others. It happened as you described it?"

"Exactly." I decided to dispense with honorifics till he insisted otherwise. Being me. Having to test the temper of whoever sat across from me. "I have no reason to distort the chronicle."

"I thought as much." He observed, "The Algardas erred when they brought those people to your theater."

"Maybe. But they were just family, worried about their kids. The theater was full of dead bugs. The Algardas wanted to show the others what their kids had been up to. They weren't there to start a war."

"I suppose. Had they been, they wouldn't have gotten so badly mauled." As though he'd forgotten me, he muttered, "Too bad it wasn't Kilsordona who got in the Bellman's way."

"Kilsordona?"

"Precisely. Yes. Oh. That would be the Nighthunter Kilsordona. The one wider than he is tall. A particularly unpleasant personality and a favorite annoyance of mine."

"I didn't know they let any Nighthunters come back from the Cantard." They'd been one of the ugliest weapons fielded by our side. Invisible and undetectable after nightfall, the Nighthunters had been insane killers, often sent out to eliminate vampires and other night predators for which the Cantard is justly famous.

"A few showed an ability to get over the need for murder. But that is nothing to do with us. Or this. A personal annoyance only."

I shuddered. His speech was increasingly creepy. "Uh . . . can you tell me what that was all about? Link Dierber going off, determined to get his brother and getting got himself instead?"

"Not so petty jealousy. The kind that happens in any family, but, for Link, magnified a hundred times. Link always made things bigger than they were. That was his psychosis." Rupert paused. He waved a hand to indicate he wasn't finished. He choked on his own words for thirty seconds before he got going again. "Many people would have lived longer, happier lives if Link Dierber had been stillborn."

"And Belle?"

"Only half as mad as his crazy half brother. Only half as violent. Thanks to his upbringing." He managed a note of sarcasm.

"What happened between them? To start everything?"

"I don't think anyone knows what the trigger was. And you could be the only one who cares. It certainly doesn't matter. We have to deal with the situation that exists today."

Don't you hate having to communicate with people whose heads don't work like your own?

I don't let it get to me. There are too many of them.

"If you weren't responsible for Dierber and the others being there, there's no need to feel responsible for what happened, Sergeant."

I didn't. The squabble between Belle Chimes and his family was an inconvenience. So were red tops who kept workmen from getting on with construction. Which I mentioned. Sourly. "What's the bottom line going to be? My principal will be extremely unhappy if he gets dragged into a vendetta he didn't start himself."

"No worries. Only Schnook Avery is likely to carry a grudge. And Schnook will be taking up residence in a special sorcerer's suite at the Al-Khar. He'll stay there till we're sure he'll behave. Or till one of my idiot older brothers has him cut loose."

Mr. Jan sewed assiduously, hearing nothing.

"What about Belle? And Lurking Felhske?"

"Felhske?" Distinctly unhappy at the mention. "Felhske isn't germane."

Damn! He sounded a little heated, even.

Calmer, "We'll see no more of him, I'm sure. The Bellman will be tracked down and arrested, though."

Understandable. "Why is he called the Bellman?"

Prince Rupert stared for a moment, as though trying to work out if I was sincere, or just stupid. "Belle? Bellman? Nickname. Goes back to when he was about ten."

"Those people load themselves down with silly monikers. I thought it might have some special meaning. Like Stormwarden. Or Windwalker."

He flinched. He wasn't immune to her magic, either. He said, "The reports about you appear to be accurate."

Great chance for a wise remark. Relway, Block, or any of their underlings would have gotten one. The prince, not so likely. "Excuse me?"

"You worry and fuss about things in no need of fuss or worry."

An unusual way of stating it but a sentiment I'd heard expressed a few hundred times before. "None of this has turned out real satisfying."

"That's life. Did you do your job? It looks like you did what you were supposed to do. That should be satisfying in itself."

I grunted. What was I doing in the back room of a tailor's shop, during a blizzard, talking to the number-three man in the kingdom, under circumstances suggesting that the meeting was part of something big and secret?

"Why am I really here?"

"In addition to matters discussed? Two reasons. What's buried under your theater?"

I shrugged. "I don't know. My associates think it's a dragon. I'm not sure I agree. It doesn't feel like what I think a dragon ought to feel like. We hope we can tame it with cold. Whatever it is, that seems to be putting it back to sleep. A few days' more winter should do it. Anyway, I'm not supposed to discuss it. The fewer who know anything, the fewer there are who will be likely to provoke it."

He eyed me unhappily. "The main reason for this is that I hope to recruit you into a new law enforcement department. In a senior position."

"Huh? Another one? Me? Be a tin whistle? I don't think . . ."

My lack of enthusiasm didn't please the prince. "I'd think this would be your dream job. Doing what you do, with the Crown behind you. Your income guaranteed."

Being told what I could and couldn't do, what I could and couldn't wear, even being told how to lace my boots.

I wanted to yell, "Get thee behind me, foul demon!" But it was better to temporize. "I was a Marine. I'm proud of that. But it isn't going to happen again."

"You not being your own boss."

"Exactly."

"You'd have more freedom than you think."

That would be true the day the air filled with live, squealing bacon thicker than a gnat swarm. "You'd have to get more specific before I'd consider it. I like my life the way it is."

"I'd hoped to make you my personal observer inside the Al-Khar. Straightforward enough?"

"Ah. . . ." Yes. He wanted to set me up to look over the shoulders of the masters of the Guard, Watch, and Unpublished Committee.

He said, "I'm gathering people who are the best at what they do. With you we'd start out using an arrangement like the one you have with the Weider Brewery. Outside the Al-Khar your Special Office would handle things we don't want the Guard or Watch seen ham-handing. Inside, you'd be Director of the Office of the Chief Inspectorate, publicly tasked to watch the watchers. You'd follow a career arc similar to Director Relway's but with your name becoming less well known. You'd have the city's most talented people reporting to you. You'd do highly important work but the public would remain unaware of it."

A snake oil salesman ought to have more facility expressing himself. The prince's tics left him sounding like a crook even if he was being honest. "What *would* I be doing if I wasn't keeping Relway honest?"

"Not yet. Not a word more than what I've said. I repeat. This isn't to become part of public discourse, now or if you accept the position."

All right. He was offering me a job. A real job. Probably doing what I do, till I weaseled my way in where I could keep an eye on the darkness at the heart of the Al-Khar.

"If you accept I'd want you to bring all your resources with you. And to disengage from private arrangements."

That killed it. Wasn't going to happen. But I wasn't ready to break his heart in front of so many absent witnesses.

He sensed the change. His eyes narrowed. "Compensation would be commensurate with your level of responsibility."

"Generous, huh?"

"Very. I'm asking you to give up a lot."

*My* eyes narrowed. But temptation remained well behind me. I couldn't imagine the king of Karenta being more generous than the king of beer. Not to mention less controlling.

"Enough to let you retain your usual associates. Though they couldn't know what you're doing. Some don't know how to keep a secret."

"You've been checking up."

"We could, in fact, set up departmental expenses separate from salaries. But you'd have to keep detailed records. You'd have to account for everything. And be prepared to argue convincingly for expenditures. I'm creating a fiscal oversight group, too."

The more he talked the more his offer sounded like a nightmare come true. "It's interesting, the turns life takes."

"Seize the night, as they say." His excitement was gone. He knew I wasn't buying.

He soldiered on, though. He asked my thoughts on the leading personalities of our day. A dozen times he said, "I never thought of it that way." Or, "Is that how the little folk see it?" He had a strong interest in the differences in thinking between his class and those of us who do the world's work. Not that he saw any particular merit in the plebian viewpoint.

He might have been slumming, or just enjoying a freak show.

He kept going back to popular attitudes toward Relway, Block, the better known human rights agitators, and the Contagues. And, more obliquely, his brother the king. I was as honest as I dared be. While growing ever more suspicious.

Morley would be heartbroken. I'd have to tell him that, as yet, he had done nothing gaudy enough to have caught the eye of Good Prince Rupert.

It would be nice if he kept it that way.

Mr. Jan did seize the opportunity to take additional measurements while I was there. Though my new coat would now be delayed till he completed the masterwork he was creating for the prince.

# 85

Back to the World? Or go home?

Home sounded good. The Dead Man could get to work making sense of what had just happened with Prince Rupert. And I could get warm.

I had some ideas about the nature of the tar pit I'd stumbled into but wasn't confident of my instincts. Old Bones could winkle out the shadowed connections.

And the house would be warm.

Everyone else had a different idea about what was going on at the World. They all agreed: We had us a dragon down below and we had to tippy-toe till it went back to sleep.

Home kept calling but there was a lot of day left. I decided to check in with Morley Dotes. I had something nagging at me. My subconscious might nail it down while my friend distracted my conscious mind.

Dotes looked so glum I decided to order a mixed veggie grill just to cheer him up. He joined me while I waited. I asked, "How come so blue? Nobody in their right mind would be out in this, anyway."

"It's not that. Not just that. I've made a deal with a devil. I can't stop thinking about the possible consequences."

"Any deal with Belinda definitely has a downside. You give up on collecting the bounty on Lurking Felhske?"

"No bounty to be had anymore, brother."

"Huh? Not even Relway?"

"Especially not Relway and his Unpublished Committee, apparently. A red top came around with a message for me, personally. He was part giant, part ogre, had fangs down to here, and made Saucerhead look like the runt of the litter."

Inspiration. "Did he drool a lot? Have one fang kind of twisted? Talked with a lisp because of what would be called a harelip if he was human?"

"Member of your family?"

"Not yet. Just an acquaintance. From afar. I doubt if he knows me. And I doubt if he's really a red cap. He'd be Urban Jack Tick-Tack. Real name, Capricious Moon. He's in the same line as Saucerhead, only up the Hill."

"Urban Jack? Tick-Tack?"

"I don't know." I preened. It isn't often that I know something about the lice on the belly of the body politic that my friends don't. "Where do nicknames come from?"

"My guess is, there's a crippled little god somewhere, sitting in his playpen, who thinks them up and slides them into people's heads when they're squatting on the chamber pot."

My mixed grill came, redolent of garlic and ginger. I dug in. It was good. Morley could tell I liked it. He was smug. He told me, "Singe and I did still give it one last half-ass try. Because I don't let anyone push."

"Singe, too?"

"My mistake. I know. I shouldn't have involved her. She decided she can't track him anymore, anyway. She says he took a bath."

"Gods! Good. If anybody ever needed one . . ."

"She didn't mean a literal soap and water bath, Garrett. Though he did that, too."

"Interesting."

"I suppose. Why?"

"Somebody wants Lurking Felhske even farther on the down low."

Dotes raised an eyebrow almost as fetchingly as I do.

"He wouldn't notice his own stench. Guys with the big body odor just don't. They live with it. Right? So somebody clued him in, convinced him, and added a little magic."

"And then sent a thug around to reason with people who might go looking for him?"

"Seems plausible to me." I recalled an unexplained pounding on my door this morning. Any connection?

Old Bones hadn't seen fit to report. Assuming he'd been paying attention at all. There were times he didn't. More and more frequently, lately.

He'd been aware enough to nag me.

"You lost in there, Garrett?"

"Some. Things started out bone simple. I had what looked like a protection play shaping. With a bug complication. I took care of the extortion and I got the bug thing under control. But one damned thing keeps leading to another. Now . . ." Now I seemed to be getting caught up in something barely even tangentially connected with the World. People involved in other things kept doing things that made getting on with completing the theater difficult.

Morley said, "On a brighter note, we'll start work on the new place as soon as the weather clears. We'll be selling lunch to your workmen by the end of the month. How can I get hold of that Rockpile person?"

I told him. Then said, "I'm not gonna get home as early as I thought."

Morley hoisted his eyebrow again.

"I'm getting a glimmer of something. Like one of those ghosts when it just starts forming." Forgetting that he couldn't see them. "I'm thinking Saucerhead might have the answer. Without knowing he has it."

"I hope that ratty coat is warmer than it looks." Said with the smirking smile he reserves for when he sticks in the needle.

I gave him my best hard eye. It ricocheted off. I put a few coins on the table and left.

# 86

Saucerhead and the others were still inside the World but huddled up close to the door so they wouldn't have far to run if they decided to make a quick getaway.

"Ghosts back, Head?"

"Yeah. Sort of. One or two."

"But they haven't bothered you?"

"Not yet. So far they're only interested in that case of yours. But that could change."

"Excellent! I'm so smart! I don't think you have to worry."

Tharpe's expression told me he was keeping a lid on his opinion only because I was the Keeper of the Coins.

I told him, "I came by to find out what you know about Urban Jack Tick-Tack. Since you know everybody."

The crowd stared at me like I'd sprouted horns.

"Ultimate badass bonebreaker, Garrett. You don't want to mess with him. But you don't need to worry. He only works for rich people. Just don't piss Weider off so much he wants to crunch you. Hell. How come you're asking? Just curious. On account of, Tick-Tack himself was here only about an hour ago."

"What? No way."

"Way. You can't imagine how big he is."

"What did he want?"

"I don't know. He didn't say. He just strolled in and started looking around. Soon as he seen all of us watching he took off."

"Been any rumors about him lately? Head? Anybody?"

"Been keeping a low profile. Any of you guys heard anything? See?"

"That's really what I expected. I guess I'm as warm as I'm going to get here. Oh. I figure the workmen will be back tomorrow."

"We got that word, maybe twenty minutes ago. Message signed by Director Relway himself. These guys are supposed to hang around and keep an eye out in case of developments."

Damn! The prince moved fast. "That's good, then." I stopped by my cases and mumbled a bit before I plunged into the great white.

There wasn't much light left. I decided to use what there was to check out the Faction clubhouse, see how busy they'd been cleaning up.

There were tracks around the steps, most going in, a few coming out. This deserved closer examination.

As I started a little voice chirped, "Mr. Garrett? Is that you?"

Took me a few seconds to locate her. "Mindie? Mindie Grinblatt? What are you doing here?"

"We were watching the place down under there for Mr. Algarda. He hired Daddy to keep people out. We would get to live there. But a little while ago this monster came. Daddy told me to get around behind it, then climb the stairs and get away. So I did. But he didn't tell me what to do after I got out. So I've just been waiting. And I'm getting worried. Mama and Daddy haven't come up to tell me it's all right."

Oh boy! ODTAA for sure.

I considered options. Most involved me going somewhere else and staying out of the way while natural dwarfish resilience took place. It would take some managing to best the Grinblatts in tight quarters underground.

But Mindie did say that a monster had come.

"Tell me about the monster. What was it? How big?"

"I don't know. Really big. I just saw tusks and a lot of hair. Or maybe it was wearing a fur coat."

Not good. Played right into the conspiracy theory I was developing.

"That's good. You're doing good so far. Here's what we'll do. You give me your ax and your sword and your shield—"

"But then I won't have *anything*. . . ."

"You'll still have your other sword, your daggers, your truncheon, your boots, your teeth, and anything you've got for your trousseau. You'll only have to go a couple of blocks. . . . Good girl. Let me see how that helmet fits, too."

It was loose. A little dwarf girl's dress-up hat.

"All right. I'm going down and see about your mom and dad. I want you to run to the World. The big building where you saw me the first time. Tell a man named Saucerhead what happened and what I'm doing. Got that?"

She nodded. Hitched her breeches. Dug something out of somewhere. "You'll need these." She handed me a couple of warm blond stones the size and shape of chestnuts. They were so smooth they felt oily. And they glowed like feeble candlelight. "Moonstones. There's a little light left in them. Take care of my stuff." And off she went, no longer troubled.

Of course. It was all on me now.

I fumbled one of the stones, but could see it through the snow. I made sure I got it back. Mindie wanted me to take care of her stuff. I shoved both stones into a right-hand side pocket of the beaver coat. Clumsily.

I was trying to manage a clutch of edged weapons. Even the shield had its sharp sides. I needed to be careful.

It got dark fast under the house. But, on the plus side, there was no wind.

I had a stroke of smarts. Brought out one of Mindie's stones. Dull, creamy light, like the light of a full moon that's gotten just high enough to have lost its autumn orange. Excellent!

Then, uh-oh! A little girl had given me moonstones. Which had to be one of the deepest secrets of her people. She'd done so thoughtlessly, as though to someone of her own tribe.

Moonstones. I'd never heard of such a thing. I couldn't begin to imagine how much they'd be worth.

So there I was—

Which is the way so many anecdotes start. Usually ones where the speaker sheepishly relates some adventure in which he came off less than shining.

But not always.

So there I was, moonstone in my right hand, dangerously

sharp arsenal in my left. I worked out a way to put the
child's sword up my left sleeve without wounding myself,
then tightened the shield's straps so it would ride my left
forearm and keep the sword in place at the same time. I
adjusted the helmet, grabbed hold of the ax handle in my
left hand, and proceeded. Holding the ax out like it was a
cobra in a foul mood.

That ax was so sharp I could hear it slicing the air.

Dwarves let little girls play with razor-sharp steel. They
never get hurt. A grown man ought to be able to . . . Ouch!
And what was that?

Somebody having trouble breathing. Given a listen, there
was no mistaking the sound, though I hadn't heard it in a
while. Somebody had what they call a sucking chest wound.

Urban Jack.

Me having had the description, this couldn't be anyone
else.

Damn, he was huge! How the hell had he gotten down
the stairs?

He was scattered around the floor of that anteroom in
the deepest basement. There was blood everywhere, tacky
but a long way from dry. Jack had suffered at least a dozen
cuts, most shallow, well distributed. Plus the chest wound,
where something had gone in deep enough to penetrate
a lung.

I held a moonstone up high, to light as much area as
possible.

Urban Jack sensed my presence. Dull eyes cracked open.
He couldn't have seen me very well, with the moonstone
over my head. He reached up, got hold of the beaver coat
for a second. "Boss? I think they were too much for me
this time." His eyes closed again. His hand fell.

He did go on breathing raggedly.

"Grinblatt! Rindt! Where the hell are you? You all
right?"

No answer.

I started with the clubhouse door. Nothing. Nobody and
nothing. The place had been cleaned out of everything but
an underground smell.

Likewise, the little trysting room. That one before any
other, most likely.

I picked the bad door for last, meaning I tried the one I

thought led to the Faction's lab. And there I found a full complement of Grinblatts. Less Mindie, gone for help.

They were all unconscious. Which meant they were bad hurt. Some dwarves can go into hibernation, or sort of an induced coma, when they suffer a life-threatening trauma. Meaning these dwarves were in a bad way but they could be saved. They wouldn't be getting out of the cellar without being carried, though.

I placed the moonstones on a naked table and started checking the dwarves. Essentially a futile gesture. They were all bundled up in their standard dwarfish apparel. I'd need a blacksmith to get them out.

The boy appeared to be in the best shape. He lay farthest from the doorway. It looked like his mother had broken bones. Rindt had more broken bones. He looked awful. I was amazed he was breathing, induced coma or no. He had to have serious internal injuries.

First things first. Mindie's moonstones were fading.

I'd just gotten a third lamp burning when I heard Saucerhead's remote bellow. "Garrett?"

"Come on down. It's safe." If there had been any spells, Urban Jack had torn them up. "Be careful on the stairs."

I slipped the moonstones back into my pocket.

The lamplight revealed a lot more nothing. The place had been stripped. Only a dozen dirty, empty tables remained. There was no seeing any wall but the one housing the door I'd used to get in. There were pillars that seemed to go out in endless ranks and files. There were echoes.

This was not something the Faction had created for themselves.

But they had gotten it emptied out fast. Them and their moms and dads.

Saucerhead came clumping down, followed by several other pairs of feet. "I'm in here. Whatever you do, don't open any doors."

Tharpe arrived. "What the hell did you do, Garrett? I know you're handy when they get you backed into a corner, but there ain't no way you took Urban Jack."

"You're right. That would be these people here."

"Dwarves? No shit?" He put down a typical human impulse to argue. "That actually makes more sense. Dwarves wouldn't fuck around trying to talk about it. They wouldn't worry about no appropriate level of response. They seen an Urban Jack headed their way, they'd go to the axes first." He added a bit of philosophy I probably ought to consider more when I get all morally judgmental. "Better to be alive and feel bad than dead and feel nothing."

"Yeah. You see that face coming at you out of the darkness, you shouldn't worry about anything but chopping it up."

"How did the asshole get down here, Garrett? Big as he is?"

"I don't know. Had to work at it, I guess. I don't care. These dwarves need hauled out. We could turn these tables into stretchers."

"Is that a good idea? What do we do with them once we've got them out in the cold?"

Not a point I wanted to hear, but a good one. "Mindie? Are you here? Where's Mindie?"

"Who? The little dwarf?"

"Her."

"I think—"

A little voice piped up in the antechamber. "I'm out here, Mr. Garrett." She weaseled between Figgie Joe and a couple red caps, looked around. "I was going to stick a knife in the monster's eye. But then I thought how bad he would start to smell, and how long it would be before there was nothing left but bones. So I left him alone. Maybe he can get out of here on his own. Then you can chop his head off."

"Sugar and spice," Tharpe observed.

"And everything nice. Mindie, what about your mom and dad and brother?"

She was looking them over as I asked. "It isn't as bad as I thought it would be. Everything will turn out all right, given time, Mr. Garrett." She knelt beside her father.

Saucerhead and his companions gaped. Me too. This wasn't the scared little girl I'd found hiding in the blizzard a little bit ago. Nor was she the girl who'd shown up at the World looking for help from Saucerhead. Now she was a girl confident of the future.

Two minutes later she was a little manager telling Saucerhead and the guys thanks for the help, and they could get back to what they'd been doing now. They smiled some and nodded some. Tharpe and Figgie Joe did go.

The red caps stayed right where they were. Violence had been done without official license. They were going to sit in here till they got official instructions from the Al-Khar. Which meant that somebody had gone to get those.

I might want to move on myself, then. I had no special desire to spend my evening answering stupid questions over and over.

Mindie accepted the presence of the law. What chance did a kid have? She came to me. "Thank you. They'll be all right. Daddy will take a while to recover, though. Did you take care of my stuff? I'll take it back now."

I pointed. Shield, sword, ax, and helmet rested on one of the otherwise empty tables. The moonstones were in my coat pocket. I slipped them to her without the red caps noticing. "You sure you'll be all right?"

"I'll be fine, Mr. Garrett. I have these men to protect me if the monster gets back up." But, for an instant, the frightened child peered out from behind the confident mask dwarves have to show us lesser species.

"All right. I don't want to be late for supper. But only if you're absolutely sure."

Fleeting dwarfish smile from behind a beard just starting to come in. "No, you don't want to miss a meal." And, as I was sliding past the red tops, "Thank you again, Mr. Garrett."

## 87

As noted, a heavy, wet snow is a quiet place. And blinding. People are vague shapes till you feel their breath.

How Lurking Felhske found me, I couldn't imagine. I'd have thought it impossible. Proof he was a genius. But he didn't surprise me, bath or no bath. Twice he came close enough for me to sense as he sized me up. Then he took a run at me less than a quarter mile from home. Coming at me out of the snow like he was just another miserable traveler slouching along in the opposite direction.

I didn't actually know it was Felhske then. There was no telltale stench. But I did realize that somebody was sizing me up.

He got the tip of the oak headknocker between the eyes as he drew even, before he could turn and jump me from behind. His knees went wobbly. I got behind him, shoved a knee into his spine while laying my club across his throat. "Be good, brother." Taking a while to realize who I had, which I did only after I realized I had hold of a very oddly constructed gentleman.

Despite the orangutan shape Felhske conceded his shortcomings as a street fighter. He resigned himself.

"What the hell are you thinking? Your principal is out of action."

He twitched. Meaning maybe his employer wasn't out of the equation after all. "Who're you working for?"

He wasn't going to talk.

I got his weird long arms up behind him, marched him toward my place. We would let the Dead Man deal.

Old Bones sensed my approach. He touched me lightly, to let me know he was there, then expressed surprise that

I wasn't alone. He couldn't sense Felhske at all. He suggested I thump the man a couple times to make sure he didn't start thinking clearly.

*His mind is extremely well protected. Bring him right to me. This should be instructive.*

"Right." Whatever that meant. Exercising my full wit and reason, in the face of the hints that had been accumulating, I bounded to an improbable conclusion. Barate Algarda had hired Felhske to punish me for lusting after the Windwalker. Or to keep quiet his illegal and immoral goings-on with his female descendants.

I had an old-fashioned, tight-ass upbringing. In my family that stuff would've been taken seriously.

So. Furious Tide of Light? She could get her daddy-lover to do something out of character and stupid. But why would she? Even to protect her baby. It wasn't that big a deal to her. Kevans wasn't particularly important in this. Was she?

*Ah. You will enjoy this.* Chuckles was in a lighthearted mood. *Come join our guests.*

Singe let us in. Her eyes bugged when she saw who I'd caught. "Look at the hair on him. Maybe he really is a monkey."

She was right. Felhske's head was a briar patch. The rest of him was damned near shaggy as a bear.

I found the full membership of the Faction crowded into the Dead Man's room, none of them thrilled to be there. Kyra Tate was on hand, too, evidently having lost the capacity to separate herself from Kip Prose. Even the apostate twins, Berbach and Berbain, were in the klatch, identifiable because their mom still dressed them alike. Old Bones must have armed Kip with some especially convincing arguments.

*All should be well soon, Garrett. The last Faction problems relating to the World have been, or shortly will be, corrected and controlled.* But he felt unsure. Something wasn't going the way he wanted. He was moody.

Did Kip look a little smug over there?

I'd see what I could do about knocking that off his clock.

I said nothing but tried to send the Dead Man the idea that I thought he'd just blown out a cloud of wicked wishful thinking.

*Not very amusing, Garrett. I am stressed to my limits.*
"Yeah? Want to share?"

*Mr. Felhske is less than six feet away, yet I can barely detect his presence. My sense for all these children is only slightly better. The only open head among them is Miss Tate. There is little of value to be found in there.*

"I'm thinking it might not be you. You're having *no* luck with the kids?"

*Very little. Every single one has a dual personality. The twins are outright frightening.*

"Have you noticed the tonsorial fashion statement?"

He can see only by using somebody's else eyes. He borrowed mine. And picked up my suspicions at the same time.

*Aha! Yes! Singe. Please pull the hair of whichever youngster is easiest to reach. As hard as you can! Garrett, stand by to deal with an outraged response.*

Singe snatched a fright wig off the gourd of a kid I hadn't seen before. She yelped, stared at her fingers. The kid turned out to be an attractive young lady with long blond hair, not a pretty boy with good skin.

*That is the answer!* the Dead Man crowed. *Garrett, bless you! You found the answer. I have been a fool. It was in front of me all the time. Once again I have failed to see what I did not expect to see.*

He was thrilled. He would've gotten up and danced if he could.

No exception but Kyra, those kids weren't thrilled. They'd been found out. Now all they wanted was to get away.

Old Bones tried to make the blonde help snatch wigs.

Painful work. Something in the hair stung and cut my fingers. The cuts burned.

*All will be explained now!* The Dead Man began trying to control the scalped in an effort to stem that tidal bore of panicky youth dedicated to getting out of our house.

He had the same luck as a cat flung into a room with fifty mice.

I felt his frustration. He had been far gone in his weakened self-confidence. Which did roar back for seconds only.

Chaos reigned. Shrieking kids trampled me and Singe. A

blast of winter air filled the hallway as Dean emerged from
the kitchen armed with a rolling pin and cast-iron skillet.

He was no help. Too many teenagers wanted out of a
place where their secrets might be exposed, all of them
at once.

A stunt had been laid on to outwit the grown-ups. It
had whipped around and bitten them. Now they were as
manageable as a troop of panicky monkeys.

Kip Prose would not be popular with this bunch much
longer.

Old Bones, despite the invaluable assistance of Garrett,
Pular Singe, and Dean Creech, lost all hope when Lurking
Felhske reassessed his resignation to his fate.

Felhske produced a blade that I'd been too dumb to look
for and take away. I hadn't looked because I'd heard the
man wasn't a fighter.

I plowed through the remaining kids and intercepted
Felhske. Sort of.

Basically, I deflected him. I didn't get in a solid hit. I did
remove part of his hair. I squeaked. My fingers felt like
they were being shredded.

I crashed through Kip and Kyra and some minor furniture. A wall slowed me down. I used the crown of my head
to soften the impact.

Dean whopped orangutan man with his skillet.

The scrambling and shrieking were done. Only Kip,
Kyra, and Kevans remained, along with Lurking Felhske.
Not an auspicious night for that part of the alphabet.

The Dead Man claimed, *I accepted the loss of the children
to ensure that we did not come absent the critical information belonging to Mr. Felhske.*

To which I said, "Bull!" But did not push because he'd
started feeling good about himself again.

Singe got the front door shut, with difficulty. Her poor
hands were more ragged than mine. Mine burned like hell.
"Dean. See what you can do about these." He's our first-
aid guru. He produced gauze and salve with striking speed.
The salve was pungent. It stung at first, then sent the
pain away.

Dean demonstrated a sea change in attitude toward Singe

by treating her first. I drank beer to pass the time while I waited. And examined one of the wigs. Sharp-edged brass wire tangles ran through what looked like hair off a woolly mammoth, up close. It was coarse and oddly colored, but that hadn't been obvious while the spells installed were crackling.

I considered Kip Prose. I considered dumpy-looking Kevans Algarda. She must be a lot more than she showed. Was she armed with some of her mother's magic?

I considered Kyra, too, but only with a passing interest. She was collateral damage. Just lucky to be in the wrong place at the wrong time with the wrong guy. She was going to tell her aunt Tinnie on me.

*This reduced assembly should be manageable.*

"The whole bunch should've been. You just needed to use a couple of kids to help us plug the doorway."

*Perhaps. However, I chose instead to collect data while panic had everyone thinking about what they most wanted to remain secret. Which will stand us in good stead should we have to deal with the Faction again.*

*The boy continues to amaze. The charged wire mesh is ingenious. A third-generation form of what began as the compliance device.*

"Kip running wild again, eh?"

*Young Mr. Prose is in the mix but on this one Miss Algarda is more responsible. Not for the physical device, but for the idea and for the sorcery used to make Mr. Prose's netting effective.*

He'd be plundering their every thought now, and mixing in fragments he had plucked from all the heads that had gotten away.

*True. And, on the whole, I am embarrassed. I was well and truly deceived.*

"You about to confess a shortcoming?"

*After a fashion. We have come full circle. Because, for the Faction, this is all about the compliance device after all.*

"Old dead guy say what?"

*Not the compliance device originally conceived. Nor the one we saw in its second iteration, that could be deployed in a proactive, pathetically hopeful manner. Not even the upgrade version we saw here tonight. No. There are newer iterations in this most ingenious collaboration between Miss*

*Algarda and Mr. Prose. The fourth-generation version moves from the purely protective to the offensive.*

"Meaning they're about to start getting into other people's heads?"

*Reading actual thoughts instead of just moods, yes.*

"Ouch!"

*Ouch, indeed. I would be rendered obsolete. Though, even more so than the three-wheel, their marketing strategy would be limited production sold to high bidders.*

I glared at Kevans. The girl didn't wilt. My thoughts became scattered as I tried to work out how her adolescent trauma, harsh as it might have been, could have brought her to—

*You are yielding to melodrama, Garrett. Although you are not wrong in thinking that Miss Algarda's relationship with her father impacts her decision-making. But greed has become more powerful.*

I suppose there had been no point when Kevans believed she might not be doing the right thing. Nor would care now if some old fart showed her the truth.

*The outstanding naiveté in all this is Mr. Prose's. Who is now being saved by the love of a good woman.*

"What?"

*So the girl thinks.*

I got it. But it was kind of corny. Kyra Tate, amateur fire goddess, saving boy genius Cypres Prose from the wiles of the dowdy wicked witch Kevans Algarda.

*There is a fifth iteration of the compliance device coming down the road. The compliance part will have actual meaning. Miss Algarda convinced Mr. Prose that she needs it as a way to manage her father when he cannot be evaded or discouraged.*

*Young Mr. Prose is a very good friend. Miss Algarda is not.*

*Unbeknownst to the Faction, initially the fourth and fifth iterations of the device came to the attention of a family acquaintance involved in law enforcement.*

"It gets better and better." A horror worse than any tentacled thing without vowels in its name, slithering through a crack in the wall between dimensions, that. "And I don't have to guess who, do I?"

*If you did you would be wrong. The man was not some-*

*one we know. Unintentionally he overheard an argument between Kevans and Kip. He did not take what he heard seriously. But he did pass it on to Prince Rupert.*

"I see, said the blind man. And all of Relway's prayers were answered."

*Given the situation, perhaps you should have taken your opportunity to become a key insider in the new order. As opposed to possibly becoming one of its earlier successes.*

"Well, yeah. I'm starting to think that. Also, I did figure out that there had to be some kind of connection between Kevans and Rupert. Or Kip and Rupert."

*You did, indeed. You have been exercising your mind, if in secret. Mr. Felhske—likely Mr. Tick-Tack, too—belongs to Prince Rupert's Special Office. Mr. Felhske was tasked both to contact Miss Algarda and to keep an eye on her. No trust on the part of the prince, who wanted an exclusive on the fifth iteration.*

That explained Kevans being unhappy to see Felhske. It explained him wearing a near full-body fright wig that he had to get somewhere. Kevans had made a deal with Rupert and thought she was in control. Felhske turning up proved otherwise. To Kevans that said the prince did not trust her.

*He allowed himself to be captured.*

"I know."

*The young lady has, perhaps, overstepped herself. Youth features impatience and overconfidence. In ten years she could have been one of the great villains. The sociopathic pieces are all there. They need experience and polish.*

*She will not laugh.*

"Say what?" He was having fun now.

*Given the opportunity to become what she has the potential to be, Kevans Algarda would make few of the traditional story villain mistakes. No windy, gloating explanations. No evil laughter.*

"Another Belinda."

*Worse. For Miss Contague these days it is about business ninety percent of the time, plus a touch of the personal. For Miss Algarda it would be personal most of the time. She would be punishing the world.*

"But selling compliance devices to the red tops . . ."

*Each including a control spell that can be tripped at the convenience of the manufacturer.*

*Consider, though. She fell into the situation but instantly understood that she was dealing with a man who might become king. She is impatient, but also capable of thinking ahead.*

"And you got no hint of any of this while the Algardas were here."

*I did not. There is an excellent chance that they know nothing.*

"Yet they wore wigs."

*Yes, they did. Algarda started at Kevans' suggestion several weeks ago.*

"She was setting him up to put thoughts in."

*She was readying him for the day when she could.*

"And the Windwalker?"

*Kevans has very little respect for her mother.* "That firecrotch bimbo!" *when she talks about her to the other kids. There is, definitely, an element of competition for Daddy's attention and affection. But, as to the parental place in this, I believe them to be exactly what they purport. Parents worried about their daughter. With reason, obviously. Their part in the scheme would be unwitting. Many people have contributed, none being fully aware. Miss Algarda has used every acquaintance as a brick in the overall wall.*

"And would've gone to wondrous places if not for the rest of the Faction."

*Those boys and their giant bugs were her undoing.*

Dean barged in with food. "I'll fetch a fresh pitcher in a minute." He looked around. Matters appeared to be proceeding to his satisfaction. But, "Has anyone thought about what to do when the parents show up demanding explanations?"

Oh. "You think they will?"

*That will depend on what the individual young people believe happened here. I suspect most will not be anxious to have their parents become further involved. We have leverage now.*

"But Dean is right. We'll hear from somebody. And none of this is what we're getting paid for."

*Correct. We will get back to the World in the morning.*

*The connection between the Faction and the theater has been severed. The young people should go their own ways.*

*Tomorrow John Stretch will make his final effort. I am confident that his rats will find little of interest. In point of fact, now we have only to deal with the dragon.*

A big Only.

The Dead Man's mood had gone through a dramatic upgrade. He was on a super high now, thrilled to be part of what, for him, was a wild intellectual adventure.

Me too. Some.

There were beautiful women everywhere, wicked and good and every possible alloy in between, along with selfish, shallow, naive, and self-destructive. What a wonderful landscape!

Old Bones went right on having adventures in the wild country behind the eyes of Kevans Algarda and Lurking Felhske. I felt his glee as he plowed the darkness and turned up curious artifacts, most of which he would never share because he wouldn't consider them my business.

*Ah.*

"Yes?"

*I have made an interesting discovery. Buried deep in the trivia cluttering Mr. Felhske's mind.*

"Which would be?" Knowing he loved to be coaxed.

*Who produced your most recent batch of clubs?*

"Clubs?" Oh. He meant the weighted headknockers. I'd bought six last fall. I keep leaving them behind. Or getting them taken away. Cost of doing business. "Ivl Verde. The furniture maker who supplies the wooden parts for the three-wheels. He has troll-powered lathes that can turn a club in a couple minutes. Why?"

*Mr. Felhske could find you in a snowstorm because Mr. Verde let someone put a tracking spell on your clubs.*

"I can guess who."

*Correct. Director Relway. And Mr. Felhske received a trace key from someone inside the Al-Khar. I would not suggest that you operate unarmed, so you should replace the Verde sticks.*

"I've still got one old one in the tool closet." My name for the household arsenal. "Which I'll save for when I really don't want to be tracked." I didn't care if the law watched me now. So why tip them off?

His Nibs radiated agreement.

I asked, "What's that smell?"

Felhske had begun to stage a comeback.

Dean brought more food. I ate some more and drank more beer.

The Dead Man sent, *I am now done with the children. You may release them.*

"Really? Even . . . ?"

*Even Miss Algarda. I have done some inspired editing of her memories. I cannot turn her into someone she is not, but I am able to manipulate the knowledge she will be able to access.*

I'd seen it done before. I expected to see it done again. "All right. Let me finish this sausage." And, a minute later, "You kids get ready to go. I'll go along, make sure you're all right. I need to see Tinnie, anyway."

Kip and Kyra eyed each other like they'd been sentenced to remote and protracted prison terms. Each silently willed the other to do something.

"Won't do any good, guys. That's the way it's going to be."

I did wonder how Kyra kept getting out. In fact, why were so many of the Faction so loosely supervised? Kevans in particular.

Kevans ought to have a parent in each pocket.

"We need to make sure Kevans gets home safe, too." That would take us a quarter hour out of our way.

I bundled up in my new fur coat and led the children outside. Along the way, in weather increasingly less unpleasant, Kip tried to distract me from what he feared was my determination to be a chaperone. He chattered on and on about ways to light the World.

For my part, I worried. I tried to make Kip understand how much he'd been used.

He wasn't that upset.

Kevans was his friend. The rest mattered a lot less.

I have a few of those friends myself.

Kyra didn't share Kip's attitude. Kevans wasn't her friend. And she was afraid that Kip and Kevans might have played at being more than just friends, once upon a time.

I cut them loose, telling Kip, "Go to the manufactory after you get Kyra home. Lie low there till I get things worked out with the Algardas."

He didn't argue. He didn't believe much of what Old Bones had dug out—he hadn't been included in all the rotten details—but he was bright enough to understand that he was out of his depth.

He paused to hug Kevans. They mumbled to each other. Kyra seethed, in redhead Tate "thou shalt have no other anyone" fashion. Then Kip joined her and they headed off. I'd bet Kyra never let go all the way to the Tate compound.

The girl had it bad. The natural way.

I hoped Kip dealt with it better than I did.

Kevans, of course, had a secret way in and out of the Algarda stronghold. And stronghold it was, as is the case with most homes on the Hill. Those people used to squabble on a deadly, daily basis. Their homes had to be fortresses.

Just as well I didn't have to deliver Kevans to her front door. I was in no mood to deal with either parent. I might've said something about bad parenting.

Me. The world's foremost authority.

# 88

Tinnie wasn't home. An unhappy cousin told me she was at the manufactory. It was all my fault she was way behind. And now there was a rumor that the situation could get worse. She'd lost her grip on reality. Garrett could end up being underfoot all the time.

I couldn't do anything about rumor and speculation amongst the Tates. Whatever I tried, I'd just equip myself with more holes dug deeper.

I took Kip along. He'd still been saying good night to Kyra when I got there. He didn't want to leave. "I need you to make drawings and write up notes. Your contribution toward helping repay Mr. Weider for damages done by the Faction."

He really didn't want to go. If he let Kyra get out of sight, she might come to her senses.

On the short walk over, I told him, "Don't worry about the girl. Tate women are a pain in the ass sometimes but they stick once they make their minds up."

Which was what he wanted to hear. Though he had trouble believing it. His self-confidence was still shaky.

"I know that only helps a little. Every day that I find Tinnie still in my life I count as another miracle. I've never worked out what she sees in me."

"Makes two of us." That was a shot, weakly delivered. I took it as a good sign.

I left him outside his personal workroom at the manufactory. It was big and full of toys for a boy genius who might spark additional money gushers.

It was cold in the building. The place didn't get warm

when manufacturing wasn't going on. It wasn't now. The weather had kept most of the workers home.

Which meant they were making too much money. In a labor market where replacements could be had by the hundred.

Ha! Thunk like a true capitalist!

"Garrett! What are you doing here? Besides sneaking up and scaring the knickers off me?"

"Don't look like I did that good a job. Why don't I try charm instead?"

"I'm working hard on getting immune to that. I think I've almost got it. You didn't answer my question."

"I needed to see you. Not for the usual reasons."

The woman can read me good. One hard look and she knew something was wrong. "All right. Spill the bad news."

"Well . . ." I wasn't sure how to tell her without sounding like I was accusing her.

"Out with it, Malsquando." She wasn't troubled. She'd concluded that the problem wasn't between her and me. "Speak!"

"You'll grant that Singe is pretty damned smart?"

"Singe is a freak. She scares me. She's not just too smart for a ratperson, she's too smart for anybody."

"Good. We won't need to debate that. So. Here's the thing. She's been studying the books, and . . ."

"And?" Eyes tight and narrow now. But still nothing to suggest that I'd tweaked a guilty nerve.

"She found a problem with the financials from the manufactory."

Tinnie seemed surprised. "How so? What kind of problem? Tell me."

"You might have to talk to her direct to really get it." I jumped in, the best I understood what I'd been told.

I didn't need to go on long. "Stop. Did she show you examples?"

I told her what I'd seen.

Tinnie was an angry woman suddenly. With the fire under fierce control.

"You believe me?"

"Of course I believe you! Why the hell would you make up a story like that? What I need to do now is figure out if it's true, or if Singe's imagination ran away with her. Go sit in the corner and don't disturb me."

I couldn't resist. "You mean I don't get to lean over your shoulder, jostle your elbow, blow in your ear, and criticize while you're trying to get some work done?"

The black look I got for that actually scared me. No good for the goose, good for the gander in this house. But she was still in that fierce, hard, rational state of anger. "Better yet, go wander around and make the night crew nervous."

I didn't need to watch over her shoulder. Not that having me there could stop her fudging anything she wanted. I wouldn't notice.

"I'll do that." I went. I made a tour of the shops. And won a full complement of growls and scowls from the few workers actually on hand. I counted the three-wheels in various stages of completion. Twenty-eight, total, of which eleven were ready for delivery. I grabbed one and went pedaling around the main floor.

After getting chewed out by a foreman who wasn't impressed by my connections, I put the big, silly toy back and went upstairs to make Kip's life miserable. But he didn't mind the company. We talked for more than an hour, of cabbages, kings, vampires, zombies, and our respective female complications. He wouldn't talk about Kevans or the compliance device, though.

I dropped a few seeds for thought. I hoped he wouldn't be able to get them out of his head.

The boy was working the nerve up to go for some intimate advice when Tinnie stalked in, saving me the need to examine my conscience. I hoped she hadn't heard anything troubling.

"Singe is right, Garrett. Grab your coat. We'll go down to your place. We can put our heads together."

She was tired and frayed and distracted. She knew what was going on and who was doing it and didn't want it to be true.

It would be family. Tates are big on family. And, given that assumption, I could name the villain. Rose Tate, bad cousin.

It had been a long time since Rose had done anything wicked.

"There's a good chance Singe won't still be up."

"Then there's a good chance I'll wake her up. Or I'll talk to her in the morning."

Oh boy! I left Kip with a parting smirk. Then I turned right back. "I need those drawings and papers to show Mr. Weider."

Kip gave them up reluctantly, and only because he knew I wouldn't steal the ideas.

As we hit the cold and darkness, my sweetie asked, "What was that with Kip?"

"He came up with a couple ways to light the World without smelly lamps, candles, or torches." Which meant the theater could operate any time, not just when the sun was available.

That wasn't what Tinnie wanted to know. She suspected me of giving manly advice.

Singe was awake. And still worrying the problem that interested Tinnie. She'd made headway winkling out the wicked numbers. So I lost the redhead for a while. Dean, though, had turned in. I drew me a mug of beer and went into my little office.

A dragon. How do you deal with a dragon with any hope of avoiding calamity?

# 89

Singe wakened us. "John Stretch is on his way. So is Play-mate. Joe Kerr and his siblings will do your shoveling for you. You'd better hurry if you want breakfast before we go."

Tinnie wouldn't let me out of bed.

Breakfast had to wait.

No one else dillydallied. John Stretch, his rats, his hench-rats, and his transportation all failed to wait. Dean's lips were pursed in abiding disapproval when we finally reached the kitchen.

He had been good enough to keep our breakfasts warm.

Tinnie didn't eat much. "I have to show my uncles." She waved papers copied from Singe's collection. "My copies. We made them before we went to bed."

I'd already been dead asleep. She hadn't wakened me. "Copies?"

"This got past me, Garrett. Maybe because I didn't want to see it. It took a ratgirl to notice. I know you. You'll tell Max. I want to be there. To try to explain. To intercede, if I can."

Intercede? The Tates would keep rescuing Rose till she scuttled them all. Yes. Max was fond of Tinnie. She stifled Alyx's worst impulses. Her presence might soften his rage enough for me to make my case. "All right. Good on you."

*See me before you leave.*

I headed for the Dead Man's room.

Singe intercepted me. "You are going to see Mr. Weider?"

"It's got to be done. I thought you went with your brother."

"I had paperwork. I would like to come with you. To explain."

I started to tell her that wouldn't be necessary.

The Dead Man stroked my mind with a feather's touch of warning. "Sure. It'll be more convincing from somebody who can add up two times three. They don't think I can count past my fingers and toes."

The redhead said, "Lucky you've got those extra toes."

"What extra . . . ?" I went to see what Old Bones wanted. That was a fast review of everything, especially what he'd learned last night, and what he'd have Penny Dreadful poking into today. He had work for Winger and the Remora, too. If I stumbled across them. They seemed to have disappeared. They were supposed to be looking out for Kip and Kyra but hadn't been anywhere in sight last night.

Vintage Winger.

Lurking Felhske had departed while I slept, but a faint souvenir of his visit hung in the air.

"That's it?"

*That is it.*

Maybe. But I was sure he had done some digging inside my head.

Singe and Tinnie were in the hallway, waiting impatiently. Tinnie was simmering again.

I wouldn't want to be Rose Tate tonight.

I could not believe that the Tates would be dim enough to let Rose get close to money. Though I would've thought she was too lazy to be this clever.

Things at the World were calm and under control. Workmen were at work. Rats were down below. John Stretch told me they were finding nothing but bug scraps and broken pupae. Saucerhead's guys were on patrol outside, cocky because they'd thwarted a feeble raid by some dead-ender Stompers during the night. They'd rounded up the gangster wannabes and handed them over to the Guard. The kids would be off to labor camp before the end of the day.

Otherwise, Tharpe's report was excellent. No inside trouble. No bugs, no freaks, and only a ghost of a ghost, seldom seen. The workmen had found nothing to bitch about yet.

Tharpe told me, "There was music last night, though.

But it was, like, contented. Sleepy. Not that loud, aggravated shit. Hell, it was purring."

The workmen were really getting on with it. I had a good feeling as I led Tinnie and Singe on toward our fateful encounter at the Weider shack.

# 90

Hector wasn't working the door. I was disappointed. I'd really built him up to Tinnie and Singe. His replacement was average size, ginger of hair, overly muscled and had the cold eyes of somebody who really missed the war. He recognized Tinnie and was concerned by the company she chose to keep. He let us in without saying a word.

Some kind of bang and crash happened, followed by shouting. Somebody launched a pompous soliloquy. Another voice bellowed, "No! No! You're not some lunatic on the steps of the Chancellery! You're in love! You're trying to seduce the unseduceable!"

All became clear once we could see the ballroom that makes up half the Weider hovel's ground floor.

A small, rude stage had been thrown together across the end whence the service staff comes and goes when the Weiders entertain. Alyx, Bobbi, Lindy Zhang, Cassie Doap, and a guy I didn't know were clustered onstage, to its right. The ladies weren't wearing a lot, in a classical sort of style. Winger stood at the left front corner, in junk armor made for somebody smaller than her. She had on an absurd helmet with big-ass shiny metal wings. It was a wonder she kept her head up. She leaned on an oversize spear and looked like her shoes pinched.

Jon Salvation paced between, muttering. He had done the shouting.

Max, Manvil, Heather Soames, Hector, and some household staff formed a small, bewildered audience.

Tinnie sputtered and hissed, outraged. "What the hell? What the hell?" Her shoes made a huge, clattering racket as she stomped down the stair to the ballroom floor, never having knocked the winter off her feet.

Singe and I were good boys and girls. We left no muddy melt water on Max's lovely serpentine floor.

That didn't help matters, of course.

When Singe and I caught up Tinnie was in a snarling match with Alyx because she hadn't been told about the rehearsal. Alyx insisted it wasn't a rehearsal because they didn't have anywhere to put on a play. They were just trying out scenes from something Jon Salvation was writing. A great historical tragedy.

Looked to me like Alyx wanted to eliminate an actress who might upstage her. "Anyway, you're always busy, Tinnie. Either working or riding herd on Garrett. You don't have time. Everybody else does."

True, mostly. But not what Tinnie wanted to hear.

I was wondering why Winger and Jon Salvation had time free.

Heather went in to referee the catfight. I climbed onstage and dragged a gobbling Jon Salvation over to where Winger was mooshing things around under her breastplate, trying to get comfortable inside armor not designed for someone as blessed as she. "The Dead Man told you guys to stick with Kip and Kyra. What happened?"

Jon Salvation accused Winger by using exaggerated shifts of his eyeballs.

Did I really have to ask?

"You just walked out on a job?"

"We got them home safe."

"And didn't let anybody know the kids weren't covered anymore?"

Winger said, "We had to get back to work on the play. *Rausta, Queen of the Demenenes* is gonna be the first play put on at the World. Jon put me in as the goddess Sedona."

The Remora told me, "Sedona was the patroness of the Demenenes. Rausta was their queen. She fell in love with the adventurer Laupher. She had to kill him to prove to the other Demenenes that she'd remain true to tribal law. Then she gave birth to twins. One boy, one girl. Demenenes were supposed to kill their male children. But Rausta didn't."

I didn't know the goddess, the queen, or the adventurer, but everybody knows the Demenenes, legendarily harsh Amazons of the plains way to the north of Karenta. They were the first people to domesticate horses. Joining one abomination with another. I didn't need Jon Salvation to tell me how the story went after the twins grew up.

Salvation told me, "Sedona may have been an earlier queen of the Demenenes. Which would make her more a patron saint than patron goddess."

Winger said, "This godsdamned armor is rubbing my tits raw."

The Remora promised, "We'll have better costumes when we open. This stuff is just for setting the tone. We will be opening, won't we, Garrett?"

"I don't see why not."

The other Amazons made a great show just prowling around. Too bad Tinnie was in a black mood. I wouldn't mind watching the rehearsal, especially if the ladies got to jumping around, pretending to fight. The legendary Demenenes were all the time picking fights. Maybe the Remora could put in some wrestling scenes.

"You rogue," I told Salvation. "Those costumes will make your play a winner." If they didn't get the World burned by the kind of loons who can't stand to look at scantily clad women. "Singe, let's get Tinnie."

Max and Manvil were headed upstairs.

Tinnie allowed herself to be removed from the stage but remained furious. Alyx had found the trigger this time.

Cunning men, Max and Manvil had noted that we came armed with masses of paper. They cleared a table away from the fury of the fireplace and established themselves at its ends. They weren't nearly as grim as I expected. I settled the females on one side of the table, went to the other myself. "These two will go first. What they've got is urgent."

Tinnie deferred to Singe. Singe managed to present her material without giving way to nerves. Tinnie nodded when she thought that was appropriate. Singe turned over her copies of the questionable records. And, almost as an after-thought, passed her expenses account to Manvil Gilbey.

Max said, "What do you call it when you mean to do one thing but you come up with something else instead?"

Gilbey wondered, "Serendipity? Or synchronicity?"

Back to Max. "Tinnie? What does the firm's treasurer say?"

The firm's treasurer had her anger under control. "The firm's treasurer admits she's a big screwup. She didn't realize her own family could steal from her."

"Is it a family policy?" Gilbey radiated exasperated disbelief.

"No! No! That's not what I meant. I meant I never thought one of my own would mess me up like this."

Gilbey turned his glower on Singe. "You've come a long way in a short time."

Singe proved it by refusing to be intimidated. She bowed her head slightly to hide her embarrassment. "Mr. Garrett has been very supportive."

"He has that reputation. Why don't we put the financials aside? Garrett, tell us what you've done at the World. Have you handled the problems we wanted resolved?"

"Things are almost wrapped."

Max gave me the fish-eye. Gilbey seemed equally dubious.

I said, "What I'm going to tell you is unvarnished truth. The way it's been told to me. You don't have to believe it but you do have to keep it quiet." Portentous enough? "As general knowledge it could lead to a huge disaster." I plunged into the story.

I've been involved with the brewery so long that Max dismisses nothing, however absurd it might seem at first blush. "A dragon." An exhalation, not a question.

"I report only what my experts are telling me. Two from high on the Hill. I don't necessarily buy it myself. You could interrogate Vilchik. He did the library research."

"Vilchik?"

"Alyx's tame playwright. Calls himself Jon Salvation. His real name is Pilsuds Vilchik. Known on the street as the Remora. My partner had him help do research. Between them Vilchik and Barate Algarda found four historical events that looked a lot like ours. So-called dragon awakenings. All long ago and far away. Fine details weren't available. My partner doesn't admit any personal knowledge but he's been around long enough to have heard about these things when they happened. I have reservations based on the fact that in none of the reports is there a mention of anyone actually seeing a dragon. The roll-up of the Cantard silver supposedly resulted from one of those events."

Gilbey demanded, "What do we do?"

"The best advice I've gotten so far is, leave it the hell alone. If we stop poking it, it might fall asleep again. Cold makes it sleepy. I'm letting all the cold air get to it that I can. But I've got a little something else going, too. In case my advisers have been talking out the wrong orifice."

Ensued a prolonged question, answer, challenge, and brainstorming session, the sum of which was that the costs of the World were mounting. The theater had begun to look like a questionable investment.

Max and Manvil suggested running ice water down under. I told them, "You have to get the water there. An uphill haul. Then you'll flood everything under the neighborhood. Which wouldn't win you any friends."

Gilbey asked, "Where do dwarves stand on the question of dragons?"

Manvil Gilbey could do two things at once. He reviewed Singe's expenses ledger while participating in the give and take. He used a company writing stick to tick items for discussion.

I said, "One more thing, then. Maybe the most important, businesswise."

Max looked like he didn't want to hear any more. "That would be?"

"Your designers didn't take into account the fact that human beings expected to consume mass quantities of Weider beer will need somewhere to set it free."

Max started to say something, stopped as the implication hit. "Really?"

"Really. How many people will you push through there?"

"Damn!" Gilbey said. "Two thousand on a good day. Why didn't anybody think of that?" He was asking himself, not me.

Max muttered, "Nobody else is worried about it. Why should we?"

Gilbey examined the elevations. He ran fingers over them like he might discover some secret not obvious to the naked eye. "It's true, Max. And it's our fault. There isn't a hint in the specs. But plenty to help beer sales go easier."

Max groused, "Must be because us divine types never have to piss. Take a lesson, Garrett. You're never so old or so smart that you can't fuck up."

Here came the rain of crap for everything that happened at the World.

I was wrong.

Max and Manvil bickered briefly, like an old married couple. I envied them. I have some solid friends but none that tight, excepting maybe Eleanor.

I couldn't take the tension. "When are you gonna jump in my shit?"

Max managed baffled perfectly but Gilbey twitched and betrayed a fleeting smirk. Max asked, "There some reason we ought to come down on your ass? Like maybe for dicking around so long getting the job done?"

"Yeah. That," I lied.

"I do have to admit, I've heard some complaints. I took into account who was whining and said, 'Good on Garrett!'" Max smirked. Gilbey likewise, again.

I got it. They were having fun. I was their proxy on the street, their beard-tugger, now that they were supposed to be too old and responsible. Now that they could afford to indulge in big amusements.

Max's gaze focused on Tinnie, *clang!* like a bear trap snapping. "What are you going to do?" His tone said more than his words. If she wanted to run with the wolves, she'd better be ready to snap and bite with them. If not, he'd take it up with one of her uncles.

"I'll keep it in the family. Same as you would."

Max glanced my way. That flicker of attention told me I'd just volunteered to guarantee my woman's work.

I said, "I have one more thing about the World."

"What else did we forget?"

I'd held on to Kip's papers to this point. I pushed them down to Max. "It's about lighting. You'll need lots of lighting. The usual methods are dangerous, messy, and unpleasant, especially for the people in the high seats. Kip Prose sent you some ideas. His way to make amends for the trouble his bunch caused."

Max eyed me narrowly. He smelled me trying to help the kid miss out on a well-deserved head-thumping. "Get with Manvil on that."

"Manvil will need to get with Kip. I'm reporting an opportunity."

Gilbey said, "Manvil needs to have a sit-down with several people before this project goes any further. So right now Manvil is going to go pry Heather loose from her hobby and put her to work." He gave me a dark look. "I do wonder if we weren't better off with vandalism, ghosts, giant bugs, and ignorance."

Gilbey left. An attendant came in to feed the fire. Job done, he left. I told Max, "So. While I'm complicating your life, here's one more thing. Your fireplace guy spends his free time at the Al-Khar."

"Really?"

"Saw him there myself." We discussed my visit with Block, Relway, the prince, me being observed by a parade of worker bees. Max wasn't surprised or angry. Relway spying doesn't surprise anyone anymore.

Gilbey came back with Heather. Soames had her business face on but was in a bright mood. She tossed a smile my way. I responded with a sign against the evil eye. She took it in good stead. Tinnie was there, after all. "I don't know what happened. I went crazy with that hat pin. I just wanted to make it stop." She forgot me, joined Gilbey, who had taken Kip's drawings and suggestions from Max.

Heather said, "There are all kinds of void spaces under that part of the city. The construction people had trouble setting foundations. Why not evacuate toilet waste into that space?"

I told her, "The stench. It would come up into the theater. And the neighbors would object when it leaked into their undergrounds. Plus, the entity down below might consider it disrespectful."

Heather grunted, turned away, slipped an arm around Gilbey's waist.

Masses of human waste are a problem wherever they occur. But the World was uphill from the river. "Hey, Max. You think we could make money with a sewage disposal company?"

"You're chock-full of bad commercial ideas, Garrett. Or

great ones for losing money." He explained why a sewer company would go bankrupt.

My feelings were hurt for seconds. Which didn't last. Most of my schemes eventually reveal big flaws. Why, indeed, would anyone pay to use a sewer system when they can throw the stuff in the street for free?

Heather said, "Tinnie, I talked to Alyx. Formal rehearsals will be held when you can attend."

The redhead put on a hard-ass look but that was the best she could expect.

Max, Heather, and Gilbey could have a social impact as profound as Block, Relway, and Prince Rupert. It would be a new world once a theater put real, virtuous, upright women onstage. Relatively speaking.

The visit to the Weider mansion lasted well into the afternoon. Nervous little men came in to talk about deficiencies in the design of the World. We found out that the absence of relief facilities wasn't entirely an oversight. Competitors had trenches out back—when they had anything. The Edge added quicklime. Infrequently. The architects hadn't been concerned so the problem hadn't gotten much consideration.

Heather insisted that facilities with a hint of privacy included would be a big selling point for women. Gilbey told us, "Trust her judgment in these things."

Kip's lighting notions generated more excitement. Though how he meant to create the flammable gas went over my head.

# 91

Tinnie insisted that she had to get home before her family disowned her. Plus, she had uncles to brief and a kangaroo court to arrange. Singe got her to tag along to the World, where they caught a ride with Playmate, John Stretch, and the rats when they headed home. The rats had found nothing bad down under, going deeper than ever they had before. I kissed Tinnie, promised I'd see her soon, then checked in with Saucerhead. Tharpe promptly warned me that one of the workmen said he'd seen a ghost. A woman. A real looker. Which nobody else saw. The man was a known shirker.

"I didn't see no ghost, neither, Garrett. But I ain't gonna spend no more time inside there than I got to." He wasn't convinced that it hadn't been a ghost who had attacked those sorcerers.

"I'll check it out. There anybody in there now?"

"That foreman guy, scoping out how to get back into full swing. He said they might hire some extra guys." The way he looked at me told me he was wondering how much longer he'd be employed.

I told him, "Unless there's a flare-up I'll be looking for work tomorrow. You should be all right. Max won't go back to the fools he had before."

"That's good. It's been a weird one, Garrett. Awful low-key."

"Yeah." Just the existence of TunFaire had been threatened. And a guy named Garrett had stumbled deep into alien territory in his personal life. In both cases the biggest show ever had stirred behind the veil, but quietly, quietly—and had not yet achieved resolution.

Tharpe grinned. "I guess if I was you . . ."

"Don't even start. I'm in a state of flying panic now."

"Flying panic, eh? So tall, so thin, and Tinnie knows who she is? That must be just about the worst kind."

Sarky bastard. "I'm going to go see Luther."

"Later, then."

I found the foreman at the edge of the finished floor, which had advanced a half dozen feet. The mess downstairs was gone. Luther seemed bemused. I told him, "Good progress today."

"You got the fear of the gods put in them."

I grunted. More likely the fear of unemployment. "Can we get back on schedule?"

"If there isn't any more craziness." He eyed me like he thought I could pass on some valuable scuttlebutt.

"It's under control, Luther. The kid gangsters are off to the work camps. Belinda Contague has developed a business interest in the neighborhood. That should discourage vandalism. The kids who created the big-ass bugs have been hammered into line. We won't see any more of those."

Luther pointed down and raised a brushy eyebrow. "And that?"

"That's still a work in progress. What can be done is being done. Inertia is our ally. It should be asleep again now. For another hundred generations, one hopes."

Luther wasn't comfortable with that. He was a guy who wanted absolute solutions. But those are the solutions that come by burying the problem in corpses.

I said, "There was mention of a ghost sighting. That what's bothering you?"

"Some. But it was Lolly doing the whining. Which didn't start till he got told he couldn't have the afternoon off. First damned day back, he's already wanting time off."

"Going forward, keep it as cold as possible in here. If it starts to warm up inside but not out, I need to know right away." That wouldn't close the matter. Max wouldn't let the dragon business slide, hoping it would go back the way it was. What had awakened once could awaken twice. He'd want some solid assurance.

"Not my problem," Luther confessed. "I'll get the place built. The rest is up to you."

I liked his attitude. It was a dramatic improvement. "I'll do what I can."

"That's good, Mr. Garrett. Hey, I've got to go. It's a holiday tomorrow. I promised I'd get home at a reasonable hour tonight." Just reminding me that he had a life when he wasn't standing around jawing. "We're having a birthday celebration for my kid."

People do go on living and changing when they're not onstage with you.

Luther left. I decided to give the World the once-over before I followed suit. One last detailed snoop before I took a quick run home for supper. I'd come right back. There were things I wanted to do when I wouldn't be interrupted.

*Creak* and a puff of cold air. I figured it was Saucerhead coming to find out what I wanted him to do. It was Tharpe, yes, but following stubby little Deal Relway himself. Tharpe's shoulders hunched in a combination expressing apology and an appeal for instructions.

I shrugged. It couldn't be too bad. The man who never left the Al-Khar had come out alone. Meaning he'd have to get back out on his own.

"Can I help you?" That most annoying of questions, usually heard when you're doing something someone doesn't think you ought to be doing even when you're not breaking any rules.

"Wanted to see the scene of the crime with my own eyes. Nice coat. Beaver?"

"I think so."

"We nabbed Belle Chimes."

"Good for you. I knew you could do it."

"Then we lost him before we could get any serious answers."

"He escaped from the Al-Khar?"

"He didn't get away. He was taken away. Custody transferred. By order of Prince Rupert. You have any idea why?"

"You're better positioned to guess than I am. You work for the man."

"I do, don't I? And I don't have a clue what goes on inside his head." He kept wandering. Was he looking for one of the infamous ghosts?

We should tame them. We could turn them into another paying attraction. Spend some quality time with your dead folks in exchange for a few pieces of silver.

Relway stopped pacing. "Then there's the guy we found way down in the underground last night. All chopped up and out of his mind. Bad actor known as Urban Jack Tick-Tack."

No way I could claim ignorance. His troops had been there with me. "He attacked some dwarves I know. Their little girl came to me for help."

"And you sent her to Tharpe. We talked to the dwarf girl. We talked to Urban Jack. We talked to Tharpe's crew. And we talked to the red tops who were there. Some curious conflicts in testimony turned up."

"That happens with witnesses."

"Yes. The dwarf claimed her family was attacked by a monster. Tick-Tack says he was minding his own business. The dwarves ambushed him."

"Five levels underground, where they were being paid to keep intruders out?"

"Jack does think he was in the right. Says we can get the answer from his boss. Who, according to him, was down there, too, but must've ducked out when the red tops turned up." Relway resumed pacing. "He can't explain how."

"He claimed to be a red top himself, earlier in the evening."

"Um?"

I told him about Urban Jack's cautionary visit to The Palms.

"Felhske again."

He was worried. And began dropping hints that he was having interesting thoughts. "A curious thing happened just before I left to come here. Urban Jack was transferred to the custody of Prince Rupert, too."

"That is curious. What does it mean?"

"That's what you're going to tell me."

"I don't think so. I'd need some idea of what you're talking about, first."

"Of course you would. Wouldn't you?"

Now he'd come at me from some unexpected direction, to get me off balance. And to give me time to get worried about what he might already know.

"You fired one of my people here. I'm not happy about that, Garrett."

"Tough. He was an asshole. Trying to provoke rightsist shit. We're building a theater. That political crap, and your games, are just ignorant bullshit."

"On the whole, I'm not pleased with you, Garrett."

"On the whole, I don't give a damn, Relway. You need somebody to please you, get yourself a wife."

He produced a smile just thick enough to be noticed. "You were at a tailor shop yesterday afternoon. Prince Rupert was there, too. What was that about?"

Thanks to a nugget found in Lurking Felhske's head, him knowing didn't surprise me. "You'd be in the know if the prince wanted you to know. Right?"

Deal Relway didn't bluster or threaten. He preferred either a direct approach, or something very subtle, when he thought intimidation was appropriate. Too, he liked knowing his footing was safe before he laid the intimidation on heavily.

I said, "I wish there was some way to get this through. We're on the same side. But I don't see that meaning I have to kowtow for us to get along." I controlled a temptation to observe that his rightsist provocateur wasn't the only asshole involved with the Unpublished Committee. I suffered another maturation spasm. "Gently put, it's not all about Deal Relway and his demons. It's a bigger world and in that world most people don't give a rat's ass about Deal Relway's personal happiness. They might applaud what Deal Relway does but figure he ought to stick to rounding up bad guys. He should forget about sculpting the realm to feed his own obsessions."

What maturity spasm was that? I was taking a two-hand yank on the king's beard. Some mad part of me must be totally confident that Rupert would bail me out the way he had Tick-Tack and Belle Chimes.

Rupert wanted his own necromancer, eh?

Relway said, "Did we know each other in a past life where we were deadly enemies?"

"What?"

"This friction. I came here with good intentions. Meant to talk a little, swap some information, try to find out what's going on behind my back. But the second I see you my hackles go up. I want to smack you around till you develop a case of basic manners and civilized behavior.

And I have the feeling that I'd shred your nerves if all I did was stand here in silence. I should've asked Block to come. He's able to deal with you."

I had so much antagonism yearning to be free I could've yammered for ten minutes. The new and improved Garrett stepped up. "It's the way you treat people." I had to say *something*.

He had an answer right there, ready to go. He saved it.

I didn't have to hear him say it to know he believed he gave people what they'd earned.

And there stood the nature of the chasm. I cherished the individual. He cherished society. He was willing to chunk anybody down a well if that would make this a better world for the survivors.

I caught movement from the corner of my eye. I spun to face nothing. Relway told me, "I'll be watching."

"I won't let it bother me."

Saucerhead, over there trying to look small in the doorway, must have gotten a better look at what I thought I'd seen. He made a frightened noise and broke trail for Relway as the little terror left.

I muttered, "Head, that must be some brutal bad memory you have." Hard to imagine a tough guy like him not being able to hang in there against what he knew was mostly inside his head.

# 92

It was like Dean felt me coming. He had supper ready. Singe had me a spot set up in the Dead Man's room. The beer was perfect and plentiful. The downside was, Dean had made stuffed cabbage.

I'm not a cooked cabbage fan. A raw cabbage heart can be tasty.

*John Stretch's efforts today proved gratifying. We have fulfilled that part of our commitment. No bugs were found. A handful of live grubs and pupea were, too few to mean anything negative. No viable eggs were discovered.*

"None?"

*The dragon appears capable of protecting itself from the younger forms. John Stretch's rat encountered their ghost counterparts doing the same work while ignoring the nutritional opportunities.*

"Ghost rats wouldn't need to eat a lot. You're sure?"

*They had no odor.*

Which would mean a lot to the rats.

*Miss Penny made herself invaluable again today, too. She acquired a great deal more information on the previous awakenings.*

"The little witch seems able to charm her way in anywhere." Sourly. That was my specialty. "She identify any eyewitnesses? Or find out what became of the dragons after they broke out?"

*No eyewitnesses. But a lot about the sort of places where dragon awakenings happen. And about what happens once they do.*

I forced cabbage down. I wouldn't taste it now. But, for sure, I'd be tasting it later.

*Because of their restrictions on information, what we can learn about the Venageti incidents is limited. But Penny did determine that the Venageti sites resembled those in Oatman Hwy and Florissant. All four lay beside broad bends in wide, slow rivers where there are vast deposits of deep, rich silt laid down atop limestone. Each roll-up exposed rich metals deposits. Silver in the more recent Venageti incident. Tin that they're still exploiting in Oatman Hwy, where they also had traces of silver, copper, and lead. In Florissant they got lead with traces of tin and silver. The first Venageti roll-up probably included a lot of copper with some silver and gold.*

I can make some remarkable connections sometimes. "Given that, maybe they caused the Great Roll-Up on purpose."

Old Bones closed in on himself. I ate cabbage and tried to smile when Dean came to see how I was doing.

*Given the essential tropes of the dragon hoard story, that could well be the case.*

*Close your eyes. I need the use of your mind briefly. And I need it undistracted by outside visuals.*

I didn't get a chance to argue.

My eyes closed, like it or not. A frighteningly detailed three-dimensional picture of the world beneath the World coalesced inside my head. I don't know how I managed to grasp it. It took all his minds to shape it. It was built of everything he had been able to dig out of John Stretch. Which was an amazing lot.

*This is still little more than speculation. Rats are not good on time, distance, or shapes. They are better on temperature, taste, and smell. Smell especially. I could not put that together inside my own head because I needed the full capacities of all my minds to translate rat sensory inputs into data a human mind could understand.*

I had to take his word for all that.

*I have built the picture now but can make nothing of it. Where is the dragon?*

My head filled with a three-dimensional hundred-gallon ink splash sprawl in saffron. Without knowing how I knew, I understood that this was a fragment of a larger whole. This was all that John Stretch had been able to see within short rat range of the World.

*This is all within the silt deposit. The bottom of that rests*

*on limestone, which lies far deeper here than it does down
under the brewing district. The dragon must be in a cavern
beneath the silt.*

"You're losing me, Old Bones. You might even be losing yourself."

*Sarcasm is a sign of—*

"A sign of impatience with those who won't admit that
they don't know what they're talking about."

*As you will, then. Go play the hand you have dealt your-
self. When you return we will begin developing a new
strategy.*

I sensed impatience with my failure to subscribe to the
dragon theory.

Might be interesting, someday, to dig around in the old
records and see if a Loghyr wasn't somehow connected to
one of the old-time roll-ups.

Though I doubted strongly that this Loghyr had been.

Singe joined me in the hallway as I shrugged me into my
new royal beaver coat. "You are going out again? At
night?"

"I need to do something at the World. When nobody
else is around."

"Really?"

"Yes. Why?"

"I was hoping to ask you about some things. I could
go along."

"I have to do this without anyone else being there.
Maybe tomorrow night." I opened the door and went
outside.

The door chunked shut behind me, anger-driven.

Old Bones didn't clue me. I guessed it had to do with
her book. She kept bringing that up, tentatively.

# 93

Saucerhead's guys were on the job. Which they proved by spindling, folding, and nearly mutilating me after I failed to check in at the guard shack before trying to go into the World. I avoided being choked long enough to let them know I was the guy who brought the money around.

Tharpe mused, "What're we gonna do with you, Garrett? I'da felt bad for days if we'da killed you."

"That's reassuring."

"So, what's up?"

"I'm going to spend some time inside there seeing what happens when there isn't a crowd."

"You sure? All right. I always said you got more balls than brains. I'll have the guys come charging in when they hear you screaming."

"I appreciate that, Head." I didn't remind him that nobody outside heard anything when Belinda Contague did her screaming. I didn't want to recall that myself.

I borrowed a lamp from the guard shack. It looked remarkably like the lamps used inside the World. I headed in there.

I found and lighted two lanterns the workmen used when they had to do without daylight. Those cast circles of light that failed to push the darkness back very far.

I built a seat from loose flooring. I sat and waited.

Not for long.

The beautiful woman in the old-fashioned clothing came out of the darkness smiling, pleased to see me. My heart spun. We were old friends. She settled beside me on the lumber, the little lamp between us. Eleanor.

I said, "I guessed right. It worked."

"It worked. But you may not be pleased by what it will cost. This may be the end."

I moved my left hand toward her right, let it hover, not sure I wanted to find out.

"You probably shouldn't."

"Um."

"It would seem real. Right now I'm as real as I was when we met. But you have another obligation today."

I did. I'd been going around blurting out stuff about her being my fiancée. "You're right. But you'll never know how powerful this was. What I had for you."

"I do know. It's why there's always so much of me still here with you."

My hand floated toward her again. She did not shrink away. All choices here would be mine.

I raised the hand, instead, to brush the moisture out of my left eye. "So what do we know about the dragon? It's clear you're in touch. He made me the woman I hoped he would."

"It's not a dragon. It's nothing like anything you might guess. It's vast and it's slow and it's more alien than you can possibly imagine. It's older than you can imagine, too. It has no sense of time. It can't remember ever not being. And it's never lived anywhere but right where it is now, down there in the ground."

I felt no special elation about having been right. It not being a dragon probably only complicated things.

Faintly, right on the edge of imagination, I thought I heard music.

Eleanor said, "You might call it a god. It has some of those attributes. But it would be the most bizarre god ever to plague this world."

"There were others like it. Still might be."

"Others?" Some inner light brightened her face.

I told her what I knew.

"Others."

I wasn't speaking to the thing directly through Eleanor's doppelganger but it would know what she knew. And she would know what it knew.

It enjoyed emotions but didn't understand their source. It had no true idea of the world up here in the light, but it did sense the feelings of the creatures that wandered in and out of that small window it had found in the part of the World that it was able to reach. It created phantoms to reflect and stimulate emotions. Mostly those turned out to be unpleasant mirrors.

Music again, a tiny bit louder.

I started to take a fright.

"It's all right. It's just concentrating hard on trying to see and understand."

"What is it? Tell me the best you can."

"I don't know if language has the means to express it. It's like a leaf-mold. Or a fungus. It lives on the organic matter in the silt, more of which comes down slowly to it as water seeps through. It's vast. It might extend forty or fifty miles back up the river."

"To where there's not much bottom land."

"Yes. It's all one great being that exists entirely in the dark and damp."

The music was a little louder. And it wasn't that harsh metallic clank.

Eleanor told me, "It isn't intelligent in any human way but it has thoughts. And it uses thoughts to shape its world." She stood. "It isn't possible for us to be what we were, love, but we can share tonight as the dear friends we are now. Dance with me, Garrett. Relax. Let the entity do what it needs to do and learn what it needs to know." She extended her arms.

"This is all right?"

"This is all right. This won't be Garrett and Eleanor. This will be TunFaire and what lives beneath the roots romancing."

Eleanor's touch was real. It was as warm as life.

That startled me. That frightened me.

I became more attuned to the music, no cruel zinc racket but a melody wisping out of a fairy wood. Music unlike any that had plagued the World before. Unlike any I'd ever heard. It was the music of beauty, not anger. It had an orchestral feel, beyond anything known in even the great playhouses.

Eleanor moved in close. She placed one of my hands on her hip. She placed one of hers on my shoulder, then held on to the other. She caught my gaze with hers. She trapped it.

We danced.

She never spoke. She just smiled that beautiful smile, crafted by angels. But we communicated because I have that opening into my mind worn smooth by daily exposure to the Dead Man.

That three-dimensional golden ink splash that Old Bones had wrought returned and expanded in all directions, including thin fibers that followed the bug and rat passages up to the World. It became a hundred times more detailed. It entered me and tried using me to find others like itself. The information was in me but useless to it because we shared no common referents.

Eleanor and I danced. And I communed with the entity beneath.

Dragon was a fine description of that prodigious intellect. Devil or fallen angel might be equally apt. Though it set no temptation greater than Eleanor before me, I had no trouble seeing how, had it had any knowledge of the world above, it might have touched receptive minds and served as the Tempter adversary resident in many modern cults.

Eleanor said it might be a god.

She and I danced. And I learned. And I taught. I couldn't fully encompass what came my way. Old Bones might, though. He had minds big enough, and a different romance with time.

Eleanor and I danced. The music! Ah, that music! I hoped the Dead Man could extract that from me, isolate it, and find a way to pass it on to someone who could bring it to life.

We danced. And I learned the secret of the metal deposits. I think.

The entity, in its glacial metabolic process, separated out infinitesimal bits of metal as it fed. Those came down the river in the mud it carried. There were caverns in the limestone way down below where it deposited those metals. It had done so for tens of thousands of years.

I could not ferret out which metals were there.

Zinc might be important among them.

The spark that remained Garrett and sane forced that out of mind.

There might be a true treasure that could lead to a city-destroying roll-up if a greedy mob started digging down through the entity, which could not possibly be recognized as an intelligent being.

It didn't suffer human-style emotions itself, however much it enjoyed those. It responded to harmful stimulation by growing hotter, like a human body fighting disease. Prolonged heat caused it to dry out. Too long dry and hot, spontaneous combustion occurred. The resulting explosion might be mistaken for a dragon wakening. And, like a mushroom, might put spores into the air.

We had missed disaster at the World by a thin margin. Cold air going down the bug tunnels saved the day.

I tried to make the thing understand that it was far too vast to suffer real harm from puny humans, however hard they tried.

Eleanor laughed. And we danced. And the beautiful music played. Music the dragon found in my true love's head.

I was possessed.

Next day was a holiday. A general, royal holiday in celebration of the accession of the current dynasty. Nobody came to work. Saucerhead and his crew were outside but they had no reason to look inside.

Finally, somebody somewhere noticed that I was missing and started asking questions. Scouts went out looking for bodies in the slush.

Eleanor and I danced. I communed with the dragon. They narrowed the search.

I wasn't dancing when they found me. I was just lying there in the dark, on wood as hard as stone. I hadn't been down long. And could not get back up, even with help. My legs were knotted with cramps. I was too groggy to make them understand what I wanted when I tried to find out what had happened to Eleanor.

# 94

I was in my own bed. My head felt pleasantly empty. The Dead Man had flushed me out while I slept. My legs still hurt bad.

Tinnie was there. Her mouth moved too slowly to shape words. I heard an inarticulate bass roar.

The Dead Man touched me. The world and I matched speeds.

Tinnie's presence made everything bearable. She told me, "We thought we were going to lose you this time, Malsquando." She struggled with something inside. "Did you really want to get out of it that bad?" Then, "I couldn't help that. I didn't mean it. You scared me so much."

I made a noise. Hoping it was good enough. Hoping she wouldn't demand explanations. I couldn't manage that. Nor did I remember what I had to excuse.

*Turn off your You. Stop being Garrett. Some things are best left untold. Some explanations, however true and sincere, are inadequate.*

*In simpler words, keep your big damned mouth shut.*

I had only one foot in the real world but had no difficulty grasping the wisdom there. And for once was able to keep it shut.

Over the next half hour every member of the household wished me well, asked if there was anything they could do, then left looking worried. Even Melondie Kadare made a drunken buzz-through, accompanied by several more serious pixies. They made up an annoying swarm of oversize mosquitoes.

Oh, joy. The pixies were out of hibernation.

So. Winter was over.

\*    \*    \*

"I spent a night in Elf Hill," I told Tinnie, thinking I was being clever. Unfortunately, rural folklore doesn't resonate in the city. People see elves every day and can't imagine them living inside mounds in the wild wood. City elves bear no resemblance to the dark, cruel folk our ancestors knew. Not in public.

Only Old Bones understood. Only he knew what I'd gone through. He promised he'd let me know what that had been, too.

He knew what happened after the dancing stopped.

*You saved the city. You and your ghost woman. The dragon . . . the entity . . . did not go back to sleep, however. It is much too excited to sleep now that it knows there may be others like it.* I sensed uncertainty. What might even be fear. *It knows there is a world outside itself now. Which it understands only through two minds and two souls, one of them a woman murdered long ago and the other a . . . a you.*

That didn't sound so bad to me.

*You became immortal that night.*

"Just a hero thing."

*Desist. This is serious. And you are not going to be pleased.*

That was his "Dire news ahead!" tone. I shut up.

*Your ghostly friend warned you that you would not like the price. You thought that might mean losing the essence that lived on in her portrait. And you were correct. But the entity did not just take Eleanor. It took you, too.*

I was too worn down to argue or question. But it sounded like he was full of something.

The thing couldn't have taken me very far. Here I was, right here.

*There is a copy of you, of the Garrett inside the flesh, identical to a percentage point so remote that it would be a waste of good numbers to state it. That Garrett will live on inside the entity forever. With Eleanor. Quite possibly never understanding that it is both a copy and the template by which the entity builds its new worldview and responds to the outside that it has just discovered.*

*No one else knows this. Nor ever will, so long as you control your tongue.*

He then fed back selections of what he had harvested

from my head once Singe and Saucerhead dragged me home.

My ratgirl had been the only one to figure out where to find me. Maybe because I hadn't told anyone else where I was going.

Tinnie sipped tea and stared at me over her cup, across the kitchen table. I gobbled oatmeal mush, taking time off to ask, "Is it all right for you to be away again, already?"

"That problem has been handled."

"You locked Rose in a cage?"

"Not Rose. Though she did do the hands-on. My uncle Archer came up with the idea. Rose is too lazy. The cage is reserved for Kyra. That girl is going to embarrass us all if she doesn't show a little more sense."

"Turning into one of the fuddy-duddies, are we?" I'd once heard her departed uncle Lester make a similar observation about her.

"Gaining wisdom. Try it sometime."

"I got wisdom coming out my ears."

"That's hair."

"And if I don't, you'll make every effort to encourage me."

She eyed me suspiciously, then backed down, smelling a trap.

She'd heard a lot of male thoughts about the futility of trying to reform men. Mostly not from me. Being a selfish weasel, I try not to say things likely to put barriers in the way of my ambitions.

Being a slick weasel her very own self, Tinnie revealed none of her thoughts about domestic reeducation.

I will stipulate that, even after all this time, she might not have a fixed strategy. A glance round her circle of acquaintances wouldn't betray any glittering example to emulate. The most successful couple either of us knows is Winger and the Remora.

I changed the subject. "If you hang around I'll put you to work. Chuckles already has Singe shackled, scribing for him." My formal penmanship leaves room for improvement. And I needed a final, formal report, full of final, formal recommendations and some creative bullshit to baffle Max and Manvil about the end of the dragon threat.

*That should be an easy sell once you explain the dragon's . . . the entity's . . . willingness to assist with the elimination of waste from the World.*

"What?"

*So much that you do not remember. Look. It lives off rotting organic matter locked in the silt and organic matter that filters down from the river. It wants to grow now, in order to reach out to its brothers. It will be thrilled to take waste matter direct, through the tunnels created by the oversize insects. It began lining those with itself before Singe arrived to rescue you.*

"Really?"

*Truly. And the World will have an exclusive.*

"Damn! I have the knack! Sweetest heart. Ready to go do some writing?"

Vaguely, I felt the Dead Man reach out to Singe.

Tinnie gave me the fish-eye again, entertaining the possibility that I was trying to run her off. She called my bluff. "I do need to stay away while the old folks work out what to do about Rose and Archer. I can do a few pages of transcription."

I didn't slump.

Dean asked, "Shall I bring a tea service to your office, then?"

Tinnie suggested, "Why don't I take care of that? That'll give him a chance to clear some of the mess away."

There would be clutter all over my little desk. She'd need room to work. "I'm going." I little-old-manned it out the kitchen door. I used the wall for support, shuffling along the hallway.

Singe met me at the office doorway. She told me, "I found your painting in the theater. We brought it back when we brought you. I hung it up for you."

"Thank you, Singe." She would know all about the matter from the Dead Man. "I don't know what I'd do without you."

I was still in my office doorway when Tinnie arrived with the tea. "What's the matter with you, Malsquando?" Irked and concerned at the same time.

"Winter is over at last."

"Huh?"

I stared at Eleanor.

The dragon had left me with an unimaginable gift.

It had duplicated Eleanor, too.

The magic was back. But all the fear and foreboding had left the painting. The shadow against the darkness in the background had been replaced by the hint of a ghost of the face of a phantom dragon. It had a mischievous twinkle in its eye, telling me it would be a dragon if that was what we needed it to be.

Tinnie couldn't see the difference.

Eleanor wasn't running from anymore. Eleanor was running *to*. Finally.

"Winter is over at last."

# 95

The World opened on time. Its first offering was that ingenious historical tragedy, *Rausta, Queen of the Demenenes*. People loved it. They survived the scandalous use of women actors.

Tinnie, Alyx, and their posse did surprisingly well. Heather Soames found her calling as a theater manager.

The Amazons wore too many clothes and didn't jump around enough, though. And Winger never popped out of her breastplate.

I couldn't shake the feeling of a presence watching over my shoulder.

After the opening show the cast, angels, day-saving heroes, and owners lurched across to Morley's Velvet Curtain and got some exercise patting one another on the back.

# About the Author

**Glen Cook** was born in 1944 in New York City. He has served in the United States Navy, and lived in Columbus, Indiana; Rocklin, California; and Columbia, Missouri, where he went to the state university. He attended the Clarion Writers Workshop in 1970, where he met his wife, Carol. "Unlike most writers, I have not had strange jobs like chicken plucking and swamping out health bars. Only full-time employer I've ever had is General Motors." He is now retired from GM. He's "still a stamp collector and book collector, but mostly, these days, I hang around the house and write." He has three sons—an Army officer, an architect, and a music major.

In addition to the Garrett, P.I., series, he is also the author of the ever-popular Black Company series.

# Glen Cook

## WHISPERING NICKEL IDOLS

In TunFaire, a city of gorgeous
women, powerful sorcerers and
dangerous magic, the beautiful,
criminally insane daughter of a
comatose crime boss has some
lascivious designs on private
investigator Garrett—who now
has to figure out why everyone
is suddenly after him.

NEWLY REISSUED

# SWEET SILVER BLUES
### Book 1 in the Garrett, P.I. Series

## by Glen Cook

It should have been a simple job.

But for Garrett, a human detective in a
fantastical world, tracking down the
woman to whom his dead pal Danny
left a fortune in silver is no slight task.
Even with the aid of Morley, the toughest
half-elf around, Garrett isn't sure he'll
make it out alive from a land where magic
can be murder, the dead still talk, and
vampires are always hungry for
human blood.

Also Available:
*Bitter Gold Hearts*
*Cold Copper Tears*

# THE DRESDEN FILES
## By
# Jim Butcher

"Fans of Laurell K. Hamilton and Tanya Huff will love this new fantasy series."
—*Midwest Book Review*

**STORM FRONT**

**FOOL MOON**

**GRAVE PERIL**

**SUMMER KNIGHT**

**DEATH MASKS**

**BLOOD RITES**

**DEAD BEAT**

**PROVEN GUILTY**

**WHITE NIGHT**

**SMALL FAVOR**

# THE ULTIMATE IN
# SCIENCE FICTION AND FANTASY!

From magical tales of distant worlds to stories of
technological advances beyond the grasp of man, Penguin has
everything you need to stretch your imagination to its limits.

**penguin.com**

## ACE
Get the latest information on favorites like
William Gibson, T.A. Barron, Brian Jacques,
Ursula K. LeGuin, Sharon Shinn, and Charlaine Harris,
as well as updates on the best new authors.

## ROC
Escape with Harry Turtledove, Anne Bishop,
S.M. Stirling, Simon R. Green, Chris Bunch, Jim Butcher,
E.E. Knight, and many others—plus news on the
latest and hottest in science fiction and fantasy.

## DAW
Mercedes Lackey, Kristen Britain, Tanya Huff,
Tad Williams, C.J. Cherryh, and many more—
DAW has something to satisfy the cravings of any
science fiction and fantasy lover.
Also visit dawbooks.com.

*Get the best of science fiction and fantasy
at your fingertips!*